PRAISE FOR *SLAYER*

"Will get *Buffy* fans up in their feels . . . A tale solidly set in the world *Buffy* stans love—and filled with all the demons, vampires, and shady folks they love to hate." —*Entertainment Weekly*

"White's new addition to the world of *Buffy the Vampire Slayer* is refreshing and hits the tone of the series at its best. . . . Slay on, Nina. Slay on." —*Culturess*

"Full of great characters, interesting plots, complex dynamics, and stakes about as high as they come." —*Hypable*

★ "Epic . . . Resplendent with quirky, endearing characters and imagination-sparking details, this novel feeds the soul of *Buffy* devotees, keeping the *Buffy* spirit alive." —*Publishers Weekly*, starred review

"White . . . taps into the ethos of the original series, mining its complicated ethics for new veins of moral dilemmas, betrayals, hidden identities, funky demons, and romance. . . . Readers familiar with the Buffyverse will find themselves delighted to be home again." —*BCCB*

"Exciting and well-plotted." —*SLJ*

"Fans of high stakes (apocalypse high), monster madness, and serious girl power will line up for this one." —*Booklist*

Also by
KIERSTEN WHITE

Slayer

SLAYER: BOOK TWO

CHOSEN

KIERSTEN WHITE

SIMON PULSE

NEW YORK   LONDON   TORONTO   SYDNEY   NEW DELHI

SIMON PULSE

An imprint of Simon & Schuster Children's Publishing Division
1230 Avenue of the Americas, New York, New York 10020
First Simon Pulse hardcover edition January 2020
Buffy the Vampire Slayer TM & © 2020 by Twentieth Century Fox Film Corporation. All rights reserved.
Text by Kiersten White
Jacket illustration by Kekai Kotaki
Series and title logos by Craig Howell
All rights reserved, including the right of reproduction in whole or in part in any form.
SIMON PULSE and colophon are registered trademarks of Simon & Schuster, Inc.
For information about special discounts for bulk purchases, please contact
Simon & Schuster Special Sales at 1-866-506-1949 or business@simonandschuster.com.
The Simon & Schuster Speakers Bureau can bring authors to your live event.
For more information or to book an event contact the Simon & Schuster Speakers Bureau
at 1-866-248-3049 or visit our website at www.simonspeakers.com.
Jacket designed by Sarah Creech
Interior designed by Mike Rosamilia
The text of this book was set in Perpetua.
Manufactured in the United States of America
2 4 6 8 10 9 7 5 3 1
Library of Congress Cataloging-in-Publication Data
Names: White, Kiersten, author. | Title: Chosen / by Kiersten White.
Other titles: Buffy, the vampire slayer (Television program)
Description: New York : Simon Pulse, 2020. | Series: [Slayer] | Summary: "Now that Nina has turned the Watchers Council's castle into a utopia for hurt and lonely demons, she's still waiting for the utopia part to kick in. With her sister, Artemis, gone and only a few people remaining at the castle—including her still-distant mom—Nina has her hands full. Plus, though she gained back her Slayer powers from Leo, they're not feeling quite right after being held by the seriously evil succubus Eve, aka fake Watchers Council member and Leo's mom. And while Nina is dealing with the darkness inside, there's also a new threat on the outside, portended by an odd triangle symbol that seems to be popping up everywhere, in connection with Sean's demon drug ring as well as someone a bit closer to home. Because one near apocalypse just isn't enough, right? The darkness always finds you. And once again, it's coming for the Slayer"—Provided by publisher.
Identifiers: LCCN 2019026228 (print) | LCCN 2019026229 (eBook) |
ISBN 9781534404984 (hardcover) | ISBN 9781534405004 (eBook)
Classification: LCC PZ7.W583764 Ck 2020 (print) | LCC PZ7.W583764 (eBook) | DDC [Fic]—dc23
LC record available at https://lccn.loc.gov/2019026228
LC ebook record available at https://lccn.loc.gov/2019026229

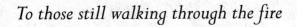

To those still walking through the fire

CHOSEN

The world is quiet now.

It used to be so loud. So much chatter, beating, drumming, buzzing buzzing buzzing. The buzzing *of it all. It used to keep him awake at night, inescapable, like mites crawling through his veins. Sometimes he would scratch at his arms until they bled, but even the bleeding never dampened the buzzing.*

Until it stopped. All the lines to and from the world, all the hungry beings clawing and sucking and pawing at it, everything cut off.

But not him. He is still here. And with everything quiet, he can finally focus. He's powerless, which is unfortunate but temporary. Everything here is temporary. He will not be.

He strokes his arms, smooth and unscarred, so deceptively human-looking. But he is no human. And this world, this quiet world, this cut-off and free-floating world, this magic-less and empty world, this unprotected and uncontested world, this waiting world—

He will be its god, and everyone will buzz with him beneath their veins, they will breathe and bleed and live and die for him, and it will be good.

Amen.

1

THE DEMON APPEARS OUT OF NOWHERE.
Claws and fangs fill my sight, and every instinct screams *kill*.
My blood sings with it, my fists clench, my vision narrows. The
vulnerable points on the demon's body practically flash like
neon signs.

"Foul!" Rhys shouts. "No teleportation, Tsip! You know
that." Even while playing, Rhys can't help but be a Watcher,
shouting out both advice and corrections. He's not wearing his
glasses, which makes his face look vague and undefined. Cillian
passes him, mussing Rhys's carefully parted hair into wild curls
and laughing at Rhys's frustration.

I take a deep breath, trying to clear my head of the impulse
to kill this demon I invited into our home and swore to protect.
"It's just soccer," I whisper. "It doesn't matter. I don't even like
soccer."

"Football, bloody American," Cillian sings, neatly stealing
the ball from me. His shorts are far shorter than the January
afternoon should permit, but he seems impervious to cold.

Unlike those of us who are translucently pale at this point in winter, his skin is rich and lovely. He passes to Tsip. Tsip is a vaguely opalescent pink, shimmering in the sunlight. She paints her claws fun colors when we do manicure nights, and I try desperately not to miss Artemis.

I stay rooted to the ground where I'm standing. Tsip caught me off guard, but that shouldn't matter. I like her. And the fact that I went from trying to score a goal to plotting a dozen ways to kill my opponent in a single heartbeat is frankly terrifying. I can't get my heart under control, can't shake the adrenaline screaming through my veins.

"Gotta take over for the Littles. I'm out." I wave and jog from the field. No one pays me much attention. Jade is lying on the ground in front of the goal, the worst goalkeeper ever. Rhys and Cillian are bodychecking each other in increasingly flirty ways. Tsip keeps shimmering and then resolidifying as she remembers the no-teleportation rule. They're all happy to keep going without me, unaware of my internal freak-out.

I've deliberately kept them unaware. Things here are going so well. I'm in charge. I can't be the problem. So none of them know how I can't sleep at night, how my anger is hair-trigger fast, how when I do manage to sleep, my dreams are . . .

Well. Bad.

They don't need to know and I don't let them. Except for Doug, his bright yellow skin almost nineties Day-Glo levels in the thin winter sun. Annoying emotion-sniffing demon. He watches me from our goal, his nostrils flared. I can't lie to him the way I can to everyone else. I shake my head preemptively. I don't want to talk about it. Not with him. Not with anyone. There's only one person I want to talk to about it, but Leo Silvera's not exactly available.

I do a quick sweep of the perimeter of the castle. *Leo loved me.* Check the woods. *Leo betrayed me.* Check the locks on the outbuildings. *Leo saved me.* Pause and just listen and look, feeling for anything pushing against my instincts. *I let Leo die.*

I keep walking. Leo loved me, betrayed us, saved us, and then died, and I can't be sad without being mad or mad without feeling guilty or guilty without feeling exhausted.

Past the meadow, the tiny purple demons are taking turns pushing each other on the tree swing. That, or they're trying to push each other off. It's hard to tell with them. With nothing else needing my attention outside, I end up at the front stairs to the castle.

"Hey, Jessi." I wave halfheartedly to our resident vengeance demon. She's leading the Littles through an elaborate game of hopscotch. George Smythe, bundled up and barely able to see under a floppy knit hat, is shouting each letter as he lands on it. "*G!*"

"What?" Jessi snaps at me.

"*E!*"

"I can take over for you." I find the Littles soothing. They might be three incredibly hyper children constantly needing snacks, entertainment, and education, but at least none of them ever randomly triggers a *kill* reflex in me.

"*A!*"

"No," Jessi says, her voice as sweet as summer fruit. "*G-E-*what-comes-next . . ."

"*O!*" George course corrects, wobbling on one short leg before jumping to the required *O*.

"Good! Oh, you're so clever. Priya, how are your letters coming?" Priya, a tiny moppet with shiny black hair, is crouched over her own chalk work, which looks more like Klingon than any alphabet I'm familiar with. "Very good, darling! You're really working hard. Hold the chalk with one hand, like we talked about. Thea, love, fingers out of noses, please—that's a dear."

And to think, we once considered these children the entire future of the Watchers. I watch as Thea spins until she falls flat on her bottom. Actually, the future of the Watchers is pretty accurately captured here. I pat Jessi on the arm. "So, you can take the afternoon off."

Everything sweet in Jessi's voice turns to ice. "I said no. I don't trust you with these three precious wonders. We have an entire day's curriculum to get through, and we haven't even done story time yet or finished our art projects. Are you going to do any of that with them?"

"I—I could?"

"You were going to turn on a cartoon and read while their fertile minds were filled with weeds."

Jessi doesn't have her powers anymore, but I'm pretty certain if she did, I would have been vengeance-demoned right into something oozing and seeping. She's already turned away from me and back to her three charges. Her whole face is full of gentle warmth and absolute love.

"R!" George declares, hopping emphatically down on it. Jessi claps like he's cured the common cold.

Thoroughly dismissed, I skulk up the stairs and into the castle. Jessi could at least pretend to be nice. She's got a lot of enemies out there—vengeance is a nasty cycle—and without her powers she's vulnerable. We took her in despite her obvious hatred for everyone over the age of ten. There was some debate, given her history, but my mom argued in her favor. It's a little easier to forgive a vengeance demon who made it her immortal life's work to avenge children than a vengeance demon who specialized in, say, fantasy league sports rivalries.

But Jessi's dismissal leaves me with nothing to do. I used to have my medical center and my studies, all my little Watcher duties. Even with so few of us, the castle ran as near to Watcher traditions as we could manage. Which in retrospect was absurd, since we didn't have a Slayer and weren't actually doing anything Watchers should.

But now everything has changed. We lost Watchers—Wanda Wyndam-Pryce, sulking off into the sunset, good riddance. Bradford Smythe, murdered. Eve Silvera, secretly a succubus demon and murderer, smushed thanks to my actions. Artemis, off to find herself with her awful girlfriend, the thought of whom makes my jaw ache as I grind my teeth. And Leo, who didn't warn us what his mother was (and what he was) but fought her to give us enough time to stop her from opening a new hellmouth.

And now we have a Slayer, again some more, thanks to Leo somehow returning the powers his mother stole from me. I don't know how he did it, and it hurts too much to think about, like everything else. I spend so much of my days trying not to think, and it's harder than it should be. I used to believe that all Slayers did was act without thinking. I was wrong, but I wish it were true. There's so little acting and so much thinking these days.

It's good. It's all good. It's good, I remind myself, over and over like a chant. Sanctuary, what we decided to turn our castle into, is just starting out, but it's exactly what we dreamed it could be. We've taken in demons who had nowhere else to go. We're keeping them safe, and ourselves safe, and we'll keep looking for those who could benefit from the generations of knowledge and abilities we have. We're protecting, not attacking or destroying.

Between our new demonic additions and existing Watchers, everyone has tasks and times to do them. It's more work than anyone anticipated, keeping everyone taken care of and fed, making sure the castle runs like it should. But so far everyone is happy. Everyone is safe.

I sink down against the wall, feeling the cold of the stone radiating outward. The unpellis demon, all four gentle eyes soft and brown and hopeful, snuggles up to my side like a dog. It's more animal than human in nature, nonverbal, and still recovering from its frequent de-skinning treatment in Sean's demon-drug manufacturing scheme. I saved Pelly from that cellar.

I didn't save everyone, though.

I wrap my arms around Pelly and close my eyes. Everything is exactly what we dreamed it could be. Except I feel Leo's loss everywhere, and I miss my twin, Artemis, with a constant, physical ache.

And, worst of all, with enough time after Tsip surprised me to calm down and remind my body there's no danger . . .

I still feel like killing something.

2

I'M ON THE FLOOR WITH PELLY WHEN Imogen finds me. With Artemis gone and Jessi taking over the care of the Littles, Imogen has shifted to the kitchen. Food quality in the castle has improved tenfold. It feels like everyone has settled into roles that truly suit them. Except me. I don't know what I want.

"You look like you could use a cookie," she says, hands on her hips. She's wearing cheerful pink lipstick and has her hair in two low pigtails. She's been in a really good mood ever since we stopped the apocalypse prophecy when I blocked Eve Silvera's new hellmouth. Preventing an apocalypse cost me my Slayer powers (briefly) and Leo Silvera (permanently). In my darkest moments, when I wake up from a nightmare alone in my room without even my sister to comfort me, I'm not sure it was a good trade. Would a new hellmouth have been that big of a deal? We've dealt with them since the beginning of time. Surely we could have handled a new one.

But I know that's selfish. Arcturius the Farsighted had a

whole prophecy devoted to Artemis and me, all about breaking and healing the world. I made the right call. It just cost so much. It took away his warm eyes and long-fingered hands and swift, sure movements. His soft lips. The most dazzlingly elusive smile. And the one person who ever really saw me.

The two people, actually. Leo died, and Artemis left. And I'm here on the floor snuggling a demon. I wish Arcturius had seen this, too. They never talk about how hard the part *after* the hard part is.

I look up at Imogen. "I could use a cookie, yeah. Actually, cookies. Plural."

"Cookies should never be singular." Imogen holds out a hand to help me stand. My phone rings. The caller ID is the number we designated for demon scouting trips. Today, and most days, my mother is on the other end of the line.

When we first started meeting with demons for potential acceptance into Sanctuary, I was always with her. But a month ago, there was an . . . incident. I hadn't slept at all that night, and I was already on edge, so when I turned around and saw the dead black eyes of a shark staring at me, I punched first and asked questions after. Turns out it was a demon with a shark head trying to escape some bad debts. My mother assured me he wasn't a good fit for Sanctuary anyway, but the fact that I attacked him didn't exactly do our reputation any favors. Word of mouth (or whatever the demon species equivalent of a mouth is) matters in finding demons who need our help. So I basically blew it.

I still feel bad about it. I like sharks! On television. Underwater. Where I am not. I can't even think about the incident without feeling roiling guilt. When did I become a punch-first-

ask-questions-later Slayer? And it made me a liability instead of
an asset. My mother tried to make it sound like she needed me
at the castle for scheduling reasons, but we both know it was to
protect me. Or to protect the demons. I don't know which is
worse.

Working together is already awkward enough. She's trying to be my mom again, but she doesn't really know how to,
so it comes across like those aggressively friendly employees at
grocery stores who constantly ask how you are and if you need
help and if you're finding everything okay, and all you can do is
smile and answer back in the same bright voice when really you
know where the cereal is, thank you very much. And there's the
added pressure of feeling like I have to reward all her efforts,
even when I don't want to. I appreciate it, I really do, but I wish I
had Artemis to share the burden of Mom Version Four, or at least
to complain to. She'd get it. No one else does.

I answer the call. "Mom? Everything okay?"

There's a popping noise in the background that sounds dis-
tinctly like a gun. I keep the phone to my ear and sprint outside.

"Hello, Nina. I didn't want to interrupt your work today,
but we've been pinned down and I didn't bring the firepower
necessary to get out." By her tone, she might as well be calling to
ask if we need more milk. My mother is baffling and also slightly
terrifying.

"Is it Sean?" I don't mean to sound so excited, but it's almost
a relief. I've been waiting for demon drug dealer Sean to make
a play for Doug again. Doug's happy-time skin secretions were
Sean's biggest moneymaker. And with ex-Watcher and worst
person ever Honora among his former and possibly current allies,

Sean knows more than enough about our operations to be very dangerous to us. Plus, I sort of destroyed his entire operation by unleashing a remora demon to crush everything. I can't imagine he thinks fondly of any of us.

Today's demon outing was a first meeting with a family of werewolves. Werewolves are low-risk, so my mother went alone. Normally, she takes Tsip, Jade, or Rhys. But we should have known better. Nothing in our world is ever truly low-risk. I wave frantically to Rhys, Cillian, and Doug. Jade doesn't even look up. She's probably blissed out on Doug right now. Useless. My sober friends jog up to me as I open the garage.

"No," my mother says. "This isn't Sean's MO. It appears to be some aggressive freelancers. I believe there are two in sniper positions. I'm using my ammunition sparingly to avoid running out, but it won't be much longer before they feel confident launching a full attack."

"We're on our way! When you run out of ammunition, hide. Don't engage. And don't risk yourself, okay?" It sounds horrible to say, but I don't want my mother to die protecting strangers. Not when I've just started to get her back after years of being strangers to each other. I want her to annoy me for decades to come.

"Thank you. See you soon. And, Nina?" Her voice gets softer, more tentative. For the first time, she sounds a little worried. "Be careful. You're not bulletproof."

The silence hangs between us. I struggle to fill it, to close that gap. Because this mom who is open about caring about me? It's new, and, like being a Slayer, or my anger or my guilt or my grief, I still don't know how to react. So instead of telling her to be careful too, I default to something less emotionally fraught. As soon as I start joking, I know it's the wrong choice, but it just keeps going, and I can't stop it.

"Yeah, we should totally take that up with our ancient ancestors who created the Slayer line. Bulletproof would have been useful to add alongside prophetic dreams, superstrength, and killer instincts. Though I guess bullets would have been an unfamiliar concept on account of this all happened thousands of years ago."

"Oh, for goodness' sake, be *careful*, Nina."

I take a deep breath. I wanted my mother to be mine for so long. Now I have to be strong enough to let her be, to trust that this won't go away. "I will be. Promise. You too." I hang up. Cillian, Rhys, and Doug are all waiting for instructions. Tsip has wandered over too.

"Can you teleport me?" I ask her.

"Yes!" The fangs jutting from her lower jaw are showcased in an enthusiastic smile. "But I can only teleport short distances. And you have to be able to reconstitute yourself after being disintegrated on a molecular level while shifting through the void beyond reality. It hurts quite a bit, but you get used to it."

"I'll drive then, yeah?" Cillian grabs the keys and starts the car.

Doug looks scared but determined. "Sean?" The fact that he's willing to come and face the man who held him captive for years speaks volumes about him.

I put my hand on his arm and shake my head. "Mercenaries. With guns. I don't think you're going to be any use. Wake Jade up and make sure you're all on alert while I'm gone, okay?"

Doug nods, holding a hand up in farewell. Tsip waves energetically as we pull away.

"The void beyond reality?" Cillian navigates the forest dirt road far faster than is safe. "Demons. Total nutters, the lot of them."

"I like Doug." Rhys checks his crossbow.

I bounce impatiently in the back. "Everyone likes Doug. He's biologically impossible to dislike." We always pick a destination with several roads in and out so we can't be traced, so the warehouse is thirty minutes away. Thirty minutes is thirty minutes too far, though.

"What are we going into here?" Cillian drives at double the speed limit. I'm grateful, and I wish he would go even faster. But we don't have our get-out-of-tickets-free Doug in the car with us, so we're risking a police encounter as it is.

"Mercenaries. Two snipers. They have my mom pinned down in the warehouse."

"Plan?"

"The plan is Cillian stops before we get there and stays in the car."

"Hey now, I can—"

I cut him off. "I can only focus on saving so many people at a time. I can't worry about you, too." It comes out harsher than I intend it, but it's true. Cillian is one of my favorite people in the world, and he almost died last fall because of it. His dark brown eyes meet mine in the rearview mirror. He nods.

Rhys turns back toward me. He forgot his glasses. His crossbow is going to be pretty useless if he can't see to use it. I want to make him stay in the car with Cillian. But he's a Watcher. This is his job too.

No. It's only my job. I'm the Slayer. "Rhys, you'll take the alleys to cut around to the back of the warehouse. Get a high vantage point and make certain there aren't any more waiting there for an ambush. I'll find the snipers and take them out."

I'm confident I can get it done before Rhys ever gets to his position. I can keep them all safe. I can keep everyone safe.

The image of Leo, unconscious on the floor, disappearing behind the ever-expanding remora demon to meet the same crushed-to-death fate as his mother flashes in my mind, contradicting me with brutal accuracy.

I can, though. I have to. I'm never losing anyone again.

Cillian slows down on the outskirts of the old fishing district where the warehouse is. I open my door and jump, hitting the ground running.

The sound of a bullet pinging off metal is all the direction I need. I don't worry about cover. I run as fast as I can, and, gods, it's fast. My red-gold hair streams behind me, my emerald-green trench coat flapping in the wind like a cape. Another shot rings out. There's a fire-escape ladder fifteen feet up on the side of a brick building. I leap, catch the bottom rung, and climb up, feeling a flash of surprise that I made that jump. I'm pretty sure I couldn't have made it when I first became a Slayer. And I haven't exactly been training—going to the castle's gym brings too many painful memories of Leo. But there's no time to wonder at my skills.

The roof is flat, rusted corrugated metal. At the far end of it, a figure is crouched, holding a rifle. A mercenary. Firing a rifle at my mother and a *family*.

"Hey!" I shout. Anger burns in me with the same devouring

intensity as the black-purple flames that nearly killed me as a child. I can feel them inside, eating away everything else, purifying me, leaving only rage. The mercenary stands and swings the rifle in my direction in the same amount of time it takes me to sprint across the roof and slam into him.

I watch in slow motion as he flies backward into thin air.

3

IN THAT ETERNAL SPLIT SECOND, I CON-
sider letting the mercenary fall.

We're three stories up. It won't *definitely* kill him. And he's
been up here, shooting at my mother and a family of werewolves
with three small children. Hidden like a coward, sending death
down to people who have already suffered and lost more than he
can ever imagine.

And a part of me, a dark burning tightness clenching around
my heart, snarls that he's my enemy and deserves whatever end
he finds as he connects with the pavement.

He's human, I think at the snarling, hungry thing.

So what? is the answer.

The spike of fear I feel about that sentiment coming from
inside of me is enough to pierce the anger. I reach out and
snatch him from the air. The rifle clatters to the ground far
beneath us. I hold him dangling as he struggles and swears.
A scan of the neighboring rooflines doesn't reveal the second
sniper anywhere.

Which means that this one was probably keeping my mother pinned down while the other one went in.

There's a jut of metal next to me. I hook him on it by his belt so he's still dangling but won't fall unless he struggles too much. Then I jump. I land hard in a crouch that a few months ago would have left me absolutely impressed with myself, and then I sprint for the warehouse. Sure enough, a side door has been pried open, crowbar left abandoned on the ground. I pick it up. The dim warehouse interior reeks with decades of lingering fish scuzz. The cold is a physical presence slamming into me.

Up ahead, next to a concrete pillar, the second mercenary has his rifle lifted. I follow the sight line to my mother, silhouetted against the entrance door, gun raised as she looks outward for the threat. Behind her, sheltered by a huge refrigerator unit, a mother, father, and three children cower.

There's a soft release of breath as the mercenary gets ready for a kill shot. I throw the crowbar.

It lands with a bone-snapping crack against the mercenary's right leg. He—she, apparently—screams. I run to her, snatching the rifle and bending it in half. Then I grab her by her black bulletproof vest and drag her behind me as I walk toward my stunned mother and the terrified family.

"Nina," my mother says.

She turns in my direction. The door behind her opens, and the first mercenary roars inside, holding a pistol I didn't know he had, gun pointed at me.

The look of absolute terror on my mother's face reminds me of our phone conversation. *Not bulletproof.* I hold the woman mercenary in front of myself as a shield. One, two shots slam into her. I feel their concussive force like I would a fly bouncing off me. I toss her to the side and launch myself at the man. He doesn't have time for another shot before I hit him, knocking him into the door so hard it swings wildly off one hinge.

He's on the ground. I lift a fist—

"Nina!"

I freeze. He's unconscious. I don't need to hit him anymore.

But, gods, I *want* to.

"Nina, the woman." My mother's voice is sharp. Chiding.

Right. The woman. The one I used to shield myself. The one I let get shot. I was so angry, so focused. It felt right at the time. My stomach twists. I'm sick at what I've done. And, inexplicably, I'm angrier than ever. How can my mom get mad at me? It was the mercenary's own partner who shot her. And she was ready to shoot my mother! Or the werewolves, who are still cowering, the children crying as the mother tries to comfort them and the father stares at me.

No one gets to shoot my mother. I let go of the unconscious man, then walk as calmly as I can back to the woman. She's moaning in pain. Her leg is obviously broken from where I hit it with the crowbar. It's too dark to see whether she's bleeding. "My ribs," she gasps.

I reach down and pick her up, hating that I have to be gentle when she deserves anything but. I bring her into the light next to her partner and set her down. No blood. The bullets both hit her in the vest.

"Your ribs are probably broken," I say. "Leg, too." I know what I could do to set it, or to check that her lungs haven't been punctured. I've studied and learned everything I can about the human body and how it breaks, so that I could help heal it. Not so I could do the breaking.

Instead of checking her lungs, I check her for weapons. I find another pistol and snap it in half. Then I gather their rifles and other weapons and make a pile on the ground next to them.

I pull out my phone. "Call the police," I tell Cillian. "Say you heard gunshots by the old fish warehouse."

"Is everything okay?"

"Fine." I hang up. We have—had—procedures for dealing with demons. But these two are humans. Which means they're subject to human laws, and Irish law doesn't look kindly on illegal guns.

"Who sent you?" I ask.

The woman's face is drenched in sweat. She grits her teeth and glares at me. From the sound of her breathing, neither of her lungs is punctured. But her ribs are definitely broken. I need this information; my mother doesn't think it's Sean, but it could be. Thinking of Sean makes me think of Honora, which makes me think of Artemis. What would she do if getting the truth meant keeping her family safe? I put one hand gently on the mercenary's vest. And then I push down ever so slightly.

She screams. "No one! No one sent us! There's a bloke, rich as sin. Pays extra for exotics. He does a big werewolf hunt for the first full moon of the new year. We'll cut you in! Introduce you!"

"Give me his name." I increase pressure.

"Ian! Ian Von Alston! Just outside London!"

I remove my hand. "If I ever see either of you again, it won't end this well for you."

I stand and turn around. It's taking everything in me to leave them there. My mother is safe, and so is the family. The mercenaries are unarmed, injured, no longer threats. But they had my *mother* in their gun sights. All so they could sell a family to be hunted. My fist clenches, twitching.

The werewolf mother, a plain woman in mom jeans and a bulky sweater, stares at me with wide, watery eyes. "Thank you. We'll make our own way."

"You'll be safe with us. They can't hurt you." I smile reassuringly. But the look of horror on her face isn't directed at them. She's scared . . . of *me*.

"We'll take our chances elsewhere." The father gathers two children in his arms, and the mother takes the smallest. They hurry away into the darkness of the warehouse toward the back door.

"Nina." My mother's voice is so even and careful, it chills me more than the building.

I didn't do anything wrong! I did what my instincts told me to. Less than they told me to, even. I acted like a Slayer. If I can't use my Slayer abilities to protect the people I love, what the bloody hellmouths are they for?

"Nina?" Rhys steps around the two mercenaries with a puzzled look. "We should find Cillian, yeah? Don't want to be here when the police arrive."

"You go ahead." I don't meet my mother's eyes. "I'm gonna run home. Got some energy to get rid of."

"But it's thirty miles!"

Thirty miles I'd have to spend with the weight of unanswered and unasked questions. I'd rather run. I sprint out of the building and into the winter afternoon, burning so hot I wonder that nothing catches fire in my wake.

ARTEMIS

HONORA IS LYING ON THE EDGE OF THE bed, head hanging over, her long dark hair draping down like shiny curtains, obscuring the light of her face. She's paging idly through a selection of brochures spread out on the floor.

". . . kind of a creep, but aren't they all? He pays well. We could make enough in a couple months for tuition for at least a year. Ooh, this is a proper campus—just look at that ivy. I know it's not practical, but I always kind of wanted to go into communications. PR. Isn't that daft?" She turns her head to look at Artemis, making a face to hide her vulnerability.

Artemis smiles so Honora knows she's not teasing. "I don't think that's daft. You'd kick ass at a PR firm. And if things didn't go your way, you'd also kick ass, just literally."

Honora laughs and goes back to the brochures. The plan is to do some demon-hunting jobs—Honora still has plenty of connections, even though she doesn't work with Sean anymore—and earn enough to put themselves through college. Artemis isn't old enough, technically, but Honora also knows someone

who can fake documents to give Artemis all the A levels and
identity requirements she needs to apply. Artemis didn't exactly
take time to grab her birth certificate before running out on the
castle, the Watchers, her mother, her sister, and everything she'd
ever known and worked toward.

"Hey, Moon, what's wrong?"

Artemis forces a smile. She stands, stretching. "Just tired."
The flat they're crashing in belonged to a vampire, and the décor
is like someone spent way too much time studying vampire films
of the eighties. The walls are painted black and plastered with
neon posters. The headboard is black leather, and Artemis tries
very hard not to think about what might have gone down in this
room. They vacuumed the carpet very thoroughly after dusting
the vampire, but she still insisted on new bedding before she'd
sleep here. And even after that, she doesn't sleep well. She constantly wakes in a panic, heart racing with the knowledge that
she's supposed to be doing *something*.

She can never figure out what, though.

Honora's excited about their plans, and Artemis wants to
be. But trying to imagine a life where she goes to college and
majors in, what, accounting? And then gets a job in an office and
wears low heels and goes to work every day like a normal person?
She's not a normal person, she's never been a normal person, she
doesn't want to be a normal person. The whole thing would feel
too absurd, knowing the evil that's out there, lurking.

Artemis, an accountant, while Nina is a Slayer.

Her phone rings with the castle cell number and she wonders if her bitterness has summoned her twin. They haven't
spoken. Artemis wasn't going to be the first to call. Not this

time. Let Nina try to fix what was broken for once. Or it might be their mother. Taking a deep breath, annoyed for how her hopes flutter fragile and pathetic in her heart, Artemis answers. "Yeah?"

"Artemis?"

It takes her a few moments to place the voice. "Imogen?" Not who she had expected. She's winded with disappointment. She wants her mother to call, to demand Artemis come back so she can refuse. She wants Nina to call and talk about how bad things are, how much they need her. She doesn't know what she'd say in that case. But Imogen?

"Hey," Imogen says. "Thank God. I was worried you'd change your number. Are you in contact with Sean?"

"No." Artemis shrugs at Honora's curious look, then mouths *Imogen*. Honora sits up and leans close. "We haven't talked to Sean since my sister destroyed his whole setup. Wait. Is the castle in trouble? Did he attack to get Doug back?" Artemis's pulse speeds up. She *knew* it. She knew they were making the wrong choice, that they wouldn't be able to defend themselves. Honora gestures and Artemis puts the phone on speaker.

"What? No. This is about something else. Bigger. I can't take it to Nina—she won't be able to handle it. And we both know she won't play nice with Honora, which is absurd. You and Honora are the best we ever had, even if the decrepit old guard were too far up their asses to see it. So this call is secret, okay?"

Artemis and Honora share a look. They've never heard Imogen talk this way. Artemis is intrigued in spite of herself. "I'm not in contact with anyone from the castle anyway."

"Good. I've done some research and there's a major new

player surfacing. We're talking hellgod level. Maybe. I can't be certain. But I think Sean is connected. You remember his tea?"

They have a supply of some of his more potent drugs, but it's dwindling. Artemis counts it every day, watching as her only access to the type of power she needs disappears. It fills her with as much terror as anticipating a life as an accountant. She wants the strength to help, to protect Honora, to fight evil, to be *more* than herself. And without Sean's drugs, she's back to the Artemis who wasn't good enough. "Yeah, I remember his tea."

"There was a symbol on it. You know the one?"

Artemis does. She glances over at the nightstand where one of his branded packages sits. Now that she thinks about it, she's seen it before. Somewhere. Where?

Imogen keeps talking. "I thought it was just his brand, but it's been bugging me. I think it's connected to something bigger. And I . . ." She pauses, and the phone is muffled as her tone changes and she answers someone in chipper tones. "Sorry. Gotta go. Nice talking to you, Liesa. I'm definitely interested in keeping chickens. I'll be in touch with more questions." The line goes dead.

Artemis holds the phone, staring down at it as she tries to process the conversation. Imogen was always on the sidelines. But they had been united by being shuffled by the Watchers to the worst jobs in the castle, Imogen tainted by her mother's choices and Artemis apparently deemed simply not good enough.

She was better than everyone in that whole damn castle. Even if the Watchers were still at full force, she'd be better than all of them.

The library! She'd seen the symbol in the library, when she had to label and catalog every single book instead of studying them like Rhys, all because she'd failed a single test.

Screw stability. Screw accounting. Artemis is a Watcher, the only real one left, and if there's a new creeping menace out there, she'll figure it out and deal with it herself. "Call Sean." She tosses the phone to a surprised Honora. "Tell him we want to come work for him."

Honora twists her lips. "You sure? I was on my way out before the whole remora fiasco anyway. Not wild about the people he's working with now. Dodgy religious zealots."

Bingo. Artemis can't help the surge of excitement she feels. Because where there are zealots, there's power to be worshipped. And where there's power, there's potential. She doesn't know what yet. Maybe they'll kill whatever it is and be done with it. But if Sean can figure out a way to take what makes demons strong and synthesize it, how much more power is there to squeeze from a potential god?

Artemis leans closer. "We work for him to work against him. Just like old times for you, right?"

Honora flinches. She doesn't talk about her time spent undercover in a demon-worshipping cult. They wrote each other constant letters back then, but Honora never, ever gave details on what she was doing. Artemis feels bad for bringing it up. She shouldn't push this. But she needs it. She needs *something*.

She reaches out and strokes Honora's hair, resting her hand on the back of Honora's neck. "This is our job, Nor. You and me. We're the only real Watchers left. And if something is happening, who else is going to look into it? Should we call Buffy?"

Honora snorts. "She's as likely to shag a hellgod as kill one.

Right, then. Can't enroll until the next semester anyway. As long as we're doing this together. You got my back, Moon?"

Honora plays it tough, but the tentative look in her eyes hits Artemis where it counts. She and Honora belong together. Nina never understood their bond, because Nina had someone looking out for her, someone protecting her. Artemis doesn't bother to fight the wave of bitterness that after everything she did to be the strongest, the smartest, the best, *Nina* was chosen. That Artemis was left missing the sister she thought she had. The one who needed her.

Honora knows what it is to never be enough, to fight and fight with no one in her corner. They're each other's corners now. Artemis takes Honora's hand in her own, locking eyes. "Always."

4

BY THE TIME I GET BACK TO THE CASTLE,
it's dark.

Rhys and Cillian will be cocooned in Rhys's room—Cillian
watching something on his battered laptop, happy to be anywhere but his empty cottage; Rhys researching, adding to his
demon encyclopedia.

Jade will be wherever Doug is. I think they're dating, but
it's hard to tell, and I don't ask for details. Jade and I were never
really close, and that hasn't changed. Plus, I try very hard to
avoid Doug and his inconvenient ability to smell when I'm lying
about my feelings.

I imagine the rest of the castle settling in. Imogen has moved
out of the nursery suite and into a room by mine. I sometimes
smell her cigarettes, but she's as quiet as a ghost. Jessi will have
the Littles all lovingly tucked in against the night. Pelly will be
curled up to sleep in the corner of the training room. The tiny
purple demons will be in the damp, humid water heater closet
they claimed. Tsip will be wherever she exists when she's not

here, sleeping in her void beyond reality as a defense mechanism. Ancient Ruth Zabuto will be in her room under a thousand pounds of blankets next to five space heaters.

My mother, whom I should go talk to, but won't, will be in her rooms. She won't seek me out and force me to talk, even if she should. We'll both pretend like the mess at the warehouse wasn't weird. We still don't know how to be a mother and daughter, not really. And we're not Watcher and Slayer, either. What we are is fragile and tentative. For a moment I'm tempted. I imagine going to her room, but then what? There's no comfy chair or couch for me to curl up on. I can't wrap my brain around trying to sit on her bed and chat. There are so many years of walls between us; if only I could use my Slayer strength to vault right over them. But emotional walls don't care one way or another how strong I am.

There are two people I could actually talk to about all this, and both of them are gone. They both left me. One by dying and the other by walking away.

Unwilling to go back to my empty room, I head for the kitchen. I'm not nearly as tired as I should be after running for several hours, but I am *exactly* as hungry as I should be. I peel off my coat, wishing I had worn one I like less to run thirty miles in, then slip out of my sneakers. At least I had the foresight to wear those instead of cute boots. In just my rainbow-striped socks, I pad silently through the castle to the dining hall and kitchen.

The lights are on. Imogen is slow dancing with herself, humming along to a song playing on the portable stereo she scrounged the money for. Her apron is dusted with flour, the fine white powder clinging to her blond pigtails, too. She stops twirling and smiles at me.

"Do you want a warm cookie?" she asks.

"Plural, remember? There is no singular for cookies."

Imogen laughs, sweeping an arm to invite me into her domain. I sit on a counter, my legs swinging. The kitchen is the newest thing in the castle, and it doesn't fit at all. It was installed back when the castle was converted to be a sort of summer training camp for Watcher kids. I never would have come here then. Imogen wouldn't have either.

But the rest of our people were blown up by followers of the First Evil, so we get to take advantage of the stainless steel counters, massive fridge and freezer, four ovens, and twelve-burner stove range. It's not a good trade-off overall, but I'm glad Imogen seems happy in here.

She provides the warm cookies, as promised. They're soft and pillowy, and taste like—

"Banana chocolate chip?" I ask, baffled.

"Do you like them?"

"They're brilliant."

She beams. "Came up with the recipe myself." She passes me a plate and a glass of milk. They're like a hug in food form, and some of my anger and tension and fear melts away like the chocolate on my tongue.

Until Imogen opens her mouth and says, "So, when are you going to admit you're lying?" Her tone is as light and fluffy as the cookies.

I freeze midbite. "What do you mean?"

"I know everyone else bought—or pretended to buy—your story that your Slayer powers came back as part of a mystical 'chosen one' thing. That when Eve Silvera died, the powers were released back into the ether, where they floated around until they found you." She takes a handful of flour and tosses it in the air. "Poof! Slayer again! Except it doesn't work like that. The Slayer power is a well, and you're either connected to it or you're not. Eve drained you. Maybe you would have refilled eventually, but it would have taken years. So what actually happened to juice you up so fast?"

I'm surprised to find it's a relief to be called out after all this time. Imogen isn't my first choice to talk to about important things, but maybe that makes it easier. My relationships with everyone else are deeper and more intense. With Imogen, the stakes are lower. I shrug. "I can't believe everyone bought it either. They shouldn't have. Even Rhys! He didn't go to any of the books, do any research to verify my claims. It's like we're not even Watchers anymore."

Imogen smiles, wiping her hands clean on a dish towel. "Oh, some of us are still watching." Her sly smile widens, and I almost ask her what she means before she gestures to a timer. "Watching so the cookies don't burn."

"Truly the most important duty." I pick at my cookie, thinking. "I think they were all just so relieved that I was back to full Slayage, they didn't want to question it."

"It does give them a purpose. Don't get me wrong, Sanctuary is lovely. Really smashing job. But getting their Slayer back makes them feel like they're doing what they're supposed to. And probably makes them feel safer, what with Sean still out there and who knows what other threats."

"I don't make *everyone* feel safer." I frown, looking at the cookie in my hand and remembering an extra cookie, years ago, delivered to me during lunch by my impossible crush. My free hand drifts to my lips, haunted by the feel of Leo's on them. It turned out my crush was not so impossible after all. And yet more impossible than I could have ever dreamed. I hate that I can't even linger on the memory of the kiss, since it happened midbetrayal.

"What do you mean?" Imogen asks. "Who doesn't feel safe with you?"

"That werewolf family my mom went to meet with. I scared them."

"You're very frightening. It's the rainbow-striped socks, I think." Her teasing tone disappears when she sees the pained look on my face. She scoots onto the counter next to me. "Tell me what happened."

It's easier to talk side by side, when I don't have to look at her. "I lost it." I pause. "No, that's not true. I didn't lose it. I knew exactly what I was doing. My mom was pinned down by two mercenaries. Guns and everything. And I took them out. Everything I did felt right at the time. But the way the family looked at me—the way my mother looked at me—it was like *I* was the monster." I flinch. "I mean, technically I did use one of them as a shield against being shot."

"You were following your instincts, right?"

"Mostly. I held back, actually."

"Don't." Imogen sounds confident, matter-of-fact. "You're a Slayer. Your instincts keep you alive. Your instincts kept your mother and that ungrateful family alive. So next time your instincts tell you to go harder, go harder. Don't question yourself."

"It felt . . . *dark*, though."

"Did it? Or were you just afraid of it because of how others were judging you?"

I frown. If my mother hadn't been there, what would I have done? "I'm not sure. It bothers me, though. Instead of looking for ways to heal, lately I've been much better at seeing ways to hurt."

"People change. You grow up. You evolve. It's okay."

For years I longed for change. Lobbied for it, even. Constantly asked the Watchers Council to do things differently. To shift the way we engaged with the world, to look for better solutions. Less violent ways of navigating potential threats. A new structure within our ranks that stopped valuing those who could kill over everyone else.

And I got what I asked for. All it took was nearly every Watcher being wiped out, becoming a Slayer, and losing my sister as she went to find out who she was without the structure of the Watchers to hold her up.

I *hate* change. No wonder the Watchers never changed anything. "Change sucks."

Imogen nudges me with her shoulder. "It doesn't have to. Also, you still haven't told me how you got your power back. Don't think I've forgotten."

I hadn't meant to derail the conversation. Or maybe I had. I don't want to say it, but it's time. "Leo." It's the first I've said his name aloud in ages. I want it to surround me like a hug. Instead, it just falls from my mouth.

"What about him?"

"He gave the power back to me."

Imogen hops off the counter. "Whoa, whoa, hold up. Leo's dead."

"Yeah." I nod, miserable. After the dream where he restored everything in a seething burst of energy, I waited for him. But he never showed up. "Maybe a cambion thing. He was half demon, after all. Might have been able to stick around in some form long enough to transfer the power. Walking on dreams to get here or something."

"Have you researched it?"

I take another cookie and shove it in my mouth. "Slayer now, remember? I don't have to research."

"You really are claiming your destiny. I'm so proud." She puts her hands over her heart, laughing, then turns as a timer announces another batch of cookies is done.

The truth is, I didn't research cambions because it hurt too much. If Leo were still alive, he would have come back. He saved us, gave us enough time to defeat his mother. Everything we're building here is because of him. I just wish he could see it. It's his legacy as much as anything else. Sometimes I let myself imagine that he survived. That we all yelled at him for lying to us about his mother, that we actually got to work through the anger to the good stuff on the other side.

But it hurts, just like the idea of researching him or probing the mess of unresolved emotions he left along with my renewed powers. I talk to Imogen's back. "Don't tell anyone, okay?" It's too sad and too special and Rhys would pull it apart to find out how it worked, and my mother would clumsily try to comfort me, and I can't deal with either option.

Imogen mimes zipping her lips. "I am a perfect graveyard of secrets. They come to me and are buried snug and tight, six feet under." She resumes waltzing around the kitchen while I finish off the cookies. She doesn't talk again until I get up to stumble to bed.

"Next time," she says, passing me a plate to take, "don't hold back. You should *never* hold back. Promise me."

I wave the cookies. Imogen is a bit of a mystery as always, but it's nice to have her on my side. Almost like having my sister back. "Promise."

5

I LINE UP THE BODIES.

One: Eve Silvera. Her lipstick is still perfect, her pantsuit unwrinkled. She should be broken beyond repair, but she looks like she's sleeping. It's nice.

Two: Next to her, Leo. I try not to look at him, but I can't help it. His dark hair brushes his shoulders, his strong jaw not softened in death or sleep. His eyelids look so delicate, like they could flutter open anytime. But they won't.

Three: Cosmina. I arrange the dead Slayer's blue hair around her head like a halo. Pretty.

Four: Myself. No. Not myself. Artemis. Does she look more like me now, or do I look more like her? I cradle her a little longer, then sigh. It has to be done. I line her up next to the others. If she's here, then she's dead, and if she's dead, then it's my fault.

I want to cry, but here, in my childhood bedroom, surrounded by the static purple-black flames that once tried to claim me, I'm not allowed to. I have to take care of the bodies. I look up toward the door. So many more bodies waiting for me, arranged in neat triangles. I can see a few I recognize—Bradford Smythe. Cillian. Rhys. My mother. Everyone from the castle. But more behind them, waiting for me to bring them in and lay them nicely in a row.

So many bodies. How did I get so many bodies?

"Hello."

I turn to see a pretty Chinese girl, late teens or early twenties, her long black hair in a single braid. "You're not dead," I say.

"No." Her eyes keep flicking to my bodies. She holds out a hand. "Ice cream."

"What?"

"You need ice cream."

Puzzled, I take her hand. She tugs me, hard, and we leave my room. With a sudden rush of awareness, the truth slams into me:

I'm dreaming. This is a Slayer dream. And I've had it before. So many times. At least the bedroom-and-bodies part. Not this new development.

"Ice cream." She points emphatically to a table with a huge bowl of ice cream and a spoon. I sit obediently, looking at our surroundings. The room is enormous, entirely white. Along the walls, childlike illustrations chase one another. One is a girl with a stake, stabbing a cartoon vampire. Another is the same girl, a monster behind her, vivid spurts of red crayon pulsing from her neck.

Oh gods, ice cream girl needs my help.

I smile encouragingly at her. But she's just standing there, staring intently at me. She hasn't sat down, doesn't have ice cream of her own. "Are you going to have any?"

She wrinkles her nose in disgust. "No."

There's a buzzing, a low pulse of noise I can feel in my bones.

I hadn't noticed it before, but it's been with us the entire time. I look behind me. The room extends forever, the illustrations continuing their macabre stories. But in the distance, a roiling nothingness creeps closer.

"Are you a Slayer?" I ask.

Her nose wrinkles in the same disgust she gave the ice cream, but she nods.

"Are you in trouble?" The last time I had a dream about a Slayer like this, it was Cosmina. She needed help, and I failed her. I *won't* fail again.

"Eat your ice cream." She folds her arms and glares.

"I can help you."

She raises an eyebrow, her full lips pursed.

"The storm." I point back at it. "Something's coming. I can help. I'm a Slayer too."

"It is not my storm." She picks up the spoon, fills it with ice cream, and stuffs it in my mouth.

I sputter around the tasteless cold mess. "Stop!"

"Ice cream helps!" She swats away my hands and force-feeds me another bite. "It makes you sick, but it helps! Giles told me! I have to help!"

I push away, the chair tipping backward and dumping me onto the floor. A new woman appears above me. Dreadlocks frame a face covered with elaborate white face paint. I recognize her! The First Slayer! Buffy told me about her. I—

She raises a blade overhead and slams it into my stomach.

6

I WAKE UP WITH A GASP, MY HANDS over my stomach. When I pull them away, I'm surprised they're not slick with dark blood. It felt so real.

I lie back. Having a Slayer dream—one where I was at least a little in control—makes me realize I haven't been having the same Slayer dreams I used to. Not since Leo gave me back my power. Though the bedroom, my old familiar nightmare, had been there too. And it was filled with . . .

The edges of the dream drift away like smoke, and I let them. All I remember is the cold burst of the ice cream and the colder pierce of the blade. Why did the First Slayer kill me? And why did the pretty Slayer lure me into that room for it to all happen?

Sleep permanently over for the night, I sit up and rub my eyes. I half turn to check if Artemis is awake before realizing, yet again, she's not in the other bed.

When I was fourteen, I got a deeply ill-advised haircut, chopping my long locks into a chin-length horror. But for months after, whenever I got into a car or lay down in bed, I reached up to pull my long hair out of the way. Every time, it surprised me to find only empty air.

When will I stop reaching for Artemis where she isn't?

I climb out of bed and throw on some clothes in the dark. I stop by the gym only to check on Pelly. It's awake and hurries to my side, gentle eyes bright. I try not to look at the gym; it was the scene of so many of my moments with Leo. Instead, we head into the darkness. I run as fast and hard as I can, even though I'm only a few hours separated from my most recent run. Pelly keeps up. It's fast—another detail that, coupled with the pairs of eyes placed on either side of its head more like a rabbit than a fox, makes it obvious Pelly's breed of demon has always been prey. Never predator. Our Watcher texts didn't bother mentioning that. I made sure Rhys noted it in his entry for *Unpellis Demons*.

We're back at the castle before the sun rises. Pelly curls up under a tree while I do pull-ups, less to build strength and more to try and exhaust it. What used to feel like potential now feels like a constant tension. Less like I'm ready for any fight that might happen, and more like I'm aching for something—anything—to fight.

With nothing else to do, I head inside and shower, then walk to the library to kill a couple hours—the only thing I'm allowed to kill, I guess—before everyone gathers for our weekly meeting. We gave up the council room, preferring the cushy chairs we dragged into the library and set up in a circle. It feels more familiar to us than a stiff, formal room anyway.

The whole castle is dark and asleep. So I stop short when I see a strip of light beneath the polished wood door to the library. I have to fight against the instant alarm and wariness that seizes me. It's probably Rhys, or my mother. Still, I open the door as silently as possible, on high alert. And then I freeze. It's a familiar face, after all. But not one I expected to find.

Artemis?

Artemis!

"You're back!" I rush into the room and throw my arms around Artemis in a hug. She came back. Seeing her here is like being able to take a deep breath for the first time in months. Things are going to be better now.

She's holding a thick book, and it presses into me between us, trapped by my hug. "I knew it. I knew you'd finally get smart and leave Honora. I'm so happy you're home! We have so much to talk about!"

But Artemis hasn't said anything. And she's still just holding that book. If she snuck in to come home, why wasn't she waiting in our room? Why is she in the library? I cringe with guilt and try to form something like sympathy on my face as I release her. "Are you okay? Was it a bad breakup?"

I don't hope it was. But I hope it was. *Get it together, Nina.* It's my turn to be here for Artemis. She must not have been ready to face everyone yet after walking out on us for Honora and having that fall apart. I will *not* let my glee show. "We've all missed you."

She still hasn't said anything, and an alarm is ringing insistently somewhere inside me. Something is wrong. Did she get hurt? Is she in trouble? I babble, trying to fill the space between us. "We have meetings in here now. Didn't want to use the old council room. Too stuffy. And we don't really have lessons anymore. Not like we used to, anyway, though obviously Rhys still spends every waking hour studying. He's working on some really great resources for us. And Imogen isn't in charge of the Littles or teaching anymore; she's mostly in the kitchen. Wait until you try her cookies. You won't have to do those duties anymore, not unless you want to. We'll work you into the schedule however you want, though everyone has to do a shift of bathroom cleaning, unfortunately. I tried to argue that it's not part of my skills as a Slayer, but no one bought it. Anyway, you'll get to pick what you want to do now, so that's good, right?"

"I'm not back, Nina."

The blow I was bracing for lands. I sit, staring at her. "Just visiting?" I keep my tone light and hopeful. But this doesn't feel like a friendly visit. You don't sneak into the castle in the dead of night if you want to pop by to check on how everyone's doing. "Lots of new residents to introduce you to. How long are you staying?"

"You know I'm not." She shakes her head, then sits across from me. But she's not slumped in a chair. She's perched on the edge of it, halfway up already. I can't put my finger on what's different until I realize she's bracing herself against me. She used to orbit around me, always busy, anticipating needs before I had them. The way she's sitting, it's not like she's half ready to get up and help me with something. It's like she's in a runner's crouch, ready to take off. Away from me.

She finally looks me in the eyes. The rest of my dream hits me like cold water, plunging me back into the memory of laying her body down. We *do* look more alike now. But that fills me with panic. I don't want that dream to be right about anything.

"You should turn them out," Artemis says.

"Who?" I ask, trying to get the image of all the bodies out of my head.

"The demons."

"Why would we do that?"

"They make you a target."

"I'm already a target. We all are. We're protecting ourselves and everyone else who needs it." I sound more desperate than I want to. I want her to be impressed with what I'm doing here. To want to be part of it. She was always so supportive of my efforts to be castle medic and to expand my skills there. I finally have my mother's approval, but it doesn't compensate for losing my twin's.

Artemis hugs the book she's holding to her chest like a shield. "No one cares about Slayers anymore. They care even less about Watchers. If you weren't running your little animal hospital here, no one would so much as lift a claw against you. All these years hiding were totally down to Watcher hubris. They couldn't imagine a world that didn't care about them, so they assumed everyone still wanted them gone, when in reality, no one even thinks about them anymore." She looks around the library, shaking her head. "It's like a mausoleum in here. You're all living with the dead, still letting them control you."

I jab a finger at her. "That's not you talking. That's Honora. This matters because it's *our* past. Our heritage. Our link to Dad."

Her eyes narrow, sharp and cutting. "You think Dad would want this? You staying hidden in a castle, isolated from the world, not doing anything to protect it? It's *selfish*."

I flinch at her words. "It is not. I'm protecting people!"

"No, you're protecting demons. You think I don't know who you've taken in? You have a vengeance demon, for hell's sake!

How much carnage is she responsible for? And now because her wish-granting is broken, suddenly she deserves help? I know you didn't like the way Watchers did things, but gods, at least Watchers protected their own. What you're doing here is irresponsible and dangerous. If you want to keep the Watchers safe, kick the demons out."

"If we do that, we're right back to what we used to be!"

"Who cares? You're exactly what you always wanted. The most important girl in the castle."

Her words pierce with more brutal force than the First Slayer's blade did in my dream. Something in her face softens seeing my reaction. She sighs and leans forward, almost against her will. "I don't mean that. But you always wanted to be a Watcher. You wanted this." She lets go of the book and gestures to the room and castle around us. "And you're holding on to it in the only ways you can. But you're wrong. You're all wrong. Be Watchers or be normal. This hybrid mess you've created will get people hurt."

Is she right? Did I build Sanctuary with myself at the center just so I could finally matter the way I wanted to? But I didn't do it for myself. I did it for Doug—kind, funny. Pelly, padding silently by my side. Jessi, who's sort of the worst but loves the Littles as much as they deserve to be loved. Weirdo Tsip. The tiny purple demons.

I think of Leo. If he had had something like this to turn to, somewhere he could admit what he was and be accepted for it— helped, loved—he might still be here.

The demons, the Watchers, even the Slayers. We're all castoffs, relics of other worlds and times and magic. If we don't protect one another, who will?

Besides which, the residents of Sanctuary are *mine*. Every demon here. I made them a promise. Buffy protected the whole world, yeah, but she stayed in Sunnydale until the end. She protected her home and the people she loved first.

"I'm doing the right thing." I'm surprised at how firm my voice is.

Artemis is too, judging by her expression. "You've changed," she says. She sounds unhappy about it.

"You've been gone awhile." We sit in silence, then I resolve to fix it. She might not come back, but that doesn't mean we have to be separated. Not totally. "If you're not going to stay, that's fine. But let's go get some breakfast. I want to hear what you've been doing. How you are."

Her hands tighten around the book, and I glance at it. There's no title, only a symbol on the cover. Three interlocking triangles. I know I've seen it somewhere. The scent of fresh produce wafts into my memory, and I place it. It's the symbol that was on all of demon drug dealer Sean's tea. What it's doing on a book in our library, I don't know. But I do know that Artemis snuck in here in the middle of the night to get it. That's what she's here for. The only thing she's here for.

"You're working with Sean, aren't you?" I clench my jaw. "He can't have Doug back."

She rolls her eyes. "This is bigger than Sean. And you can't exactly criticize me for who I choose to associate with, given your little demon menagerie here."

"Sean's a creep! You're better than this!"

She stands, glaring at me. "I *am* better than this. I'm better than Sean, and I'm better than the Watchers, and you have no idea what I'm doing, so keep your judgy eyebrows to yourself."

"My eyebrows are not judgy!"

"Your eyebrows are so judgy they might as well have a gavel!"

We both glare at each other. I crack first. "Can they have a frilly white collar like Ruth Bader Ginsburg?"

She tries to hold her stern look, but the edges are trembling. "No. Your eyebrows have to wear a huge gross wig because we're not in the USA, we're in Ireland."

I snort, which turns into a giggle. Artemis was never one for giggling, but even she grins at me, and for a few precious moments we're each other's again.

Then she sighs and tucks the book under her arm. I shouldn't let her take it. It feels urgently wrong. Maybe that's just my long-standing friendship with Rhys speaking, or maybe it's some deeper instinct. But if I tell her no, I don't know what will happen. And I need Artemis to be okay, I need her to be okay with me, so that when things fall apart for her—which they will—she'll come back. She'll be my twin again. We'll paint each other's nails and watch bad movies, and then I'll have my mother *and* my sister.

I shove down my feelings and choose to ignore the fact that she's stealing from us and I don't know why. "Should I tell Mom you were here?"

Artemis shakes her head. "I didn't want anyone to see me." She bites her lips. She didn't mean to admit that. If I hadn't come into the library, she would have been in and out, and I never would have known.

It stings, and the aftertaste of laughing with her turns bitter. "Rhys will never forgive you for taking a book."

She smiles, but it's tight and full of tension, just like her ponytail. "It's my library too. You said so yourself. Our heritage. I'm owed a lot of back pay for years of free labor. I'll consider this a down payment."

"Don't give it to Sean. Please." I can forgive her sneaking in, stealing the book, but not for that. Not for him.

"It's for me, dummyrabbit." She pauses, then straightens her shoulders like she's settled something internally. "It's for all of us. You'll understand."

"What does that mean? Please. Talk to me. Tell me what's going on." I pause. "Stay," I whisper. She pretends like she doesn't hear me as she zips up her leather jacket.

"I have your other coat," I say, flinging out any words I can think of that might hook her. "In our room."

"I'll get it next time." The words linger between us to soften the tension. Next time. She's coming back. I lean toward her for a hug, but she turns and walks out into the dark hallway, not even a scent lingering in her wake. She's just gone. Again.

7

I STAY IN THE LIBRARY AS THE SUN RISES. My mother is first in, of course. I wonder if she'll somehow be able to sense that Artemis was here. And she does look uncomfortable as she sits across from me and sips her tea, but then I remember what happened at the warehouse and realize it's all about me.

I can't leave. It would be too obvious I'm trying to avoid her. Which is funny, because I used to be desperate for one-on-one time with her. I pick up a book at random and pretend to be absorbed in it. I wonder what was in the book that Artemis stole. She said she wasn't giving it to Sean, and I trust her on that. I have to. I can't tell Rhys she took it, though. He'd never forgive her. And I know they'd judge her, speculate about what she's doing. She'll be back. She said so. I won't let our people turn themselves against her in the meantime. Artemis spent a lot of years protecting me; I feel fiercely protective of her even when I'm hurt and pissed off at her. I get to feel that way, but no one else does.

"We should talk about yesterday," my mother says, surprising me. I really didn't think she'd bring it up.

"What about it?" I don't look up from the history of a minor hellgod. It might as well be a fairy tale now. Wherever this hellgod lives, it can't get here to find more sacrifices. No more portals, thanks to Buffy.

Buffy. I wish I had been able to see her in the Slayer dream. I haven't run into her in the dreamspaces, not in months. I really *want* to talk to her. It's a stark change to how I used to feel about her. If I can't have a Watcher, can I at least have the reigning Slayer?

"I'm concerned about your tactics," my mother says.

I put the book down, defensiveness rearing in me like a snake ready to strike. First Artemis telling me I'm being selfish, and now my mom questioning my fighting. "What about them?"

"They were . . . excessive."

"I held back! My instincts were telling me to do much worse." Imogen told me I should have done exactly what my instincts told me to. Why is my mom giving me crap for it? "And besides, are you saying they didn't deserve what they got? They were trying to shoot you! They were hunting a family. For money."

My mother takes another prim sip of tea. "I think they did deserve much worse. From a tactical standpoint, your actions were both effective and reasonable."

"Then why are we talking about them?"

"Because I'm not speaking from a tactical standpoint. I'm speaking as your mother. Your actions would have made sense for a mercenary. Or even another Watcher. But you're not either of those things. You're Nina." Her voice gets soft, almost tentative. "My Nina. And that didn't feel like you. Lately you've seemed . . ."

I can't listen to my mother tell me who I am. Not after so many years of her deliberately hiding who I was, trying to keep me from becoming what mystical forces had chosen me for. I know she's trying, I do, and I want her to try, but she has no right to make these judgments. I'm already raw and stinging from my encounter with Artemis. I open my mouth to snap something I know I'll regret, but I'm saved by the door opening.

"Why is it so early?" Jade enters the room, trailing sleep like car exhaust in her wake. She slumps in the chair next to me. "Can't we have these meetings in the afternoon?"

"Good morning!" Rhys is bright-eyed and perky, even his curls not flopping over his forehead. Doug joins us, sitting next to Jade, and finally Imogen walks in, bringing a tray of fresh pastries and fruit.

I'm immensely grateful my mother and I can't keep talking now that our complete Watcher-Sanctuary Council group is here. Ruth Zabuto doesn't care. Jessi only wants information if it affects the Littles. Tsip sometimes appears in the middle of the meetings, but disappears just as quickly. The tiny purple demons understand English but can't speak it and were banned from the library after eating several irreplaceable volumes. It's the only time I've seen Rhys look genuinely terrifying. He's been trained to kill, like every Watcher, and he was a heartbeat away from ending their violet lives. Another reason not to tell him about Artemis.

Cillian is always invited, but he spends his mornings tending his shop in town. With his mom still gone on a months-long soul-searching trip, he's got to keep it up in order to pay their bills. It sucks that he has to work to afford a house he barely stays in now, though.

Rhys runs through the morning itinerary. Finances—always tight, but okay for now. Task assignments. I imagine where Artemis would be slotted in, but it hurts, so I stop. Rhys moves on to a review of those with invitations for Sanctuary entrance interviews.

"We can cross off the werewolf family." I avoid eye contact with my mother. "They decided to go in another direction." The opposite direction of wherever I am.

"Just as well. Children are expensive." Rhys makes some notes, then talks with Imogen about how the kitchen food stock rotation is going, and whether she needs to add anything to our purchase lists.

"What about the chickens?" Jade asks.

"What?" Imogen frowns.

"That woman you were talking to on the phone about chickens. Are we getting chickens?"

Imogen's frown slips into a slightly vacant smile. "Oh, right. I'm looking into it. Fresh eggs every day. And they're better for you."

Rhys makes a note. "Draw up a plan and we'll review it." It's all very efficient and boring. The light in the library is warm and golden, dust motes winking in the air. I half expect Imogen to get up and begin our next lesson on demonology, or instruct me to translate a prophecy from Ancient Sumerian into Latin into English.

But we don't do that anymore. It's weird how suddenly and fiercely I wish I could be slacking off, copying Artemis's notes, and heading to my little medical center to tidy up and organize. As much as I wanted more back then, it's hard not to think about how much I actually had and took for granted.

Rhys clears his throat. "Which brings us to outstanding threats."

"Outstanding like phenomenal?" Doug asks, frowning.

"Yes, all our phenomenal enemies," I answer.

"We really do have some excellent ones," he agrees.

I shrug. "We could do better. I mean, look at Buffy. Our enemy caliber is nowhere near hers."

Doug pats my shoulder. "I have faith that you'll get there. Give it some time. She's had years to build up her rogues' gallery."

Rhys clears his throat in a decidedly annoyed manner. "Back to the subject at hand of outstanding *as in still active* threats. Any word on Sean?"

I stay very, very quiet, hoping Doug can't smell my inner conflict. Artemis said the book wasn't for Sean. Just because it has the same symbol as his tea doesn't mean she's working for him. It could be unrelated. Or she could be fighting him! Maybe that's it. Artemis is taking out threats that might harm us. Imagining that makes me feel better. It does seem like an Artemis thing to do. Behind the scenes, making sure everyone is safe. She said she was doing it for all of us.

My mother shakes her head. "I send out feelers whenever possible, but Sean has been relatively quiet. And I've never encountered him or any agents working for him during my meetings off-site. Mind you, he's still active. But his activities have never conflicted with our movements."

Jade waves a hand lazily through the air. "If he's not bothering us, why do we care? He only goes after demons, anyway."

The awkward silence hangs in the air, a palpable weight. Doug shifts in his seat. "Oh. Only demons."

Jade sits up straight. "No! Obviously I didn't mean you. That's different."

"Love, it really isn't." Doug retracts his hand where Jade reaches for it.

"I agree with Doug," I say. If Artemis is going after Sean, we need to stay out of her way. I can't let the council decide to start investigating him. The last thing I want is for us to mess up Artemis's plans and keep her away even longer. "But at the same time, we aren't in a position to launch a preemptive offensive. And even if we were, I don't know that we should. It's not that I don't think what he does to demons is wrong. I do. But if we start going on the attack, we'll be right back where we used to be. Watchers and Slayers deciding who gets to live and who has to die based on archaic criteria. That's not who we are. Who we want to be." I remember how close I came to letting that mercenary fall, and twitch against a shudder. "Anyway, we chose to be a sanctuary. Not a militia. We're better than that, right?"

Doug nods. He hates Sean, but all Doug wants in the world is happiness. He doesn't have a predatory bone in his black-and-yellow body. Even his horns are rounded.

"So let's come up with ideas for how we can help more demons *and* people." Whatever Artemis said, this isn't selfish. This is right.

"And werewolves?" Rhys adds with a raised eyebrow. He still doesn't know why the family ran.

"Sure, whatever."

"What about Slayers?" my mother asks. "I'd like to bring

more in. Surely there are girls out there who need our help, or a
support system. Even just a safe place to live. Do you know, your
father lobbied to give Slayers a stipend for living expenses. He
never could understand how with the expansive Watcher budget, we couldn't find room to ensure that Slayers didn't have
to worry. It seems too much to ask that they spend every night
patrolling and fighting the forces of evil and every day trying to
provide for themselves. Though Buffy herself derailed any dis-
cussion of financial support when she refused to work with us.
Still. Even before that, look at the conditions Faith Lehane had
to endure. Is it any wonder she—"

Rhys clears his throat, cutting her off. I'm oddly touched that
my mother is so passionate about the ways Watchers failed Slayers.
It feels like she's taking my side in a roundabout way.

Rhys doesn't care about that, though. "We hardly have the
budget to subsidize additional Slayers, much less the one we already
have." He frowns down at his paper. "Crossbow maintenance alone
threatens to bankrupt us. I vote we move the tiny purple demons
to stake-carving duty. We live in a forest. We should take advantage of existing resources."

My mother looks at me. "I'm not talking about funding Slayers.
I'm talking about taking them in."

I squirm in my seat. That was my job. The big one assigned
to me from day one of Sanctuary. I was supposed to find other
Slayers in my dreams. But last night was my first real Slayer dream
in months, and all I found was a blade in my belly. "There was a
Slayer in my dream last night. Didn't get her name. And honestly,
I can't figure out if she needed help or not."

My mother sets down her teacup. "What happened?"

"She brought me to a weird room. And then, uh, fed me ice cream."

Jade snickers. "Bow-chicka-bow-wow. What happened next?"

"I got stabbed."

Jade wrinkles her nose. "Not sexy anymore."

My mother frowns, concerned. "She stabbed you?"

"No, someone else—it doesn't matter. It was unrelated." I don't want to tell them it was the First Slayer who stabbed me. I don't know what it means, and it doesn't relate to our meeting. Also it's kind of embarrassing. "There was a big storm coming. Which could be a threat to this girl, right?"

My mother jots down notes in a leather-bound journal. "See if you can find her again. Get some concrete details so we can track her down."

"Will do." Except I don't know that I can. I seem to have lost control of my dreams along with everything else. "What about the name the mercenaries gave us? Ian Von Assface? Or whatever it was."

"No." My mother's answer is shockingly curt.

"What do you mean, 'no'? We know he's collecting were-wolves for a hunt. And the full moon isn't far off. Shouldn't we at least look into who he is?" I'm certain we could figure it out. Aside from our library, we have Cillian, who's good at finding information online. It's not a skill Watchers ever developed.

"I know who he is," my mother says, surprising me. "He's worked with us—with the Watchers—in the past. It's not something we should pursue at this time."

"Why not?"

Her expression closes like a door. This is the mother I used to know. Cold and distant. "Because we can't afford to lose any allies."

"With allies like that, who needs enemies?" I lean forward, heart rate rising. "He buys werewolves to hunt them. I think we should look into it."

"Do you know where we got our cars, Nina? Who financed those? Who donated this castle and the land it sat on before we moved it here? Ian Von Alston. So unless you can afford to replace a car if we lose one, or buy next winter's clothes for the Littles, or keep up repairs on this absurdly old castle, I suggest we not attack one of our only potential sources of future funds."

Doug toys with one of the delicate gold hoops he always wears in his ears. He's maintained the distance between himself and Jade. "Right. Well. I might have a lead on demons who need help, or at least a way to get some leads. There's a sort of convention every year in London. A get-together of emotion-eaters. It's a combination networking, advice, and matchmaking event."

Jade scowls, jealousy twisting her face. "Matchmaking?"

"Do you think anyone there would need our help?" I ask, ignoring Jade.

"Maybe. And even if not, they might have scoops on demons who are in a bad way. We deal in emotions; we tend to know where to find the best *and* worst ones. It's tomorrow, though, so we'll need to leave right away."

The idea of taking a trip away from the increasingly claustrophobic castle fills me with relief. "Let's do it."

Rhys adds it to the agenda. "Who do we want to send?"

"I'll go," Doug says. "I'm your way in."

"Are you sure that's safe?" my mother asks. "If Sean still wants you, he might think to look for you there."

"Sean knows where to find me here, too. If he wants to come for me, he's going to."

"I'll be with you," I say.

Doug smiles. "Thanks. That makes me feel safe."

His sentiment warms me, and I beam. Then I roll my eyes as his nostrils flare. He shifts defensively. "What? You give me hardly anything to eat these days. Can't blame a guy for taking advantage of a good meal when it's available."

"I'll come too." Jade reaches out and aggressively takes Doug's hand.

I see the flicker of discomfort behind his hazel eyes. I can't smell emotions, but I can read them. I shake my head. "No. I have to focus on keeping Doug safe. I can only do that if I'm not distracted."

"I can handle myself!"

I backtrack. "Yeah, which is why I need you here. So I'm not distracted worrying about the castle. I want every trained Watcher here when I'm not."

Jade slumps in her chair, scowling. "Fine."

Imogen clears the remains of the breakfast platter. "I'll pack snacks for the road." She hums as she leaves the room. Doug blinks, a bit dazed watching her. Rhys finalizes his notes and asks for a few more details from Doug. My mother watches me too closely. I stare up at the window, tired and sad and angry and only certain why I feel the first thing.

I know I should be focused on helping others, but all I can think is that a demon convention is exactly the distraction I need. I push down the fear lingering at the back of my mind that I might want more than a distraction. That I might be looking for a fight. I'm not that person.

The memory of the fight with the mercenaries—and, worse, my instincts to hurt Tsip when she surprised me—disagrees with me, though.

Whatever. I'll find more demons to help. I'll figure out how to contact Slayers who might need me. I'll prove to Artemis that we made the right choice, that we aren't just hiding. That we're doing good. And when she comes back next time, she'll stay.

ARTEMIS

ARTEMIS HAS TO ADMIT THAT SEAN HAS upgraded. His subterranean office beneath a health-food storefront was fine, but the building in front of them is nearly blinding. It's all windows and steel, something elegant in its surprising angles. The windows are interlocking triangles. The effect is oddly disorienting.

"The old building is cordoned off for being an environmental hazard," Honora says, squinting up at the gleaming new one. "They're filling the whole area in with cement."

"A remora demon that expands to fill whatever container it's in is pretty hazardous." Artemis tightens her ponytail. "How did he afford this?"

"This isn't Sean's building. This is the guy Sean started partnering with. I only met him once. He was . . . weird. Big weird. Bad weird. I did my best to stay clear. I can smell a toxic power complex from two kilometers." Her hands twitch, her fingers going to her wrists.

Back at the main Watcher compound, before everything and everyone blew up, Artemis had asked Nina how to treat bruises and welts. Nina was more than happy to show her. And then Artemis had found Honora and they hid in a cool, dry pantry while Artemis treated the damage Honora's mother did. It was the first time Artemis had felt what the other girls giggled and whispered about when they had crushes. But hers felt so much bigger, so much more important.

A surge of protective instinct wells in Artemis. "You don't have to do this."

Honora bites her plum-colored lips. Her voice is neutral, but so *carefully* neutral Artemis can sense the hope behind it. Honora's cool act is her biggest tell. The more she cares, the less it shows. "We could go to California. My cousin is still there, I think. We stake the vampire he works for, take over the PI company, then Nancy Drew the shit out of America."

"How would Wesley feel about that?"

"Wesley Wyndam-Pryce," Honora says in an exaggeratedly stuffy voice. "We could take him. I can't imagine Los Angeles has changed him that much."

For a moment, Artemis lets herself imagine it. Running away with Honora. Building a new life somewhere bright and warm, the environmental opposite of cold, closed-off Watchers. But there would still be the problem of power. Other people would have it, and Artemis wouldn't. And then how could she protect Honora? How could she protect herself? How could she face what she knows is in the world as just herself? She needs to be more. And this is how to do it.

"Maybe someday." She pretends to miss the slight fall of

Honora's shoulders. "But you don't have to do this. Get me in and then if you want to leave, you should."

Honora slides mirrored aviator sunglasses into place, and her lips part in a smile. If she's devastated, she doesn't show it. She never does. "It's you and me against the world, right?"

Once, Artemis would have said the same to Nina. The memory of Nina's disappointment in the library sits heavy alongside Honora's dashed hopes. But until Artemis is what she should be, she's going to keep disappointing everyone. It's all a means to an end, and then they'll understand and everything will be right. She has the book. She knows what to look for, what to wait for, what to do.

"You and me." Artemis squeezes Honora's hand. "You're my girl."

"Damn straight. Or damn gay, if we're being accurate." Honora beams and holds open the door. As soon as they enter the sleek lobby, Honora's demeanor shifts. Her walk is deliciously sexy and somehow snide at the same time. Artemis doesn't know how she does it. Honora goes straight to the receptionist's desk and hops on it, sitting there and leaning back on her arms.

"Can I help you?" The receptionist's pinched face threatens to pinch completely closed on itself in shock.

"Tell Sean I'm here."

The receptionist glares. "And you are?"

"He'll know." Honora winks at Artemis over the top of her sunglasses. Artemis leans against a wall, unable to be flippant like Honora. She folds her arms and sets her face in stone. She can't reveal how she feels. Because she's not nervous. She's excited.

The receptionist makes a call and not a minute later a man

who could only be described as a born minion—small with rat-
like eyes and greasy hair—leads them to an elevator and pushes
an elaborate series of buttons. They glide up the building to the
penthouse floor. All the walls along the hallway are glass, so they
see the meeting before they reach it. A huge oval table is surrounded by men in suits. They're watching a screen filled with
graphs and charts. Sean himself is the one presenting, using a
stupid laser pointer to emphasize certain points.

Artemis and Honora slip into the back of the room, standing
next to a bound and gagged demon cowering in the corner next
to a potted plant.

"—projected margins are—" Sean stops midsentence, then
points to Artemis with the laser pointer. "Which one is she?" His
face has gone several shades redder.

"The good one," Honora says with a shrug.

"Good as in morally good as in a Slayer, or good as in—"

"Good as in here with me. So what do you think?"

Sean glares but goes back to his droning speech about projec-
tions and quarters and other nonsense. All the men at the table
are rapt, nodding along and tapping notes onto their devices.

But one of the men, a white guy with black hair and piercing
dark eyes, is staring into space. Artemis can't quite look away
from him. He's like when an older movie is shown on one of
those super-high-def televisions, so everything looks somehow
too real, which then makes it look fake. Like he's 3-D on a 2-D
background.

"It's all imaginary," he says, his voice a soft, melodious tenor.
"All these numbers, all this money, all these things you fight and
die for."

Sean smiles patiently. "Right, yes, but we like our imaginary numbers to be very, very high." The rest of the men laugh uneasily. Sean keeps talking.

The man turns toward them. Artemis's breath catches. She was right. This is *him*. This has to be him. He's not a man at all. He frowns, his eyes lingering on Artemis's hair. "Autumn is the saddest season. All seasons are sad. Time is death. It's so quiet here. Do you ever want to pierce the silence?" He has a slender knife in his hands, one finger running up and down the edge.

"Can't say as I do," Honora says. Her arms are folded, and she's not betraying any fear.

Artemis isn't afraid either. She's thrilled. If only Rhys were here, he'd pee his pants at this real-world research opportunity. The book she took was right. It's all going to work. She smiles, and the Sleeping One, the one with no name, the three-form god, tilts his head as he considers her.

"Right, so, supplies." Sean switches the slideshow off. "Big opportunity coming up. Honora, if you're back, I'm assuming you'll lead?"

Honora snaps her gum. "Not a problem."

"We can't guarantee we'll find the right specimen, but there's a good chance something like this will draw one out. Or at least provide someone who knows where to find what we need. And, hey, maybe we'll luck out and find another option. Gotta be flexible. It's how we stay young." He grins the desperate *please acknowledge I am still young* grin only a man in his early thirties would.

"I have never been young," the Sleeping One says. "I have always been here. I will always be here. I cannot stay here under these circumstances. To know infinity and be powerless to touch it is the cruelest fate of all."

The demon bound in the corner whimpers. Artemis feels a pit of dread in her stomach that they're going to see a crueler fate in a few minutes.

The Sleeping One slides the knife right into his own ear, as far and deep as it will go. Sean turns a shade of green more often found on demons. Honora pops her gum. Artemis watches. The Sleeping One slowly withdraws the knife. It oozes with a shimmering luminescence that fades to nothing in the air.

"Still so quiet," he says.

"Time for the quarterly sacrifice." Sean straightens his tie and tries to brusquely move them back to business as usual as he pulls out a sword and approaches the demon in the corner.

Means to an end, Artemis thinks to herself, not taking her eyes off the hellgod she's going to defeat all on her own.

Suck it, Slayers.

8

DOUG AND I DRIVE TO THE PORT IN Dublin, where we steer onto the cheapest ferry to England. I didn't want to take a car at all—with this one gone, the castle only has one vehicle left, and apparently sleazebags are our only options for enough money to replace them—but public transportation isn't really an option with Doug's obviously not-human face.

As it is, he sits in the passenger seat with a hoodie on, hood up over his horns and his face as shadowed as possible.

I climb back into the car in the bottom of the ferry with two Cokes and some snacks. I hold out one of the Cokes, and Doug looks at me as though I'm daft.

"Right. Sorry." I forget sometimes just how demon-y Doug really is. He fits in so well at the castle. The differences between us don't seem to matter. Differences like the fact that I eat food and he eats emotions.

His stomach rumbles in response to my thoughts. "No offense, Nina, love, but you are barely a snack these days. More like an after-dinner mint. One of those unwrapped buttermints that's been in a tin for years, and when you try to pull it out, it's stuck to three others, and you know you don't want it, but you've already committed, so you pop it in your mouth and regret every decision you've ever made that brought you to that point."

"I think I *should* be offended by that."

Doug shrugs. "I think you and I should talk about why you're so unhappy."

"Or we could enjoy this ferry ride with an incredible view of the backside of a Mini for the next several hours. What do they call the bigger Mini Coopers? Maxi Coopers? Mega Coopers?"

Doug doesn't take my desperate topic change bait. "I never officially met Leo," he says. "But judging by the pain, he was pretty special."

I groan, slumping in my seat. I can't talk about it because then I'll have to think about it, and I can't think about it. "Am I prying into your personal life? Asking questions about Jade?"

"Actually, I wouldn't mind talking about it. At first it was flattering, yeah? She's cute. Her happiness had a nice sort of lemon twist to it. Tart and surprising."

"That's weird. But also intriguing. What does everyone else taste like?"

"Rhys tastes like freshly cut grass smells. But when Cillian is around, he tastes like bubble gum. And Cillian tastes like— mmm, let's see. Have you ever been starving and walked into a bakery and the first deep breath in almost hurts, it's so good? That's him. Imogen . . ." He pauses. "You know, it's weird. I don't like smelling her."

"Bad?"

"Not bad. Just . . . off. She makes the back of my throat itch."

"Maybe you're allergic to her! Is that possible?"

He shrugs. "Maybe."

"What does my mom taste like?"

"I rarely get anything from your mom at all. Good or bad. That woman has worked very, very hard to be emotionless. She's been through a lot."

I scowl. I don't like feeling bad for my mom, because it means I have to feel less bad for myself and everything Artemis and I went through being raised by her. It's petty, I know, but it's true. "We all have. What about Jessi?"

"She smells like hand sanitizer. Actually, that might just be hand sanitizer. And Ruth Zabuto smells like English breakfast tea."

"Well, that's going to make drinking that tea weird now. But back to Jade. You like the way she tastes. Gods, that sounds dirty. Keep going. But no dirty details, if there are any, please."

He toys with one of his gold hoop earrings. "I like the castle. I like all of you. I like that Jade likes me. It's been a long time since I had any real human contact other than Sean and his ilk taking advantage of me. And I'm glad she's happy. But I worry about how much she's using. It's one of the things I want to talk to some of the fellows at the convention about. There's a reason my type don't usually stay in relationships or even friendships. We can be a bit addictive." He sighs, rubbing his face. His skin still looks like a cracked desert floor, neon yellow with black beneath. But he seems healthier than when I first found him after he escaped from Sean. His cheeks are fuller, his pretty and incongruously brown eyes clear.

"No one else in the castle uses you like that, do they?" I should have been paying more attention. Doug's skin secretes a psycho-tropic substance. It has to be ingested to have an effect, which I assumed would mean no one taking advantage of him. But for all I know, they've been lacing their tea with Essence of Doug.

"No, no one. Which isn't to say I haven't been tempted to give you a dose every now and again." He holds up his hands at my horrified expression. "But I would never do it, because I know what it's like to have choices taken away from me, and I only use it as a defense mechanism when absolutely required."

I laugh, relieved. "I used it that way once too."

"Really? How?"

It was right after Sean and Honora had found Doug where my mother was hiding him in the forest. His torn and beloved Coldplay shirt was left behind in the struggle. Leo had been try-ing to kidnap me to get me away from his mother, but I didn't know that. I grabbed Doug's shirt and shoved it in Leo's mouth, blissing him out long enough to get back to the castle . . . and right into his mother's claws. Which led to Artemis getting hurt, me sacrificing my power to save her, Leo sacrificing himself to save all of us, and then Artemis leaving anyway.

I don't like to think about this memory. With Leo dead, I try to only think about the good ones. Because this memory pisses me off. He was lying to me, letting me run around chasing false leads when he knew all along where the real threat was. And I don't want to be angry with him. It makes it so much harder to mourn him when I also want to throttle him.

I open my mouth to tell the story, but Doug lifts his arm and covers his nose with his sleeve. "Don't tell me. Stop thinking about that right now. I'm going to lose my lunch if you keep smelling so impossibly sad and angry."

I turn on the radio, settling back into my seat. I don't want to feel this way any more than Doug wants me to. I try to think about something else. "The thing I liked best about Leo," I say, staring out the window at the corrugated metal wall of the car bay, "is that he saw *me*. Sometimes better than I could, even. No one else saw me in the middle of the mess of being a Watcher and a Slayer, where we're only our jobs . . . or in my family, where I was just this broken thing my mom and Artemis devoted their lives to protecting. It was nice, you know? Knowing that he liked me. Not what I could do, or how I could do it, or what he thought I needed from him. When he looked at me, I liked the person he saw."

"That's lovely," Doug says. "But now you're sadder than ever. And I'm starving."

"Oh, for the love of the gods, give me a hit." I hold out my hand. If it keeps him full and keeps my brain off this sadness and anger threatening to swallow me whole, I can pull a Jade for the duration of this ferry ride.

"No, it's true!" My stomach hurts from laughing. "Our ceiling fan is so sharp it would decapitate someone! But only if they stood on exactly the right floorboard for us to trip the spring-loaded thingamajig to shoot them upward! And now that I think about it, it might not decapitate them. It might just sort of take off their scalp. And then fling blood everywhere. Gods, we did *not* think that one through."

"You always seem so sweet." Doug laughs with me and passes me my second Coke.

"I am! I really am! I'm, like, the only Hufflepuff the Watcher society ever had! Everyone else is pure Ravenclaw and Slytherin. I just want everyone to be happy! And love each other! And love me! Except lately, I also want to hurt and kill and maim things. But that's okay too, right? I mean, if you're good at something, it's important to develop your talents."

Doug sounds dubious. "Some talents might be best left buried, Bible be damned."

I snort soda through my nose. "You can't say that! That's, like, double blasphemous."

"Demon, remember?"

"True. I guess you're allowed." I sigh dreamily, remembering happier times. "We had so much fun booby-trapping our room, though. Decapitation fans, flamethrowers, holy water snow globes. We armed the whole castle."

"Is *that* why all the wooden spoons in the kitchen have pointy ends?"

"Yes!"

"You're terrifying."

"I am! I really, really am." I lean back, toying with my Coke bottle. "Not as terrifying as Artemis. Gods, I hate her girlfriend. I hate that I even have to think about Honora as her girlfriend. Maybe they'll break up soon. Maybe Artemis will kill her!"

"You know, most people get mellower when they're high. You get more murdery."

"Ooh, maybe they'll fight and Artemis will kill her and then Sean will get mad and so Artemis will kill him, too, and if they're both out of the picture, Artemis will come home. Wouldn't that be great?"

"It would be great if it involved less murder."

"That's true. That's a good point. Murder is bad. Generally. I dunno. I mean, as a Watcher and a Slayer, can I really say that murder is bad? Why would it be murder if Artemis killed Sean, who is a bad dude, really bad dude, hate him, but it's not murder that I killed Eve Silvera? Because I think it is murder. I think I murdered her. And I think I murdered Leo."

"You didn't kill them." Doug sounds so serious. I don't feel serious. I feel loose and floppy inside. All the coiled-up tightness is gone. I can look right at what I did without it making me want to curl up into a ball and never move again. Without wanting to gather up everyone I have left and lock them in a room and never let them out where they might get hurt or die or leave me.

"I mean, but I did kill them. Eve, at least. I for sure set her up to die horribly. On purpose. And what I did killed Leo, too. So doesn't that mean I killed him?"

"Oh, for hell's sake, girl, even when you're happy you guilt spiral."

"You're right. Let's not think about that. Let's think about Honora and Artemis getting in a huge fight and Artemis kicking her butt and coming back home so sorry she ever left because it was totally the wrong decision." I lean across the space between our seats to rest my head on Doug's shoulder. We've switched places so he can drive when the ferry lands. "I'm so glad I didn't kill you. Whatever else ended up happening, I made the right decision to keep you secret long enough to protect you."

"I think so. But I am quite selfishly attached to the idea of being alive. And being free."

"Selfish, selfish Doug. Always wanting to not die horribly or be someone's drug captive. I like you. I'm glad we're friends."

"That's the drugs talking."

"No! I'm always glad we're friends. I just avoid you because you sniff out how I'm feeling when *I* don't even know or want to think about it."

"But we should talk about it."

I yawn, closing my eyes. "Later." I'm so happy and warm and perfectly content. And I know when I sleep, this time there will be no bodies waiting for me.

The First Slayer chases me from dream to dream to dream, and I run. And the other Slayers run from me. And the storm follows, the churning emptiness racing right behind us. I don't know where we're going or what will happen when we arrive. And so I run.

When I wake up, it's with a mild headache and the same sort of fuzzy discontent that comes with caffeine and sugar withdrawal. I can see why Jade likes Doug's effects, but in retrospect it feels so . . . foreign. Like I was watching a movie of someone else being happy and having a good time, not like I experienced it myself. And all the things I felt okay about are right back to that crawling, tentacled black void threatening to drag me in and swallow me whole.

"Feel all right?" Doug's driving carefully, following every traffic law to the letter. I don't remember the ferry landing.

"Eh." I wish I had another Coke to soften this crash.

"Yeah, sorry about that. Everything's got a price."

Don't I know it. The price of being a Watcher was never fitting in. The price of being a Slayer is never fitting in. And the price of an hour or two off from all my stress is a pounding headache. "So, where is this demon convention, exactly? Sewer? Cemetery?"

"A Marriott."

"A what?"

"You know, the hotel chain?"

"Yeah, I know what a Marriott is. You're holding a demon gathering in a moderately priced business hotel?"

"They've got good conference spaces, which can be hard to find in London."

"Yeah, but . . . I mean." I gesture at his face. "Are the other demons more human-passing than you?"

Doug grins. "Just wait. You'll see."

9

DOUG WAS RIGHT. I DO SEE. I JUST CAN'T believe what I'm seeing.

In the middle of the tastefully bland Marriott lobby, demons are . . . hanging out. Several are at the bar. A few are in the lobby chairs, laughing and talking. Most of the business travelers barely glance at them, or if they do, it's with amusement and confusion rather than fear.

"Welcome to the Annual Makeup and Mask Special Effects Experts Conference." Doug sweeps his hand to encompass the lobby and the hallway leading back to the conference area. His hood is down, his black lips parted in a huge smile. "AMMSEEC, if you're a regular. Jokingly referred to as AMSEEKING, if you're here trying to find a mate."

"God, those horns are brill," a young woman with a gorgeous Afro says, pausing to admire Doug's rounded black horns. "And how do you get that cracking effect with your skin? It's seamless. I can't see any makeup lines anywhere!"

Doug winks. "Tricks of the trade. Did you visit the show floor?"

"You even did your teeth! Your whole look is deadly. Haven't been on the floor yet. Just waiting for my mates. We come every year. Hopefully we run into you in there so they can see."

"Enjoy!" Doug guides me through the lobby and into the hall-way leading to the conference space. He breathes in deeply, eyes dilating as he sighs in satisfaction. "I missed this. Haven't been in years. Not since—well, Sean wasn't big on outings."

"Speaking of, how do you know he won't hit it? I'd think this would be like fish in a barrel for him."

Doug nods to two massive shadows lurking by the open double doors to the largest conference room. I can barely make them out, they blend in so well.

"They sense malice or violent intent. I wouldn't fancy trying to get past them. They're at every door in or out. AMMSEEC has a perfect attendee safety record."

I freeze midstep. "Um. Remember how I'm a Slayer? Some-how I'm guessing this isn't a real Slayer-friendly venue."

"Do you feel violent right now? Have malicious intent toward anyone in here?"

"No! No. We're here to help. I want to help." I really do.

"I can always dose you up again."

"No. I need to be sharp." Plus, I don't want another head-ache. I'm still feeling a little Doug-hungover. I guess this will test whether being a Slayer means I'm inherently full of violent intent, though. I've felt so different since I got the power back. I walk stiffly, nervous, but the two shadowy figures don't move. When we get through the door, it feels like I passed not only their test, but one of my own. I'm okay. I'm still me. Some of the tension between my shoulders eases.

"Of course," Doug says, "a lot of the demons in here are violent. And malicious. You just can't have any *active* violent or malicious intentions."

Okay, test not passed, then. I'm too overwhelmed and distracted to care much, though. The conference floor is bonkers. A few humans—or human-passing demons—wander, eyes wide and amazed. There are tables, displays, some full-on professional booths. Demons are hanging out on bar stools, in meeting spaces, laughing and talking and trading cards. It's a sea of horns, tails, and even a few sets of wings. Every color of skin imaginable is represented. Doug isn't even that cool in here. If I thought it was actually a makeup special effects conference, I'd barely bat an eye at him compared to the woman with her blue hair piled on top of her head to reveal three distinct faces. She turns in front of us, the face on the side of her head raising an eyebrow at me, and the face on the other side of her head winking.

"Let's walk. I'll look for anyone I know." Doug strides confidently forward, and I stay close, though it's hard with how much I'm staring. Rhys would kill to be here. We should have brought him. All this in-person research! I'm giving myself whiplash trying to take it all in.

"Can I read your palm, love?" A woman at a booth holds out both hands. She looks normal, except for the third eye in the center of her forehead. Other than that, she's wearing a nice pin-striped suit with a jewel-green blouse on. I lift my hand.

Doug takes it and pushes it firmly back down. "Don't want to do that. She'll suck five years from your life." The woman scowls, flipping him off. But as she puts her hands back down, I notice they're covered in octopus-like suction cups. Which reminds me of someone else who seriously sucked.

"Any incubus or succubus demons here?" Not that it would matter if there were. I couldn't exactly ask them for details on how Leo came back long enough to return my powers without admitting that I killed his mom—a succubus—and prevented his incubus father from coming back to earth. I doubt any relatives would be fans of mine.

"They're quite rare, yeah? Heavily hunted in the last few centuries. Endangered species."

"Well, that makes me feel *great*."

Doug sniffles. "I can tell."

There's a booth ahead of us covered by a thick velvet curtain. A man—human—stumbles out with a dazed expression. He blinks several times, then catches us staring and blushes deep red, hurrying in the other direction.

"What's in there?" I reach for the curtain.

"I wouldn't." Doug gestures for me to follow. We duck behind the booth and see a grublike creature getting plumper as we watch. It's as big as my thigh, and the impulse to step on it is almost overwhelming. Except then I'd have it all over my boots, and I really like these boots. Also, I'm trying really hard not to have violent impulses in here, just in case the door guardians can come inside.

It's . . . harder than I want it to be. None of these demons are hurting me—or at least actively hurting me, because sucker-hands definitely didn't have my best interests at heart—but I can feel something building in me the longer I'm in here. My hands crave a weapon. It's not that I'm nervous or worried. I'm ready. Eager, even. And that *is* enough to make me nervous and worried.

"Feeds on lust," Doug says about the maggoty thing. "Go in that booth and it'll project whatever will trigger the most lust in you. I mean, if you want to find out . . ."

"No. Nope. Super nope. All the nope in the whole world." I don't even want to imagine what I would see in that curtain. And I definitely don't want to imagine whatever I see and feel making this horrid, bristle-covered grub fat and happy.

I know the only person I've ever truly lusted after. The idea that I might see Leo makes me feel sick inside for any number of reasons. I want to see Leo again, but not like this.

"Most of them work in the high-end gentlemen's clubs. This one is probably young, using the convention as an audition." Doug leads me back out to the floor. Then he brightens and shouts. "Jason! Jason!" He waves to a demon with the same coloring. They cross the floor and grab each other's necks, pressing their foreheads together so their horns touch.

"Doug! We thought you were dead!"

"May as well have been. How are you? How's Janet?"

"Fantastic! We had a litter!"

"No! How many?"

"Twelve! Eleven boys and one girl. Here, I have photos." The other demon pulls out his phone and swipes through twelve identical photos of neon-yellow babies carefully swaddled and staring solemnly at the camera. Their skin is solid, no black cracks running through it, and their horns have barely broken through.

"Cute," I say. And I mean it. They are pretty cute.

"Thanks! And you are . . ." He wrinkles his nose and looks in alarm at Doug. "She's a dine and dash, right? You're *not* feeding off that regularly. You'll make yourself sick."

"Rude." I'm more offended than I should be, but it gets old being told you're not delicious.

Doug covers quickly. "Sorry, right, Nina, this is my cousin, Jason. Jason, Nina. Nina's my friend. She saved me."

"Saved you from what?" Jason asks.

I shuffle awkwardly. "Do you two need to catch up? I can give you a few minutes."

Doug squeezes my shoulder gratefully. "Don't wander too far. Don't let anyone touch you if it seems like they really want to."

"And be sure to hit booth seventeen," Jason says.

"Do not hit booth seventeen," Doug corrects, glaring at his cousin.

"What? She could use some."

Doug points out where they'll be—a group of chairs near the far wall—and I agree to meet him in half an hour. I don't mind wandering on my own. Doug can get info on anyone Jason might know who needs help, and I can stare. I recognize only a handful of the demon varieties here. I'm a little offended on my Watcher heritage's behalf, but the truth is we only focused on the most common and most threatening. There are more demons and more hell dimensions than we could ever truly catalog. That won't stop Rhys from trying, though.

At first it's fun, like wandering through a department store all decked out for a baffling holiday. But after a while I notice the bright exteriors and fun booth designs aren't matched by the general tone of the demons.

I catch several hushed conversations trying to locate missing friends and relatives. The closing of all portals and hellmouths left so many demons orphaned here. Two demons huddle, their heads close and their fingers linked. I could swear they were crying, and the waves of sadness coming off them are almost palpable. I reach up to find tears streaming down my face.

The waves of sadness *are* palpable. I turn directions quickly, needing to get away from them before they suck me in. A booth ahead has the biggest human crowd of any I've seen. There's a banner above advertising autographs and photos for twenty quid a pop. I can't figure out who here would be able to charge that. The signs all feature a beautiful blonde and a stylized title card for something called *Harmony Bites*.

I edge around, trying to get a peek at the blonde to figure out why she would be here. But it's not her behind the table. It's a demon, pinkish, with big floppy ears and folds upon folds of drooping skin. He's totally bald but wearing a garish suit and holding a kitten in the crook of his arm.

"Clem!" a woman shouts. "Clem, marry me!"

"Get in line, sweetheart," he says. "No, seriously, get in line. There's a line."

"How long are you going to be filming here?" A young man leans against the table, all eyes on the blonde in the photo above Clem's head.

"Just as long as it takes us to finish up the special, *Vamping London*."

"She's not really a vampire, though, is she?"

Clem winks. "No, and I'm not really a demon. I just wear

this every day for fun." Everyone in front of the table laughs, but it's an uneasy one, and I can see several of them frowning as they try to puzzle out whether he's joking.

A vampire has a reality show? Really? We have *got* to get cable at the castle. Vampires were messed up by the end of magic too. They can't sire any more like themselves. Any new vampires turn out as zompires, mindless beasts. No old vampires are willing to sire now; the more notoriety they get, the more dangerous it is for their survival. Apparently this blonde didn't get that memo, or doesn't care.

As a Slayer, do I have a responsibility to hunt her down? If she seems to have a body count, I guess maybe I should. I decided to be a different type of Slayer, but if I let a known vampire go free and she kills even one person, isn't that death partly my fault?

"Come closer." A gaunt, grayish man leans in my direction, and I'm grateful for the table between us. His booth has a large sign that says DIRECTIONS. DIRECTORY. TRANSLATION. ANSWERS. Underneath are a series of incomprehensible pictures that seem to be giving instructions, but I can't for the life of me understand them. He breathes in deeply, licking his lips.

I don't want to know, but I ask anyway. "What do you eat?"

He grins, revealing bare gray gums. "Confusion. Usually I linger at tube stops frequented by tourists, but I could live for *years* off you. How much you want?"

"What?"

He reaches into his pocket and pulls out a wad of bills. "How much? You're here as a pet, right? Whoever's your leech,

I'll pay more. One-year contract. All you have to do is exactly what you are."

"Nah, girl, listen here!" A demon with skin the color and texture of white mold growing on bread has stopped and leans too close for comfort. I take a step back. "You're guilty." He grins, leaning in even closer. "You reek of guilt and shame. I'll take all your guilt. Every last drop of it." His tongue flicks out, thin and purple and forked at the end. "Think of how lovely it would be to live free of that."

I fold my arms over my chest protectively. Much as I'd love to give up this guilt, I need it. It drives me, directs me. And combats the anger. If I could live guilt-free with what I've done, I'd be a monster.

How many of the humans here actually know what's going on? How many of them sell their emotions and feelings for a wad of cash? It's one thing for Doug to feed on happiness without taking it away. This is something else. That new viciousness nestled inside me flares, and I see these two demons for what they are: predators. They might not kill people, but if they really can permanently suck away my guilt or confusion, they're taking something that makes me *me*. That makes me human. Just because it isn't blood doesn't mean it's not part of me.

I take a step forward, eyes narrowed, and think of the last time I saw Leo alive. The moldy demon suddenly puffs up like a sponge absorbing water.

"Too much," he gasps, turning and stumbling away.

The gray demon has backed against the wall of his booth, hands up pleadingly. "Go. Just go. Don't want nothing from you."

I walk on. Apparently now I give off enough spiky, angry

energy that the majority of the demons turn quickly away from me, giving me a wide berth. I duck between booths, trying to catch my breath. Who here could need my help? Who here even deserves it?

Maybe Artemis is right. Maybe I really am only helping myself.

10

DOUG IS IN A GOOD MOOD WHEN I MEET back up with him. Which makes me worried for a new reason. Will I have to let another friend leave? I don't think I can handle it right now. "Do you want to go with him? Your cousin?"

Doug must feel my concern. "Aww, you'd miss me! Don't worry. We're generally solitary. Makes it easier—more food that way, less likely to draw attention. Plus, he's got a lot of mouths to feed now. Lucky strike, finding a mate. His kids are pretty accurate of the gender breakdown of our species. Not many girls. I'm just glad I know he's okay. And he gave me a lead."

"Oh yeah?"

"Course there's the usual disappearances. That's normal. Loads of missing demons ever since the portals closed, but that's down to being cut off with no communication. I asked him about incubus and succubus types, though, because you got me wondering. And he said there's a rumor that someone is hunting for them. Lots of demons going into hiding because of it, but no one can say exactly who it is they're afraid of. No name."

"But we know someone who looks for specific types of demons!" I snap. "The dude the mercenaries were hunting for! Van Alston!"

"*Von* Alston. The one your mother told us not to go near. And wasn't he only looking for werewolves?"

"Yeah, that we know of. But if he's in the market for one type, doesn't it make sense he'd be in the market for others?"

"Does it, though?" Doug seems genuinely puzzled by my leap. But it's the only lead we have, the only connection. I know it isn't a *solid* lead, but I want it to be. I need it to be. And it really does make sense that if some dude pays for one type of supernatural creature, odds are he's paying for others, too. Or at least knows how to find them.

"Is there somewhere quiet we can go? I can't focus in here." My mother was very clear that we should stay away from Von Alston. But who knows how many demons or werewolves or other vulnerable creatures he's holding? If I can't go after Sean, why can't I go after some rich creep? Are we really going to take more money from someone like that?

Then again, my mother was right. We don't have many—or really any—allies these days. We've been in hiding for so long, everyone assumes we're dead. Which we meant to happen. So is it worth potentially saving a demon or two to alienate one of our only remaining contacts? Am I only doing this on the off chance I can get information about succubus and incubus and cambion demons out of guilt for letting Leo die?

I glance over my shoulder, paranoid that the confusion demon will smell me from across the floor and come to eat.

Doug leads me out a back door and we end up in an alley

between buildings. A few demons are smoking near us. Literally smoking, the smoke trailing up from their skin instead of from cigarettes.

I pace. I don't know what the right choice is. Do I go against my mother—with whom I'm finally beginning to develop trust? In the past when she told me not to do things, she had her reasons. And I know she cares about demons. She's the one who helped Doug in the first place.

Would I be endangering us if I went after Von Alston? All for the chance of finding a type of demon I know we can't take into Sanctuary *and* who probably won't give me answers about Leo even if they have them?

Artemis's accusation punches me in the gut. This really is about me. This whole trip. I don't care about helping any of the demons here. I just want closure, desperately, and I'm willing to paw through the absolute dregs of demon society to find it. Gods damn it all, Artemis left! She doesn't get to show up for twenty minutes and be right about everything.

The door we came out opens and the drooping-skin demon, Clem, nearly stumbles into me. He has a kitten half pulled out of his pocket. It mews frantically. He leans against the wall, stroking the kitten and lifting it to his face.

A drawing in one of my research books flashes in my memory. Before I can stop myself, I snatch the kitten out of his hands and hold it against my chest. "No!"

He flinches, then stares guiltily at the ground. "Sorry. Sorry. Terrible habit. I keep trying to give it up, but the pressures of my life, I tell you. And the camera adds twenty pounds of skin folds." He rubs his face. "Thanks. Yeah. No more kittens. Just fear from now on." He looks up hopefully. "You aren't scared of me, are you?"

I raise a single eyebrow. He sighs.

"Your Harmony vampire," I ask, reminding myself that whatever else I am, I'm a Slayer. "Does she eat people?"

"Harm? Nah. I mean, she's not as vegan as she pretends to be. But you can't quote me on that. Still, she's careful. Only kills in self-defense. She likes fame more than blood. And more than me." His droopy face droops further, every line a frown.

At least I can cross that off my to-do list. I don't have time to hunt a reality-show star. Besides, it's not like I'm the only Slayer out there. Someone else can worry about D-list celebrity demons. We really should have a text chain or something to assign tasks.

Doug ignores Clem. "Any idea where this Von Alston lives? Maybe we could snoop. If he *is* the one they're whispering about, he's bad news and we should do something. And if he's not, we haven't hurt anything."

"Are you talking about Ian Von Alston?" Clem asks.

I narrow my eyes. "Yeah. What do you know about him?"

"Oh, he's dreadful. Kept trying to hire Harmony to do a private party. You know what *that* means with these rich humans. I didn't even send her the offer. She has no idea how much I protect her from."

"Do you have an address for him?"

He eyes the kitten in my hands. "What'll you give me for it?"

"I'll give you a heaping serving of not beating the crap out of you." The edge I say it with surprises me. More Artemis than me. Or maybe . . . more Athena than Nina. I lean into it.

Doug coughs to cover up a laugh. "She's a Slayer, mate. You should probably tell her."

"A Slayer!" Instead of looking intimidated, Clem brightens. "Do you know Buffy? I haven't seen her since Sunnydale was swallowed whole! It was a simpler time back then. Just a demon, trying to make it on a hellmouth. None of the cameras and the fame and the love of my life who can't see me, you know?"

Doug and I share an awkward glance. We actually do know. We both nod encouragingly.

Clem continues. "Anyway, you should have said you were a Slayer. Slayers and I go way back. Here." He pulls out one of his cards, scribbling an address on the back. "If you see Buffy, tell her Clem says hello, would you? And if you see that good-for-nothing peroxided nightmare of a vampire, tell him I haven't forgotten he owes me ten Scottish Folds and three Siamese. Gets a soul and thinks all debts are crossed off. I'll have those cats from him, diet be damned." Muttering to himself, he heads back inside.

"That was really weird." I stare at the door. The three smoking demons have gone back in as well. Only one demon is left out here with us, a human-looking woman in a black cloak leaning against a wall. "Right? It's not just me. That was weird."

"Demon conferences tend to be." Doug holds out the card. "Let's go see whether this collector has managed to nab any nasty incubuses or succubuses—succubi? Incubi? Succubussesses? No wonder they're going extinct, what a nuisance. Hopefully it turns out Von Alston has something less nasty and easier to say. Or that he actually is a friend, he's not the nameless threat hunting for demons, it's all a misunderstanding, and he gives us a check for no reason."

"One of those giant cardboard ones. With lots of zeroes. Maybe then we can finally fix up the tower section of the castle."

"I call dibs if we do. Always wanted a room in a tower."

"No way. I'm the Slayer. I get the tower room. Assuming it ever isn't a total crumbling safety hazard that would get the whole building condemned if anyone actually knew the castle existed." I pause, nuzzling the purring kitten. "Aw man. Now I really want a tower room. Let's go see about that imaginary check. Or demons, I guess. Whichever."

We turn to find our way blocked by the woman in the cloak. "Doug!" she says brightly. "Fancy meeting you here!" And then, knife in hand, she lunges.

I shove Doug out of the way so hard he slams into the wall and slumps to the ground, winded. The woman dodges me, blade winking wickedly in the sun. I'm still holding the kitten. It purrs, a soft warm ball against my chest. I duck a slash of the knife, spin left, and kick at the woman's leg. She jumps, landing neatly and punching me hard in the side. I shift to protect the kitten, then toss it gently onto Doug's chest.

"Okay." I hold up my fists. "Now I'm ready."

She comes at me with a flash of menace and metal. I twist and turn, working backward, leading her away from Doug. When she's far enough that she can't hurt him—or the kitten—I stop so abruptly she stumbles, confused.

"You sure you want this fight?" The need for a fight is roaring inside of me, begging for it. Nobody gets to hurt my friends. Nobody gets to take someone I love. I tremble with the effort of holding it all back.

She snarls and slashes. So I don't hold back anymore. I catch her arm, twisting until it pops. She screams and drops the knife. I let her hit me with her good arm, barely feeling it as I lift her and pin her against the brick wall. She kicks and I press against her dislocated shoulder.

Sweat breaks out on her face. She groans in pain, gritting her teeth, but there's nothing she can do against me, and we both know it.

I hold her there. "You can tell Sean he's never touching Doug again."

She laughs, pain making the laughter sound discordant and unhinged. "You think I take orders from Sean now? He's little leagues, love. And you're in over your head. Everyone you love is already *his*. You just don't know it yet."

I grab her neck. Rage so ancient it defies understanding pulses through me. It's ready to devour something. Better her than me. Something slips from her sleeve into her good hand, and she slams it into my side. I seize up, grabbing her collar as she electrocutes me. Time seems to pause in brilliant, bright white pain. She twists away, her necklace coming off in my hand, and then she runs. I stumble, falling to my knees as the memory of the current makes it feel like it's still happening. But she ran in the opposite direction as Doug. I glance back.

He's sitting up now, holding the kitten. Safe.

I don't know what I would have done if she hadn't tased me. Shaking from the adrenaline and the electricity, I shuffle to Doug and take the kitten, holding it against my chest. I wrap the necklace around its neck and fasten it like a collar, the triangle pattern familiar. The woman was lying about not working for Sean. It's the same symbol from his demon-power-infused tea. The same symbol that was on the book Artemis stole. I hope that means Artemis is fighting him. If so, why didn't she ask for my help? I can do so much now!

I almost did something very bad, though. The kitten purrs, unaware how close I came to murdering a woman. Doug's expression makes me think he isn't so oblivious.

"Let's go get the car." I turn to the alley exit, quite certain in this state the guardian demons wouldn't let me anywhere near their conference.

That's when the screaming starts.

11

THE SCREAMING IS COMING FROM INSIDE the conference center.

I hand the kitten back to Doug. "That woman must not have come alone. Looks like Sean's going shopping for new merchandise, after all." I flex my fists, shaking off the remnants of the tasing.

"Jason's in there." Doug looks at the door with a stricken expression.

"I'm on it." I fling open the door and take a step inside—

And am thrown back into the alley with such force it leaves me winded. The way in isn't even visible anymore. It's solid shadow. "I'm trying to help!" I shout.

"They can't sense motivation." Doug paces in front of the door while I stand and brush myself off. The screaming hasn't stopped. There's definitely a brawl going on inside. There are so many demons in there. Humans, too. "The guardians have no way of knowing that you want to go in to help, only that you're going in with violence on your mind."

"Oh, you bet I am. All the violence." I can't punch a shadow, and I don't see any way around them. They're at every door. Guess I won't use a door, then.

I back up as far as the narrow alley allows. I close my eyes, reach for that well of power inside me. And this time, on purpose, I reach for the darkness swirling around it. I breathe in. Breathe out. Focus on all the rage that I've been trying so hard to keep under control. Then I open my eyes and *run*.

I slam into the wall shoulder first. It cracks and gives, and I'm through in a shower of brick and plaster. My elation at my success is more than dampened by how much that hurt. But I'm inside. And, good news for my strength and bad news for Sean's creepy cloaked minions: I'm more pissed off than ever.

Doug climbs in behind me. "Why didn't I think of running straight through a wall? Oh, right, because I'm not completely off my trolley."

The conference floor is utter chaos. Booths and tables are overturned and scattered. Demons are trying to flee, but most of them can't get past the guardian bouncers, which unfortunately seem to work in reverse, as well. If the demons are feeling violent—which they should be—they can't get in *or* out. In the midst of the melee, more black-cloaked Ren Faire rejects are tasing everything that moves. A few of the attackers are lying prone and unmoving, though. Some of these demons are more than capable of handling themselves. But not all of them.

"First priority is Jason," I say. "Stay close. When we find him, you two get out and go to the car. You're not violent; you shouldn't have a problem."

Doug tucks the kitten safely into his shirt. "Second priority?"

I crack my knuckles, shake out my sore shoulder. *Fun*, I almost say. Then I run straight into the middle. There's a whole group of the black cloaks surrounding several stunned demons, including my new friend Clem.

"Hey!" I say brightly. They turn to look at me. They're all human, as far as I can tell, and each holding one of those stupid shock sticks. "What do you all have in common with vacuums?"

"What?" the man closest to me says, confusion shifting his placid expression.

"You suck."

One of the women gives me a witheringly dismissive shake of her head.

"Oh, come on," I say, a little hurt. "I'm a new Slayer. I'm still working on the banter. But I'm good at this part." I pick her up and throw her into the others. Three of them go down in a tangle of limbs and cloaks. Bad idea, all that extra material.

I hear the crackle of electricity and duck as a shock stick jabs where my neck had been. I could break her neck, smash her ribs beyond repair.

People, I remind myself with gritted teeth. A well-aimed kick results in a crack and a scream of agony. Dislocated knees aren't fatal, and they're very effective. And satisfying. I duck and roll and spin among the remaining attackers, taking out knee after knee after knee. The incapacitated demons are recovering, scurrying away. I give Clem a hand up.

"I'm so full I might puke," he says, holding his stomach. He eats fear, and every demon trapped in here must be positively reeking of it. "Thank you, pet. You're a good girl."

I backfist a cloaker trying to sneak up behind me, and he goes down screaming, clutching his broken and bleeding nose. Clem seems to know this space judging by the professional level of his setup. "If you were trying to kidnap—demonnap, I guess?—in bulk numbers, how would you do it?"

Clem points to an area blocked off by curtains at the back of the conference floor. "Loading dock there. That's how we got my booth in. I'm not getting the deposit back on that, am I?" He looks morosely at the wreckage of materials and steps gingerly over the nearest cloaked woman. "How did you get past the bouncers?" he asks her.

She laughs, a hollow, unnerving sound. "Our intent isn't violent or malicious. It's essential. You'll see. You'll all see." She jabs at him with her shock stick.

"Okay, creeper." I take her shock stick and snap it in half. "Clem, I've got more punching to do. I'd recommend running away." I glance over the group I've already taken out. I feel bad for how bad I don't feel. It's not like me. But I don't want to be me right now. I want to be Buffy. Even Artemis. Someone who knows what they're doing and doesn't stop to feel bad about it. The darkness inside of me agrees. This is who we should be.

The injured cloakers are surrounded by demons now. The woman in the pin-striped suit with suction cups on her hands has an evil glint in each of her three eyes. She reaches out to help the nearest one stand. He lifts a hand, confused but grateful.

"She's going to . . . ," I start, then stop. Well. They *did* kind of ask for it. And the cloakers mostly still have their shock sticks. They just can't drag demons away now. I feel comfortable with my decision to leave them on their own in the middle of the convention they were terrorizing. Once I've made certain no demons are being hauled off and after I've stopped whoever is out there, I'll come back and keep the cloakers from being totally sucked dry.

Probably.

A flash of yellow catches my eye, and I whirl to see Jason dragged past the curtains toward the loading dock. There are twelve adorable baby demons waiting at home for him, and I will not let them be hurt the same way I was. Leaping over tables and chairs, I tear through the curtains to see a huge corrugated metal door has been opened. A moving truck is in the loading bay, doors open, several demons already inside.

"Need some help?" I ask.

The nearest cloaker, the one awkwardly dragging Jason, smiles gratefully at me. "Yes."

"Gross. Not you." I kick her knee and she falls, screaming. Doug appears behind me and grabs Jason under his arms. "Go. I'll make sure no one follows you."

Doug nods and drags his semiconscious cousin away. I turn back to find five cloakers, each armed with shock sticks, moving to surround me.

Imogen was right—I should follow my instincts. All this time I've been trying not to feel the way I feel. Embracing it is awesome. So much easier. This must be what it's like to be Buffy! No more worrying and overthinking and being afraid of doing things the wrong way.

I hold up a hand; I'll at least give them a chance. "I'm going to stop you right there. You're already looking at a massive physical therapy regimen for your friends back there. It's gonna be months before they regain full movement in their knees. And they'll need help in the meantime. They're not going to be very mobile. Depending on which knee I took out, they're also not going to be driving, so they'll need rides to and from their appointments. What I'm saying is: Do you want to help them? Or do you want to join them?"

"When the Sleeping One reaches his third form," a turnip-faced man says, raising his eyes to the ceiling rapturously, if a turnip can ever be said to be rapturous, "we will live in his light and walk across the backs of the prostrate masses and—"

"Wait—hold up. The *what* masses?"

He looks at me, glaring at my interruption. "Prostrate."

"Oh, okay, whew. That is not what I thought you said. Whole different meaning there. I would choose a different word if I were you. One that's not quite so easy to confuse with certain reproductive organs. Anyway. You guys are zealots, apparently."

"All should be zealously engaged in—"

"Cool story about zealots. They blew up almost everyone I'd ever known or cared about. So guess who gets to have more than their knees broken?" I punch him square in the face.

A shock stick gets me in the side. I push through the disorienting jumble of pain to grab the arm holding it. I jerk up, dislocating the arm. She drops the shock stick, and I kick her knee. And then I punch her in the face too, for good measure. The remaining three come at me at once. I grab the first and throw him into the other two. It feels dirty to kick them while they're on the floor. I do it anyway, one-two-three knees, no one able to follow me out.

The truck is idling. Whoever is driving it can't see what's going on behind them. They're in for a nasty surprise. I jump and catch the top of the truck, pulling myself up. I walk across the roof of the back of the truck, then jump down onto the hood. I crouch there and turn around.

"Nina?" Artemis stares at me in shock from the passenger seat. She rolls down her window. "What are you doing?"

"What are *you* doing?" She must have gone after the cloakers and been kidnapped! But . . . she's wearing a seat belt. And Honora is in the driver's seat. No. No no no. This isn't how it was supposed to be. Artemis was supposed to be out there fighting evil in her own way. Not chauffeuring for it. I feel sick.

"Hey," Honora says. "How's things?"

My fists clench. I could punch through the windshield. Rip Honora out and throw her to the side like trash. Artemis shakes her head once, somehow anticipating my thoughts.

I focus on her instead. "Artemis, how could you?"

She lifts an eyebrow. "How could I help capture demons? It's literally what I trained for my entire life. Did you forget?"

"When we talked in the library, you said—I thought—"

"You have no idea what's going on here. Get down. You look like an idiot up there."

I flinch. I had imagined how I would look leaping onto the hood of the car, and in my imagination I was Buffy. I was badass. I was . . . like Artemis. But she saw, and she's embarrassed for me.

Honora looks in the side-view mirror. "Hell's bells, Wheezy, what did you do in there?" I want her to sound scared or impressed, but she just sounds annoyed.

"Get in." Artemis opens her door.

"What?"

"Get in. Come with us. I'll explain on the way."

"On the way to free these demons?" My voice can barely muster a hopeful tone.

"On the way to deliver them." Honora drums her fingers on the steering wheel. "Come on, Wheezy. In or out. We have a schedule to keep and loyalty to prove. We'll give you this one chance to join."

Artemis frowns at her. "No, we'll drop her off somewhere safe. I don't want her to be part of this."

"Part of what?" I want to stomp my foot, but it feels petulant and immature.

Honora wrinkles her nose in distaste. "I hate to admit it, but if it's all as big as you say, we could use her help."

"No." Artemis turns toward me, and her face is set in such hard lines I can barely see my sister there. "Floor it."

Honora blows a huge gum bubble. It pops. She grins, and then she does as she's told. I'm thrown off the hood and roll, tumbling hard against the asphalt. The truck wheels squeal as Honora careens out of the alley, the back doors flapping wildly, several demons still inside.

Artemis. What is she doing?

I stand with a groan. I can still catch them. I can—

A blinding jolt of electricity freezes me. Someone has a shock stick against my spine. They hold it there. The edges of my vision start to go fuzzy and black. And then I fall to my knees as the current is cut off. The cloaker slumps to the ground next to me. A neon-yellow hand reaches out to me, and I take it.

"I got Jason in a cab," Doug says. "He'll be fine. And I didn't see any other trucks, so they're not going to be hauling off more demons. But we should get out of here. I don't like any of this,

Nina. This wasn't Sean's MO at all. Too big. Too coordinated. Something else is going on. And I don't think it was about me, either. They grabbed Jason, yeah, but so many others."

"It was Honora," I whisper. "And Artemis. In the truck. They're helping."

Doug doesn't say anything. But he puts his arm around me for more than just balance as I limp and stumble back to our car.

12

DOUG EYES ME CRITICALLY. "ARE YOU sure we should be doing this right now? We have no idea what kind of threat Von Alston is, and you were jolted with so much electricity you could power the castle for the next month. Plus, you ran through a wall and got thrown off a moving vehicle."

I pull down the sun visor and look in the little mirror there. There are bits of brick and plaster still in my hair. A bruise is forming on one cheek—I don't remember what caused it—and now that it's been an hour and all my adrenaline is gone, my shoulder is so stiff I can barely move it. "It's fine. Except for my shoulder."

"That's why people generally use doors instead of walls."

"I'm a trendsetter." I pick as much of the rubble out of my hair as I can. Doug is probably right. This Von Alston might be more than we can handle right now. If he was behind everything and can launch an offensive that big, I don't feel safe about the castle being without my protection. I thought Sean was our biggest foe. It could still be him—the Honora connection, plus the symbol from his tea. But the last time I saw the ponytailed wonder, he was running a drug-dealing business out of the basement of a health-food store. No cloaked zealots in sight. He had mentioned something about powerful allies, though. Maybe it's Von Alston.

All I have to go on is the triangle symbol on the necklace, which is still on the kitten curled up asleep on our backseat. I should never have let Artemis take that book. I thought I was making it easier for her to come back. Not easier for her to hurt me.

We need more information on everything. But going home means reporting on what we found. And that means telling everyone that I've seen Artemis twice now and let her walk out with one of our books. Rhys will never forgive me—or her. And slightly graver than taking a book—though Rhys will disagree— is that apparently she's working with Sean's crews. And she told Honora to throw me off a moving vehicle.

Saying it out loud will make it hurt so much worse than my shoulder does. For so long it was Artemis and me against the world. And I can't let go of the idea that we can return to that. Like if I can figure this out fast enough, I can get her out of whatever she's mixed up in and no one will ever have to know how she's betrayed us.

How she's betrayed me.

I've lost so much. I refuse to lose Artemis or the hope that she's going to be my sister again. We'll rule Von Alston out or in, and then we'll go from there. I'll find Artemis before she's in too deep. No one has to know but me. We let the Watchers tell us who to be and how to be it for so long. I'm keeping this just the two of us.

I sigh and try to rotate my shoulder to ease some of the stiffness. "This is our only possible lead on the nameless threat, right? If we go back, we'll have to talk it over with my mother, and she'll say no to confronting him. But if we play this right, we'll get the scoop on Von Alston without revealing we're with the Watchers, in case we do need him as an ally in the future." I turn to Doug and wait expectantly.

He puts his hands out. "I don't like this plan at all. It didn't work in *A New Hope*."

I tie his wrists together, making sure the rope is tight enough to look convincing but loose enough that he can slip out. "They rescued Princess Leia!"

"Obi-Wan Kenobi died, though, even if it was on purpose. And I'm not really sure who's who in this scenario. I'm obviously a Han Solo type. You're maybe a Luke Skywalker. Good hair. Better at fighting than you have any right to be. A bit on the whiny side."

"Just for that, I'm declaring you the C-3PO of this mission."

"Hey now! That's not fair."

"Whatever you say, 3PO." I fiddle with my ruined hair in the rearview mirror. I'm not really sure what vibe to go for. Polished and professional? Gritty and tough? Probably the latter, given the visible bruising. And, sadly, I know exactly who to channel. It's not hard. We have the same face.

I pull my loose red curls back into a ponytail and grimace in pain as I slip on Artemis's nicest black leather jacket. She left it behind . . . on account of it was hidden at the bottom of my closet. With my hair in a severe ponytail and the black leather zipped up, I'm my twin. Stronger. Tougher. Willing to throw her own sister off a moving vehicle in pursuit of her own goals.

We could have been doing this together. *Should* have been doing it together. Instead, she's somewhere with Honora and a truck full of pilfered demons. I should have punched through that windshield after all. Imogen was right again—my instinct was correct. I can't understand why Artemis is doing what she's doing. You don't have to love demons to know you shouldn't work for zealots and drug dealers.

I put the car into drive with more force than is strictly necessary. We debated putting Doug in the trunk of the car, but that seemed too mean. Even having his wrists bound is obviously triggering for him after all his years in captivity. Especially after such a recent run-in with Sean's people.

I reach over and squeeze his hands. "I won't let anything happen to you. I promise."

"What about Chewie?"

"Chewie?"

Doug nods toward the kitten.

"First of all, we are not naming our new cat Chewie. Second of all, I don't intend to stay in there long enough for her to miss us. And I'm not letting you out of my sight. You're only how we get inside. We're not keeping up the ruse any longer than that. I won't risk you for anything."

Doug swallows audibly, but he nods. "Thanks. I'm sorry for complaining about how you taste so often. I really do trust you."

That makes one of us.

I drive carefully, every nerve on alert. I learned how to drive in the last couple of months, but I don't technically have a license, which is why we always have Cillian or Imogen drive. The Von Alston address is in a posh, sprawling neighborhood of estates outside the city. It takes ten minutes of winding up a narrow lane before we even get to the gates. The decorative iron flourishes have protective runes and symbols worked in. Not much use now that magic's dead, but this Von Alston fellow obviously knows his stuff.

In addition to the runes, there are several cameras, a far less magic-dependent protection. I roll to a stop in front of a control panel. There's a camera mounted there, and a small television showing the feed of us.

"May I help you?" a polite voice asks over a surprisingly smooth intercom.

"I heard you buy exotic animals. I'm looking to sell."

"Do you have an appointment?"

I reach for Doug's shirt collar and yank him closer to the camera. "Yeah. Here he is." I'm met with silence. "Fine, there are other buyers." I shove Doug back into his seat, mouthing *sorry* when my head is turned away from the camera, and put the car in reverse.

The gates buzz and open. "Master Von Alston will see you."

"Lucky me." I put the car back into drive and ease through the gates. They snap shut like a mousetrap behind us.

After another ten minutes of driving through lush forest-land, we emerge into sunlight and I'm convinced we drove out of London and into Jane Austen's imagination. A massive golden-brick mansion sneers at us with stately disregard. White pillars decorate the exterior, and a series of fountains line an expansive, perfectly manicured green lawn. I half expect to see Mr. Darcy emerge from one of the ponds. "It is a truth universally acknowledged," I whisper, "that a single man in possession of a good fortune must be in want of a demon."

Doug snickers next to me. He's remained carefully limp in case there are more cameras.

"Oh my gods. What if—what if it actually *is* Colin Firth? If Colin Firth wants to hunt you, I might let him. Well, I'd let early- to midnineties Colin Firth hunt you. I'll have to see how he looks in person now."

"I can support that."

We pass a gatehouse where an armed guard watches us impassively. I assume that means I keep driving. The road leads around the back of the house, where stables have been converted to a series of garages. I pull to a stop, gravel crunching beneath my tires. I've parked in an area where it will be easy to pull out for a quick escape. I didn't see any extra gates or anything, but the entrance gate will need to be reckoned with. We'll burn that bridge when we get to it.

An aged butler comes out a side door with a look on his face like he's here to clean up after a dog. I try to keep my mouth still as I talk to Doug. "He doesn't have anything to transport you. Be unconscious. I'll carry you in. That way I'll have to go wherever they want to take you, and we can get a look at whether they're holding anyone else here."

Doug raises one cracked patch of skin where his eyebrow should be, then shrugs.

I climb out of the car and stretch as though this is a normal day's work for me. "Hey, Jeeves." Without thinking, I'm not even pretending to be Artemis. I'm channeling the worst person I know: Honora. This morning she would have been the only person I could think of who would willingly sell Doug to someone else. But now I have to add Artemis to that list.

Grimacing and then scowling to cover the pain in my shoulder, I walk around to Doug's side of the car and open the door. He half falls out, fully committed to the charade. I drag him free and throw him over my injured shoulder.

"Stake me," I hiss. I am only using doors from now on.

"Is he damaged?" Jeeves asks.

"I'm careful with merchandise. He's drugged."

"Very well. Follow me. Try not to get . . ." Jeeves gestures vaguely, then settles on "Try not to get *him* on anything."

Doug tenses in offense, and I shift him to cover.

"Right, no chaise lounges for the sticky demon. Now can we finish delivery so I can get paid? He's not exactly a lightweight. And I'd like to talk with the boss about future jobs."

"Follow me." Jeeves turns, the tails on his coat so stiff and formal they don't even move in the wind. He'd be at home in a period piece on the BBC. Doug and me, not so much. Though that's one I'd actually be interested in watching. *A Demon Dines in Downton.*

I follow Jeeves through a servants' entrance. The hallways are narrow, paneled in dark wood with faded wallpaper. The lights on the walls look like they were converted from gas lamps. We pass a large, modernized kitchen, then several hallways that lead off in various directions. Finally we come to a narrow stairway. I follow Jeeves up two flights, then down another hall, then down a flight, then up two more, then down another two, then up two more.

I'm pretty sure we're going in circles. I keep waiting for a threat, but we haven't seen a soul except this ancient relic of a British butler, and I'd sooner punch the Museum of London.

Finally, after going up three flights to the top floor, he leads me to a room at the end of another dim, narrow hall. He unlocks and opens the door. I follow him inside a room that's been converted to a cell. Half of it is covered with bars, the walls are metal, and everything is bolted to a reinforced floor and ceiling.

"You can set him in there." Jeeves points to the tiny cell portion, turning to observe me.

"I'm not putting him anywhere until I get paid."

"Very well. Wait here." He shuffles to the door. As soon as he's gone, Doug and I will start snooping. Maybe we won't have to talk to Von Alston at all, which will mean I haven't disobeyed my mother's wishes. Everyone wins. And with the pace the butler takes, we'll have more than enough time to check the house out, rescue any stray demons, and bolt.

Jeeves steps over the threshold and reaches for the wall to steady himself. The panel he grabs makes a clicking noise. A thick set of bars slams down from the ceiling, blocking the door and locking us in.

He turns, looking me up and down. "You didn't perspire." His teeth are crooked and tea-stained, his smile downright gleeful.

"What?" I can't believe this. The room has no window and no other door. Just that idiot butler, grinning at me.

"I led you around the entire manor carrying at least twelve stone's worth of demon. And you look as fresh as you did when you got out of the car. You're not human. Oh, he's going to be so pleased." Jeeves clears his throat, trying to regain some of his decorum. "We do not do business with demons. I'm afraid you'll be joining us instead of getting paid."

Doug has stopped pretending to be unconscious. I set him down and take a step toward the bars. "See, here's the problem, Jeeves."

He bristles. "My name is Smith."

"Good to know, Jeeves. Here's the problem. I'm not a demon." I punch straight through the panel he pushed, grabbing and pulling out the wires. They spark and sputter . . . and nothing happens with the door.

"Nuts," I mutter. It would have been so cool. Jeeves smirks at me.

"Wait," Doug murmurs. He puts a hand on my shoulder and I stop where I was about to reach down and try to bend the bars by hand. "Listen, Jeeves. Go fetch your boss. He'll want to talk to us."

Jeeves sniffs dismissively. "I am going to announce your presence, but not because you requested it. I do not work for you."

"Yeah, my butler is way better at his job." I fold my arms petulantly.

"Handsomer, too. The way he fills out his waistcoat. Mmhmm." Doug nods, smiling dreamily.

"And did you see the dust on this wainscoting? I'm embarrassed for Jeeves just thinking about it. Righto, chap, stiff upper lip and all that. Not every butler can be a good one these days."

He harrumphs away.

"What is wainscoting?" Doug asks.

"No idea. Why didn't you want me to rip the door off? I'm pretty sure I can. Or I can go through the wall again." I rub my shoulder in anticipation of the pain.

"I'm not defenseless. I can weaponize happiness if I need to. Between the two of us, we can leave anytime. But breaking out right now will draw attention and we won't get any info. Let's meet this bloke, get a feel for what's really going on here and whether he's the nameless one that has the demonic community so shook up. Maybe he's reasonable. Maybe he's not. Either way, we'll have more info than we came with. Break out now and we detoured for nothing."

"Ugh. That all makes sense." I don't want it to. I sit in the middle of the floor and pull out my cell phone. I almost dial my mother, then change my mind and dial my safest option. Cillian.

"Nina?" He sounds bored. "Shop is dead, as usual. How's things in London?"

"Um, fine. We got a kitten."

"A kitten? No! You didn't! Oh my god, I'm so excited. What does it look like? I've been brainstorming perfect kitten names for years. But I think I need to see it in person first. Don't they say that? You need to see the baby before you can name it?"

"Well, they might say that. About babies. But this is definitely a kitten. Orange. Female." I lower the phone. "The kitten's going to be okay in the car, right?"

"It's not that cold," Doug says. "She'll be fine."

I switch back to Cillian. "Anyway, I wanted to check in. See how everyone is."

"Jade's a right nightmare. Please take her with you next time. I wasn't even going to come into the shop today, but I couldn't handle another minute of her barking orders. Rhys barricaded himself in the library with his grandma. Your mother was sharpening blades in the gym last I saw. Everyone's fine. Any luck at the convention?"

"It was . . . surprising. Sean attacked. I think. Might not have been Sean. It's complicated." So very complicated.

"What? Are you all right? Should I call Rhys?"

"Nah. I handled it." Mostly. Not at all, really. "Anyway, we're making sure Doug's cousin gets home safely, so we'll be later than originally planned. Let the others know? I'll text when we're ready to head back."

"Sounds good." He pauses. "You sure you're all right?"

I pause too. Cillian's my friend. I could talk to him about Artemis. He won't judge her. But why am I so worried about people judging her? She's the one making reckless choices.

It's a sister thing, I think. I can be pissed off at her and judge her and we'll still be sisters. And she knows that. So it won't stop her from coming home.

"Oh!" Cillian interrupts my thoughts. "Her*meow*one Granger! No. The cat's a ginger. And I don't want to name a cat after Ginny. No offense to Ginny. Too bad it's not a male, then we could make a play on Prince Harry. I'm on it, though. Don't worry about a thing. I'll have the perfect name by the time you get back."

"That's a load off, then. Thanks, Cill."

"Cheers!" He hangs up. I pocket the phone, then lean back.

"They say the truth will set you free," Doug says.

"So will ripping this door off its hinges."

"So will I," a pleasantly clipped voice says as a man steps into view and takes us in with a curious glance. He's white, his thinning salt-and-pepper hair slicked back, dark eyes as sharp as the lines of his suit. "Assuming you're in the mood for a game." He smiles, and though he's one hundred percent human, all my instincts scream *threat*.

"Okay, but I'll warn you right now, I'm really good at Monopoly."

He laughs. "I had something in mind that's a little more suited to your skills, Slayer."

13

IAN VON ALSTON STIRS HIS TEA WITH A
delicate silver spoon. The china is so fine it's almost translucent,
hand-painted with delicate flowers. "None for you?"

"I prefer root beer. Also, I don't generally sit down for tea
parties with people who are holding my friend captive."

He *tsks*, setting his cup in its saucer. The room we're in looks
like the Queen of England vomited Buckingham Palace's rejects
into it. It tips right past impressive into absurd. A few years ago I
would have been afraid to even breathe in a room like this; now,
I kind of want to wander around and "accidentally" break things.
But he has Doug for the time being, and I need information.

"You can hardly chide me for my behavior," he says, "considering you came here under false pretenses. Clearly you had no
intention of selling that demon to me. But I'll give you a chance
to get your friends."

"My friends?" I raise an eyebrow. Plural. Does he have
someone else from the castle? How did he know we were coming here? My heart races, and I look at the entrances and exits

to the room. I could grab him, threaten him. I tense, but he raises his hand.

"Calm yourself. The other Slayers are perfectly well."

"The other Slayers. Right. My friends, the other Slayers." It turns out it's a good thing we came, after all. I want to ask more questions, but I'm trying to pretend I have any idea what's going on. So instead, I criticize. "You can't just *take* people."

"Did you know it's illegal to bring undocumented animals into the country? They brought a creature all the way from the Himalayas. Imagine what strains of disease they might be introducing. What they might expose our beloved country to."

"What kind of animal?" I ask, wary. What gets the attention of this dude?

"The kind that is best hunted on nights like tonight." He pauses, waiting for something. The look of expectation on his face sours. "A full moon."

"My Slayer friends brought a werewolf into the country?" I pick up a teacup to cover my confusion, accidentally snapping the delicate handle off. "Whoops. Slayer strength. You know how it goes." I smile innocently.

His left eye twitches. "That cup was hand-painted by King George's mistress."

"Shouldn't have given it to me, then. You know how Americans feel about King George's tea."

"Not *that* King George, you imbecile."

"I mean, you've had one King George, you've had 'em all, am I right?" He's not amused. I wanted to channel Buffy, or Artemis. Hells, even more Honora at this point. It's hard when you're trying to project an impression of someone other than yourself. No one is intimidated by Nina the Vampire Slayer. All I'm doing is annoying him. Last I checked, irritating enemies is not among my innate Slayer strengths. Or maybe I'm just special.

I half wish the seething darkness that keeps popping up at inopportune times would roar to life, but it seems semi-sated by what I did at the demon conference and deeply unconcerned about this sitting room. I set down my teacup. "So you're hunting a werewolf. And you need me for what?"

"To be part of the hunt, of course."

"Didn't you already capture him? Seems a little unsporting to capture him, let him go, and then hunt him. Doesn't your particular brand of wealth prefer birds? Foxes? Much younger women? Go buy an island or something." I lean back, folding my arms. "Werewolves are people, you know."

"You could say the same of vampires."

"That's different! Vampires are always vampires. The person—the soul—is gone. They're only predators. Werewolves can't help it, and they're people most of the time."

"Ah, but they're infectious. You draw a distinction that I don't think exists between vampires and werewolves; both are victims of a, shall we say, *condition* that robs them of their humanity and turns them into monsters. That's bad enough, but they can also infect others. If I had someone with Ebola, would you argue they should be set free to do what they would?"

"I would argue you should get them the best medical care."

"Well, until we have an antidote for lycanthropy, or a way to restore souls to vampires—"

"Actually—"

"Do not interrupt me. In the absence of a medical way to

intervene, the only humane choice—the only moral choice—is to prevent the spread of infection and end the suffering of the afflicted."

"By hunting them."

He shrugs, taking a sip of his tea. "A man must have hobbies."

"Again, *buy an island.* Do you see Richard Branson running around hunting humans?"

"Actually—"

I hold up my hands. "No. I don't want to know. Werewolves are people. They have souls. You don't get to decide that they should be hunted out of existence."

"I do, in fact. You understand about power. About the responsibilities that come with it. And my responsibility is to use the power and privilege that I collected over my lifetime to prevent the supernatural from becoming natural. From becoming accepted. You of all people should understand. You're a Slayer. A killer. This is your job."

And just like that, it hits me. How wrong he is. All these years, I thought the first Watchers were a bit dense for giving power to only one girl. One Slayer to fight everything? One Slayer to make impossible choices? But . . . that's the beauty of it. Because the Slayer is young. The Slayer is a girl. The Slayer isn't some rich dude, insulated from life and pain and struggle, sitting in his Mr. Darcy house deciding who gets to live and die.

The Slayer is on the streets, in the dark, in the night, walking right alongside the things she hunts. So when she makes life-or-death choices—they're life-or-death choices for her, too. Not just for the things she's hunting. She's not a committee, a council, a group working at a remove.

She's part of the darkness.

And when you're already in the dark, you can see the subtle differences in the shadows. Some things are so absent of light that there's no question. And other things, like werewolves, like the Dougs and Clems of the world, they're delicately shaded.

I think of Artemis and Honora behind the wheel of that truck. All those shades of darkness in demons. Just like in humans.

My ancient ancestors actually got this one right. The whole one-Slayer thing wasn't a flaw. It was a feature. The fact that there are more of us now doesn't change that. This is my calling. My duty. My right.

I don't have to pretend to be anyone else right now. Nina the Vampire Slayer is exactly who I am and should be. I'm going to play his game, and I'm going to win, and he's going to regret everything.

I lean back and prop my booted feet up on the mahogany table. "So tell me the rules, Mr. Most Dangerous Game."

All noble pretense at civility is gone, revealing a face with less humanity than Doug's neon-yellow one. His tone goes cold. "You're hunting a werewolf. The other Slayers will be in the trees before you. They want to protect him. Your job is to kill him, if you want to see your little demon pet again. You'll have a ten-minute head start over the other hunters. They'll be hunting the werewolf . . . and anyone in the woods before them." He smiles, his veneers catching the light to show the ghosts of his tiny gray teeth behind them. "Kill the werewolf and make it out alive, you'll win a prize and get your demon back. If not, well, can you really call yourself a Slayer?"

I can't believe my mother considers this man an ally. He's

like the veneer over his teeth—wealth and privilege covering up rotting waste. He thinks he understands what Slayers are? He has no idea. None of them do. No one gets to threaten my friends. No one gets to make decisions that are mine.

Something in my expression must reveal my thoughts, because he smiles sharply. "Before you do anything rash, remember that I have your friends. If you harm me now, none of them make it out alive."

"Can't wait for my prize." I smile at him with such blankly intense cheer that he finally shudders and calls for Jeeves to return me to my cell until the game.

ARTEMIS

HONORA PULLS ARTEMIS INTO AN abandoned side hall. The basement level of the shiny building is far less shiny. Their failure to snag more than a handful of demons at the convention means that they'll have to go hunting instead of buying in bulk. Sean has some leads—he always does—but it's dirty, dangerous, aggravating work.

And Artemis doesn't want to be far away from the Sleeping One. She needs to be close to him, watching. Ready. Nothing can be done now, but when it happens, she'll be there.

Honora checks up and down the hallway, drained of life by the flickering fluorescent lights above them. When she's certain they're alone, she turns and folds her arms. "I read the book."

Artemis has pored over the book of the Sleeping One. Maybe Honora found something she missed. "Most of it is incomprehensible, right? But he has to go through three forms, and the third and final form will be the most powerful. Like, *all shall love me and despair* levels of powerful, minus being as hot as Galadriel. Also probably minus the love and plus a whole lot of despair."

Artemis is rambling, she knows she is, but she can't focus. She paces. Seeing Nina threw her off. She keeps remembering the look on Nina's face, the shock and betrayal and hurt. Artemis was never the person who put hurt on Nina's face. She was the one who protected her sister from it. She shakes her head, trying to move past it.

"Right," Honora says. "So my question is, why are we waiting? We've got a hellgod here. He's not at full power, or even close if his ramblings about the cruel ravages of time are any indication. And he can't juice up until he finds the right battery size of demon. So I say we make with the stabbing and end it *before* things get precarious."

"No!" Artemis backtracks from the force of her exclamation. "No. You saw him stick a knife all the way into his brain and not even bat an eye. How do you propose we kill that?"

"I mean, hard to recover from a decapitation."

"But not demonically unprecedented. And what happens if we don't get him on the first strike? Once he knows we're attacking, that's it."

"So what, we help him get what he needs to find his third form? It will be a lot harder to defeat him when he's at full power."

"We'll never let him get there. But we need his guard all the way down. That's the perfect moment. He's going to be so focused on changing that he won't see us coming. And by the time he realizes what we're doing, it'll be too late."

"And what, exactly, are we doing?" Honora frowns, searching Artemis's face.

Artemis hasn't exactly told Honora this part yet. Honora has been operating under the assumption they were here to assassinate the hellgod. But they're a team. Honora needs to know. "We're stealing it. The hellgod's power."

Honora's eyes go wide. "Moon. Baby. *Why?*"

"If there's power up for grabs, we should be the ones who get it! Aren't you tired of being powerless?"

Honora's face shifts, becoming fierce. Her eyes narrow. "No one gets to make me feel powerless without my permission. Not ever again. I'm not powerless, and neither are you."

This is so much harder than Artemis thought it was going to be. She thought Honora would understand. Honora has to understand, because Artemis doesn't have anyone else now. Tears prick in her eyes. She holds her arms out and Honora comes in close, their arms around each other, foreheads pressed together. "I am, though," she whispers, trying not to let her voice break. "The whole world makes me feel powerless. That's why I have to change it."

Honora reaches behind Artemis and undoes her ponytail, letting Artemis's hair down. The relief of the constant tension of her ponytail is immediate and she lowers her head to Honora's shoulder. "Change what?" Honora asks. Her voice is soft in a way it is only ever for Artemis.

"The world."

Honora sighs. "You need this."

Artemis nods, her face still against Honora's shoulder.

She lets go and pulls out her phone. "My girl wants a hellgod's power, my girl's getting a hellgod's power." She holds up a finger as someone answers on the other end of the line. "Yeah, it's Honora. We're in the market for something special of a demonic variety. Looking for rare species. What've you heard?" She makes some noncommittal noises, and then draws a sharp breath. "Yeah. Yeah, that's the one. Who has him? Thanks. We're square now."

Artemis resists the urge to bite her nails. "Well?"

Honora's mouth is pursed. She pauses before answering, something about what she heard troubling her. "We're going back to London. Should have called my guy *before* we made it all the way home. This might get messy, though. Personal too."

"I don't care. It's worth it. Thank you. Thank you. I promise, this is going to work out. Trust me."

"I do. It's the rest of the world I worry about. But we're going to change it, right?" The line between Honora's brows shouldn't be there. Artemis presses a kiss to smooth it out. They're going to win. They have to.

14

A DIFFERENT SERVANT FETCHES ME when the sun sets. Doug and I have talked; he's confident he's not in any danger and reassured me he has his own plans for while I'm busy. I still don't like leaving him—and if anyone hurts him, they'll pay—but I trust that he can handle this.

My shoulder is almost better, and the buzzing anticipation in me isn't nervousness. It's excitement. Which should worry me, on account of I am not only hunting but being hunted. But I don't let myself look too long or hard at it. I don't have time to question myself. I might not have been able to figure out how to face Artemis and Honora, but I can do this. I'm a Slayer. I'm made for this kind of nonsense.

Out on the far edge of the perfectly manicured lawn, Ian Von Alston is waiting. He's in a different sharp suit, his hyperpolished dress shoes reflecting the full moon back at us. A maid holds a tray of drinks near a half circle of chairs. Three other men are with Von Alston. They're all wearing full tactical gear and adjusting night-vision goggles. Like gentlemen, they remove the goggles when I approach, ogling without goggling.

"Ah, our other Slayer." Von Alston gestures to me as I walk up. I've got my hair down. Ponytails are Artemis's signature fight look. I don't want to be her right now. It didn't really work out for me before, and channeling her means I have to think about her. Besides which, I had psyched myself up to pretend not to be afraid, but now that I'm out here looking at these men, I'm not afraid. I'm disgusted. Maybe it's dangerous not to be warier, but I can't muster any fear of these men who hunt the vulnerable to make themselves feel powerful. They don't have any real power. They have to know it. If they don't, they will by the end of the night.

"A redhead?" One of the men, a white guy with more beard than face, snickers. "Did you know redheads have a lower pain tolerance?"

"You're right." I smile, gritting my teeth. "And you're *really* hurting me to look at."

Beard slides a compensating-for-something-size knife into a sheath, glaring at me. "She's mine," he growls at the other two.

"Cool, bye." I walk to the tree line.

"Ten minutes!" Von Alston shouts after me.

I wave without turning around. As soon as I'm in the trees, I stop, ducking behind a tree and taking stock of my options. I could wait here and take out the hunters as soon as they enter the trees. But they'll probably be spread out, so it'll eat up some time. And I'd risk one of them finding the werewolf first and killing him.

My best bet is to find the werewolf first, get him to safety,

make sure the other Slayers are safe, and then take out the hunters. Easy. All I have is several acres of forest to cover. Before
three trained hunters do it. And an unknown number of Slayers
to locate and manage. And a werewolf on a full moon.

"Uggggh." I pick a direction and start running. My cell rings,
and I startle, pulling it out. Von Alston never even checked for
phones or weapons, the smug ass. "Cillian? Is something wrong?"

"I'm trying to think of a play on Lucille Ball. But I can't
figure out a way to make any cat puns with it. I wish you had
consulted me on cat colors before. A ginger cat makes things so
much more specific and complicated. I feel like you can't overlook that detail."

"Oh my gods, Cillian. I cannot talk to you about the cat
right now."

"Did you already name it? That's not fair!"

"No, I can't talk to you about the cat because I'm currently
prowling through a forest hunting a werewolf who might also be
hunting me in addition to three toxic masculinity poster boys
who are definitely hunting me."

"*Nina*. What is going on?"

I sense movement on either side. I can't say how I do—I don't
see or hear anything. But I know there are two people closing in
on me.

"Listen, I don't like people names for animals. It makes it
so awkward when you meet people with the same name. 'Oh,
Nina! We named our hedgehog Nina!' Like, how am I supposed
to respond to that? I can't even . . ." I throw my phone hard to the
side. Someone squeaks in pain as it connects with a face. I drop
to the forest floor as a large stick swings through the air where

my head would have been. I sweep my leg, tripping someone. She curses in Spanish as she goes down.

I hop to my feet and whirl to find myself face-to-face with the ice cream Slayer from my dreams.

"You!" I say.

"You!" she says. And then she punches me in the face.

"Ow! Gods, I actually prefer the ice cream." I dodge another punch, then kick her in the stomach. She doubles over, stumbling back. "I don't want to hurt you! Any of you! I've got to get to the werewolf."

"We won't let you hurt him!" The Slayer with the stick pushes herself up. In the darkness, she's an indistinct mass of gorgeous curly dark hair and whirling kicks and fists. I dodge, jump up, grab a low branch, then swing a double kick into her chest. She flies backward, landing hard. The third one I hit with the phone is still on the ground, crying. It was a phone. I can't have hurt her that bad.

The ice cream one has recovered. "He is our friend."

"I'm not going to kill him! I'm trying to save him! And I'm trying to save you three, assuming you stop punching me." I dodge a fist from the curly-haired Slayer. "Seriously! Stop. I'm on your side. I'm not going to kill the werewolf. I might have to knock him out so he doesn't bite anyone, but that's it."

"It won't be a . . ." There's a whistling noise and we all throw ourselves down as a tranquilizer dart sings past us.

"Three hunters," I hiss. "I promise I'm on your side. Let's work together."

"Taylor's going to be useless," the curly-haired Slayer whispers, gesturing at the crying Slayer. "And I—I don't want to do any of this either."

"Grab her and get her somewhere safe, then." I look at the ice cream Slayer. "I'm Nina."

"Chao-Ahn." She frowns at me. Then she turns to the other Slayer. "Maricruz, get her out. Cling to the edges of the trees. We'll find you when we've finished this."

But Chao-Ahn's hands are shaking, her full lips trembling. Come to think of it, all their attacks were clumsy, and their faces in the moonlight look terrified. Something's happened that I don't know about. Maybe Von Alston drugged them, or hurt them before releasing them as some sort of a handicap. My protective instinct flares, momentarily overpowering my punch-kick-kill instincts.

I shake my head. "No, you three should stay together. You'll be stronger that way, and then I won't have to worry about stumbling into one of you and attacking by accident again. I only have one job if you three are safe, and that's getting the werewolf out alive. I can do it. I promise. Go to the edge of the tree line. I passed a huge dead oak on my way in. Climb it and wait."

"For what?" Maricruz, the curly-haired one, asks. Taylor is wiping her face and standing with Chao-Ahn's help.

"My signal."

Chao-Ahn hands me my phone. "What signal?"

"The bat signal. I don't know. I'll figure something out. You'll know it's me on account of I'm not a dude. Go!"

They hesitate for only a second, then take off running in the direction I came. I hope the hunter who shot at us doesn't follow them. "Oh no," I cry out, rolling my eyes. "I twisted my ankle. Don't leave me behind! Wait for me!"

I jump for the lowest branch and silently pull myself up. It's not long before the clumsy footsteps of a man trying for stealth in brand-new combat boots announces the presence of one of the hunters. I watch as the beard steps right beneath me, then two steps past. I drop to the ground and tap him on the shoulder.

"What the—" He whirls around, his face finding my fist.

"How's that for pain tolerance?" I step over his prone, unconscious body, then relieve him of his weapons. I pick him up by one arm and a leg, swing him a few times to get momentum, and then launch him straight up into the trees. He catches on several branches about fifteen feet up, suspended like a rag doll. "Sleep tight," I sing, then hurry deeper into the trees. As I run, I check over his gear.

"Bloody cheaters!" I curse, looking at a small device with a green dot blipping regularly. They know exactly where the werewolf is. What kind of a hunt is that? I adjust my course and pick up speed. I have to beat the other two. Beard took a detour, more determined to get me than get the werewolf, but I can't count on that for the other hunters.

I watch, nervous, as the green dot gets closer and closer. Well, as I get closer and closer to it. It's not moving at all, and hasn't since I started looking. Did they drug the werewolf, too? It wouldn't surprise me. None of these creeps would actually risk their lives for this. They want the imitation of life-and-death struggle, the pretense of it.

I slow down. I'm almost on the dot. Another possibility occurs to me—the other two have already killed the werewolf, and I'm about to run into them and a dead body. Do werewolves turn back into humans if they die? Or does their body stay forever in that state? Rhys would know. I hope I don't find out.

Holding my breath, I creep up to a small clearing bathed in the cold light of the full moon. Sitting cross-legged in the middle, eyes closed, hands on his knees, is . . . a rather petite white man. Spiky reddish hair, nice face, flowing baggy clothes that could either be skater chic or Eastern mystic in origin. I look around, confused, but there's not a slavering, fanged were-wolf in sight.

"Hey," I whisper. I have Beard's big knife in my hand. This guy could be a hunter? He doesn't look like one, though. The other two were in full gear. "Who are you and why are you here?"

"Wow. Those are big questions." He opens his eyes and stares at me, nodding slowly. "Is it harder or easier to answer them as a Slayer? Because on the one hand, chosen! On the other hand, didn't choose. Wow. Wow. Oh, you were probably asking my name." He glances upward where the moon shines over us. "I'm trying really hard to stay calm right now. So if you could not stab me, I'd appreciate it. But this is fun. They told me there'd be another Slayer who would probably kill me. I liked my odds, though. I have good luck with Slayers, generally."

"Are you—the werewolf? Did Von Alston mix up his order forms or something?"

The man stands, stretching. "I'm of the wolfish persuasion on occasion. But I didn't feel like it tonight. Are we gonna go? I think we should go."

"Right. Yeah." I'm so confused. "Actually, before we go, they put a tracker on you."

He checks his pockets, then pulls out a tiny metal cylinder the size of a pill. "I just thought the butler had wandering hands."

I take the tracker. "Go to the edge of the tree line. There's a huge dead oak. Can't miss it. The other Slayers are waiting there for my signal."

"Cool." He sticks his hands back in his pockets and meanders out of the clearing.

Tracker on me, I go the opposite direction. In the end, it's too easy. I climb a tree, wait until I hear two hunters approaching from either side, and then snap a branch. They both shoot their tranquilizers at each other, and then two bodies go down with loud thuds.

I drop back to the ground, relieve them of their weapons, and then give them the same tree treatment as Beard. *Too bad they're human*, I think. Then I cringe. Where did that come from?

Feeling a little dirty with the realization that I would have liked to hurt them a lot more than I did, I run toward the dead oak. I don't want to leave Doug in that house any longer than I have to, and my work is almost done.

I pause at the base of the tree, looking up.

"Hey," I call.

"What's the signal?" Maricruz calls back down.

"Um. Me? Calling hey?"

"That's a terrible signal. You didn't even try." She drops to the ground next to me, her rather glorious eyebrows writing disappointment all over her face.

"That's not fair. I took out all three hunters and saved your werewolf . . . ish . . . guy."

"Whatever." She turns away from me, arms folded. Chao-Ahn lands in a crouch, and then Taylor, a tall, lanky blonde, slowly climbs down. The not-werewolf is last.

"I have questions for you," I say.

"Math? I'm good at math. Oz, by the way."

"Oz?"

"I'm. And I'm pleased to meet you."

"Oh. Nina."

"Nina. Well, we can worry about the math later."

Still confused and also oddly disappointed and unsettled, I walk out of the trees with the three Slayers and the alleged werewolf. Von Alston stands, and I can't see whether he's surprised, but I sure hope so. He's flanked by three security guards. I shoot tranquilizers at all three before they can draw their own weapons.

I walk up to Von Alston and grab him around the throat. "Monopoly would have been easier. For you. Now let's go see about my friend and my prize, and then we can play a fun game called Hostage Negotiations, where I use you to get all of us out of here without any problems."

He sputters until I release some of the pressure. "No prize. The werewolf is still alive."

"Do you see a werewolf here? Because I don't. Besides, alive is such a temporary state of being." I tighten my grip again, a small, mean thrill of pleasure coursing through me seeing panic on the face of this man who threatened my friends and tried to kill innocent people. Something pushes me to go further. To squeeze harder. Because I can.

I let him go and take a step back, shuddering. That's not me. That can't be me. Where did that come from? "Come on. No funny business or I'll let the nice man bite you, and then we'll see if your stance on werewolf rights changes."

"I'd really prefer not to bite you," Oz says. "We've only

just met, and I don't think we're at a biting stage of our relationship yet."

Chao-Ahn and Maricruz each take one of Von Alston's arms and frog-march him back toward the manor. Two figures appear on the distant steps of the front door and I lift the tranquilizer gun to use the scope to view them.

One is Doug, having obviously freed himself. But I can't even wonder how, because I can't process who the other person I'm viewing through the crosshairs is.

Leo.

Leo Silvera.

Who is not dead.

I twitch. My finger pulls the trigger. Leo collapses.

15

"HEY," A SOFT, EVEN VOICE SAYS. A HAND comes down on my shoulder. "Hey. Deep breaths. Focus on your breathing."

Leo is there, lying on the porch, unconscious. And even though I know we're outside, we're safe, I can almost feel the remora demon expanding all around us. I know what will happen if I try to drag Leo away. I won't be able to, and he'll die, just like he did before.

Just like he didn't before.

"Breathe," Oz says again, moving to stand in front of me. He blocks my sight of Leo, and I feel like I've surfaced from too long underwater. I gasp for air, gulp it desperately. "Good. Breathing is good. I really dig breathing." He smiles but doesn't move, keeping one hand on my shoulder.

"I'm okay," I say. I'm not okay. I'm not. I haven't been okay since Leo died. And Leo isn't dead. All the anger I've been suppressing, all the grief I've been avoiding. The floodgates are open, and I feel it all. Along with joy and also absolute confusion. And rage. So much rage. Because Leo is alive. Leo is alive!

Leo is alive?

"Yeah." Oz almost smiles, an odd expression that is both reassuring and unnerving. He's like Doug, I think. Only instead of smelling emotions, I suspect Oz just sort of . . . gets them. I wrap my arms around myself and focus on breathing. Oz removes his hand and steps to the side. "Can I get my van back now?" he asks Von Alston.

"I don't understand," Ian Von Alston says, staring at Oz.

"I get that a lot." Oz wanders toward the garages. "It might be hard to tell which one is mine. My van blends in pretty well with Aston Martins."

"How is he still human?" Von Alston asks, frowning.

I can't look at the porch. I can't feel what I'm feeling. It's too much. So I pick the nearest thing that I understand. And that's Von Alston, the rich weasel. All my rage focuses, contained. "Why do you have Leo? How long have you had him? Where were you holding him?" *That's* why he never came back! Von Alston took Leo. All this time, thinking Leo was dead, blaming myself, hurting *so damn much* every day. My hand twitches. I want it around Von Alston's throat with an intensity that scares me.

"Nina," Doug says, walking up. His face flashes with alarm, and he steps between Von Alston and me. "Let's redirect whatever's happening here."

"Demon!" Taylor squeaks. Maricruz and Chao-Ahn both shift to defensive stances.

"He's my friend," I snap. I hate that everyone is still talking, still here. I don't want to talk to any of them. I want answers. I want answers that will solve the way I feel right now, because I can't handle feeling like this. There's too much input; I'm fraying at the edges.

"Do we have to fight anyone?" Maricruz asks. Chao-Ahn and Taylor are standing next to her. They're all flicking their eyes between Doug and the mansion.

Doug shakes his head. "All the household employees and security guys are too happy to care about much of anything right now."

This gets my attention, at least. "You took out the whole *house?*"

Doug shifts, obviously uncomfortable. "I told you I wasn't defenseless. Sean kept me near-starving, but now that I'm healthy, I'm back in fighting form. My spit is hyperconcentrated, and I have this, uh, muscle? It lets me spit at great distances with startling accuracy."

"Eew." Maricruz twirls her hair around a finger. "But also rad."

Doug shrugs. "I don't like using it. But it comes in handy."

"Where did you find Leo? What kind of cell did this monster have him in?" I want to know the details, need to know them. They feed the churning black mass in my chest, and it's easier to be furious than think about Leo lying there unconscious because of me, again. To think of all this time I spent in bleak despair over being the reason he was dead when this *human* had him. Rage is simpler. Cleaner.

"About that." Doug eases himself more in between Von Alston and me. "Leo wasn't in a cell. He was in a sitting room, near a fireplace. Reading."

"Wait, what?"

"Leo is my guest," Von Alston says. "I was friends with his mother. She belonged to an organization I traded information and favors with for many years. Young Leo showed up at my gate a few months ago. I'm afraid there's nothing I can do for him, but I've done my best to keep him comfortable out of loyalty to his mother."

I shake my head. None of this makes sense. Why would Leo come here instead of coming back to us? Why would he stay, knowing we would all assume he was dead? Knowing how much it would hurt?

He let me think I was responsible for his death all these months. Maybe I don't feel so bad about accidentally shooting him with a tranquilizer. Maybe I want to shoot him with another one. But what Von Alston said needs more explaining, since Leo himself can't explain it right now.

"What do you mean, there's nothing you can do for him?"

"He's dying."

I push past Doug and throw Von Alston to the ground, my hand around his throat. "Don't lie to me." Leo can't be dying. He was dead, and now he's not, and my heart can't take any more.

Von Alston's voice is strained. "I've been nothing but truthful with you this whole time. Without his mother, he's starving to death. Take him, if you wish."

"Nina." Doug tugs on my shoulder until I release Von Alston. "Let's talk."

"No. I don't want to talk. We need to finish up here. You owe me a prize," I snarl, yanking Von Alston to his feet. "I take cash."

"We should go." Chao-Ahn eyes the dark grounds nervously.

"Can't leave until Leo wakes up." I know from deeply painful experience that Leo cannot be budged or carried. I stalk toward the house, my hand around Von Alston's wrist. I'm probably squeezing too tight. I can't care. Von Alston hurries to keep up and avoid the indignity of being dragged. "Might as well make our time here worthwhile."

"I am a man of my word," Von Alston huffs. "I suppose you did win, even if it was unconventional. The prize is fifty thousand pounds."

"Bully for me." Although it's a massive windfall for the castle, I can't begin to feel giddy over it. We've gotten to the porch, and I can see Leo now, bathed in the warm yellow light from the house. He looks . . . awful. His jawline, always strong, stands out in stark contrast now, his cheeks hollow and the circles under his eyes so dark they look more like bruises than anything else.

But he's here. He's alive. And I'm so angry my vision is pulsing at the edges.

"Should we take him inside?" Taylor asks, trembling like a purse dog.

"Literally impossible. Hopefully he wakes up fast." I try not to look at Leo's prone body as I step around him. It's too close to my nightmares of when I had to leave him behind.

I follow Von Alston into a study where he retrieves a leather satchel. He opens it to show me neat stacks of pound notes. "If you get a chance before he dies, you should ask Leo to train you," he says, his tone sneering and pedantic. "He's a Watcher. Pity they're all gone now. You could certainly use one."

"What do you mean by that?"

"I've known rogue Slayers. No control, all violent instinct without any training. Like feral animals without Watchers to direct them."

My hand finds the place on his neck already marked by my fingers. I push him against the dark-wood-paneled wall. "Do I seem like I don't have control right now?"

His eyes are wide. He shakes his head.

"Good. Are you the nameless threat demons are terrified of?"

He tries to shake his head again, but my hand must have tightened. He can't quite manage it.

"No," he whispers. "Everyone knows my name. I've never made a secret of what I do."

I have to admit he's right. It wasn't hard to find his name. I got it twice—from the mercenaries, and from a demon. Much as I want it to be Von Alston, Doug searched the mansion and found only one demon. Half demon. And he was here by choice, which I still can't reconcile. Plus, Von Alston doesn't strike me as the type to inspire zealots, much less tolerate them. He's far too British.

I don't loosen my grip, though. "If I ever hear your name again in connection with anything or anyone under my protection—and that means werewolves and demons and Slayers, *all of them*—it won't end well for you. Are we clear?"

He nods. I mean to let him go. I really do. But my fingers stay where they are, and I lean closer, staring at his neck. Such a fragile thing, a spine, separating life and death. Every part of humans is so breakable.

A strained wheeze escapes him. I let go, backing away. Disgusted with him. Disgusted with myself. And more than a little scared of how I keep thinking of him as a human. As something separate from me.

"You know I'm not in the wrong," he says. "They don't belong here." He adjusts his tie, smooths his waistcoat, then raises one eyebrow over his aquiline nose. I'd like to break that nose into aqui*lines*. See how regal he looks then. "I do a tremendous service to my country. You have no place to judge me if I sometimes seek sport while rendering those services. I don't expect you to pity me, but you'd be astonished at how dull being this wealthy can be. I want for nothing, I need nothing, I—"

His need for my fist in his face is answered with a resounding thud. He goes down, clutching his bleeding, broken nose. I try to feel sorry, but I can't find it in me.

If anything, I want to punch more things. I half hope the other hunters will wake up and come after us. But I'm afraid of what I might do. I know I'm overreacting. I'm not even being a Slayer right now. I'm being . . . me. But not me. And that's what's scary. I don't recognize this Nina, and I don't know how to feel any of the things I'm feeling without being taken over by them.

I close my eyes and let myself imagine my tiny medical center back in the castle. The neatly organized cupboards. The drawer full of tongue depressors. Artemis laughed at me for that. *How many tongue depressors can one castle need?* The truth was, I just liked having them. I liked all of it. I liked being the one who fixed things, who healed things.

But I don't know how to fix Artemis. Or Leo. Or myself. And thinking about my medical center doesn't calm me. It makes me feel even more lost.

I walk out to check on Leo, but something else catches my eye. A serial killer's dream van is parked on the grass. It's covered with dings and scratches and a long-faded decal for something, but I can only make out the letters for GO AT BABY. There are tire marks all over the formerly perfect lawn, far more than would have been required just to get the van here. The side door slides open, and Oz sits there, legs out, bathed in the light of the moon.

I stay on the porch, not touching Leo. Not looking at him.

I can't. Chao-Ahn stands in front of me, considering me with what I assume is disapproval. We might be here for a while, and I need to talk about something that doesn't matter. I need to do anything other than think about what I'm going to say to Leo when he wakes up.

"So. Uh. What brings you all to London?" I ask her.

Chao-Ahn has the most beautifully judgmental glare I've ever seen. "Sineya."

"I'm sorry?"

Her glare deepens. "Sineya. The First Slayer. You know." She gestures to her hair, then hunches a bit and scowls.

"Oh, right! She tried to stab me. She *did* stab me." I used to have such good control of my Slayer dreams. But I've lost that, along with control everywhere else in my life. Buffy told me about the First Slayer. She said Sineya was judgy. She never mentioned stabby. It feels like a pretty big oversight.

"Why are you here?" Maricruz asks. She's sitting on a decorative stone wall, braiding Taylor's hair.

"Thought there was a threat. Bigger than Von Alston, I mean."

"So you're hunting it?"

Am I? Wasn't I the one who said if we started going after potential threats, we would stop being Sanctuary? And if it's something that's only threatening demons, do I get involved? Because not all demons—or even most of them—are benign like Doug. I want to help the ones who are, but the ones who aren't definitely don't belong here. My head doesn't ache, exactly, but it feels like it should.

"Um, not really. We're looking for people—werewolves—well, anyone of a bump-in-the-night persuasion. It's a long story."

"Why are you looking for them?" Maricruz's wariness is

understandable, considering most people looking for beasties are hunting them, as evidenced by Von Alston.

"I run a sanctuary. A safe haven. For werewolves, or demons, or anyone who needs it and won't harm anyone already there."

Chao-Ahn's eyes widen. "You offer sanctuary?"

"Yes. Yeah. We're the sanctuariest." I'm a bundle of nerves. I almost want to run into the trees and find the hunters, give them a few more punches for good measure. Something to do with my hands while I wait for Leo to wake up and decide whether I'm going to hug him or strangle him.

"What are the odds?" Oz asks.

"Odds of what? Wait, is this the math you were going to help with? I don't actually want math advice."

"No, dingbat," Maricruz says, but she softens with a smile. "What are the odds we'd find a Slayer with a safe haven when that's exactly what we came to London for?"

"Seriously?" I was always supposed to bring Slayers in. I thought I'd find them through my dreams. And I guess I did, in a very roundabout sort of way. After all, Chao-Ahn and I already know each other.

Oz nods. "I was taking them to another Slayer. But she's actually the one outlier in my general good luck with Slayers. I think this might be a better option."

I'm excited in spite of myself. Everything is messed up and confusing, but I did something right! I found Slayers. "Oh yeah! You should totally pick us. We have a castle. I'll bet that other Slayer doesn't have a castle."

Oz rubs his chin. "Castle, huh? I've been looking into getting one of those. But the market is tough right now."

"I need to pee," Taylor says. Maricruz follows her inside. There's a weird dynamic there. Taylor can't be much younger than Maricruz—in fact, I think she's slightly older than I am. But it's like she needs a babysitter.

"Where are you all from?" I ask.

"The Himalayas, by way of a lot of places," Oz says.

Chao-Ahn seems annoyed. Or maybe that's her permanent state of being. "That is not where any of us come from. That is where we were. Maricruz is from New York City. Taylor is from Iowa. Idaho. Ohio." She frowns. "Somewhere smaller than New York City."

"What about you?"

"You do not know it."

"Try me!"

"Guangzhou."

"Oh. Um. Yeah. I don't know it. It's in . . . China?"

The breath she releases sounds sharp enough to cut me. "I will tell you enough, and then you will ask no more questions. A British man came. He tried to take me. Then other men came. No eyes." She gestures to her own. "They almost killed me. I went with the British man. He brought me to California."

"Sunnydale?" I ask, my heart racing.

"Home sweet hellmouth," Oz says.

"Yes. Very sunny. Very bad part of California. No movie stars. Just monsters. No one learned Cantonese. So many Slayers, and I was always alone." Some of the anger fades and she talks as though trying to find her way through the words like navigating an unfamiliar room in the darkness. "And after, when we won, I had to keep fighting. Always fighting. I have not been home since

Mr. Giles took me away. And I wonder. I am a Slayer for a reason. Guangzhou must have demons. Vampires. Monsters. Who is protecting them while I fight Buffy's fights?"

"Wait. Did *Buffy* send you here?" There was a period of time when Buffy ran an extensive network of Slayer operatives. Basically a big Slayer army. But a crap-ton of them died, and after Buffy destroyed the Seed of Wonder and killed magic, she kind of retired. Went back to solo Slayage in San Francisco. Is she still working internationally? We should have known if she was. This idea worries me and also makes me feel a touch left out that I haven't been recruited.

"No." Chao-Ahn packs an entire history I'm not privy to in that one word. "We don't speak. I was in Tibet with Oz and a Slayer army. So close to home." She stares into the forest as though she can pierce the distance through sheer determination. "But I could not leave the girls, after the fight. No one takes care of them."

I cross my arms, not in defiance but to hold myself against the shame. I believed so much in the Watchers. In my heritage. It took becoming a Slayer for me to realize how deeply they failed in their calling. I told Eve Silvera that I was going to be the Watcher for every Slayer out there. I haven't done a very good job of keeping that vow. But I will. "I'm trying to change that."

She nods brusquely. "We fought gods. We got hurt. Maricruz and Taylor and me and many others. We stayed when Buffy left. And she never came back. She never— Well, we stayed there. But they need to heal and move on. So we came here to find somewhere safe."

"They haven't healed? They should have healed by now. Slayers heal fast." I rub my shoulder, which is almost totally better. I wonder if there's something with the loss of magic that's changed our powers. They've all been Slayers longer than I have. Is it fading? Panic sparks through me. If we stop healing quickly, does that mean we'll also lose our strength? Our instincts? I've lost it before, and the memory keeps me awake at night. It's one thing to never know power. Another entirely to have it and then lose it.

Chao-Ahn shakes her head. She gestures to her body. "Not here. Here." She taps the side of her head. "Sometimes we break here. And no one can help us, because no one understands."

I *feel* what she's saying. One of the worst parts of navigating the last few months is how alone I've felt. Is that why Artemis left? Because she got hurt, and no one could understand except Honora? I would have understood. I will understand. I just need her to come back. To talk to me. To give me a chance to be there for her. Like I'll be there for these Slayers.

Leo groans, ending the conversation as we all shift to look at him. I want to stare at him until he wakes up. I never want to look at him again. I never want to stop looking at him. I want to tear out my hair.

Doug pulls up in our car. "If you all want to come to the castle," I say, calculating, "Oz will have to drive too. We don't have room in our car for every extra passenger."

"But we do have a kitten!" Doug holds up the tiny orange fluff ball. "Meet Trouble."

"Better than Chewie, but trouble is what we're going to be in when Cillian finds out you already named her." I toss the case of money to Oz. "Check that for, I don't know, booby traps or trackers or something."

"All money is a trap, if you think about it," he says.

"What?"

"Don't think about it," Maricruz answers, coming out of the house. "Trust me. Don't ever think about anything he says, or you'll lose your mind. Ooh, kitty!" She rushes Doug and snatches the kitten away. It crawls on her shoulder, disappearing into her hair. "Taylor, come see the kitten."

Taylor drifts to Maricruz's side. She seems to relax a little. "We're riding in the catmobile," Maricruz declares, climbing into the back and settling in with Taylor.

"Your friend doesn't look so hot," Oz says, pointing to Leo. I don't look. I don't want to acknowledge how bad he seems, because it makes it harder to settle on being livid or being devastated or being happy.

Oz closes the money case and shoves it into his van. "He can lie down in here. Is it a long trip?"

"Ireland," I say. "We'll have to take a ferry."

Oz pats the side of his van fondly. "She'll get us there. Slowly but surely. But more slowly than surely."

"What happened?" Leo groans. His voice triggers memories of training in the gym. Fighting side by side. And not listening when he was trying to kidnap me to get me away from his mother, whom he had known was a killer and still let live in our castle.

I crouch next to him. His eyes, so dark they look black but with a hint of violet when you get close enough and the light is right—and I *have* been close enough, and the light *has* been right—focus on my face.

"I thought you were dead," I whisper.

"Not quite yet." He tries to sit up but doesn't make it. Chao-Ahn leans down and together we help him stand. We take him inside to the nearest sitting room.

"Go get snacks and water and whatever else you can raid from the kitchen?" I ask Chao-Ahn. She nods and disappears.

I'm still shaking inside. I can feel it in electric bursts of white-hot anger, more powerful than the jolts I got at the convention. Leo looks winded from the effort to make it this far. My anger flares even brighter, seeing how vulnerable he is. "You came to *him*? When we were right there, this whole time?"

"I couldn't," he whispers.

"You most certainly could have!"

"The things I did . . . the things I hid from you all."

I throw my hands in the air. "Oh, join the club. We would have gotten over it. You didn't give us the chance to."

"It wouldn't have mattered. You can't help me."

"I can help anyone," I say through gritted teeth. A pained moan from Von Alston's study contradicts me. I flex my hands, then ball them into fists. Today has nearly broken me. First Artemis proved that when she left, it wasn't so much to discover herself as it was to get away from me. And now Leo—Leo, who I mourned and blamed myself over—has been alive this whole bloody time and he didn't think I could help him.

I'm going to help him if it kills him. Chao-Ahn reappears with some full bags, and Doug clears his throat from the hallway. "Good to go."

"We're taking you with us." I hold out my hand to help Leo stand.

"Athena, I don't—" Leo starts.

I cut him off. No one has called me that since he died—since he didn't die; gods, I have got to stop thinking of his death that obviously didn't happen. "I swear to every deity listening, if you say one more word, I will get you to the car by throwing you out the window."

Leo's lips twitch like they want to smile but can't quite remember how. "You can't."

"Fine, not throw. Push. I can definitely push you out the window. And the likelihood of me doing that is getting higher every moment we—"

"Right, then." Doug grabs Leo's hand and maneuvers him up. He puts Leo's arm around his shoulders. "It's been a rough day. Let's all walk calmly to the car; no defenestration necessary. Sweet hells, you are a heavy skeleton."

Leo's half human, half incubus. The earth recognizes he belongs in a hell dimension and pulls on him a little harder. Gravity is greedy like that. Doug and Leo stumble and make agonizingly slow progress down the hall. I follow, glaring at their backs.

"What about our host?" Doug asks, looking back.

"I took care of it." I help Leo get into the van, avoiding his eyes. I'm glad I'm not riding with him. I don't want to talk to him. Not yet. It's still too raw, and I feel so betrayed. And part of me wants to snuggle in next to him and forgive him and not talk about it, which I refuse to do.

Chao-Ahn gets into the van. I take the passenger seat of our car, and we lead the way. Doug steers us out of the estate as dawn breaks on the horizon. We leave unchallenged, the gates gaping open from the happy-dosed employees' neglect. I close my eyes and take careful breaths. Never mind that my sister is working with demon-snatching zealots, or that we didn't figure out what this nameless threat is, or that I went against my mom's wishes and confronted Von Alston.

Leo is alive. We saved the world's weirdest werewolf and three Slayers. I should be relieved. I should be happy.

I should be.

ARTEMIS

AS SHE GETS OUT OF THE CAR, ARTEMIS thinks Ian Von Alston's estate is like something out of a Jane Austen novel, if Jane were writing about a man who bought his nobility and used his wealth to hunt demons for sport instead of falling in love with someone slightly inappropriate. Actually, she would read that book. Nina would like it too.

Or she would have, before she went Team Demon. Artemis understands her sympathies, she really does, but there's still a difference between humans and demons, and that line has to stay there. Pretending that her little demon utopia is even possible shows how naive Nina still is, how incapable of handling everything mystical forces have given her. And she accused Artemis of turning her back on their past? Artemis can't forget, won't forget what demons and vampires have cost her. Cost their family. Cost the whole world.

Just because some are benign doesn't mean they aren't still tumors growing where they don't belong.

"Remind me why we had to bring the entourage?" Honora

glares over her shoulder at Sean and three huge goons, plus the Sleeping One drifting distractedly behind them.

"Pardon me if I want to make sure we get what we need." Sean smooths his ponytail. "*Someone's* sister cost us a lot of supplies yesterday."

Honora rolls her eyes. "Yeah, and *someone* threw her off a moving vehicle. You had better not be questioning our loyalty. I'm the one who found this lead."

Sean holds up his hands. "Certainly not questioning you, pet. But this demon is the key to everything. Boss wants to make sure we get the right merchandise this time. No more mistakes or false hope."

The Sleeping One makes eye contact with them. "I am without so much. I cannot stand the emptiness, the silence. Can you feel time eating at you? An infestation, like maggots, devouring you from the inside out." He holds out his hands, long fingers splayed. "I can see the decay that will claim me in another thirty, forty years. The blink of an eye."

"Can the decay hurry up so we don't have to listen to you anymore?" Honora lets out a long, annoyed breath, then pounds on the front door to the manor. An ancient butler answers it. "We're expected." Honora walks in right past him. Artemis follows with the rest of their entourage behind them.

A white man with a severely broken nose and some suspect bruising around his neck is sitting in a leather chair in a study. He stands, shocked, when Honora and Artemis enter.

"You!" he says, pointing at Artemis. She's never seen him before in her life. Which can only mean . . . he knows Nina. And judging by the damage to his face, she's guessing their acquaintance is recent. Which is bad news for all of them. She can't let Sean and his people decide to go after Nina. It would be a lot easier if Nina would stop sticking her nose where it doesn't belong.

"Nope, not me," Artemis says, shaking her head. Honora makes a slashing motion over her throat, then puts a finger over her lips. His eyes widen and he shuts his mouth. The rest of the men shuffle in, the Sleeping One wandering to the window.

"We're in the market for something in your possession," Sean says.

"I'm, ah, afraid my inventory is depleted." Von Alston keeps looking nervously at Honora and Artemis, licking his dry lips. "We had a mishap last night. If I had known you were coming, I would have held it for you."

"You do not have what I need?" The Sleeping One doesn't turn around, but his voice is as cold as the depths of winter.

Von Alston tugs on his collar. "I have many useful contacts. I own half the House of Lords. You'll find working with me is most advantageous. You want me as an ally."

The Sleeping One shakes his head. "I do not even want to breathe the same air as you. Filling your greedy lungs and then spewing poison to corrupt me."

Von Alston laughs nervously. He looks at Sean instead of the Sleeping One. "You know me. My reputation. I can get him back. I will get him back. Let's sit down, discuss terms. I have a feeling we'll see eye to eye on everything."

The Sleeping One turns and crosses the room to Von Alston. He reaches out and puts his thumbs through Von Alston's eyes. Artemis jumps at the screaming, startled by the sudden, unannounced violence. Honora has stepped forward, an arm out in front of Artemis, a knife in one of her hands.

Von Alston drops to the floor, twitching and screaming. The Sleeping One holds the two eyeballs in his palm. "Ruined. I cannot see through these. Everything gets ruined. Everything decays." He drops the eyeballs on the floor, then wipes his hands clean on Von Alston's suit. "Everything dies." He steps on Von Alston's neck until it snaps.

And Artemis stands there and watches it all. She knows she should stop it. But if she does, she'll lose her chance. She just watched a man die—a human man, however dubious his business—and she did nothing. Make the hard decisions. Make the acceptable sacrifices. She learned those lessons well as a Watcher, but she knows this moment will haunt her for the rest of her life. She has to make sure it's worth it.

When it's clear the Sleeping One is not going to murder Artemis, Honora quietly sheathes her knife. "No leads, then. Dead end."

Things have to progress. She wants to protect Nina, but how can she without power? It's Nina's own fault. Artemis warned her about taking in demons. "He recognized me," Artemis says. Honora shoots her a look as sharp as a knife. She was lying to protect that information. Artemis gives her a tiny shake of the head. "Which means he's met Nina. She must have beaten us here and taken what we need. So we know where he is."

Sean lets out an exaggerated sigh, staring up at the ceiling. "That Slayer is a pox. Always nicking my things. And this is bad news for us. You're still vulnerable right now, pardon me for saying so, your, uh, unholy grace." He waits, tense, but the Sleeping

One merely nods. "The ginger Slayer isn't vulnerable. We've got to make sure we know exactly what we're facing. No mistakes this time."

"Where?" the Sleeping One asks.

"Our old home. Two hours north of Dublin, along the coast." Artemis feels less guilt for saying this than she should. Sean knows where the castle is. She's not telling them anything new, and she has to be the one in charge. Because if she's in charge, she's in control. She can protect those fools even if they refuse to protect themselves by making smarter choices. "Honora and I know that castle inside and out. We'll make the plan and lead the raid. Safest if the Sleeping One isn't there. The Slayer doesn't know about him, and there's no reason to let her."

Honora relaxes slightly next to her. She gets it now. They're protecting the Watchers by attacking them. By keeping this monster out of their home.

"The coast," the Sleeping One says. His eyes are fixed above her head. "I cannot go there. The call of the ocean, the weight of the stones, the press of humanity. If I go, will I want to stay? I stayed once. Longer than I should have."

"Right," Sean says. "We're keeping you far away from the little ginger Slayer. Let's get you back to Dublin before the bobbies get wind of *this*"—he gestures with disgust toward the still-warm body—"and then you leave it to my girls."

Artemis struggles to hide her disgust at Sean's possessive words. Honora looks at her nails, stained nearly black with her favorite fingernail polish. Artemis tries not to think about how her own nails used to be cheerful rainbows once a week thanks to Nina and their manicure and movie nights. She tries not to imagine how much blood must be under the Sleeping One's fingernails right now.

Sean pulls out a handkerchief and gingerly retrieves the eyeballs. "Did you want these for some reason?" he asks the Sleeping One.

"I want only the power to save this corrupted world and this corrupting form."

Artemis is even more bothered by how much she relates to that than she was by Sean's possessiveness. She brushes it off, though. One of them wants power to dominate the entire world. One of them wants power to protect it. She's nothing like this monster.

"Cheers to that." Sean hands the eyeballs to one of the goons. "All right, ladies. Demons to steal, gods to recharge, bills to pay. Don't disappoint me." He tries to sound intimidating, but he's not the threat and they all know it.

The Sleeping One fixes his eyes on Artemis's. "This one is hungry," he says. "She *needs*. She will bring me my prize."

"I will." She'll attack her own family to do it. She'll break Nina's heart forever. And she won't apologize for any of it, because a Watcher makes the hard sacrifices. A Watcher makes the choices no one else can. The test she failed was a simulation; she won't fail the real one.

16

MARICRUZ LEANS INTO THE SPACE between the front seats. Doug is driving, and I'm in the passenger seat losing my mind. "Wait, so you are a Watcher, or you were a Watcher, or . . . ," she asks.

"It's complicated."

"Okay, but Watchers have, like, a crap-ton of research, right? So tell me this: Mermaids. Real or not? Because if all these other monsters and demons are real, can't we at least have mermaids, too, to balance the scales?"

"Not mermaids exactly, but I'm pretty sure I've read about something similar. Carnivorous, though."

"No way!" Maricruz leans back, almost bouncing in her seat.

"How do mermaids do it?" Taylor asks, staring out the window at the night. We're almost at the ferry. "Do they lay eggs like fish? Or do they . . . you know, *do* it?"

"Rhys can tell you. *Stake me*, Rhys. I forgot." I pull out my phone to see dozens of texts and several missed calls. This was way longer than we were supposed to be gone, and we haven't checked in with him at all. Not to mention my last call with Cillian was probably quite alarming. I text Rhys the details of our London trip. I hesitate, then leave out Artemis and Honora. Too much to get into. It'll be easier to explain in person. I include the Slayers and Oz with a sinking feeling. No way to avoid mentioning that we hit Von Alston. Which means my mother will know I deliberately went against her advice. Even though I'm glad we did—who knows what would have happened to Oz and the Slayers otherwise—that old fear of displeasing her is hard to get rid of. I spent so many years desperate for her to acknowledge me, to approve of me, that disobeying her is terrifying.

But all those details about the trip are lost to context when I send the last text. My terse line about finding Leo is met with many, many *non*terse texts back, which I ignore. At least their minds being blown over Leo might distract them from when I tell them about Artemis. I still don't know how I'm going to do that.

On the ferry, I pace the deck and try not to think about Leo, who is sleeping in the van. The Slayers keep to themselves, which I get. They still don't know me, not really. And I'm positively radiating my angst—a fact Doug let me know very unsubtly by keeping the windows rolled down on the drive, even though it's January.

Between the drive, the wait for the ferry, and the ferry itself, it's dark again when we finally get to Ireland. Rhys texts me as the ferry docks and I slide back into the car. I frown at my phone. "They're here."

"Who's here?" Doug asks.

"Rhys and at least one other person, unless he refers to himself using the royal 'we' now. Said to meet them immediately.

Parking lot one street over." I give Oz directions to follow us. The few humming streetlights bathe the parking lot in eerily flat orange light. We pull in to find the only other car is one of ours, and standing outside it are Rhys, Cillian, Imogen, Tsip, and my mother. And then ancient Ruth Zabuto, she of the knitting needles and openmouthed snoring when she's supposed to be watching the Littles, comes around the side *holding a sword*.

I'm out of our car before Doug puts it in park. "What's wrong? What happened?"

"Get out of the van," Rhys shouts. Doug climbs out of our car, the same look of confusion and fear on his face. The Slayers follow him, Taylor holding the kitten in front of her face like a shield.

Maricruz looks pissed, but I suspect it masks fear. "What is this?" she demands. "Did you set us up?"

Rhys is holding a crossbow. My mother has one hand in her suit pocket, where I'm almost positive she has her brutal handgun. Imogen doesn't look tense; she's casually leaning against their Range Rover. Tsip is shimmering in and out of existence. And Ruth has her feet apart in a fighting stance. How is she even holding the sword up? It's got to weigh almost as much as she does.

I hold out a hand to Maricruz, who looks ready to run. "No! I have no idea what this is about."

"I knew I should have RSVPed," Oz says, climbing out of his van. "I always forget."

Chao-Ahn slides free from the passenger seat with a stake in her hand and daggers in her glare as she looks at me.

I point at the well-armed castle denizens. "I didn't tell them to show up here like this! Seriously, what's going on?" I ask Rhys. "Is it the Littles? Are they okay? Oh gods, did—"

"Step away from the van." Rhys crosses the space to us and yanks open the sliding door to the van. "Leo, get out and get on your knees."

"If this is about tall, dark, and semi-unconscious, can we get back in the car?" Maricruz opens her door and ushers Taylor back inside. Chao-Ahn stays out and on alert.

I swat away Rhys's crossbow. Leo is struggling to sit up. I shake my head at him. "Stay where you are. What in the many, many hells are you doing, Rhys?"

"Ian Von Alston is dead," my mother says. "He was murdered."

"What? When?"

Rhys jerks the crossbow free of my grip. "The last time we had Silveras in the castle, people died. We won't risk that again."

"But Leo warned us, remember? He told you the truth, and he saved us all by taking on his mother and stopping her hell-mouth progress! He's one of us!"

Rhys looks grim. "So was his mother. So was Imogen's mother. A past as a Watcher cannot and will not excuse betrayal in any form. And how do we know he's not like his mother? A man is dead."

Doug takes a step toward the van. "Ian was alive and well when we left him. Leo was already outside, with me. Nina was the last one to . . ." He pauses. Rhys and my mother turn toward him, the silence weighted and pressing down like the night around us. Doug clears his throat. "The last one to talk to him."

"No, you mean Nina was the last one to see him alive," I say. "Do you think I killed him?"

"No! No. But you pushed him back into that room in the house, and when you came out, you . . . I . . . well, it's just, Leo was unconscious, and as soon as he woke up we were with him the whole time, so it couldn't have been Leo, could it?" Doug looks down and to the side, avoiding my gaze.

"I left him alive." How could he think otherwise? I cringe, closing my eyes. He knows better than anyone how I feel on the inside. He can't get away from knowing, not trapped in confined spaces with me like he has been. And the truth is, I could have killed Von Alston. Part of me might have even wanted to.

Gods. Do I smell like a murderer? What is wrong with me?

"Nina?" My mother puts her hand on my arm. If she had the gun, it's gone now. "Tell us what happened and why you went to Ian Von Alston's estate."

"We went to the convention. There was an attack. Sean's people, I think, though there's a new element. Humans, black cloaks, necklaces. Seem like zealots. I stopped the attack. I ran into . . ." I pause. This doesn't feel like the right time. Everyone is literally up in arms already. If I tell them about Artemis, who knows how they'll react? Rhys told me himself he doesn't care about our past with someone if they betray us. And I can't imagine they'll view Artemis working with zealots as anything other than a betrayal.

I have to be careful. I can be as pissed off at her as I want, but when things crash and burn for her, which they will, I need her to feel terrible and guilty but be able to come home. She's still my sister. My *misguided* sister, but mine. I won't leave it up to other people whether or not she deserves her place in my home.

When we get back to the castle and I have a minute to breathe,

I'll call her. Explain that I haven't told on her. That she can give the book back and there won't be any consequences. It'll help fix things between us and prevent complications at the castle.

Besides which, Artemis might be messing with things she shouldn't, but it's not like she's my enemy. She can't be. I continue, deliberately leaving her out. Doug stares at me, but I trust he won't contradict me. "I ran into a few weird demons. Anyway, we got some information that led us to Leo. And to Oz, and these three Slayers, all of whom were in immediate mortal peril thanks to your *ally*, Von Alston." My mother's face twitches, but she doesn't interrupt me. "I didn't leave him on polite terms, exactly, but I definitely didn't kill him. And he didn't know I was a Watcher. He thought I was a rogue Slayer."

"So you didn't gouge out his eyes and then snap his neck?" Rhys asks.

I give him the most brutal glare I'm capable of. Chao-Ahn would approve. "Pretty sure I'd remember it. A girl never forgets her first eye gouging, or so I've heard."

"That's true!" Tsip chirps cheerfully.

"And you're positive it couldn't have been Leo." Rhys peers into the van, then deflates and lowers the crossbow. Leo is in no state for neck-snapping. And that wouldn't be his method, anyway. Incubi and succubi drain life force from victims, but usually only when they're sleeping so there's no resistance.

"His eyes were gouged out?" I ask, puzzled.

"Gone." Rhys pushes his glasses back into place. "They were either taken for some reason, or eaten."

"Eew," I groan.

"What? We were all thinking it."

"No. Nope. None of us were until you said that."

"Well, I can research demons that consume eyes. Though none of the guards had their eyes removed. So it might have been for fun, rather than a specific pathology. Which, unfortunately, doesn't narrow down suspect species. If only I knew whether the eyes were eaten." Rhys stares into space, already absorbed with his theories and doubtless planning the research he'll do as soon as we get back to the castle.

"Doug, Rhys, help Leo into the other car," my mother says.

"I can help," Oz says. "Don't be fooled by my elfin good looks. I'm quite handy with demon transportation."

I shake my head. "No, he's okay where he—"

My mother takes my arm and gently steers me away from the others. "We debated whether or not to allow Leo back in the castle at all."

"What? You made a decision without me? That's not fair! Besides, I—"

"Nina. Might I remind you that *you* made the decision to go to Ian Von Alston's estate after *we* made the decision not to. Sometimes you have to do the best with a situation as it presents itself. I wish you hadn't, but—"

"Mom! He is—was—a creep of the highest order. We can't want or need him for an ally." I think of the money in the van and feel a twinge of guilt that I took it. Won't do him any good now, anyway.

"We can't fight every battle."

"You're still acting like a Watcher! Picking and choosing who's worth fighting based on the benefit to us. I don't care if I have to get a job, or if we have to send Jade out to work—actually, can we? That's a great idea. But we'll get money another way. Keeping allies like Von Alston because they might potentially help us someday, knowing they're hurting vulnerable people and demons and whatever in the meantime? That's wrong. That's old-school Watcher crap. I won't do it."

My mother stiffens, and I instinctively cringe, bracing myself for her rejection. But instead of telling me I did wrong, she takes a few breaths and closes her eyes. I can see her physically changing course, trying to find a place where we can talk instead of fight.

And while Nina of the past would have been thrilled, I'm not. I *want* to fight. I want her to tell me I messed up. Because if she does, then I'll feel justified in keeping secrets from her again. Secrets like what Artemis was doing. But my mother being understanding and working to meet me in the middle leaves me riddled with guilt over keeping things from her.

She finally smiles, but it's sad. "You're right. I made a decision like a Watcher. It's the only way I know how to make decisions, and the only way I know how to protect you. You care so much, you love so hard, and I don't understand it. It terrifies me."

There it is. I fold my arms. "You think I'm stupid, or naive?"

"No. No, I think it's tremendously brave. Braver than I've ever been." She closes the space between us and presses a quick kiss to my forehead. It's awkward but not unwelcome. But it hurts, because it reminds me of what I'm missing in our family. Artemis was my ally, my companion, my friend. I'm still acting like she is, in spite of evidence to the contrary, because it's the only way I can hope she will be again.

My mother smooths my hair back, but she can't do it like Artemis used to. "You were right to look into what was happening

at Von Alston's. And I'm glad you saved those Slayers and that
odd man, and that you found Leo. But we have an entire community to worry about. And while your points in defense of Leo
remain true, his heroics do not erase the fact that he knew his
mother was a demonic predator and never told the Council or
warned us until it was almost too late."

She's right. I know she is. But she's also wrong. "If we kicked
people out of the castle for keeping secrets, none of us would be
there."

My mother surprises me by laughing. It's soft, almost more
an exhalation, but it's not the reaction I was expecting. "That's
very true. And it's why I argued that Leo should be allowed to
return. But under very specific, guarded conditions, until we can
determine whether he poses any threat."

"He can barely move!"

"We'll also research how to help him. And we *will* help him.
But I think it's best if you leave Leo's care—which will be protective both for and against him—to me."

"But I can—"

"Can you be impartial when it comes to him?" There's no
accusation in her tone. She waits for my response. And I want
to insist that I can. But when it comes to Leo, I've never been
capable of that. Even now knowing he's right there fills me with
every emotion imaginable, none of them rational or impartial.

My mother takes my silence as confirmation of her suspi-
cions. "Right, then. We're agreed. Leo is my responsibility. You
have enough to deal with. Part of the agreement to allow him
back in the castle is that he has to be restrained and under guard.
We have the cells on the bottom floor of the castle."

"Absolutely not. He's already sick, Mom." I went down there after Artemis left. I had no idea the prison existed; another dark secret of Watcher Society I was never privy to. The scent of damp rock, rust, and the lingering sense of despair and pain were not really my taste in decoration. "We can't keep him down there. Put him in his mother's old rooms. Or Wanda's. Or Bradford's. Or any of the rooms in the dorm wing." We have so many empty spaces. Though I guess the Slayers will need some of it. And Oz, if he's staying. I never asked.

"I'll make a decision. But it won't be the cells. I can get chains from storage."

"That's *so* excessive."

"His mother preyed on people during their sleep. If it's night, Leo is secured. That's the trade-off."

I remember the handcuffs from Cillian's shed. The ones we used on Doug after we found him last year. "I'll get a pair of hand-cuffs from Cillian's. That should be enough. Leo can barely stand."

"Fine. It's a good compromise." She squeezes my shoulder, then takes the keys from Cillian. Everyone from the castle but Cillian and Doug go in that car. They transferred Leo while I was distracted. The Rover pulls out into the darkness, the taillights staring at me like burning eyes.

"So, about the kitten!" Cillian rubs his hands together, excited.

"You mean Trouble?" Doug sounds innocent. That's when I realize his Coldplay CD is playing on the car speaker, and the song is called "Trouble." What an absolute nerd.

"You named it without me!" Cillian's never looked this angry. "I can't believe this."

I put my hand on his arm. It's my fault for not vetoing the name as soon as I heard it, like I did with Chewie. But I was a little distracted. "I promise, the next time we save a kitten from being eaten by a demon, you get to name it. And I'll try to get one that isn't orange, to make things easier on you."

"Fine, whatever." He sulks, full lips in a pout.

In all the drama, no one even got introduced. "Cillian, Slayers and also Oz. Slayers and also Oz, Cillian. We're going to Cillian's place first," I say to the remaining group. "Gotta get something from his shed. Maricruz and Taylor, do you want to ride with Oz now? I'll tell you how to find the castle; that way you can get settled in."

"Fine by us." Maricruz and Taylor climb out. Cillian takes the kitten from them. It looks more like a tense hostage negotiation than a friendly feline transfer. I'm going to have to get another cat or two for the castle at this rate. I give Oz directions.

Chao-Ahn gets in the van last. "Is it safe?" she asks. "The castle? Or more weapons?"

"Oh, loads of weapons. But they won't be directed at you. I promise. That was a misunderstanding. Ish. I mean, they shouldn't have done that. But they had a reason to. It's complicated?"

"Yes." Her tone is flat.

I lean close to Doug. He didn't bring Artemis up, but I need to make sure he knows not to going forward. "What happens at demon conventions stays at demon conventions, okay? I have my reasons."

He nods and relief floods me. I'll deal with Artemis on my own. We get into our car so they can follow us to Shancoom and the turnoff to the castle.

Cillian takes the passenger seat. "What do we need from my shed?"

Doug looks quizzical, catching my eye in the rearview mirror. Realization dawns on his face. "They're not bad," he says, his voice gentle. "Really. I've even thought of getting a pair of handcuffs to wear decoratively."

Cillian passes me Trouble, unbuckles, and climbs back in a jumble of elbows and knees and exclamations of dismay from Doug. "We have doors!" Doug says.

Cillian puts his arm around me. "Rough day."

I can feel the tears threatening, but I refuse to cry over Leo Silvera. Not again. And I won't cry over Artemis. I'm still too hurt and confused to even be sad. I lean my head on my friend's shoulder. "A little, yeah."

"It'll come out right."

"How do you know?"

"Because it's you. You'll figure it out." He kisses the top of my head.

Tsip pops into existence in the passenger seat. I put a hand over my racing heart. "Sweet hellmouths, Tsip, you have *got* to stop doing that. One of these days I'm going to hit you, and I'll be sorry, but it'll be your fault. I thought you left with the other car."

"Did you bring me a souvenir?" Her voice drops into a conspiratorial whisper. It whistles around her tusklike fangs. "If you took the eyes, can I have them?"

I rub my forehead against the exhaustion pressing there. I'm not looking forward to this drive or what we have to do at the end of it. Miles to go before we sleep. "I didn't take the eyes, Tsip.

And I didn't exactly go shopping. All we brought is betrayal, a broken half-demon boy, and a kitten."

She frowns at me, clicking her teeth together in disappointment as Doug puts the car in drive. "Next time," she says, "bring candy. Or eyeballs."

"Deal," I mutter. Either would be easier to deal with than the return of Leo Silvera.

17

"FECKING HELL!" CILLIAN SLAMS ON THE brakes in front of his cottage. Doug is thrown against Cillian's seat as Tsip pops out of existence. I'm out of the car before anyone else has recovered, fists up, ready for a fight. Oz's van has already turned off toward the castle, so it's just us.

Cillian's charming cottage is on the end of a narrow lane abutting the forestland. All I see that's changed is an unfamiliar car parked in front. And inside, several lights on.

"Who is it?" I ask as Cillian climbs out. There's a stake in my hand. I don't remember pulling it out of my jacket. "Have you invited anyone in you shouldn't?"

"It's my mum."

"Your mom?" She's been away since magic died. I've gotten so used to it I kind of assumed it was permanent. She used to go on trips a lot, but the last few months she was just . . . *gone*.

"Are you going to stake her? Because that might be a wee overreaction to bad parenting." He scuffs his shoe against the street, hands shoved in his pockets and shoulders turned protectively inward.

I put the weapon away. "If we staked people for being bad parents, none of us would have any."

"Is it okay if I stay in the car?" Doug leans out the window. "I don't have the best memories of the bondage shed, and I don't fancy explaining myself to Cillian's mother." He gestures at his face.

Cillian's mom was a witch before magic went *poof*, but Cillian didn't know about demons, so I assume she won't either. "Yeah, probably easiest. Where did Tsip go?"

Doug shrugs, then settles back into his seat with the music on, kitten curled up and purring in his lap. The faint sounds of Chris Martin drift toward me like a tinny echo. One of these days, I'm getting Doug Coldplay tickets if it kills me. It's Doug's fondest dream in life. Most of our dreams are messy and impossible; it'd be nice to fill one.

I close my eyes with a pang of emotion. One of my dreams was Leo being not-dead. And it's come true, for now. Which should have been more impossible than backstage passes to Coldplay, but is definitely not as simple. When he was dead, it was easy to think of only the good things. But my mom's right. The others are totally justified in remembering everything else Leo did, and holding him accountable.

The front door opens to reveal Esther, Cillian's mother. "That you, Killy-my-love? Come inside! I've been waiting for you!"

"Gee, you've been waiting for me," Cillian mutters to himself. "What must that feel like."

I follow him to the porch, where Esther stands in the pool of warm light spilling from the house behind her. Her braids encircle her head like a crown, and her skin betrays no hint of aging. It's easy to see where Cillian got his good looks.

"Is that Nina? Goodness, you've grown!" She frowns, looking me up and down. "No. You haven't. You seem taller, though. I can't put my finger on it." I used to be the one to go into town and pick up supplies from her shop back when it was a magic shop. I always liked her. I like her less now, though. She hurt my friend.

"We've got things to do, Mum." Cillian tries to angle past her, but she holds out an arm to block him.

"Things that are more important than catching your mother up on the last few months?"

"Yeah, actually." Cillian pushes past her arm and stomps straight through the house to the backyard, where the shed is.

"So." I wish awkwardness were a demon I could punch, instead of an insurmountable, suffocating atmosphere. "How was, uh, Colorado?"

"Monks are boring." She moves to the side to let me by. Her flowing ruby-red dress looks elegant and comfortable at once. "I learned what I could, though. How is he?" She nods toward the backyard. "Besides angry."

"He's good. Stays with us a lot now." I'm pretty sure she knows about Cillian and Rhys, but if she doesn't, I'm not going to tell her. Not my place.

"I thought your compound was off-limits."

"A lot has changed. You were gone awhile." I try to keep my voice neutral, but I can see her stiffen at the assumed accusation.

"I'm doing this for him, you know. Ever since we lost his father, I've been trying to prepare. I don't know what will happen with Cillian. If I can connect with something bigger—something greater—maybe I can find direction." She looks at me as though I'll understand.

I don't. I have a mother who did things in what she *thought* were my best interests, and it nearly broke us all. "Try connecting with him instead."

I hurry past Esther before she can ask me any more about her son. Outside, Cillian is throwing things around in the shed, nothing gentle or careful in his movements. "Where is that fecking box?"

"Here." I push aside a stack of traditional Irish fairy-tale collections and tug the box free. But, forgetting my own strength in my haste, I tug too hard and it flies across the room. It hits the far wall and drops to the floor. The contents spill out.

"Sorry." I kneel and begin replacing things. Cillian grabs the handcuffs and shoves them into his pocket. My hand freezes on a weird metal puzzle I vaguely remember from the last time we went through his dead father's things. It's a series of interlocking triangles. The same design as the necklace I took from the woman in the alley and put on the kitten. And . . . I hold the triangles out, getting a different angle. It's the exact image stamped on all of demon-drug dealer Sean's tea. And the symbol from the book Artemis stole. What is it doing *here*?

"Everything in this box was your father's?" I ask.

"Yeah." Cillian's distracted and on edge as he stares through the night at the house. I can't tell whether he hopes his mother will come out here after him, or whether he hopes she won't. I doubt he knows which he prefers either. But his mother is illuminated in the kitchen, dancing slowly as she makes tea.

"Even this?" I hold it up.

He barely glances at it. "Yeah, it's a toy or something. A puzzle. I used to play with it, but it was his."

"Are you sure?"

He finally focuses, frowning. "Why does it matter?"

"Because I've seen it before. At Sean's place, branding his demonic tea. And a woman who attacked me in an alley was wearing a necklace with it." And it was on the book Artemis stole.

"That exactly, or something like it? Kind of Celtic, innit? Could be a similar design."

I have enough room for doubt. I was sure, but maybe I'm seeing it everywhere because I have sisterly betrayal on the brain. "The necklace is on the kitten. We can go check." I keep the puzzle in my hands. "Do you want to—I mean, are you going to stay here tonight?"

"I want to be with Rhys." He sounds miserable, and it hurts me to know I can't fix it. But Cillian still hasn't moved to leave. He's standing in the doorway, staring through the window at his mother.

"I could send Rhys back here."

Cillian takes a long time to answer. Then he shakes his head and abruptly moves as though being tugged by strings, his gait forced and unnatural. "No. Nothing here that needs doing." He opens the back door.

"I've got tea on!" His mother turns with a tray already set with three pretty pale-green cups. Her eyes shift from Cillian to me, then to what's in my hand.

She drops the tray on the floor with a clatter of metal and a shattering of ceramic. "Where did you get that?" She steps right through the shards to me.

"Mum! Your feet!" Cillian tries to steer her away from the

sharp pieces, and I can see smears of blood where she walks bare-
foot. But she doesn't pay him any attention, instead grabbing the
triangle thing out of my hands.

"Where did you get this?"

"In the shed. It's a puzzle? Cillian wanted to, uh . . ." I look
at him for support.

"I wanted to show it to my boyfriend. He likes puzzles." Cillian
grabs a broom and dustpan and sweeps up his mother's mess.

Esther's gripping the interlocking triangles so tightly her
hands shake. "This isn't a toy. You shouldn't have it."

"Da used to let me play with it," Cillian says.

"No, he didn't!"

Both of their jaws are set in rigid, angry lines, but his mother
also looks scared. She used to be a witch. Maybe not everything
in the box belonged to Cillian's dad, after all. My eyes flick to
her neck to see if she's wearing a necklace, but her dress neckline
is too high to tell. Where has she really been going all this time?

Cillian sets down the broom. "Yes, he did. I remember."

"You're remembering wrong."

"I'll show you. I can do it with my eyes closed." Cillian grabs
for the puzzle, but Esther jerks it away, holding it behind her back.

"No! You stay out of your father's things!" She takes a deep,
shuddering breath. "Now go sit down. I'm making food."

"Give me the puzzle!"

"No."

They're standing close, both of them breathing hard, faces
set in mirrored anger and determination and hurt.

I could get the puzzle from her. Easy. And part of me is
tempted to. I want to take this from her, because it obviously

means something and taking it would hurt her. Like she hurt him by leaving so easily and for so long. People shouldn't get to leave you behind and not hurt like you do because of it.

I close my eyes, force my breathing to slow. She's not Artemis or Leo. She didn't do anything to me.

I just want to figure out what in all the hells is going on here. And I hope—sincerely—that Esther isn't involved in it. She's a bad mom, but that doesn't make her evil, and after Leo's mother's betrayal, I've had my fill of dealing with evil moms.

I put a hand on Cillian's arm. "Come on. There are other puzzles. We don't need that one."

He stays where he is for a few more seconds, then turns sharply on his heel and storms out of the house. I don't apologize to his mother. I didn't take the puzzle from her, which was more than generous of me. I can feel her watching us, waiting in the light of the doorway. I pause in the yard. Cillian is already in the car.

"I won't let anyone hurt him," I say, my voice low. "Including you."

"Excuse me?"

"Whatever you're involved in, get out of it. He needs you."

"You have no idea what you're on about."

I ignore her and climb into the car. Cillian peels out. Neither of us looks back.

Doug coughs and rolls down his window despite the frigid temperature. "Wow. What did I miss?"

"Give me the kitten," I say.

Doug reflexively holds it against his chest. "Why are you so angry?"

I roll my eyes. "I'm not angry at Trouble! I need the necklace."

He unfastens it and hands it to me, keeping the kitten to himself. I hold it up, trying to catch enough light. Cillian pulls over halfway to the castle. It's pitch-dark out here in the forest. He turns on the overhead light and takes the necklace from me.

"The same." His voice is flat. "What does it mean?"

"I don't know. Maybe nothing?" It doesn't mean nothing. I know it doesn't. But my instinct to protect my friend makes me want to shield him from the looming bad I can feel building on the horizon. The looming bad that now somehow involves his mother.

"Right. I'm sure it's a big whopping coincidence that we happen to have the same triangley thing in my shed that was on Sean's tea and a madwoman's necklace. Maybe they all visited the same souvenir shop."

"Wait, you had one of these?" Doug leans forward. He narrows his eyes at the necklace. "Sean had a tattoo of it. Most of his people did. What was in the shed? A necklace?"

"A bigger version of this. Not a necklace. More like a puzzle thing."

Doug frowns, his cracked skin shifting so the black lines between the yellow pieces almost disappear.

"What?" I ask.

"Nothing."

"I can't smell emotion, but I can see it. What are you thinking?"

"Just—there was a reason I picked Cillian's shed, yeah? Out of every place I could hide. I was half dazed with hunger and exhaustion and pain, but something . . . something called me there. I chalked it up to fate. Like I was supposed to meet you, Nina." He ducks his head, and I swear if he weren't neon yellow, he'd be blushing. "So you'd care about me. So it wouldn't only be your mom on my side. But maybe it was something else. I can't smell power, exactly, but most demons are sensitive to it."

Cillian's staring at the necklace as though hypnotized by it. I turn toward him. "Your mom *was* really weird about the puzzle."

"You two want me to believe that my dead da—a fisherman and local police volunteer—was dealing in, what, demonic artifacts?" His voice is cold and so unlike him that I shrink closer to my window.

"No! No. Could it have been your mom's instead? From when she practiced witchcraft? And that's why she was so upset?"

Cillian finally looks away from the necklace, holding it out and dropping it into my waiting palm. He shrugs. "Could be." His tone becomes deliberately lighter, but there's a forced edge to it. "Good thing we know an incredibly sexy Watcher who excels at research. He'll be even happier to have a new project than to see me again."

"Never," I say, trying to match his tone and almost succeeding. I already know Rhys won't find the research material he needs.

Cillian slows down as we catch up to Oz's barely limping van. It'll take us forever to get to the castle at this rate. Doug yawns, stretching out in the backseat. "So we've got a symbol that may or may not be demonic and/or powerful, and that is linked to Sean, but we don't know how. Goodie. Just what we needed. *Another* mystery."

I don't correct him that this isn't another mystery. It's all the same mystery. And my sister has the answers. I know what I need to do. I'll make a deal with her. My silence on her activities in exchange for getting the book back. I'll get the information we need and protect everyone from themselves in the process.

18

THE VAN PULLS TO A STOP IN FRONT OF
the castle, more garble than roar to the engine. I'm waiting in
front of it. I can't help the flutter of nerves and the fear that invit-
ing three more Slayers into the castle is a bad idea when I can't
even control my own Slayer impulses. What if they attack my
demons? I know the demons—I like them—and I've still found
myself fighting a kill instinct that seems to be growing stronger
by the day.

Chao-Ahn, Maricruz, and Taylor climb out, eyeing the castle
dubiously. Only a few windows have lights in them, and we don't
have any outdoor lighting. I try to see it through their eyes. It
looks menacing. Blocky and black, and somehow unbalanced.
The eyes naturally want a tower where there used to be one, but
now that whole wing is ruined and we don't go there.

"It's safe," I say. But . . . it hasn't always been. Just a few
months ago, Leo Silvera's mother was stalking us all during the
night, feeding off us, and killing poor Bradford Smythe. And now
Leo's back. Knowing he's somewhere inside the castle feels like

the moment before a blow lands, when I can see what will happen but can't dodge it. Everything is on high alert, and it doesn't hurt—yet—but I know it will.

"Nina, will you introduce me?"

Chao-Ahn and I both jump, turning to find my mother has materialized out of the darkness behind us. My mother holds out her right hand to Chao-Ahn. Her jacket has parted to reveal a glimpse of her gun.

"You are scary," Chao-Ahn says.

"You have no idea," I mutter. "What are you doing lurking out here?"

"I wanted to greet the new Slayers. Also, we have a procedure to follow. None of them have agreed to the rules or completed the entry interview yet. Ladies, if you'll follow me to the library, Rhys and I will get you processed and settled into rooms."

"Is there a test?" the timid blond one, Taylor, asks. She looks terrified. "I'm not good at tests. Or interviews."

"Just some basic geometry," I say, "and a few essay questions."

"Really?" Maricruz's dark eyes are wide with alarm.

"No. Sorry. All you have to do is hear the rules and agree to them. We need a simple majority to allow you in, but I don't think that'll be a problem."

"I'm certain it won't." My mother smiles, but she's never been good at reassuring. Maricruz and Taylor look appropriately intimidated as they follow her in. Chao-Ahn lingers for a few seconds, like she wants to speak with me, but Cillian grabs my arm and draws me to the side.

"Let me talk to Rhys, okay? I'll take point on this mystery. You've got enough going on."

I nod, melting into his offered hug. It's a lie for me to accept his reassurances—he's not taking over this mystery, but he can at least handle his family's ties to it. I'll be there to support him, though. "Sure. Thanks."

One of the van doors closes and Oz comes around the front of it. "Watchers, huh? Anyone related to Giles?"

I shake my head. I have complicated feelings about Rupert Giles. My dad was Buffy's first Watcher, but Rupert Giles is the one she bonded with. The one who left the Watchers in protest of their policies, and who probably influenced Buffy to turn her back on them as well. I get it now—I really do—but it doesn't change the weird spikes of resentment I feel when I hear the name Giles, may he rest in peace. "Last of his line. Most of us are."

"I knew another Watcher. Wesley—"

"Wyndam-Pryce," we say together, imitating the pretentious pride with which all Wyndam-Pryces deliver their names.

"Sadly, he's not the last of his line." My glower is colder than the night as I think about Honora and how she's corrupted my sister. "Come on. I'll get you some food, and if you want to spend the night, you're more than welcome." He said he was dropping the Slayers off in London, so I assume he's not looking for a permanent situation here.

"I like food. Thanks." I lead him through the dim main hall. Which room is Leo in? The dorm wing, where I live? The Council wing, where he stayed with his mother the last time they were here? Not the dungeon, at least. My mother promised.

Imogen isn't in the kitchen, so I make the only things I know I won't mess up: toast and tea. I want Oz to leave so I can figure out how I feel in the solitude of my own room and so I can practice what I'm going to say to Artemis when I call her with my demands. I also don't want him to leave for that exact reason—I don't want to confront her again. Or, worse, to face my feelings about Leo being alive even though I was never able to face my feelings about him being dead.

Oz sips tea, looking around the dining hall. "I like your castle. I like it better knowing it's broody vampire–free."

"Don't like vampires?"

"Nah, I'm cool with vampires in general. But the broody ones. They make things complicated."

I should probably go call Artemis right now. But I keep remembering the look she gave me as I was crouched on the hood of that truck. Like I was *stupid*. She never treated me that way. Honora did, though. What if Artemis rejects my offer?

She won't. All I'm asking is that she return a book. Or, barring that, tell me what it's about. She did say she'd fill me in, but I refused to get in the truck. Maybe I should have.

Gods, I'm tired. I haven't slept in so long. Maybe I'll wait until morning to call her when I can think more clearly. We all need some rest. I wonder where the Slayers will stay. It seems weird to stick them in the dorms, but also weird to give them the fancy rooms. I briefly considered taking one of the Council wing rooms when we changed everything, but it felt like I was promoting myself. And if I left the dorm wing room I shared with Artemis, it was too close to admitting she was never coming back.

So those rooms stayed empty. I think the new Slayers should take the old Wyndam-Pryce suite. Good riddance to its former occupants. I hope they don't take the Silvera suite. Though I don't know if Leo will want to stay in there, surrounded by memories of his mother.

Where is he right now? I can't believe he's not dead. And he's here. And I can't see him. And I don't want to see him. But I do want to see him.

"And that's how I got the nickname Oz."

"What?"

"I was telling you my life story. It's a pretty good story. Some dull bits, but I kind of like those."

I grimace. "Sorry. I have a lot on my mind right now."

"I noticed. It's okay." He finishes his tea and then stands up. "Well, long drive ahead of me. Gotta get home."

"You sure you aren't staying?"

"Why would I?"

"Because you're a werewolf. Are you, though? It was the full moon last night. Wasn't it? Did Von Alston miscalculate by a day?"

"No. I'm a werewolf. But it's fine. I'm pretty zen about the whole thing."

"Really?"

He shrugs. "We all have monsters inside. Mine's just more literal. You understand."

I do. More and more lately. If a werewolf is two different things—human and monster—but he's figured out how to live with both, maybe he can teach me how to be the two different things I am. The healer who wants to fix everything, and the Slayer who increasingly wants to break them.

I lean forward. "How do you stop it taking over?" I've never heard of a werewolf being able to avoid transformation.

According to our research, it's not possible. But I've learned in the last few months that just because something is written in fancy calligraphy in an old book doesn't mean it's true.

"Think of the darkness like a river. If you try to dam it, it might work for a while, but eventually the dam will burst and then it's all fangs and claws and chasing your ex-girlfriend's girlfriend through a campus and getting caught and sent to government labs and being experimented on."

"That . . . feels like a really specific example."

"No, I think it's universal. But back to the river of darkness. Don't dam it. Channel it. Direct the darkness, let it flow through and past you. Feel it and then release it."

"But how?"

"Have you tried meditation?"

I wrinkle my face up. "Mm. No. Slayer energy doesn't really lend itself well to sitting still and letting your mind go blank. That's when all the *maybe we should go find something to kill* thoughts sneak in."

"Well, my other suggestion is moving to the Himalayas and finding yourself a beautiful wife. That one worked out really well for me. For a while, at least. But the darkness always finds you, and things get Slayer-army-and-giant-goddess-level complicated again."

"So by darkness finding you, you mean Buffy?"

He laughs. "The Buffster messes things up, yeah, but she always shakes out the truth, too. And the truth was, we needed to help instead of isolating ourselves. I thought I had found peace, but really I was letting the darkness gather and pool. So here I am. Helping. Channeling that river. And here I go, back home, until I find another way to help. You can't stop what's inside you. If you fight it, it'll win. Figure out how to live with it, how to direct it instead of letting it drag you in its current. And only you can do that."

"Moving to the Himalayas and finding a beautiful wife seems easier."

"RSVP if you decide to visit." With an enigmatic smile, Oz grabs the bag of snacks I threw together for him. I walk him out and watch as he drives away, back toward his life. I sit there for a long time afterward. Alone. In the dark.

I know the Slayer energy. I know the contours of that power, the feel of it. What I don't know is the new jagged edges, the sharp bursts and spikes that feel foreign. The ones that I've had since Leo gave the power back to me. When I first became a Slayer, the power would wash over me in a fight and I'd become something— someone—else. But I always snapped back to myself.

Ever since I stopped Leo's mother and thought I lost him, I can't seem to find myself to snap back to.

If I want to understand, if I want to channel this darkness instead of being washed away in it, I need to talk to the one person who has held exactly what I have now. And it isn't the other Slayers.

It's the boy who stole what had been taken in order to give it back to me.

It takes me until the next afternoon to work up the guts to decide to talk to Leo. I'm so mad at him, and so relieved he's not dead, and so mad he let me think he was dead, and so relieved I didn't accidentally kill him, and a teensy bit afraid I might on-purpose kill him for the last few months of guilt and sadness he let me go through.

I've been trying to get ahold of Artemis all morning, but her number keeps going straight to a voicemail box that hasn't been set up yet. I don't know what I'll do if she doesn't pick up soon. But I can't delay seeing Leo any longer.

Unfortunately, I need to find him before I can talk to him. I don't want to ask my mother. Not after she made such reasonable points about why I shouldn't see Leo. So instead, I choose the person least likely to question or hassle me. Rhys is, unsurprisingly, in the library.

"We voted the Slayers in," he says, not looking up from his book. "They're all settled in the Wyndam-Pryce rooms. They seemed very reluctant to agree to learn our castle defense plans, though. It's concerning. The castle only works if everyone does their part."

"I'll talk with them." *Just ask where Leo is. Just ask.* "So, um, have you found anything about the puzzle thing?"

"The necklace?" Rhys has it on the table in front of him. Cillian is sitting in the corner, curled up in an armchair with the kitten purring on his lap. He looks half asleep.

"Yeah, and the matching puzzle from Cillian's shed."

"Where is that one?"

"His mom wouldn't give it to us."

"His mom?" Rhys looks over at Cillian. Cillian's eyes are suspiciously closed now, where I swear they were open a second before. "His mom is back?"

"Yeah, he—we saw her? Last night? She said the puzzle was Cillian's dad's and I'm not sure why he didn't tell you this . . ." I trail off. Cillian's eyes are open now, and he's glaring at me.

"I told you I would take the lead on this one," he says.

Rhys has set down his book. Always a bad sign. "Your mom is back? You didn't think that was worth mentioning? And this is all connected to your father somehow?"

"No! I don't know. Maybe. Probably not. Just find something in your books."

"Shouldn't we go to a source who already has information?"

"We're not talking to my mum."

"Why?"

"Why would we?"

"Because I could spend weeks looking through books trying to find something, when your mother could point us in the right direction in a single conversation."

He could and will spend weeks looking through the books, because the one he needs is gone. But I'm fixing that as soon as Artemis answers the dang phone.

"I don't want to talk to her."

"What a privilege, to decide you'd rather not speak with your parent. Some of us aren't so lucky." Rhys's jaw twitches. Both of his parents died when acolytes of the First Evil blew up Watcher headquarters. I put a hand on his shoulder. He shrugs it off.

"You don't get it." Cillian sets the kitten on the floor and stands, turning his back to us as he pretends to examine book spines.

"You're right. I don't. I'd give anything to be able to ask my mum for help, or advice, or even to just say hello."

Cillian whirls around, eyes blazing. "But your mum was taken! She didn't choose to leave, for weeks and months at a time, because you weren't enough for her!"

"You don't know that's why! You haven't even talked to her!"

"And I'm not going to! I don't care why she left. God, I can't believe you're taking her side. You're supposed to be on *my* side."

Rhys softens. "I am. I always am. But I also know that living mothers—even complicated, messy mothers—are better than the alternative."

"He has a point," I say. My own relationship with my mother is fraught and fragile, shifting daily. But I'm glad she's still around to have a relationship with. "We can talk, if you want, about—"

"No, I'm good. I don't want to talk with either of you about any of this. If we can't find out about that symbol in one of these fancy books, then obviously it's not important and I can keep my memory of my da exactly how I want it to be."

Ah. Some of Cillian's anger makes more sense. This isn't about his mother at all. Not really. If this symbol is something bad, and his father had it, what does that mean for Cillian's memories of him? I worked so hard to protect my memories of my father. Artemis and I used to trade them back and forth like precious possessions, holding them close so we wouldn't damage them. And then I became a Slayer and had his Watcher diary and, in a way, grew closer to him than she ever would. But she had always had Mom in a way I didn't—or at least, that's what I thought. I didn't want to give her Dad, too.

Oh, Artemis. Come back so I can fix things. I clutch the phone in my pocket, waiting for it to ring.

"Even if your father was somehow involved, he's obviously not anymore. Where's the harm in investigating?" Rhys is trying to be gentle, but I cringe in horror at this tactic. Cillian's eyes are wide, his mouth a single tight line.

I opt for an abrupt subject change. Talking to Leo can't be any more charged and awkward than hanging out during what I suspect is Cillian and Rhys's first real fight. "Hey, where's Leo?"

"You can't see him." Rhys looks down and calmly turns the page in his book.

"What do you mean?"

"I mean, you can't see him."

I snatch the book Rhys is determinedly staring at instead of looking at me.

He glares, pushing his glasses back into place. Cillian is conspicuously silent, sitting back in his corner and turning pages on a demonic bestiary with slightly more aggression than is required.

Rhys tugs his tweed jacket around his trim waist, nervously buttoning and unbuttoning it. I'm always surprised when I catch him in his pajamas and they're not tweed too. "I mean, your mother specifically instructed us that Leo needs to be kept in isolation."

"From me?"

"Well, obviously."

"Last I checked, you and I decided to take over the Watchers Council. We don't follow them anymore."

"It's not the council. It's your mother. And . . . I agree with her."

I flinch away from him as though he's struck me. "What the hells, Rhys? Why are you so anti-Leo now? You were the one who helped him when he tried to kidnap me to get me away from his mother!"

Cillian slams his book shut. "I'm with Nina. She deserves answers."

"Sometimes people look for answers in the wrong places!" Rhys snaps. "Or they refuse to find the *right* answers because it might hurt!"

"Sometimes other people don't want to help you get answers because they're being selfish and think they know better than you do what you need!"

"Sometimes other people's parents are both dead and they can't ever talk to them again, so excuse them if they think their boyfriend should talk to his own mother instead of consulting Watcher texts for what seems to be a family issue!"

"Sometimes you should mind your own business!"

"That's it! I'm not researching a thing for you until you stop pouting and go speak to your mother!"

I can feel my anger rising, and I don't have time to deal with wanting to murder someone. Especially not two of my best friends. "Can you two focus?"

"No!" they both shout, turning to me.

Rhys recovers first, looking back down at his book. "Nina, Leo let his mother come here, knowing she was a demon. He let her prey on us. And yes, he helped us in the end, but I don't think that wipes his slate clean. That day when he told the truth, I was helping him because that meant helping you. And now I'm *not* going to help you, because it's the only way I know to help you. Leo is poison. You've not been yourself since he 'died.' We can pretend otherwise, but it's true. I don't want to see how you'll change now that he's back. We'll all be better off once he gets well and we can send him away forever."

"You know that's not going to fix things. We have to face our problems. Pretending issues aren't there when they so obviously are is what got Watchers where we are today. Nowhere. Gone. I'm not going to pretend like Leo isn't here, or wait for him to get better and leave. He's one of us, Rhys. If your dad had been a demon, I wouldn't turn my back on you. If Cillian's mom turns out to be mixed up in something bad, we're not turning our back on him."

"That's irrelevant."

"It's perfectly relevant!"

"You haven't had to watch yourself suffer for the last few months! He hurt you, and now he's back, and I won't see you hurt again!"

I laugh, a sharp, harsh sound. "I didn't have to watch myself suffer, I had to feel myself suffer. I had to live it. You don't know what's best for me."

Rhys adjusts his glasses again. "My mind is made up. There's a reason Slayers had Watchers. Sometimes someone less close to the problem needs to make the decision."

Cillian drops his book on the floor. He may as well have slapped Rhys. Rhys stares in horror, but Cillian leans back, folding his arms. "Maybe some people need to decide for themselves what will help them be better off." Then he slowly, deliberately puts his feet on top of the book like it's a footrest.

Rhys stands, sputtering. "Get out of my library!"

"Gladly! Nina, let's go."

"Where are you going?" Rhys demands.

"Why don't you research to find out?"

I follow Cillian. I have to figure out where Leo is on my own, and I'm so mad at everyone in this garbage castle for thinking they know what I need more than I do. We nearly run into Jade.

One look at her face shows she's in as bad a way as we are, at least emotionally.

"Misery, meet company. Come on," Cillian says, gesturing to the massive front door. "We're going out."

Jade never gives up a chance to sleep. She spends most afternoons napping. So I'm surprised when she twitches and then nods. "Yeah. I wanna come."

Jessi peers out the door to the gym. "Where are you all going?"

"Out. Wanna come?"

"Yes, I'd be happy to leave three innocent children alone so they can get themselves fed dinner and bathed and tucked into bed with a story and a kiss. Honestly. If I had any powers left, you'd—" She slams the door.

"I'm not really sorry she passed," Cillian says.

"Yeah, me neither." I link my arm through his and we walk straight out of the castle. A figure is lurking right outside the door, and I have a stake in hand immediately.

"There's gonna be a lot of blood to clean up if you stake me." Maricruz peels herself free from the shadowy alcove of the castle steps. "Needed some air. I'm assuming that's okay?"

Taylor, her blond shadow, is nowhere to be seen. "Come with us," Jade said.

"Am I in trouble?"

Cillian looks determined. "Not yet, but the afternoon is young."

The car is where we parked it outside the garage. I have the phone with me, and I'm powerless until Artemis calls back. Might as well kill some time. I toss the keys to Cillian. He starts the car and we peel out. He does a terrible job street parking on the cobblestones in front of his shop, but it's Shancoom. Traffic is like something out of a fairy tale here. Far away and make-believe.

He unlocks the shop and we tumble in. I love it in here. It used to be a magic supply shop, but when magic died and Cillian's mother took off, Cillian needed a way for it to make money. He converted it to a soda and sweets shop. Shancoom gets a mild number of tourists, which means he sells just enough to keep the lights on at his house.

"Oh! I have fifty thousand pounds!" The fact that I almost forgot is a testament to how much else has been going on the last few days. Oz brought the bag in before he left, and I tucked it away in the gym. Without telling my mother, maybe a little because I felt like the fact that I had a freshly murdered man's money might not reflect very well on my innocence.

"Then why the hell are we at Cillian's soda shop and not on a tropical island?" Jade gestures at her heavily coated self. "I look really good in a bikini! I think. I've never actually owned one."

"Bikinis not standard Watcher-issued clothing?" Cillian asks, pulling out several glass bottles of Coke from his fridge and popping the lids off. He also grabs a root beer, which he keeps on hand only for me because no one in this country appreciates the delicious American taste.

"They don't come in tweed," I snort, imagining Rhys in tweed board shorts. Cillian must be doing the same, because he collapses with giggles.

"Instead of a three-piece suit, he'd wear a three-piece swimsuit." Cillian gasps for air, and I lean over the counter, holding my stomach.

"You two are ridiculous." Jade takes a long swig of her Coke. Her eyes are heavily lined with turquoise, maybe to distract from the bags under them. She looks rough. "Seriously, though, where did you get fifty thousand pounds and what are you going to do with it?"

"I share this question." Maricruz sits at the counter and looks around the room.

"Got it from the rich dead guy because I won his hunt. And I'm going to use it to fund Sanctuary for the next few months until we figure out ways to generate more income."

"Well, that's . . . responsible, I guess." Maricruz taps her black fingernails against the side of her Coke bottle. Then her face lights up and she raises one eyebrow. "Too responsible. I'll be back." She slips out the door. Cillian, Jade, and I shrug at one another, then proceed to design Rhys's ideal bathing suit. I check my phone obsessively, but it remains stubbornly blank.

Maricruz reappears with a bag. It clinks ominously. "Guess who remembered the legal drinking age in this country is lower?" She pulls out a bottle of whiskey and a bottle of absinthe.

"Absinthe?" I ask.

"No way!" Jade takes the bottle and holds it out, gazing at it. "It was my coven's favorite." She spent several months undercover in a coven that subcontracted for Buffy back when Buffy was leading an army of Slayers all across the globe. It disbanded when magic died. "Absinthe is awful, but I kind of miss it. And them. It was nice, you know? Having a purpose."

"Spying on Buffy?" I ask.

"You spied on Buffy?" Maricruz seems less alarmed than curious.

Jade pushes her hair out of her face, then pulls three glasses from under the counter. "Yes, but I was also part of the coven. We did all sorts of stuff. I really liked it. Like having sisters."

"Sisters are overrated." I scowl at my glass as Jade fills it with just a bit of whiskey and then pours in Coke to dilute it.

"Amen," Maricruz mutters.

"To rubbish families, dead fathers, absent mothers, and lost sisters," Cillian says, holding up his glass.

We all cheers to that. The whiskey burns, and not even this much Coke can cut through it. But I drink it anyway. An hour later, we're lying on the floor in a square, heads on one another's stomachs. I have the phone balanced on my forehead, willing it to ring.

"Bollocks," Cillian says. "Joan of Arc was not a Slayer."

"She was so!" I gesture aggressively, spilling half my drink down my arm. The phone slips off and clatters to the floor. "The Siege of Orléans was actually a vampire siege. It was one of the only known organized vampire armies in history. Generally vampires are solitary, but they had a very charismatic leader who saw the upheaval as an opportunity to place kings and rulers who were sympathetic to them and would turn a blind eye to their activities. Orléans contained a Watcher outpost, and they wanted to burn it down. One of the Watchers was an advisor to the French regent, who the vampires were hoping to sire. But they knew they had to get rid of the local Watchers first."

"You're lying."

"She's not." Jade has both her hands in the air, admiring her manicure. "We have a whole series of books on it. The Watchers were heavily involved in the Hundred Years' War and the War of the Roses. Richard the Third was half demon."

"No!"

"Yes. That's why his skeletal structure was so odd."

"You're all such nerds," Maricruz says in a dreamy, affectionate tone.

"Anyway," I say, "Joan was a Slayer. I've never run into her in my dreams, though. I'll have to look for her. Except my dreams seem broken lately."

"To broken dreams!" Jade picks up her glass and lifts it in the air.

"Are your Slayer dreams working?" I ask Maricruz.

"I don't like dreaming."

Cillian interrupts. "So did the queen ever have her own Watcher to advise her on supernatural threats?"

Jade turns her head where it rests on my stomach and makes eye contact with me, slowly winking one eye. "Oh yes."

I pick it up. "For centuries. Queen Elizabeth had an affair with hers. It was very scandalous."

"No!"

"Mm-hmm." Jade pauses. "Though obviously it didn't produce Charles. He's all Philip's. Which means my crush on Prince Harry is not at all incestuous."

I nod. "An important point."

Maricruz narrows her eyes. "Wait, was it your—"

"A great-great-uncle or something." Jade shrugs casually.

I keep going. "So her great-great-uncle was out, but they put another Watcher in after. It was a very prestigious position. The queen's Watcher had a number assigned so the queen's forces could talk about him without giving away his role. Some numbers have magical significance. This one was an infinity symbol followed by a seven."

Jade manages to keep her voice even. "They called him Double O Seven to simplify, though."

Cillian sits straight up, dislodging my head from his abdomen. "No fecking way. Watchers were 007? Watchers? It was real?"

I lean back on my elbows. "Well, yeah. Most things are real. Normal people catch rumors and make them into stories. Myths. Spy novels."

Maricruz's lips are pursed, and her cheeks are getting steadily darker from holding back a laugh. I flash my eyes at her, and she gives a minute nod. She's onto us, but she's not spoiling it.

"But Ian Fleming got it mostly wrong." Jade sits up too, pouring herself a new drink. "Double O Seven wasn't dealing with Russians and spies, he was protecting the queen from an order of vampires who planned to use her in a sacrifice to end the sun and bring about eternal darkness so they could ravage the land at their leisure."

Cillian's dark eyes are almost circles, they're open so wide. He shakes his head. "I can't believe this."

"You shouldn't," I snort, finally breaking.

Jade cackles. "None of it was true." Maricruz throws her head back as she laughs, though I don't know how she knew we were lying.

"You absolute cows!" Cillian grabs a handful of crisps from a bowl and throws them at us.

"But the Joan of Arc thing was true!" I say.

"Like I'll believe anything out of your mouth now."

"Double O Seven!" Jade laughs until she falls over. I can't stop either.

Cillian finally joins us. "*You Only Live Twice* was obviously about vampires."

Maricruz claps her hands. "*On Her Majesty's Supernatural Service.*"

"*The Watcher Who Loved Me.*" I laugh until my stomach hurts, until tears stream from my eyes.

Jade does too, until I realize her laughter has shifted from laugh-crying to actual crying. I turn on my side to look at her. "What's wrong?"

She takes a few breaths to calm herself down until she can talk. "I think I really do like Doug. Not just because of the happy stuff. He's so funny and kind. And he has the prettiest eyes. But I blew it, and I wish I could go back, and I used to know a spell for that, but it won't work now, so it's broken and it's my fault and there's nothing I can do."

"We can never go back." Maricruz looks haunted.

"Are you and what's-her-face a thing?" Jade asks, sniffling.

"Taylor? No. She's my friend. She's the reason I was hiding outside. I love her. I'd do anything for her. *Have* done anything for her. But sometimes it gets too heavy, you know? I keep waiting for her to get better, and she doesn't. And I'll always love her and be there for her. But I'm tired. And I can't let her know I'm tired, or it'll hurt her, and I won't ever be the one to hurt her."

Cillian squeezes her hand. "You're a good friend. How did you end up in Buffy's army? Why did you leave New York?" Cillian asks.

She shakes her head. "There are lots of kinds of monsters. I don't want to talk about it. I wouldn't go back, even if I could."

Jade is still crying. Cillian sits up and pulls her over so her head is resting on his leg. He strokes her hair gently. "Sometimes I wish the world hadn't changed. If magic hadn't gone away, my mother wouldn't have left to chase it. But then I never would have known the truth about you guys. And finally gotten close to my boyfriend. Rhys is it for me. I know he is. But sometimes he gets so rigid, and it's like he disappears behind his glasses and books, and I don't know how to reach him."

"It's how he was raised," I say, my tears real now too. "None of us were taught how to have healthy relationships." I sniffle unattractively. "My ex-could-have-been-boyfriend stayed with a predatory creep instead of coming back to us for help. And now that he's not dead anymore, he's maybe dying."

Jade's still crying, but she also snorts a laugh. "Cheers. You win."

Cillian nods in agreement, lifting his empty glass. Maricruz doesn't look up.

I meet Cillian's glass with my own. "Bully for me."

On cue, my phone dings. I scrabble for it, thinking it's Artemis. But it's an angry text from Rhys, demanding to know where we are. I text back. "Drunk at the soda shop," I mumble aloud, squinting at the screen. "Can't drive back. Come pick us up."

PICK YOURSELVES UP is the response.

"Looks like we're walking." I stand, my leg half asleep from being against the hard linoleum floor. The door chimes, and Cillian's mom observes us with her hands on her hips.

"One of you is not old enough to drink." She gives me a heavy

look. I can feel my face burning. One thing I haven't been able
to shed from my Watcher upbringing is the absolute shame of
breaking any rules. We lived by rules, and frequently died if
those rules weren't followed.

I hang my head. "Sorry."

"I won't tell your mother, if you promise not to do it again."

"Oh, bugger off." Cillian scowls.

His mother seems to grow somehow, her braids wrapped
around her head like a terrible crown of power and authority.
"Young man."

"Can you give us a ride back to our castle?" Jade asks, hiccup-
ping. "We're all very drunk."

I shove her. But I'm tipsy and not paying attention to things
like extra strength. She goes careening into the counter. "Sorry!"

"Bish," she slurs, glaring at me and rubbing her hip. Maricruz
helps right her.

"Well. I don't approve of this, but I'm glad you all had the
sense not to try and drive. I'll give you a ride back." She waits as
we slink out and Cillian turns off the lights and locks up.

"I like what you did with the shop," she says.

His silence is more aggressive than my Jade shoving. When
we get to the castle, he climbs out of the car.

"You aren't coming home?" his mother asks.

He doesn't respond as he stomps away toward the front door.
Maricruz and Jade follow him, weaving. Esther turns off the car
and climbs out. Her voice is low and sad. "I'll walk back. Here
are the keys."

"He's angry," I say.

"I know."

"You should talk to him."

"I know."

"My mom never talked to me."

She reaches out and pats my cheek, her hand soft and warm. "Motherhood is far more complicated than you can even imagine."

"Then make it simple. We need to know what the triangle thing was. Even if it hurts."

"What if it hurts *him*?" She's watching him walk away with a look I can't interpret.

"I'll protect him."

"Keep him away from this. If you want to know more, come talk to me about it. Without Cillian. The Sleeping One worshippers have been around for centuries; they're not going anywhere now. But tell Cillian whatever you have to in order to keep him out of it. Okay?"

I don't know why she needs him excluded, but there's an intensity and desperation to her plea that I respond to. And the Sleeping One is a name I haven't heard before. It might be enough to find information even if butthead Artemis never calls me back. "Okay. I'll visit tomorrow afternoon." I have castle meetings in the morning, and I still have to visit Leo.

She nods, then walks back into the woods.

I catch up to the others, bid Maricruz good night, and help a staggering Jade inside to her room, then follow Cillian to mine.

I throw myself onto my bed and squeeze my eyes shut. I have so much spinning around me. So many questions and problems. What I need is a Watcher. Leo was supposed to be my Watcher. I should be able to turn all this nonsense over to him so I can focus on the important, punchy bits. But I can't even talk to him, apparently.

Slayer stamina means most of the alcohol has already left my system. That hardly seems like a fair side effect. If anyone should be able to get good and sloshed on occasion, it's Slayers. But as it leaves, I realize I know exactly where Leo is. Which means I'll talk to him tomorrow.

I fall asleep listening to my phone ring and ring and fail to connect me with Artemis.

19

CHAO-AHN IS IN HER CARTOON HALL OF horrors, waiting for me.

"I don't want any ice cream."

"You are always gone. You don't talk to me." She jabs at me with a spoon.

"It's not a slumber-party scenario! You three can stay as long as you want. We'll protect you. But I kind of have a lot going on right now."

She mutters something in Cantonese that feels like swearing at me, even if I don't understand the words. I grab the carton of ice cream and shovel it into my mouth. "Happy?" I mumble around it.

She shakes her head. "This would be easier if we were awake."

"And we'd be less likely to be stabbed by her." I nod toward Sineya, prowling on the edges of the dream.

"She never stabs me. She likes me."

"Congratulations." I salute her with my spoon. "Have you seen Buffy around? I can't find her lately."

Chao-Ahn scowls. "No."

"Fine. Whatever. I got this on my own." I spend the rest of the dream sitting there eating ice cream, while Sineya repeatedly stabs me in the back and Chao-Ahn throws her hands up in exasperation.

The next morning at breakfast, it's clear Chao-Ahn remembers the dream very clearly. She glares at me from across the room during the entire meal.

Cillian rubs his head, his close-cropped hair unmussable. He looks rough. I pass him a bottle of ibuprofen. It takes everything in me not to stare aggressively toward the pantries and give away that I already know where Leo is. It was pretty obvious as soon as I thought about it. Not the dorms where I am. Not the Council wing, with its connection to secret passages. The one place in the castle everyone wants me to stay out of for other reasons, namely my atrocious cooking.

"What is wrong with you?" Chao-Ahn asks, dropping onto the bench across from me.

"Where to start?" Jade mutters from where she's slumped on my other side. I pass her the ibuprofen. I feel fine. Yay, Slayer powers.

Cillian jabs in her direction with his spoon. "Hey now."

"No, that's fair." I pat Jade on the shoulder. She flinches as though being touched hurts.

"Has anyone seen Doug?" She straightens, looking hopefully around the room. "I need to talk to him."

I change the subject. I feel for Jade, but I'm also Doug's friend. And if he wants out of the relationship, she needs to get over it sooner rather than later. It'll be best for both of them. "So I got today's schedule from Rhys—shoved under my door; I think he's mad—and this morning I'm taking the new Slayers on a tour of the castle and assigning you castle defense and lockdown positions." That still gives me the afternoon to go visit Cillian's mother. I haven't stopped trying to call Artemis either, but there's no timeline on that being successful, apparently. And at some point I'm going to break into the pantries to talk to Leo.

"What?" shrieks Taylor, her tray clattering to the ground behind me. "Castle defense? I thought this was supposed to be a safe space!"

Jade stands up. "Clearly *someone* has never researched Watcher history. I'm making bombs in the weapons shed, so be sure to knock. If you see Doug, tell him I want to talk to him."

"Did she just say she's making bombs?" Cillian watches Jade walk away with wide, worried eyes.

"Is everyone here very stoned?" Maricruz takes Jade's place. "Because if so, it's rude not to share." She tugs Taylor's arm and forces her to sit down too. "What's going on today?"

I give them the basics. It doesn't go over well. Cillian slides in to detail lockdown procedure. Taylor pulls on the ends of her blond ponytail, face flushed and breathing coming fast. She's on the verge of a panic attack. I have some things to help soothe her in my medical center. Xanax, kava, even some Rescue Remedy for the most natural option. I think I'd go that route with Taylor.

This flash of old Nina hits me hard, and I close my eyes. I've felt so removed from myself lately. And even now, most of my mind is on my other plans, when this—finding someone who needs help and giving them that help—is exactly what I wanted to do. What I wanted to make.

I flex my fingers, make fists. I will beat everything back into submission. I can. I'm strong enough, I know I am. I'll fix it all. I'll talk to Leo and figure myself out. I'll talk to Cillian's mom and get information. And I'll talk to Artemis and get that book back and maybe—maybe, maybe—get her back too.

Cillian has finished filling them in. I'm impressed. He's really stepped up to become part of the castle. Taylor, however, is trembling like a reed in the wind. "Wait, why is so much of the castle defense plan centered around protecting a demon? If someone came here just for this Doug guy, why would we all risk ourselves to protect him?"

We made these specific defense plans under the assumption that, at some point, Sean's going to make a play to get his prize moneymaker back. "Doug put himself on the line at Von Alston's so I could help you all. I would no more turn *you* back over to someone hunting you than I will betray Doug. I'll fight to the death for both of you. If you can't accept that, you can leave." It comes out harsher than I intend. I take a deep, steadying breath. "You don't have to fight. I wouldn't ask that of you. You always have a choice here." It's the only thing I can offer her, the thing that all Slayers were denied. A choice.

"What are our options?" Maricruz's wide-set eyes are steady, but I can see the tension around them. I have no idea what these three went through, fighting at Buffy's side. I can only imagine.

"If you really don't want to be part of it, you can leave. I don't want you to go, though."

"Maybe we'll be safer," Taylor says.

"We are Slayers," Chao-Ahn says. "Nowhere is safer than anywhere else. At least here we are not alone."

I nod at her. "We can assign you to the Littles. Their rooms are so far out of the way, and there's nothing in there anyone would want. Plus, you'll be with Jessi, and she's scarier than anything that might attack us."

"So we'd hide?" Maricruz doesn't seem any happier about this option. I can see the tension in her, and I know exactly what she's feeling. She's a Slayer. Even when she doesn't *want* to fight, it's hard to deny the instinct.

"You'd *protect*. The Littles and each other."

She nods, reluctant. Taylor still seems extra on edge, so I decide our first stop on the castle tour will be the medical center, where I can give her some natural anxiety reducers. I don't have anything powerful—I'm not a psychiatrist or a real doctor—but something's better than nothing.

The tour takes way too long. I show them the grounds, avoiding the shed where Jade is apparently making bombs. I always wondered what she'd be like if she weren't sleeping all the time. This was not on my list of possibilities. We visit the gym, where Doug is hanging out. It's a clever place if he wants to avoid Jade, who has always avoided the gym. Taylor doesn't disguise her glare. I shoo them out, but Doug holds up a hand for me to wait.

"I overheard her this morning when I was passing the kitchen. And she might have a point. If me being here makes everything more dangerous . . ."

"Nope. You being here is exactly the point of everything. You're not going anywhere, and no one is taking you. Ever."

Doug nods, then sniffs, then looks confused. "Why—why do you smell so happy all of a sudden?"

I shouldn't be. I have a looming conversation with Leo once I can ditch enough people to make it happen, and I've started texting Artemis because maybe she'll respond to that, then I have to go visit Cillian's mother to find out more about this potential baddie. But last night, when I was drunk, I decided to use some of my ill-gotten funds for a good cause. I can't keep it secret anymore. "Guess what we're doing next month?"

Doug lifts one patch of cracked skin where an eyebrow would be. "Inventory. Training. Housebreaking the tiny purple demons."

"Eew, no. I got tickets to Coldplay."

The sound he makes doesn't register on any human scale of notes. He rushes to me, throwing his arms around me and spinning me in a circle. "You didn't! You didn't!"

I laugh. "I did." To prove to him, and myself, and everyone else that we're okay. We're normal. Nothing bad is going to happen to any of us. Including knucklehead Leo. I got a ticket for him, too.

"But how did you get the money?"

"Von Alston is treating us from beyond the grave."

Doug's smile is even better than a hit of his artificial happy. "You're a good friend, Nina. Whatever it was that brought us together—fate or demonic power object or luck or—"

"My mother?"

"Or your mother, I'm glad it did." He hugs me again, and I rest my head against him for a few heartbeats. If I were a bad person, if I were all the way broken, Doug would know. He wouldn't be my friend. Leo will give me answers about the darkness of my power, and we'll figure it out, and everything will be fine.

I head back out to the Slayers and introduce them to Pelly. The tiny purple demons are harder to track down, but eventually we find them. It . . . doesn't go over well. The Slayers are clearly on edge around the chaotic energy of the three little demons. I hurry them along, moving on to the kitchens—where the pantry nags at me, knowing that Leo is there—and then the bathrooms, the Council wing, the dorm wing, and finally the secret passages. Sufficiently impressed, I leave them to explore on their own.

It's been hours. I send another text. The first one said I had a deal for her. These ones are just question marks and exclamation points and random letters to make her phone chime with notifications. And now I can't wait any longer to go visit Leo. I hurry to the library to check if my mom is there, mostly so I'll know where she is when I'm defying her wishes.

When I open the door, my mother and Rhys are in there. But they both look . . . twitchy. Guilty. Rhys slams a book shut. I step forward and look down at the cover. "Why are you wasting time reading Arcturius the Farsighted's prophecies?"

"Just checking something." Rhys pushes his glasses up and slides the book off the table.

"No. Tell me. Why are you reading that?" It would be nothing if he were reading any other book. This one is personal.

My mother sets her hands on the table, regarding me coolly and calmly. "We had some questions about the last prophecy."

"That one's done. We can check it off the list." It was about Artemis and me, how one of us would break the world and one of us would heal it. But we already stopped the hellmouth from being formed.

"It doesn't quite line up," Rhys says.

"What?"

"The details of the prophecy and what you did. For example, Artemis had very little to do with stopping Eve's hellmouth."

"Yeah, but I lost my powers because I protected Artemis, so that led to the breaking part. And then the healing, when I plugged up the hellmouth with the remora demon."

The noise Rhys makes is one I'm deeply familiar with: a low hum of *that's not right, but I don't want to fight, so I'm not going to correct you.* I've heard it many, many times during our years of studying together.

My mother has her Watcher face on. She's perfectly calm and collected while delivering brutally upsetting information. "We thought it best to make certain we aren't overlooking anything vital."

I throw my hands in the air. "We don't have time for an apocalypse. It's going to have to reschedule for another month when I'm not trying to settle in three new Slayers and keep an eye on Sean and whatever his new minion associates are up to. Maybe pencil an apocalypse in for May. It seems like a nice spring activity."

"No one said anything about an apocalypse," my mother says, her mouth twitching with the hint of a smile. "But I do agree that spring is a nice season for apocalypses to be triggered. Come to think of it, most of the near-apocalypses in recent memory have happened in May." She frowns thoughtfully. "I wonder why that is."

I shrug. "Like seasonal allergies. The earth trying to sneeze itself out of existence. Anyway, the Slayers have been slotted into our plans and chore rotation. Arcturius is low priority." I want him to be. I need him to be. I can't worry about another thing. "Have you been looking into cambions so you can help Leo?"

Rhys glares at me. "We're worrying about Leo. You don't need to."

"Come on, Nina." My mother stands and gestures for me to follow her out of the library. As soon as we're in the hall, she stops and turns to me. "I change my mind. I think you should talk to Leo."

"What?"

"Leo is important to you. He always has been. And with Artemis—well. I never spoke to her when I should, and she left. I've been very guilty of letting people I care about slip away because I was angry, or because I was scared. I won't see you repeat my mistakes. Go talk to Leo."

"Seriously?"

She smiles. It's sad, but strong. It's exactly who she is. "I would give anything for another chance to speak to the love of my life. Which I'm not saying Leo is—you're much too young to settle into a love for your entire life just yet—but you never know what will happen. Don't let words go unsaid. That's what Watchers do, and you're not a Watcher." She puts her hand on my cheek. It doesn't feel like Esther's hand. It's colder, not as natural a fit. But I appreciate it all the more for the effort it takes my mother to think of a comforting gesture and then do it.

"Okay, okay," I grumble, but I smile at her. "The pantries?"

"How did you know?"

"Pretty obvious. It's where I'd hide something from me too."

She scowls. "Well, I suppose it doesn't matter. Go ahead."

I hurry to the kitchen and then pause outside the pantry rooms, taking a deep breath. Time to talk to my not-dead not-boyfriend.

ARTEMIS

"ARE YOU SURE ABOUT THIS, MOON?"
Honora is leaning close to the mirror, applying her eyeliner with
a steady hand. It's fascinating to watch Honora work with fingernail polish and makeup as efficiently as she checks and loads her
weapons.

Artemis sets down her phone. It feels like a bomb. She just
hasn't detonated it yet. "I'm sure. We'll do the least damage possible. But it has to be done."

"Does it?"

Artemis sighs and looks at the gun she's loading very, very
carefully. "If we don't do it, someone else will. If it isn't today for
this demon, it'll be next week for another one. It's only a matter
of time. At least this way, we can save them from themselves. We
won't kill anyone. We won't even hurt them, if we can avoid it."

"I've fought your sister before. She's not going to be careful
not to hurt me."

"I know." Artemis hates how much Nina hates Honora. It's
unfair and selfish of her sister. But she has a plan for that. She has

a plan for everything. She just hasn't been able to make herself hit send yet. "Don't worry. We'll eliminate the potential source for the most damage before we even get there."

"You want to kill Nina? I never liked her, but still. Harsh." Honora is smiling slyly.

Artemis rolls her eyes and pulls out her phone. Two calls to make. This is the easy one. She's got her argument all ready. Why it has to happen this way. Why they have to take who they have to take. Imogen picks up on the third ring.

"Sanctuary, this is Imogen speaking, how may I direct your call?" There's a laughing quality to her voice.

"It's me."

"I know. What's up?"

"You have something we need. Someone." Artemis takes a deep breath, ready to launch into her arguments.

"Cheers, what do you need me to do?"

"What?"

"What do you need? They're keeping a close eye on things. I could drug them all, but I can't guarantee everyone will eat the same thing. Hard to gauge how much it will take to knock out the Slayers, too."

"Wait, Slayers—plural?"

"Yeah, but the three new ones are duds. They won't factor in. Here, do you have a pen? I'll detail where all the humans will be in case of a lockdown. That way you know where to avoid. I'm not sure where your target will be, unfortunately."

"We can handle that." Artemis gestures for a notebook and a pen, and Honora scrounges in a drawer until she comes up with them.

"First, though, you'll need Nina out of the way."

"I've got that." What she's doing is unforgiveable, but at least Nina will be gone. She'll be safe. And more than that, she won't be there to see what happens. Who's doing it. And who she's losing.

It's for the best. For everyone. Artemis takes careful notes as Imogen details the castle lockdown procedures, what their defenses are, and which areas Artemis will need to instruct her more lethal forces to avoid.

When she has enough info, she sets down her pen. "Thanks, Imogen. Hey. Why did you stay?" She really never knew Imogen well besides their occasional commiseration as they did the worst tasks the castle had to offer. But Imogen had as much, if not more, reason to leave.

"Got a job. I have to see it through. You understand. Hey, Nina." Imogen's tone shifts, becoming the more familiar, sweet one she used in the castle. Artemis freezes, as though somehow her twin will be able to sense her on the other end of the line. "Okay, sounds good! I think this exchange of goods will benefit everyone. Can't wait for the chickens." The line goes dead.

Artemis is seized with a sudden urge to call Nina with the truth. To tell her everything. To avoid this entire mess.

But it wouldn't help them in the end. She has to make the hard choices. "Call the goons," she says to Honora. "We have a plan."

"No fatalities," Honora says, her voice firm. She hasn't said anything about Von Alston's death, but she keeps washing her hands. "We don't kill any humans." Her voice softens. "And we have to give him a choice, okay? We can be clear about the consequences, but it has to be his decision."

"What if he says no?"

"Then we figure out another way. Promise me, Moon."

"Promise." It's the first time Artemis has ever lied to the girl she loves. Another on the increasingly heavy list of acceptable sacrifices. She holds her phone and stares as another series of meaningless punctuation marks from Nina comes in. It's almost time to make the call that will break her sister.

20

THE CASTLE HAS MANY ODD ARCHITEC-
tural features. It was never intended for how the Watchers used
it—as a sort of summer camp for trainees—so the conversion
had to make do with what was available. The dining hall has soar-
ing ceilings and exposed stone to contrast with the long, chipped
Formica picnic-style tables. The kitchen was totally redone.
There wasn't any pantry or closet space there, though. So they
took the next three rooms and converted them.

I try the door to the pantries. It's locked. My mother must
not have let anyone else know I was going to visit Leo. I'm not the
only rule breaker in the family.

I stand outside the door for several minutes. I still haven't
sorted through how I'm supposed to feel about Leo. But I *have*
to talk to him. I didn't kill Von Alston, but . . . I could have.
And I think Leo is the only person who can help me work
through why.

Having the other Slayers here has made me realize that I
still feel separate from them. Different. And I don't know if it's

my Watcher background, or if somehow the power inside me is wrong. Besides which, Chao-Ahn already seems weirdly suspicious of me. I don't want to talk to her about all my murdery impulses.

I twist the doorknob until it snaps, then push the door open. The first pantry leads to the next door and the next pantry. This one is filled with cereal, pasta, bread, canned goods, and Imogen.

"Hey, Nina," she says, holding up a finger. "Okay, sounds good! I think this exchange of goods will benefit everyone. Can't wait for the chickens." She hangs up and lowers her cell phone. "Trading some of the excess weapons for a coop."

"Really? Big market for used swords and the like?"

"LARPers. Anyway, you broke in."

I don't know where Imogen falls on the Nina-seeing-Leo sides—with Rhys or my mother. I study the shelves as though I were looking for a snack of . . . pickled beets. I pick up the jar. It's dusty, the contents floating in a vaguely menacing manner. "I was hungry?"

"I agreed to guard duty to keep Leo in. Never agreed to keep you out." She gestures to a set of keys on a shelf next to her chair. "Feel free to not break the next doorknob. Hard to explain to Rhys and Ruth."

"Thank you." I take the keys, my fingers betraying me with a slight tremble as I unlock the door.

"I've got your back." Imogen smiles.

I push the door open and slip inside, closing it softly behind myself and resting my forehead against it, trying to calm my breathing. Maybe Leo is asleep. Maybe I can't talk to him right now. Maybe I'll come back tomorrow. Maybe—

"Athena?"

I'd rather face a horde of vampires right now. Even broody ones. But I turn around. Leo's propped up on a cot, and the sight of him is like a blow to the stomach. He looks worse than I remember. His eyes are sunken, the skin around them the color of old bruises. His jawline is sharper than ever, cheekbones sticking out over hollow cheeks. He's wrapped in a blanket, but even his position screams frailty and illness. Leo was always so assured, so confident. Even the way he moved. He's so much *lessened* that my nerves are swallowed up by concern.

I want to lie next to him and stroke his hair until he's strong again. The impulse is almost overwhelming. But we're not there yet. Maybe we never were. Maybe we never will be again.

"Hey." I cross the tiny room in two steps and sit on the chair next to his cot instead of crawling on and holding him. "You look awful."

"You look lovely."

I laugh. It comes out sharp and braying because of my nerves. "Sure. So. Last time I saw you in person, you were unconscious on the floor and about to be crushed by the remora demon. Mind filling me in?"

He closes his eyes and smiles. His eyelids look too thin. I remember how soft his lips were; they still look the same.

"When I woke up and saw the remora filling the room, my first thought was how proud of you I was."

"Really?"

He cracks one dark eye open. "Well. No. My first thought

was *Oh god, I'm going to die.* But my second thought was how proud I was of how clever and strong you are. You stopped her with nothing but yourself. No powers. No mystical Slayer abilities. Just you. And then my third thought was a refrain of *Oh god, oh god, I'm going to die.*"

I try not to laugh, and instead put on my sternest face. "But you didn't."

"No. There was a door along the back wall. I made it in time."

"Why didn't you come out and find us?"

He sighs, sinking deeper into his pillow. "I never should have come to the castle in the first place. I put you all in danger. I knew what my mother was, who she was. But . . . she was still my mum, you know?"

Instead of my own mother, I think of Artemis in that truck. I could have stopped them. I didn't. I was so distracted by the fact it was Artemis doing the bad thing that I didn't do everything I could to stop it. "Yeah. I know."

"When she promised that she wasn't going to hurt any of you, I let myself believe her. Both because I hoped she was something other than a monster, and because I wanted to come back. To be part of the Watchers again. I wanted to be with you. With all of you. And I let that selfishness blind me. People died. People got hurt. *You* got hurt. So I decided I'd never let myself be the reason you get hurt again."

"Didn't you think your death would hurt me? I haven't been the same since! I've been—" My fists are clenched so tightly they ache. I'm almost shaking. Somehow instead of feeling sad, I keep diverting to rage.

He shifts, grimacing. "I figured you'd get over it."

"It took me *years* to get over you the first time, and you didn't even die then!" I flinch, biting my lip and wishing I could take that back. A ghost of a smile parts his lips. He lifts a hand like he might take mine. Then he looks down at it—slender fingers rendered near-skeletal—and puts it back on his cot. I almost reach for it, but I don't.

"Well, I did come back. I had to return what was taken. I owed you that much, at least."

"And that gave me hope! But then you never came back for real, so I was just confused and alone dealing with . . ." I run my hands through my hair, then I stand, pacing the tiny space. "First of all, thank you. That was nice of you to return my things. Pretty standard breakup procedure, I guess. Bringing back a box of sweaters. Books. Ancient demonic-based powers."

"Wouldn't fit in a cardboard box."

I snort. "Not so much." I have to ask him about why the Slayer powers feel different. I have to find out if it's me, or if he felt it too. Maybe they got broken from too many transfers. Or maybe they were always this, but I hadn't suffered enough to really feel what they were like. I wish I could talk to Buffy. At least I have Leo now. "But here's the thing. When you—"

"I'm sorry I kissed you," he rushes. "I shouldn't have. I didn't deserve that moment. But I really thought I'd never see you again. And it was the only way I could think of to transfer the power. I've never really done it before. Transferred power, I mean. Obviously I've kissed you before." His pale skin flushes, and I could almost laugh at making Leo Silvera blush. Almost.

The cell phone rings in my pocket, and I jump, startled. My

eyes were locked on his lips. *Honestly, Nina.* I pull out the phone. "Hello? Artemis?"

"I'm—I was told you help demons in trouble?" Not Artemis. I deflate.

"Sort of. Sometimes. What kind of demon, what kind of trouble?"

"Oh. Right. Well, I'd rather not say what kind, and the trouble is I think I'm being hunted. A lot of us are."

"You have to tell me what kind."

"I'm nonlethal. And I barely have any power at all since magic died. I promise you won't even notice I'm around."

I'm suspicious that he won't tell me what kind he is. Leo shifts to the side, and I sit on the edge of his cot, painfully aware of how close he is. "How did you get this number?"

"A friend of a friend. Tsip."

"I'm sorry, it's absolutely against the rules to even meet with you until you tell me what type of demon you are. I'm really not trying to be speciesist or judge you, but we have an entire group to think of. Like, I'm not going to bring a lilliad demon here. We for sure do not offer broth made from the bones of children on our weekly menu."

"Right. Right. I get it. I'm . . ." He sighs heavily, then mumbles, "I'm a chaos demon."

"Oh." I let the word out in a long exhalation. "Right. Chaos demon. That's—that's nonlethal. Right."

"You don't have to pretend. I know."

Chaos demons are . . . slimy. They have giant antlers that drip a steady stream of slime. The slime can be used in various magical spells—or could be, at least—and the demons themselves are drawn to chaos and help foment more of it. They're most typically found in countries with civil war, or riots, or very full and understaffed daycare facilities.

"Totally fine with the slime! It's not—we're not—how is the chaos end of things, though?" I'm not totally fine with the slime. I can imagine the protests about the chore rotation if we had to clean up his trail. And the laundry from his bedding. Oh gods, the laundry. But we already have more chaos here than we can manage.

"The chaos was a magic-based connection to my hell dimension. I'm all dry." He lets out an awkward laugh. "Only figuratively. Literally, I'm still. Well. You know."

"Yeah. Okay." I rub my forehead. "We need to meet in person so I can check everything out." And get a sense for whether he's still all chaosy. I'll have to send Rhys and his grandma Ruth. They're the least prone to chaos in the whole castle. I once saw Rhys's sock drawer, which was organized by color, type, and level of wear.

"Great! Thank you! I can only meet at night. It's hard for me to be out during the day."

Giant antlers would definitely make staying incognito a problem. Poor guy. "When can you get to the Dublin area?"

"Dublin? Hmm. Next week sometime."

"Okay. Call when you're there and we'll arrange a meetup." I hang up. I'm not sure where I'll meet him, but we decided after the warehouse attack we needed to range even farther away from Shancoom.

"Your mother told me what you're doing here," Leo says. "It's good. It's what Watchers should be. What we should always have been."

"Thanks." I stand, needing to move for this next part of the conversation. I wish we could go for a walk. My phone rings again, and I sigh, answering it. "What?"

"Nina."

My heart stops. It's Artemis. "Hey."

"I got your text. You want the book in exchange for not telling everyone what I've been doing? You're blackmailing me?"

"No!" I pause. "Yes. But I'm also protecting you. I should have told them."

"You should have." She pauses for so long I want to reach across the static distance between us and strangle her. "Fine. I don't need it anymore, and you should know what's going on. Meet me tonight. Outside Dublin. Bring Rhys." She pauses again. "And Mom."

"Won't that defeat the purpose of them not knowing?"

"I don't care if they know, Nina!"

"I do!" I cringe at how I shouted it. "I do. You need to be able to come back, and you can't if everyone votes against you because you've joined some demonic zealot group. You picked the one thing we can't overlook. Why would you do that?"

Her voice is neither soft nor vicious. It's just far away. "I'm never coming back. I'll text you the address." The line goes dead. I leave the phone pressed against my ear for way too long, hoping she'll say something, anything else. It dings, startling me. The address stares at me. I'll see Artemis. I'll get the book. But it feels so . . . final.

I look down at Leo. I need more time with him, but if I'm going to get to Artemis when I'm supposed to, I have to leave now. Artemis told me to bring Rhys and our mom, but I hold my

hand out to Leo. "They said you can't have free range of movement in the castle." He isn't handcuffed to the bed. I'm assuming
they'll save that for nighttime.

"I understand."

"No, I mean, they said you can't have free movement *in* the
castle. So let's go."

"What?"

"Gotta take a partner on every trip out of the castle. Even
one to meet with my sister." I'm not done talking to Leo yet. Not
by a long shot. And maybe it will distract me from my nerves
over going to confront Artemis. Plus, this way she'll still have
the option of coming back, even if she thinks she doesn't want it.
"I could . . . I could use a Watcher."

His face softens, and he grabs his blanket, wrapping it
around his shoulders. I open the door to find the next pantry
room empty, Imogen's book lying facedown and open. "What is
she, a sociopath?" I close the book so the spine won't break, then
peer out into the kitchen. The coast is clear. My mother gave
me permission to talk to Leo, but I'm pretty sure she wouldn't
approve of this. Leo walks far too slowly for my needs, but we
make it through the great hall and down the front stone steps
without being caught. I get him in the car.

"One second." I sprint back inside to my room and grab
Artemis's favorite leather jacket out of the closet. A peace offering. And a reminder. I saved my meager pocket money and sold
half my novels to buy it for her for our last birthday. Once I'm
back in the car and we're on the way, I text Rhys that I got a call
from a chaos demon—not technically a lie—and I'm going to
check it out and I took Leo with me.

Then I turn my phone off.

Leo leans back in his seat, closing his eyes. The dappled January sunlight, as weak as he is but just as lovely, plays on his face, and something in my chest loosens for the first time in months.

21

"AND YOU'RE SURE YOU SAW WHAT YOU saw?" Leo asks as I slow down, scanning the streets for the address Artemis texted me.

I nod, miserable. I brought him along to talk about my power, but he overheard my conversation with Artemis and asked what's been going on. I told him the truth. Talking it out almost feels like what we were getting close to before everything went to hellmouths in a handbasket. What we should have been: Watcher and Slayer. Except he's still wrapped in a blanket and can barely keep his head up, and we're worrying about my sister instead of a demon or vampire. "Kind of hard to mistake her intentions when she told Honora to throw me off a moving vehicle."

"Maybe she'll have a good explanation."

"She had better. But at least we'll have that book back and we can get some answers about this nameless one or Sleeping One or whoever he is. Cillian's mom—shoot, I was supposed to meet her this afternoon—knows some stuff too." Maybe we'll stop there on the way back to the castle. I have a feeling I'll be in no hurry to get back and face the music.

"What will you do if you discover danger beyond just the zealots?"

I shrug. "I don't know. Slayers should have some sort of sign-up sheet where you post a threat and whoever is best equipped to deal with it steps in."

"So, Buffy. Every time."

I laugh. "Yeah, she probably wouldn't appreciate it."

"It's going to be fine. You'll figure it out."

"Which part? Artemis, or the potential looming monstrosity?"

His smile has more faith in me than I deserve. "Both."

"It might get messy, though. Oh gods, speaking of mess, I told that chaos demon we'd meet with him next week. What if he's telling the truth and he isn't chaos incarnate anymore? And we have to give him sanctuary?"

"How would he fit in the car?" Leo asks, staring at the backseat where the chaos demon would presumably sit.

"Oh no, you're right. We'd need a sunroof open or something. Maybe if he turned to the side? And his antlers came up between the seats? But then he'd drip slime on us and . . . yuck. Maybe he'll have his own car. Or we'll get lucky and he'll try to kill us, so we can deny him entry."

Leo laughs. It's soft and dry and a bit rattley, but still makes me happy to hear. "That's a weird definition of getting lucky."

"Only type of getting lucky I manage these days." I cringe. *Do* not *talk about getting lucky with the only boy you've ever liked.* Fortunately, Leo's laugh has turned into a cough, and he didn't catch what I said or can't respond.

I slow down even more as we get close to the address, looking from side to side for a house, or an abandoned shack, or a
lair. Whatever Honora might have picked to live in with my
sister. Instead, I pull up alongside a cemetery weeping with the
gently falling rain. Even the trees are heavy and bowed with
time, nodding over the worn and age-pocked monuments.
An angel with her head lowered, hands covering her face, is
wrapped in her own stone wings as though trying to find comfort in cold granite.

The fence around the cemetery is old and rusting, and it
doesn't look like anyone new has been buried here in at least a
few decades. It probably doesn't get a lot of foot traffic on dreary,
drizzling January days. We couldn't have met at a coffee shop?

It's not quite sunset, and I don't really relish the thought of
standing in the rain freezing my butt off, so I put the car in park
but keep it running. This feels like my last chance to fix things.
But I'm also defensive and angry and worried I'm going to snap
and shout at Artemis like she deserves.

Leo rests a hand gently on my shoulder. "She's your sister,"
he says.

"Let's hope that's enough." I lean back in my seat, surveying
the cemetery. It must go on for some ways. The heavy trees and
low gray drizzle keep me from seeing too far inside, but I don't
see any movement. I'll wait until the sun actually goes down.
Artemis said sunset. And I kind of like the idea of making her
wait for me after what a jerk she was.

The windows quickly fog up, sealing us in the dim, warm
interior. I turn my head so I'm looking at Leo. With the light
fading and his face in profile, he looks like himself. I want to talk

more about why he didn't come back. I should ask him about what my power was like when he held it, if he can help me figure out why it feels different. But I don't want to do any of that. I want to be a normal girl sitting in a car with a cute guy. Like a date. At the cemetery. To have a tense exchange of stolen goods with my sister. Total normal girl stuff.

I know I'm avoiding facing my problems, but I'm tired of life and death, of darkness and threats. I got Leo back. Maybe I'll get Artemis back too. And then things can be normal and I can stop feeling terrified that I'll lose someone else, or feeling so angry that I'm terrified I'll lose myself.

"Have you ever met a chaos demon?" I ask.

"One, in Brazil. He didn't speak English, but I think he had a crush on my mom." Leo smiles, but his smile fades as quickly as it appeared, the weight of his mother's memory too heavy.

Must change the subject. "Did I tell you we almost let a Roehrig demon into Sanctuary? We thought he was a half-Brachen demon. Turns out he was just wearing a half-Brachen's *skin*. That was messy."

"What did he want?"

"Dinner."

"Did you—"

"No, Jade and Rhys were the ones who met with him. Honestly, I probably would have brought him home. But Rhys knows his demons and realized something was off. Plus, Rhys isn't as trusting as I am." I scowl, thinking about how Rhys is anti-Leo.

"He's not wrong." Leo's voice is soft. "His first duty is to protect all of you. Listen, I don't want to make things complicated. I never did. That's why I—"

"Doug and Jade are dating," I blurt, not wanting to give Leo the chance to tell me why he shouldn't be at the castle. I'm keeping him. I'm not letting anyone else go.

"That's . . . something."

"Yeah, I guess it's complicated. He's worried she's using him for his skin secretions."

Leo makes an appropriately horrified face and I laugh.

"I know. I never thought interspecies relationship counseling would be part of the deal when I decided to make Sanctuary. But here we are. Although if Imogen starts dating one or all of the tiny purple demons, I'm out. She can handle that on her own."

"I can't imagine Imogen dating anyone."

"Me neither, actually." Imogen is so self-contained. She doesn't really seem to need anyone at all. It would be weird to see her connect with someone on that level. I almost wonder why she stays. The rest of us are anchored—I have my mother, Rhys, and Cillian, not to mention being a Slayer. Rhys has Cillian and his grandmother Ruth and the library he would never give up. My mother could never be anything but a Watcher. Jade is staying for Doug, doubtless. The demons have nowhere else to go. But Imogen is in a similar position as Honora. The Watchers were never good to her. I wonder if she stays because she has nowhere else to go? She's a bit of a mystery. But I hope she doesn't leave, because I really like her cooking.

"What about you?" Leo says, deliberately not looking at me. "Any demon love interests?"

"Just the one."

He glances at me and I can't handle the hope and sadness in his dark eyes. If it were one or the other, I would know what to do or how to feel. My heart squeezes and my throat burns, warning me I might cry. So I deflect again. "I mean, *hopefully* just the one if things work out next week. I'm really into chaos demons. Love a good slime antler. Mmm."

"Athena, I—"

"Nope. Whatever you're going to say, I don't care and it doesn't matter. You're back home. That's what's important. We're gonna get you better, and once you're healthy *then* I'm going to rip your head off for letting me think you were dead."

"I want—"

"Don't take this the wrong way, but I don't care what you want. I let Artemis have what she wanted, and now she . . ." My fists clench. "No. Nope. No. You might have thought you were being noble staying away, but you weren't. It hurt. It hurt me so bad, and I've had to live with the guilt of killing you every single day since then, so no. I don't care what you want. I don't care about your feelings, or whether you think you're doing the right thing. I'm a Watcher *and* a Slayer and you're a half demon, so I'm doubly pulling rank on you. You'll stay right here in the car while I go get our book from my sister and talk some sense into her. Then when I get back, we'll drive to the castle, where you're not going to stay in a stupid pantry anymore, you're going to take a real room because you're part of the castle and you're not going anywhere. We still have a lot we need to talk about."

He doesn't look at me. "It's the best thing if I don't fight this. For everyone."

"Wow. You're being a selfish prick."

He turns, shocked. "What?"

"You think you're protecting us by giving up? Protecting me?

I was devastated when I lost you. You were the only person who ever saw me for *me*. When no one else noticed me, or when they saw me as the lesser Jamison-Smythe twin, or when they only saw me as a disappointing Slayer. You've always seen me. I see you too. And yeah, you made bad choices. Really so super bad, and it's okay for you to feel guilty about that. But you made them out of love. She was your mom. And she was kind of evil. But she was still your mom."

I think about Artemis and how I've been lying to everyone to protect her. If I were a good Watcher, a good Slayer, if I were *only* those things, I could have and would have stopped her at the conference, or even in the library. But she's my sister. And it's so much more complicated than a vampire or a demon or anything else in the world.

Like my relationship with Leo. I think it might never be simple between us. But I don't care. It's worth fighting for, and so is he. "So reconcile what you did however you need to. Figure out how to come to peace with it. But you dying is not the right way. That wouldn't fix what your mom did, or make the world a better place. It would just make it emptier, and with everyone and everything we've lost, isn't it already empty enough?" The darkness inside me—the darkness I tried to channel, to feed, to ignore, all to no avail—seems like emptiness to me now. A gaping void that I can't fill with violence and I can't fill with happiness, and I'm so scared it's going to devour me one of these days. "If I can figure out how to live with what's inside me, can't you do the same?"

"It's not that simple."

"It is. And I refuse to let you die again." I open the door

and climb out, slamming it behind me. I love so many people, and they're *all so stupid*. I'm sick of it. I'm sick of them hurting me and hurting themselves and hurting each other. I stomp into the cemetery, my cute purple Docs squelching through mud. I'm wearing Artemis's nicest leather trench coat and an emerald-green sweater underneath, but I can still feel the bite of the evening. There's a mausoleum with an overhang, and I make straight for it, standing out of the drizzle and surveying the night. A few stubborn lamps burn overhead, giving dim illumination to the landscape of sleeping dead.

I still need to ask Leo about my power. About the ways it's changed. The Artemis situation felt more pressing, and then Leo being an idiot took over the conversation. He's not allowed to die. We have a lot more fights we need to get through.

I pull out my phone and turn it on, not opening all the unread texts from the castle. Nothing new from Artemis. I text her. *Here.*

A dark figure swoops toward me, ducking into the shelter before turning and staring at me in shock. It's not Artemis. She's wearing an elegant dress, long and flowing and black, with a high neck. Her hair is pinned up in elaborate swirls, and her lips are painted very red. There's something classic about her face and the way she stares at me, like a portrait of her could be hanging in the national gallery.

"Vampire?" I ask. Less because of how she looks and more because of the instant *KILL KILL KILL* buzzing through me, so I really hope she's a vampire and not human, otherwise I'm in trouble.

She nods slightly, and I'm more than a little relieved. "Slayer?"

she asks. I nod in imitation of her. Neither of us moves. "Patrolling?"

"I don't really do that. Hunting?"

"Not tonight." She pulls out a cigarette and then one of those long black cigarette holders like I've only seen in movies. "Do you mind?"

"Nah." I used to. Smoke was very triggering for me. But I've stopped having nightmares about almost burning to death in my old house in Phoenix. I still visit that room, but it's different ever since I found out my mother left me behind because she knew I would survive when Artemis wouldn't.

The vampire smiles as she lights her cigarette. "Smoking forces me to breathe. I find it deeply nostalgic."

"And bonus, none of that pesky lung cancer to kill you."

"Perks of the undead." She blows out a long, slow stream of smoke.

"Don't suppose you've seen me wandering around this cemetery tonight?"

She looks puzzled but intrigued. "No?"

"Twin sister. Meeting her here."

"Ah."

I should probably stake her, but I don't want to be midfight when Artemis gets here. Or maybe I do. Is it creepy if I hold off fighting this vampire until Artemis can see? Her witheringly dismissive look at the convention tugs on my pride. I'd look really cool in her leather coat fighting and dusting a vampire before turning to her and calmly asking for the book and some answers.

"I love that coat. Interested in selling it?"

"It's my sister's." I brought the coat as a peace offering, but Artemis is late. She's making me stand here in the rain. It would serve her right if she showed up and a vampire was wearing her favorite coat.

"Think she'll sell it to me?" She reaches into the lace-lined bag where she keeps her cigarettes.

"No! I gave it to her. As a gift."

A smile seeps across the vampire's face. "And yet she left it with you, apparently. I bet she'd sell it to me." She takes another drag of her cigarette.

I shouldn't be talking to her. I'll stake her. Talking to her now is going to make it weird. Vampires are so good at being human . . . until they're not. And performing a slaying for Artemis is gross of me. What is this vampire doing here, anyway? "Did you rise tonight or something?"

"I'm here to visit a very old friend." She puts her hand on the plaque on the side of the mausoleum. It has several names, but her fingers trail along the one that reads SARAH McCABE 1801–1823.

"Is she a vampire too?"

"No. I was the lucky one. She's in there, and I'm out here, and somehow it's been nearly two hundred years, but I can still hear her laughter. Neither of us changed after that day. Well. I suppose there is the decay to take into account. And this." Her face briefly shifts into the monstrous, fanged vampire visage before shifting back. She smiles wryly. "Sarah would have found that hilarious. I was always so worried about getting wrinkles. Vain Jane, she called me." She holds out the cigarette.

"Not a fan of smoke." Even with my progress about the fire, the scent has me on edge.

She shrugs, then removes the cigarette from the holder and puts it out on the wet stone. It hisses softly.

I check my phone. Nothing from Artemis. Maybe I got the cemetery wrong, or Artemis is in a different section. But if I go look, I'm leaving a vampire behind. And if I fight her, I might have to range through the cemetery and miss Artemis that way. Ugh.

"Hey," I ask, remembering the conference and my thoughts about my responsibility to kill any vampire I'm aware of. "Do you know a vampire named Harmony? She has a reality show?"

Jane hisses. "That idiot child. There's a reason we live in the night, in the dark. The more people know about us, the more likely they are to kill us. Anonymity is a vampire's best friend. How many famous vampires can you name?"

"A lot, actually. The Master, Kakistos, Angelus, Dracula, but that one's obvious, William the Bloody, Drusilla, and are we counting cults, because if we are—"

She rolls her eyes. "Right, I forgot about your line of work. But for most people, up until now, it was Dracula."

"And Edward."

"Personally, I prefer Lestat." She laughs, the sound low and throaty. "But that bastard Dracula, telling his story for fame. And now Harmony. She has no idea what the weight of centuries is. No concept of eternity. Give her a few decades and she'll come to know and accept the absolute burden and *boredom* of immortality. We survive not so that we can bask in adulation and glory. We survive and feed and hide so that we can survive and feed and hide. There is no thriving for vampires. Especially now that we are denied even the power of siring new vampires."

"Oh, right, the whole zompire thing." With magic dead, new vampires don't have the connection to the ancient demon that infected the very first vampire. They turn into mindless hivelike zombie vamps. I check the time. Artemis is definitely late.

"That is a disgusting term, and I refuse to use it." Her nose wrinkles in distaste. "Abominations, all of them."

I sigh, putting my phone away. "So you sire so you aren't alone?"

"We are always alone." She folds her arms, looking out into the darkness. "Friendship requires love, and love requires a soul. We sire so for a few moments we can pretend we have power over life and death. So for a few moments we can savor that moment between dead and undead and remember our own change. And because it's funny." Her lips twist in amusement. "Cemeteries used to be so amusing. I'd wait after a burial to see the new vampire emerge, covered in dirt and baffled. Like a baby deer learning to walk."

"Baby deer don't kill people."

She shrugs. "Well. It is a pleasure I no longer have and never will again. It's all hollow anyway. The only person I should have sired, the only one I would have liked to spend an eternity with, is beyond my reach and forever will be." She puts her hand over Sarah's name again.

And, weirdly, I get it. I get her. Because if I thought I had a way to bind the people I love to me, to keep them forever, safe and mine? I think I would. I know it's wrong. Is it wrong, though? It would be if I were making them vampires. But that impulse—to change someone so they can't be hurt, so they can't grow old or grow away from you, or die, or seem to be dead but really be hiding because they're absolute idiots—that, I understand.

"Who's in the car?" she asks, nodding toward my car. "You keep looking in that direction."

"Old friend. Sort of." Where the hells is Artemis?

"Sort of?"

"We were kind of a thing? Or going to be a thing. I'm not really sure. And now it's all messed up and complicated and he's sick and I don't know how to fix it."

"Oh, I used to love couples like you. The sick lover! Modern medicine is a plague. Back in the day, I had but to wander through a park a few evenings before I'd find some lad doting on his ailing sweetheart, or some sweet pretty lass placing a blanket on the lap of her wasting beau. I'd offer to save them. The hope and desperation in their eyes! My own Faustian play, over and over, knowing as soon as I turned the dying lover, they'd kill the human one! Such sweet tragedy."

"Are all vampires this chatty?"

She purses her red lips. "You try living in the shadows of the night for decades; tell me how you entertain yourself then. Besides which, Artemis isn't here yet. What else do you have to do?"

I half nod in agreement, then I freeze. "I never said her name."

She freezes, a half smile on her lips. "Didn't you?" Then she lunges.

22

I TWIST, USING JANE'S OWN MOMENTUM to throw her against the side of the mausoleum. Her head cracks against her dead friend's name. "What did you do to my sister?" I scream. If she took Artemis—if she hurt her—

"Oh, you sweet thing." She stands.

"Did you hurt her?" Artemis can't be dead. She can't be. "Where is she?"

Jane leans in close, licking her lips. "The devastation is going to taste so sweet on you." I grab her and throw her against the mausoleum again. She laughs. "Don't you want to know the truth? Don't you want to know why I'm here? Why you're here? And why Artemis isn't?"

I pause, and she uses that moment to slam her fist into my stomach. I stumble backward.

"We have our orders. No killing the Slayer," a male voice in the darkness calls out.

"But what if she trips and her throat accidentally falls on my teeth?" She prowls, catlike, angling around me.

"Where is my sister?" I ask, not wanting any answer this vampire could possibly provide and increasingly terrified it's not Artemis who is hurt. It's me. I just don't know it yet.

Jane jumps, and my stake is out and in hand by the time she lands on me. She poofs out of existence.

"Look, we don't want to hurt you." The male voice steps into the light. It's another vampire, tall and broad-shouldered, face already vamped out in contradiction to his statement. Next to him is a shorter vampire whose spiky Mohawk has gone limp in the rain.

"Why are you here, then? Who said not to hurt me?"

He shrugs. "I was all for making you sit quietly in the rain waiting alone for a few hours, but Jane likes—liked—to chat."

Every alarm bell in my body is going off. No no no no no. There was only one person who knew where I'd be tonight. "Whose instructions?"

He reaches into his jacket and pulls out one of those shock sticks the cloakers used. He hasn't touched me with it, but it jolts me to my soul nonetheless. "We need another hour. So we all wait calmly, and then everyone leaves. No one gets hurt. We get paid, you go home with all your blood safe and warm on the inside, where you want it."

The only reason I can think that Artemis—oh gods, Artemis— would want me stuck in a cemetery in Dublin was so that I wasn't at the castle. The castle filled with people I love and demons I swore to protect. That crawling black thing in me roars to life, darker than the night, soaking me from the inside out. The vampire doesn't have time to dodge before my foot connects with his head.

The second vamp lunges for me. I duck under his arms,

twisting free and lashing out with a vicious kick that sends him flying. I see a moment—one perfect, clear moment—when I can stake him and be done with one of them.

But the growling thing inside me doesn't want this to be done. I turn and kick the first vampire in the head again. He stumbles backward, and I jump, switch-kicking the Mohawk vampire. I throw him into the lamp, the bone-on-metal sound ringing through the night. The tall vampire, shock stick lost, grabs me around the waist. He lifts me off the ground. I slam my head back into his face, hearing bones crunch.

I get my feet down and tug him over me, throwing him flat on the ground and dusting him with a single, brutal stab.

When the Mohawked vampire lunges for me again, I drop to my back and use his own momentum to propel him up over my body and down onto the ancient, peeling picket fence around a small burial plot.

He moans in pain. But moaning is a very different sound from poofing.

The fence impaled him but missed his heart. He kicks and bucks, trying to get free. I walk to him, standing over his snarling, monstrous face. And I feel nothing. Not anger. Not elation. I finally gave in to it all, and instead of being relieved to finally let go, I'm hollowed out and empty. I channeled the darkness, used it, and nothing changed.

I could be wrong. I could be wrong. I have to be wrong.

"Who wanted me here?" I ask.

He grabs for me, but he's still stuck on the fence. I take a small step back, and his hands claw at the air in front of me. "You can stake me. I won't tell you anything."

"Okay." I stake him. I'm once again alone. I already know the answer.

All this was a ruse to get me out of the castle. The castle where Doug—Sean's lost prize—is, where my mom is, where Rhys and Cillian and everyone I love is. I dial my mother as I race back toward the car. "Someone's coming. It's—" I choke. "It's Artemis and Honora. Don't trust them. Go on lockdown."

There are a few heavy seconds as she processes what I told her. "Done." She hangs up.

I throw myself into the car. "Setup," I say, slamming it into gear and flipping a very illegal U-turn. "Artemis. She set me up. She set this all up." I toss the phone at Leo. "Tell me the second you get any texts." The phone dings, and I resist lunging for it.

Leo reads it quickly. "'Everyone accounted for. Lockdown initiated.'"

Maybe they haven't had time to launch an attack yet. The vampires did say they needed to hold me there for another hour. Hopefully, talkative Jane blew it for them. "They were proba-bly hoping they could just walk in. But the castle knows they're coming. And Artemis and Honora haven't been there since we created the lockdown procedures. They won't know what to expect." I shake my head, disbelief numbing me. "Artemis. She's going after the castle. I never should have let her leave with Honora. This is my fault."

I clench my jaw, strangling the steering wheel imagining Honora's perfectly lush and thick dark hair, that smug smile, those clever eyes.

"You're not okay." Leo's eyes are heavy on me, even though my own are glued to the road blurring beneath us.

"Of course I'm not okay! The castle is probably under attack, Artemis is behind it, and I'm not there!"

"No, I mean, more than that. I saw you in that fight. It didn't seem like you."

I wanted to have this conversation. Needed to. But I couldn't make myself because it felt too important and scary. With this news, it feels less scary. "Ever since you gave my Slayer power back to me, it's felt different."

He sits up from his slouched position. "What do you mean, different?"

Another ding.

"'All clear.'"

But I don't feel all clear. I feel like I'm flying apart at the seams. I drum my fingers against the steering wheel. "Not that I was an expert before or anything, and the powers are demonic in origin anyway, so there's a certain amount of darkness that accompanies them, right? But I've been having these flashes of *rage*. And sometimes I want—I want to hurt things. Not to stop them or fight them, but to hurt them. And that's new. That's not me." My voice breaks. I stop and clear my throat. "You had my power for a little bit. You felt it. Did you feel *that*?"

I finally look over at him. And then I wish I hadn't. His face is frozen in a mask of horror.

"What?" I ask. "Tell me."

"I—oh, Athena. I'm so sorry. I didn't think—I didn't even consider it."

"Consider what?"

"When I took the energy from my mother. It was over-whelming. So much of it. I assumed that was what it felt like to have your power. But—god, I should have died. I should have died when I was supposed to."

I pass a car with barely enough space, an angry horn following us. "Leo, tell me. It can't be worse than what I'm imagining."

"My mother drained others before you. Bradford Smythe. Cosmina. Several incredibly old demons. And I assumed that power would have burned off. She was using so much of it. But . . ."

"No, that's worse than what I was imagining. That's for sure worse. You're telling me I got an extra demoned-up cocktail of power? That my demon-based Slayer power wasn't demony enough, so I got several shots of demon espresso to really bump me to the next level. And Cosmina! And Bradford Smythe! Oh gods, I have part of Bradford Smythe's life energy force free-floating around in me! I need to take a shower. I need to—"

"I should never have been part of your life. I thought I was helping. I really did. But who was I kidding? This is who I am. What I come from. I corrupt everything I touch, and I always will. I'm so sorry. I wish you hadn't found me. I should have died alone in Von Alston's house."

"You're not going to die." The tires skid as I take a curve too fast but somehow keep control of the car. "No one is unless I say so." It comes out a snarl.

He slumps in his seat. His voice is exhausted. It sounds like it's coming from much farther away than it is. "I never took any energy myself. It was always my mother. And she's gone. I'm dying. Starving to death. But it's only incredibly slow and painful, so, all things considered not a bad way to go." He tries to laugh. It doesn't work.

His mother's fate hangs in the air between us. His mother, who stole power and energy from others while they slept, and then passed it to him. That's how he got my power back from her. Before I killed his mother and left him for dead.

"I refuse to let you die." I hit the road that will take us to Shancoom. Every mile is torture. "I had to leave you before. I didn't have a choice. Now I do. And you don't get to die because you feel bad about what your mother did or who your father was."

"I'm sorry to do this to you," he whispers. "But you don't get a choice in this one either. I'd rather die than be a predator or hurt you again."

The phone dings. Leo takes way too long to relay the message. I already know before he says it.

"They're under attack."

23

"HERE'S HOW IT'S GOING DOWN," I SAY, the engine roaring as it devours the road beneath us. I run through the plans over and over in my head, like thinking about them can protect the people involved until I get there. "Jade, Cillian, and Rhys are on the grounds. Jade will have had enough time to set traps. Doug is locked in the gym, where there's only one way in or out, so they'll have a hard time getting to him. He can defend himself, but I'm not risking him with how badly Sean would love to get him back. We don't know their objective, but we can guess they're after the demons as retaliation for how many I cost them."

"Athena," Leo says.

"Tsip will be in and out, wherever she's needed, though mostly centered around the gym. I don't know how she is in a fight. She'll keep the attackers focused on the main portion of the castle, though, and out of the wings. The Littles are staying in their suite, but we have a false back to their closet built in so they can hide there. I'm assuming the other Slayers will be there with Jessi to protect them. Jessi would be more than happy to let them die, but she'll do anything to protect the Littles." Artemis won't go near the Littles. She won't. Whatever else she's doing, she won't hurt them.

"*Athena*," he says again.

"Ruth will be in the library with Imogen protecting the books. You know Ruth will die before she lets someone take any of our resources. And my mother—" My breath catches. My mother gave me permission to see Leo, and instead I stole him and ran away for the day. And now she's protecting the castle on her own, and I'm not where I should be, and if she dies it will be my fault. Artemis specifically told me to bring our mother and Rhys. She set me up to get the only people in the castle she cares about out.

Oh gods. People are going to die. And Artemis knows it.

Leo's hand rests on my forearm. "They all know what to do. They've all trained for this."

"If something happens to any of them—"

"Nothing will happen to them."

"Something happened to you!"

He detaches one of my hands from its death grip on the steering wheel and laces his fingers between mine, bringing it to his lips and pressing a gentle kiss against my knuckles. "And it wasn't your fault."

He releases my hand. I turn onto the forest road that will lead us to the castle, my heart in my throat. I reach for the darkness inside, but all I find is fear.

I slam on the brakes before I hit the smoking ruins of a van tipped over on its side. Jade must have actually pulled off a bomb. I don't know if I'm impressed or worried. And I can't help the spike of fear for Artemis.

"On foot from here," I say, because I don't know where any more bombs will be. I get out, stake in hand, and hurry forward. *No bodies*, I think as I peer into the interior of the van. *Please, no bodies.* There aren't any, and I can move again. Leo is behind me. His breathing is heavy, but he's moving fast.

There's a snapping of a branch, and I gasp as I'm doused with water. A water balloon, to be precise.

"It's me!" I shout.

"Sorry!" Cillian is somewhere in the trees. I can't tell his exact location, which is good, because it means no one else can either. But it also means he wasted one of his few holy water balloons on me. "We took out five vampires who climbed out of the ruined van, but there were two other vans that didn't get damaged!"

"Where are Rhys and Jade?"

"Rhys is chasing down two stray vamps, and I haven't seen Jade yet. I'm supposed to stay in my tree."

"Good!" My hair dripping, I hurry forward around the next curve. There are two vans stopped in the middle of the dark forest road. I hold up a fist to Leo. "Stay here," I whisper. I close the distance to the vans. The first one is empty, doors gaping open like mausoleums. No hostiles, no Jade, and no Honora or Artemis.

Or at least that's what I think, until I'm electrocuted from behind.

"She's down," a woman's voice says. "There's one in the trees. No, up in the trees, not on the ground. Another deeper in the forest with a crossbow. He should be neutralized soon."

"Nonlethal force," another voice says over a crackling feed, and this one hurts more than whatever they did to me that's left me flat on the ground, blinded by pain and unable to move. *Artemis.* "Remember our goal. Full team converge on the castle; the Slayer is out of play."

"The hell she is," I say, my face against the dirt of the road.

"What?" the woman over me asks.

"Playtime is just starting." I stand and punch her and she falls back, unconscious. Human. One of the creepy cloakers. I tear the door off the second van. Jade is in there, her head bleeding and her hands and feet bound. My favorite crossbow has been tossed in the back, so I grab that, then break the ropes. Jade groans, sitting up.

"Where is she?" Jade demands.

"Who?"

"Honora!"

"She's mine."

"First come, first serve!" Jade pushes past me and runs for the castle, stumbling and limping.

I'm about to follow when I remember that Cillian and Rhys were being pursued. I scream in frustration, then run into the trees around where I was doused. A vampire is halfway up the tree. I aim, but before I can pull the trigger, he poofs into dust from another crossbow bolt.

"Cillian!" Rhys's glasses are askew, and his hair has abandoned all pretense of order. There's a cut along one of his cheeks, and his eyes are wide with adrenaline and panic.

"I'm okay!" Cillian shouts from above me.

I turn on my heel. Rhys isn't going to let anything happen to Cillian. "They're at the castle!"

"Go! We're behind you!"

"Bring Leo! Go in the back way, put him in the tower with Pelly, then converge on the great hall."

Leo is leaning against a tree. "Athena, I want to——"

"Follow your orders!" I snap. "I can't wait for you!"

I sprint, and Jade curses as I pass her easily. The front door is closed, still intact. They didn't come in this way. I do a quick mental inventory. The dorm wing is the easiest point of access. The windows are lower to the ground, and half of them are missing. I race around the side of the castle. There are two vampires in the trees. I fire two bolts, and then there are none.

Leaving the crossbow on the ground, I jump up and catch my own window ledge, then break my window and fling myself into my room. In the hall, I hear the furtive, creeping sounds of several attackers.

"Doug!" I shout. "Come on, this way! Hide in my room!" Sure enough, I hear footsteps running toward the sound of my voice. I slam the door. A few seconds later, it bursts open to reveal two vampires. I'm standing in the middle of the room between my bed and Artemis's. The fan whirls in a blur overhead.

"Oh no. Two vampires. Help. Help." I pull out a stake.

The first vampire, her bumpy, tortured face incongruous beneath perfectly coiffed blond hair, charges at me. I stomp on the floorboard beneath me. The spring-loaded board . . . does nothing.

I've faced a lot of disappointment in my life, but this is right up there with the worst of it. I stomp once more in petulant disappointment. That does the trick, though. The spring-loaded board is tripped, and she flies in almost slow motion upward toward the fan blades. With a cut-short shriek and a showering of dust, she loses her head.

"Holy hellmouths, it worked! It actually worked!" I laugh in shock, jumping up and down. "I have to tell . . ." *Artemis. I have to tell Artemis.*

The other vampire has frozen in disbelief, staring at the remains of his companion floating lazily down toward the beds.

All my giddy triumph sours. Artemis is the reason I got to test our booby traps. I pick up a heavy book and throw it at the vampire's head. He stumbles, stunned. I kick him, and he flies directly into the large stone fireplace. The switch is hidden behind the mantel. I flip it, and he's consumed in the jet of pressurized flame that shoots directly into him.

And look, I didn't even catch my room on fire. That was our one concern with that method, but I figured out a way to keep it contained. Just put the vampire directly in the fireplace. "Go me," I mutter, then step back into the dark passageways.

If the attackers are working under plans from Artemis and Honora, they'll know about the secret passageways. I walk toward the nearest entrance. Sure enough, the closet door is ajar. I lean toward it.

The screams echo down the narrow stone passageways. Definitely several vampires' worth of screaming.

I can't quite imagine what the tiny purple demons are doing in there, but whatever it is, they're good at it. No secret passageway movements for hostiles. I hope Artemis isn't one of them. I almost call the tiny purple demons off, but I can't afford to protect her. Creeping around secret passageways isn't Artemis's style. I sprint back toward the main hall to make sure my mother has it under control.

There are two vampires writhing on the floor, clawing at their now-empty eye sockets. Tsip looks up at me, beaming. "I got some eyes, Nina! And it's my birthday!"

"Great job, I guess?" I stake the vampires, knowing even sightless vampires have enough killer instincts to be threats. My mother must still be hidden outside in the alcove, protecting the front door.

I peer out the window to see several hellhounds converging on the entrance. I open the door, grab my mother, and yank her inside before slamming it closed again.

"Thank you, Artemis," she says, straightening her jacket. "Nina!" she corrects.

The fact that the first name on her tongue while being rescued was my sister's hurts even more. I know it was a mistake. But it was a mistake born of habit. Artemis is the one she relies on when things get bad. And now Artemis is the one making things bad.

We share one silent, agonized look. We don't have time to say anything, though. Rhys and Cillian run in from the dorm wing, Leo behind them. He looks beyond winded.

"Leo, into the tower section. Pelly's there. Keep it safe. Sean did bad things to it for a long time, and I'm sure he'd love to take it back."

I can see the struggle on Leo's face. It's killing him to have to leave this fight to us. But he nods and heads toward the kitchen, where he'll access the door to the condemned tower section.

"Why now?" Leo asks, pausing.

"What?" I'm peering out the window. The hellhounds are circling. There's no sign of Artemis or Honora, which is troubling.

"Why did they attack now?"

"Because I pissed them off at the convention!"

"No, he's right," Rhys says, reloading his crossbow. "You pissed them off a long time ago. What's changed?"

"I don't know! They have Artemis and Honora on their side now. They had room in their calendar for a quick castle assault. They threw a dart and it hit 'screw over Nina' on a board. Does it matter?"

"It might!"

"Well, we don't have time to figure it out now! Leo, get into the tower wing. Rhys, Cillian, take up sentry in the Council wing. You should have a good view out of Bradford Smythe's old rooms. Pick them off if they come near."

"Anyone who comes near?" Rhys asks, hesitant.

I almost say yes, that's how focused I am on protecting the castle. But Artemis. And, hells, Honora. I don't want her dead. If only so I can rub her defeat in her face. "Legs until you can see their faces. Then heart shots, assuming vamps or demons."

"On it."

"Be careful," Cillian says.

"Oh, I don't plan on being careful. I plan on being vicious."

Jade appears from the dorm wing. Her head is still bleeding, but she has my discarded crossbow and looks terrifying as opposed to terrified. "Took out two more. If you can cover me, I'll go to the shed and get supplies to blow up their vans so they can't get away."

My mother cuts a hand through the air. "Too risky. There are hellhounds out there. Post yourself at the far end of the dorm wing. Guard our backs."

Jade scowls, but she nods and disappears where she came from.

"We do need to neutralize the hellhounds." My mother checks the safety on her gun. "I seem to recall we're both pretty good at—"

That's when the front doors blow up.

24

MY HEAD RINGS, AND I COUGH AS BITS of dust and plaster and centuries-old stone particles invade my lungs. I scramble to my feet, blinking away the grit and expecting a hellhound to lunge at me from the gaping hole where the front doors are hanging wildly by one hinge. But no hellhounds are prowling.

"Hey, Wheezy! Catch!"

I turn just in time to have my own mother thrown into me. I catch her, stumbling backward and nearly falling. I set my mother on her feet. She straightens her suit jacket and pulls out a sleek black club. "Thank you."

Honora stands across from us, one of those wretched shock sticks in her hand. I'm going to take it from her, and then I'm going to shove it down her—

"You were supposed to be unconscious." Honora's hair isn't even mussed, a sleek high ponytail showing off her lustrous dark locks. She's wearing perfectly fitted black pants, combat boots, and a black sweater. She's like an advertisement for traitorous assholes—*betray your people, but look good doing it!*

Now it's not the grit that's making it hard to see. It's the pulsing red on the edges of my vision. "Yeah, well, you were supposed to be screaming 'my arm!'"

She tilts her head in confusion. I rip one of the heavy doors the rest of the way off and throw it at her. She only has time to raise one arm to protect herself, and the door slams into her forearm with a bone-shattering blow.

"You bitch!" she screams, clutching her arm and dropping to her knees.

I shrug. "It's not 'my arm,' but it's close enough."

"Nina." My mother's voice is sharp. "Careful."

"Not with her." I refuse to try and hold myself back. Not for Honora. I take a step toward her, then twist to the side as a dart whistles through the air, hitting the wall behind me.

Artemis reloads. Judging by her position, she came from somewhere else in the castle—the dorm wing, or the Council residence hall, or the kitchen. I don't know which. I was too focused on my prey. Artemis is holding a pillow, of all things, in one hand. But in the other, she has the dart gun trained directly on me.

"Artemis," our mother says, "you are grounded."

Honora laughs, her normally low voice high and tight with pain. "You're all lunatics. All you had to do was give up some demons. Now look at us."

I don't take my eyes off the dart gun, but I'm trembling with rage. "You came here! To our home!"

"This isn't a home," Artemis says. "It never was." She tosses the pillow to Honora and then fires three darts at me. I twist out of the way, jumping and somersaulting across the floor. None of the darts hit me.

"Oh." Our mother stumbles to the side, then leans against the wall and slides to the ground. One of the darts is embedded in her shoulder. "So grounded," she slurs before her eyes close.

"You tranqued our mom!" I point accusingly at where she's lying on the floor.

Artemis reloads. "Yes, I did."

"Why are you doing this?"

"You wouldn't understand. You're the last person who could understand." She circles. I follow her, not letting her get behind me or to the door to the gym where Doug is.

I used to be the only person who understood her. Now? She's right. I don't. "What happened to you?"

She laughs wildly, gesturing to the castle. "This happened to me, Nina. You happened to me. You have no idea how it feels to be powerless. To know as much as we do and be totally dependent on others to fight it."

"Of course I do! I had to watch you be the capable one, the strong one, the one who always got picked. I was powerless for sixteen years of my life!"

"No! You were *always* chosen. From the day we were born. *You* were chosen. Well, I'm choosing myself. I don't need ancient mystic forces determining I'm worthy of power. I'm going to do it myself. And then no one will be able to hurt me, or hurt you, or hurt any of us."

"*You're* hurting us!"

"Means to an end." She lifts the gun and fires several darts so fast I barely have time to dodge.

"Don't think I don't see what you're doing."

She raises an eyebrow. "Oh?"

"You're angling me away from Honora while she sneaks off." I stop moving, raising both my fists. "She can't get away. I'm faster and I'm stronger and I'm better than her. Not only is Doug staying here, but she is too. We have a whole dungeon waiting for her."

"Actually," Honora says, sweat beading on her forehead from the pain of her arm, "she's angling you in front of the door so that this can happen."

The snarl behind me is just enough warning. I turn and catch the hellhound as it barrels into me. It takes me to the floor, and I hold its jaws where they're desperately straining for my neck. Hot, sticky saliva drips down on me. I kick up into its stomach, launching it off me and through the air. It hits the wall with a thud and lands with a yelp, scrambling to right itself. I pull out a stake, but the hellhound changes direction and lunges for my unconscious mother.

Two darts stick out of its back before it gets there, and it stumbles, then slumps down.

Artemis doesn't lower her gun, instead firing another dart at me. I dodge, then run at her, hitting her stomach with my shoulder and carrying her across the great hall with my momentum before tossing her down. I'm about to grab her—and do what, I don't know, but my heart is racing and my anger is eating me alive, hotter and fouler than the hellhound's saliva. But a popping sound precedes Tsip.

"Nina!" she says, crying. "It's terrible!"

I whirl around. The door's intact! No one could have gotten in to Doug! "What? What happened?"

Tsip holds out her hand. Her palm is lined with dust. "Their eyes turned into dust! All the pretty eyes! And it's my birthday."

I grit my teeth and clench my fists. "Tsip. Get back to your post right now, or so help me, I'll take your own eyes and gift wrap them for you." It's not an empty threat. I know as I'm saying it that I'd do it. But I don't have time to feel disgusted with myself.

She scowls, her lower lip trembling. "That would totally defeat the purpose." She disappears, and I turn back to Artemis to see her slip something into her mouth. Doubtless one of their demonic booster drugs.

"It won't matter." I fold my arms and watch her stand up. "You can't beat me. And yes, I noticed Honora is gone. I'll catch her."

A hellhound howls. Artemis turns sharply toward the sound. It's not coming from this side of the castle. It howls again. It's coming from the back corner.

The tower.

The pillow Artemis stole. She must have come from the kitchen. Which meant she stole something there that had a scent. And the only person they could possibly want to hunt who had a pillow there—

"Not the demons," I whisper. *Leo.* They're after Leo. He was right to question why they'd attack now. Because it was never about Doug, never about the other demons or revenge or anything. It was about the one new factor at the castle. Leo.

Artemis launches herself at me in a flurry of punches and kicks so fast I can barely block them. She drives me back across the great hall toward the dorm wing, the opposite direction I need to go. The tower is through the kitchen, which is accessed via the entrance to the Council wing.

I dodge a punch and then grab her arm, spinning her and throwing her into the wall. I sprint across the great hall and into the Council wing, whipping around the corner to the kitchen. I can get to the tower through an old door and passageway here. But someone could get in from the outside if they scaled the side up to a few of the gaping holes we didn't have money to fix. I have to beat them. I have to—

Artemis slams into me from behind, sending me flying into one of the fridges. The metal dents. I don't. I pick up one of the rolling stainless steel counters and throw it at her, knocking her down. I'm almost to the door. She grabs my foot and tugs, tripping me and climbing onto me to hold me down. I flip onto my back and kick her off. The door is locked, so I break the handle and shoulder it open, the wood splintering and my shoulder screaming in agony.

It's almost pitch-black. We never bothered wiring this part of the castle, for obvious reasons. I sprint down the damp stone passageway, my heart in my throat. I just got him back. No one gets to take him away from me.

The hallway curves ahead of me, and I can see dim light. Pelly yelps, and I push for another burst of speed. But my foot catches on a stray jumble of stones. I go down hard. It's enough time for Artemis to catch up to me. She jumps on me, trying to pin me. I throw her off and scramble to my feet. Turning the corner so fast I skid and nearly fall again, I'm greeted with a wide circle of a crumbling room, half the floor covered in rubble. Moonlight streaks in from the gaping holes twelve feet up the wall. One of the holes reveals a vampire scrambling up a rope, Leo following. Honora is standing at the top. She takes Leo's hand to help him out—he's climbing out of his own free will—and then they disappear out of my sight.

I run and leap for the hole, but Artemis grabs my foot, interrupting my trajectory. I slam into the wall instead, falling on her.

She rolls so she's on top, pinning my arm behind me. "You never took the real Watcher lessons. They were all about acceptable sacrifices. Demons are always acceptable sacrifices. Even Leo knows that."

I slam my elbow up and back, catching her on the jaw. She falls off me, and I jump to my feet. "He's not a demon! He's one of us!"

"But it was okay to hurt Honora? She's one of us too!"

"She chose to leave!"

"So did he! So did I, for that matter! Are you going to break my arm?"

We stand across from each other, chests heaving.

She rubs her jaw. "I'm making the hard decisions. The ones you never could. You have to trust me."

"How can I?"

"Because I'm your sister. I've always protected you." Artemis sounds hurt. After everything she's done, she still expects me to trust her? To let her do these terrible things for terrible people? She lured me out of the castle and set vampires on me. She brought hellhounds and vampires into my home. Against people I love.

Leo wanted so desperately to trust his mother that he kept the truth from all of us, and Bradford Smythe paid the ultimate price. I nearly did too.

I don't trust Artemis. I won't let myself.

My posture betrays my intentions as I lean toward the hole to go after Leo. Artemis leaps at me. I catch her and throw her against the wall. I spin with the motion, fist raised, and punch as hard as I can. She dodges, barely, and my blow goes against—and into—the crumbling tower wall. It rumbles and cracks.

Artemis and I share one wide-eyed look. I throw her out of the way before half the wall comes down on top of me.

25

BUFFY STANDS ON THE SHORE. I TRY TO
reach her. I need to reach her, to talk to her, to get her help. But
every time I get close, a roaring wave of darkness grabs ahold of
me and drags me backward. Drags me under. I can't breathe, and
I can't move.

I crawl. I'm almost to her. She stands like a beacon of light,
her blond hair brilliant and shining.

"Some things you can't fight," she says, crouching low and
fixing her sad green eyes on me. "Some things you have to just
survive."

I reach for her. She extends her hand, but the darkness sinks
its claws deep into me and pulls me under.

Something nudges insistently at my shoulder, which in turn
makes my shoulder scream in pain. I crack my eyes open, but I
can't see anything.

I also can't breathe.

Panic surges through me, and I push out with all my might,

dislodging the stone and bricks that blanketed me. They tumble down, a small avalanche freed by my movement. I roll away, pretty sure I'm bleeding in more than one place and bruised in every single place possible. But nothing's broken that I can tell, and Artemis's coat saved a lot of my skin.

Pelly nudges me again, putting its arm out and making a low chirping noise.

"It's okay, Pelly. I'll heal fast. You keep your skin for yourself." I push to standing, shaking off the dust and bits of stone still clinging to me.

And then everything crashes back down on me in a rush of memory. Leo, climbing out. Artemis, fighting me. Artemis, who is gone, leaving me buried in the rubble.

I sag against the nearest intact wall. Because as much as that hurts, it hurts more that it was my punch that brought down the wall. My punch that was aimed at Artemis. If she hadn't dodged . . .

Gods. What happened to us? What happened to *me*? I could have killed her. If I don't know her anymore, I know myself even less.

I limp out of the tower section, broken more than physically. I don't know how much time has passed. I could run out and see if I can catch them before they escape with Leo, but—

I miss a step, nearly falling. Nope. I could not run out. Not right now, at least. The kitchen is empty, but the Great Hall isn't. My mother's still unconscious, but she's been dragged in front of the door to the gym. Jade is standing guard over both my mother and the door, bedraggled and bruised and armed to the teeth. She lifts a sword, watching behind me for enemies.

"No one gets Doug!" she shouts.

"No one was trying to." I kneel heavily next to my mother and check her pulse. It's steady. No telling how long it will take her to wake up, but she will, at least. I remember the tranquilized hellhound, but a wicked knife at Jade's side is thick with black blood. She made sure it wasn't a threat anymore. Good for her.

"Call Tsip." I lean against the wall next to my mother. "It's over. We lost."

"But Doug—"

"Leo." His name coats my tongue like the dust of the tower; I almost choke on it. "It was Leo they wanted all along. And they got him."

"Oh." Jade has the grace to sound sorry. She knocks twice on the door before pulling out the walkie-talkie and announcing the all clear. Cillian and Rhys will have a walkie-talkie, as will Ruth Zabuto and Imogen in the library and Jessi in the Littles suite.

Tsip pops up in the middle of the hall. She looks around eagerly, but there are no enemies with available eyeballs. Her shoulders deflate, and she scowls. "Is it over?"

"Yeah." It's over. It's all over. Everything. Sanctuary. Me. Because if I couldn't protect Leo, and I couldn't stop myself from almost killing my own sister, how can I claim to protect anyone? I'm not a Watcher. I'm not a Slayer.

I'm a failure.

I'm a monster.

All that extra demon in me has nothing to say now. It won. There's no reason for it to gloat or try to take over. It already has me.

"What should we do?" Jade asks. The sound of boards being

pried free from the door behind us is the only noise in the cavernous Great Hall. It'll take Doug forever to get out. Not that it matters. There's no rush. We have no plan. No way of making one. And I'm certainly not going to try.

Leo is gone. Artemis is lost to me. Sean and Honora and their zealots won.

"Nina?" Imogen rushes into the Great Hall. I stand so fast I almost fall over. She's covered in blood and shaking.

"Where are you hurt?" I look for a wound, but I can't find one.

"It's not—it's not my . . ." She takes a deep breath. "Ruth is dead. It was Artemis."

"*No.*" No. I run past Imogen, careening off walls, my balance not quite back yet and my speed too much for my battered body. I get to the library to find the door ajar. That crack of light spilling from inside slices me open. I push the door, not wanting to see. Needing to see.

Ruth is splayed on the floor. Her plaid skirt has ridden up, revealing baggy nylon panty hose, and I want to sob at how much I know she'd hate that I saw that. Instead of her favorite pair of fake pearls, her throat wears a jagged red line, the dark pool beneath her rippling.

Rippling. Which means there's still blood flowing into it. Which means Ruth's heart is still beating. "Pelly!" I scream. "Pelly!"

Pelly races in behind me. It doesn't even pause. It crouches next to Ruth and pulls off a strip of skin from its forearm, the skin thin and translucent. It puts it over the slit in Ruth's throat, stopping the blood.

I kneel in the pool, feeling it soak into my pants. I put my fingers against Ruth's repaired throat, hoping, praying. Her own skin is papery thin, Pelly's replacement smooth. But there's no pulse. No pulse. The darkness inside me wells, threatening to swallow everything, but then, there! A flutter. The tiniest brush of life. Ruth isn't dead.

"Rhys is O-negative!" I shout, not knowing who I'm shouting to.

Jade answers. She followed me. "I'm on it. I'll get him and a stretcher." I hear her sprinting away down the corridor. There's nothing I can do for Ruth until I have Rhys and some supplies.

"Tsip!" I scream.

She pops up next to me. "Yes?"

"Go check on Jessi and the Littles and the other Slayers. Come back immediately and tell me they're okay." They have to be okay.

She nods and disappears. When she comes back, she's scowling. "They almost staked me! They're so jumpy."

"Did you appear in the closet next to them?"

"Yes, obviously. That was fastest."

I take a deep breath, my heart hammering, my soul as bruised as my body. "But everyone there is okay."

"Yes. Jessi yelled at me for scaring the small people, though."

"Go back—through the door this time—and tell Jessi to take them to Cillian's house. Tell them to leave through the window. I don't want the Littles seeing any of this." Not the hellhound corpse, not my unconscious mother, and certainly not this horror in the library.

Oh gods, what will I tell the Littles if Ruth dies? She's Thea's great-great-aunt and basically a grandmother to all of them. We never should have kept the Littles here. We should have sent them away years ago. My idea for Sanctuary was not only inherently flawed, it was deeply selfish. I'm as bad as the old Watchers. I decided it was going to be what I wanted it to be, and I barreled forward, not considering the risks.

Now Ruth Zabuto still might die, Leo is taken, and these little kids could have been kidnapped or worse. Because if Artemis did this to Ruth, then I was wrong to assume she'd leave the Littles alone. I have no idea what she is capable of. Maybe I never did.

And it is all—entirely, every bit of it—my fault. I let Artemis do everything she did.

I can't wrap my head around the image of my sister slitting ancient Ruth's throat, though. Why? Why would she do this? What happened to her?

"Nina," Imogen says. She eyes Ruth with shock. "She's not dead? I thought she was dead. There's no way someone could survive that."

Rhys gasps a sob, taking his grandmother's hand. I help Cillian load her onto the stretcher.

"She's stronger than anyone," Cillian says. "She'll make it."

"Rhys, we're giving her your blood."

He nods through his tears. I know the basics of how to do a blood transfusion. It's one of the things I studied more than anything else. I thought I'd have to use it someday because of a vampire attack.

Not because of my own sister.

"Cillian, I'm sending the Littles to your house. But I need to know. Is it safe?" I can't discount the fact that his mom has items connecting her to all of this. She was willing to talk to me, but I never got to visit and find out what she knows. And Artemis pretended to be willing to talk to me too. We can't trust family anymore. We can't trust anyone.

Cillian squeezes my shoulder. It hurts. "She's not a bad person. I'm sure."

Jade picks up one end of the stretcher. "Come on, let's get to the medical center. Then I'll come back to help . . . clean up." She used to work closely with Ruth. They both specialized in magic before it died. Jade stares down at Ruth, who is so much lighter than her mounds of shawls would have hinted at. She barely feels here at all. It makes it seem that much more likely she won't stay. Cillian gently nudges me out of the way and takes the other end of the stretcher. I follow them down the hallways, both moving as fast as is safe while Rhys pads alongside his grandmother, still holding her hand.

Artemis. My sister. My mirror image. Attacking wrinkled and perpetually beshawled Ruth Zabuto, whom we've known since we were little girls. Putting a knife to her throat and cutting.

I try not to picture it, but I can't picture anything else as we hurry through the hallways toward the place where maybe I can still help at least one person.

Two hours later, Rhys is down quite a bit of blood and his grandma seems stable, as far as I can tell. I debated sending her to the nearest hospital, but it's an hour away. I don't doubt she would have died before getting there, and I don't know how we'd explain her injury or the way it was closed. I've got her on a fluid IV, and we're monitoring her vitals. Her pulse is weak but steady. She hasn't woken up, though.

I'm sitting in the hall outside the medical center. Having Ruth on a cot inside with Rhys sitting next to her takes up nearly all the space, but I don't want to be far in case she wakes up.

Imogen seems surprised to see me there. She must be here to check on Ruth. She peers inside and sees Rhys there. "You two should go rest. I'll watch her."

"No," Rhys says. His voice is raw but determined.

She hesitates, then joins me on the floor. "How are you?"

"I can't figure it out. Why would Artemis try to kill Ruth? Can you tell me exactly how it happened?"

Imogen sighs. "Artemis came into the castle through the library window. Ruth tried to stop her. I was behind the false shelves in the secret room guarding the passage. By the time I got out, it was too late."

"*Almost* too late," I correct. I need that "almost" more than I've ever needed anything. "She's too old. I should never have kept her here. Or the Littles. I put everyone at risk." I hang my head and put my hands over my eyes. "You were all at risk this whole time just by being around me. I threatened Tsip, and I meant it. And I almost—I could have—Imogen, I could have killed someone today. A person, not a vampire."

Imogen reaches out and takes my hand, squeezing it. "But you didn't. Your sister did, though. Or at least tried to. She cut Ruth's throat, Nina, and she left you for dead too."

"When are we going after her?" Rhys asks. He's standing in the doorway. His face is grim and cold, the bandage on his arm evidence of what he was willing to sacrifice to keep his grandma alive.

"I don't know."

"Not good enough," he snaps. "You knew, didn't you? You knew she was working with these maniacs. And you didn't tell us."

"I knew," I whisper.

"And now my grandma is—" He chokes on the words. When he can speak again, his voice is cold. "You protected Artemis, and we all paid the price. No more. We need a plan."

Imogen laces her fingers through mine. "We're going to get Leo back, which means we're going to face her again. And we need to know that you understand."

"Understand what?" I don't understand *anything*.

"She chose a side, and it wasn't ours. She's our enemy. We can't afford to think of her as anything else now. I'm worried— hell, I'm terrified—that next time you go against her, she won't be satisfied with burying you under a tower wall. We almost lost Ruth. We still might. We can't afford to lose you."

I want to cover my face again, hide from this, but Imogen has my hand. "She's my sister."

Rhys snorts an ugly sound. "Didn't stop her from leaving you buried under half the castle. She doesn't care about you. She doesn't care about any of us."

Imogen's voice is softer. "I know she's your sister. Which is why it has to be *you* who stops her. Promise me that if it comes down to you and Artemis, you'll make the right choice."

"We owe it to my grandma," Rhys says. "You know she would have died to protect any of us. Even to protect Artemis." He spits her name.

"Promise you'll make the right choice," Imogen repeats.

Artemis once made me promise the same thing. That I'd choose myself over her. I didn't, and we nearly got a new hell-mouth. I thought we'd averted the end of the world, but it feels like it quietly ended in the last few days and I didn't notice until it was too late.

Artemis chose Honora and Sean over us. Artemis tried to kill Ruth. Artemis could have killed me. And Artemis took Leo. I can't meet the pain and fury in Rhys's eyes, or the weight in Imogen's.

"I promise," I whisper to the floor.

ARTEMIS

THEY HAD A CAGE ALL READY TO GO FOR him, but Leo is in no shape to run or fight. He can barely even stand. It hurts Artemis to look at him slumped in there. She always liked him. Admired him. Envied him, even.

But he should never have passed his Watcher test. He proved he would choose his mother over the world, or at least over the Watchers. He knew what she was and he let her continue. Did he know what *he* was, even back in the days they trained together? He must have. He was always the most careful, the most precise. The most controlled. Because unlike the rest of them, his inner demons were literal. Does that make them easier to fight, though? When they have a name, a species, a neat little Latin classification?

Artemis's own demons aren't so easily defined. She can't forget the look on Nina's face as she pushed Artemis toward safety. Yes, Nina brought down the wall by trying to hit Artemis so hard even Artemis doesn't know if she would have recovered, but Nina also shoved her out of harm's way. And then Artemis left her there. Buried.

It's gnawing at her, wriggling inside like an infection. Maybe she's doing the wrong thing. Maybe she betrayed her sister and stole a friend and manipulated the only girl she's ever loved and none of it will work out. She wasn't chosen, after all. She never wins. Not really.

She looks away from Leo in the cage, focusing on her girl-friend, who's checking the other cages in these caverns and marking down demonic inventory. "How'd you get him to go with you?" Artemis asks Honora.

Honora looks up from her pad. "Same way someone could make me willingly walk to my doom." She looks back down, swallowing but keeping her expression light and disinterested. "Threaten the person I love most in the whole world."

It's the closest Honora has come to saying *I love you*. Neither of them has. Maybe neither of them is capable of it, after the ways they were raised. Maybe Artemis doesn't deserve it and never will. Artemis's throat aches, her eyes burn.

Her voice comes out a whisper so she won't cry. "What if it's the person you love most in the world who's leading you to doom?"

"Then I would die like I wanted to live. Believing in her. Fighting at her side."

Artemis wipes under her eyes. She will win. She has to. For Honora. For Nina. But most of all for herself, so she can be the person she needs to be to deserve any of this. To be strong enough to keep it. "For the record, I love you too."

Honora closes her eyes. The look on her face is so raw and private that Artemis knows to turn away. To give Honora time alone to feel everything she needs to. Artemis just hopes they have enough time left.

She walks across a catwalk and sits next to Leo where he's leaning against the rough stone wall of the cavern that forms the back of his cage. On one of the metal catwalks nearby, chains are being welded to the platform in front of the thing that will solve all of Artemis's problems. Including the pain she feels thinking about Nina. When Nina sees the results, she'll understand. And Honora won't have to worry about anything, ever again.

There's scraping and moaning and a few sharp snarls. A line of chained demons is being arranged, prodded into place by the black-cloaked zealots. Artemis hates the Sleeping One worshippers with an instinctive self-preservation and has done what she could to avoid speaking to any of them. How long have they been working on these caverns? Or have the caverns always been here, ready and waiting?

"Why?" Leo asks.

Artemis doesn't look at him. "What would you do to protect my sister?"

"Anything."

"Me too." Artemis is only half lying. She *would* do anything. Has done everything. And it didn't matter. Ever since the day she had to watch Nina get left behind in that fire, she's been trying to protect her and failing at it. She couldn't protect Nina from the pain of her crush on Leo, from the rejection of the Watchers, from the dismissal of her healing interests and efforts to improve things. She couldn't protect either of them from the heartbreak of a cold, distant mother. Or from the death of their father. She would love to be able to protect Nina. *Will* love to be able to.

But more than that, she wants to protect *herself*. She can't deny it. Not after what she's done to get to this point.

Artemis doesn't want to hurt anymore. She doesn't want to have to watch these things happen and not be able to fix them. She doesn't want Watchers like her father to die, or people like Honora to work every day to undo and hide the damage done by her own mother. She doesn't want Nina to have to be a Slayer, to risk her life because she can't stop caring about everyone and everything.

The world is *so broken*, and it hurts too much. She has no desire to be its god, not like the Sleeping One. She just wants enough actual power to change things. Maybe if she had been the Slayer, it would be different. But it's not. Not yet. Not until she *makes* it different.

She doesn't want to hurt Leo, but she will. In his Watcher test, he once chose the world over what he loved most. She's hoping what he loves most now is Nina, and that he makes the wrong choice.

She nods toward the demons. "You know all those breeds. You know what they do. Each and every one of them is a mindless predator."

"Then kill them. Don't ask me to drain them. It's cruel. It's wrong."

"But you're dying without it."

"I don't care." He looks haunted. "Once I start, what if I can't stop? What if I turn into my mother? I won't risk it. Better to die."

Artemis rolls her eyes. "Gee, that's noble. So glad you—a perfectly nice, nonmurdery mostly human who knows enough about the world to actually protect the innocent in it—are choosing to die rather than let all these vicious demons die instead.

You know that one drinks bone broth made from children, right? Judging by the rings on his claws, he's been alive for a few hundred years. Imagine how many children that is. How many bowls of soup. But sure. Better that you don't risk maybe someday hurting someone."

"You're twisting this. Me choosing not to benefit from killing these demons is not the same as turning them loose." Leo regards her with a calm gaze. He was always good at seeing through people. It's inconvenient. She doesn't want to be seen right now.

"Fine. Don't do it. You're right, I won't let them go even if you don't drain them. But what do you think will happen to Nina?"

"She'll get over me." The words hurt for him to say, but he believes them.

"No, you arrogant dolt. It's not about her *feelings* for you. It's about Nina herself. If they can't get power transferred from you, they're going to go looking for new sources. And who do we know—who do they know—who's positively bursting with power?"

"No," he whispers.

"They'll see the same thing your mother did. Helping them was the only way I could steer them away from Nina. But if you don't work out, there will be nothing I can do. I can't fight a hellgod, Leo. And I don't think Nina can either." She leans close, almost pressing against the bars, and whispers. "I have a plan. Do what they tell you to. Take the power. Transfer it. Charge up his amplifier. And *trust me*. It's the demons or it's Nina."

It's not. She would never let Nina get close to the Sleeping

One. It wouldn't work anyway, without an incubus- or succubus-type demon to transfer the power. But Leo doesn't know that. And thankfully he's too depleted, too exhausted, too desperately in love with her sister to see through Artemis's lie.

She softens her voice, makes it more like Nina's, then puts her hand through the bars to rest it on his arm. "You were going to let yourself die to keep her safe. Live to keep her safe, instead."

This—feeding on other living creatures—is the line Leo chose, the one he wouldn't cross. If she were really his friend, she would find another way to make this all work.

She can't afford to be his friend. She sees the moment on his face when Leo breaks. He nods. "I'll do it."

Artemis squeezes his arm, then stands to inform Sean they can start. She's waited long enough. This is the end, or the beginning, or both.

26

THE CAR BUMPS ALONG THE DIRT ROAD toward Shancoom. I'm in the back sandwiched between Jade and Doug while Rhys drives and Cillian sits in the passenger seat. My mother is slowly waking up, guarded by the purring kitten and Imogen, and I've left Tsip in charge of still-unconscious Ruth with a strict no-eyeballs mandate. The demon is still bitter over the dusty fate of her vampire trophies, and I don't want to take any chances leaving her up to her own devices. Imogen offered to be in charge of Ruth, but Tsip can get to me in a heartbeat if something is wrong.

Facing Ruth's mortality feels like the end of a Watcher era. She's the last of the old guard, two generations ahead of my own mother. The amount of experience and knowledge we almost lost today—could still lose—is too overwhelming to even think about. And I certainly can't think about who tried to take that knowledge and experience and crotchety old warmth from us.

Ruth is already working on next year's Christmas scarves

for the castle. The current one must be sitting unfinished, her needles still in it, waiting for her wrinkled, deft fingers—

The silence in the car is palpable. Everyone is hurt and everyone is angry. At Artemis, yeah, but also at me. And I don't blame them. I couldn't have known she was going to attack the castle, but I absolutely made it possible.

Rhys clears his throat, Cillian taps his fingers on the armrest, and Doug, who made certain I was sitting between him and Jade, twitches but keeps his eyes firmly on the window, staring out at the dark forest only now softening with the dawn.

It's a new day. A terrible, empty new day, ushered in with loss and failure.

We pull up to Cillian's and Rhys puts the car in park. It's obviously hard for him, but he turns around to address me. "We should talk about the plan to get Leo back."

"Didn't you want him locked up?" Jade asks. "Why do you care if Artemis took him? Our plan should be to go after her, not him."

I want to argue, but I have no right to. Not on this subject.

Rhys scowls. "Yes, I did want him locked up. By us, so we could take care of him. I didn't want him kidnapped by these fanatics for whatever nefarious purpose they have in mind."

"No one in a black cloak has ever been good news," Doug mutters in agreement.

"Magicians?" Jade offers.

"Case in point." But Doug smiles, and Jade brightens at this softening.

"It doesn't matter," I say. "Artemis will be wherever Leo is, so the goal doesn't change. And Rhys is right. Whatever they want him for, we have to stop. Our only hope is that Cillian's mom can give us a lead to track down Artemis and the zealots."

"Because someone let the zealots steal our book that could have shed light on the problem." Rhys's jaw twitches. Normally, Cillian would reach over to soothe him, but Cillian has his arms folded tight, his face unreadable. I don't know who in the car he's most angry at. If it's me, he's not alone. I'm most angry at me too.

Cillian pulls out the necklace we took from the cloakers and holds it in his palm. I know how much it's going to cost him to face whatever we're going to find out. It means letting go of his memories of his father, potentially replacing them with bad things. His mother asked me to keep him away from it all, but thanks to my choices, that's not an option anymore.

"Cillian." Rhys lifts a hand toward him. Rhys is pale, and his hand shakes slightly, but he seems okay in spite of having donated so much blood. Cillian takes Rhys's hand and squeezes it.

"Let's do this." We follow Cillian inside. The Littles must have been bundled into Cillian's room with Jessi, and this early it's still quiet. But the light in the kitchen is a warm island in the chilly ocean of the dawn. Cillian's mother dances around the kitchen humming as she prepares food. We shuffle in. The space isn't large enough for all of us, so Doug and Jade sit at the table for three, while Rhys, Cillian, and I block the entrance and exit to the kitchen. I don't know if we stage it this way on purpose, but she can't get out without going through us.

Jessi appears on the stairs and glares at us all. "Be *quiet*," she hisses, before disappearing back upstairs.

"Oh, hello!" Esther beams and her eyes sweep over us. They pause on Doug, but only long enough to register mild surprise and then move on. She does know about demons, after all. She continues bustling about, pulling things from cupboards and the fridge. "I wasn't sure what the little ones would like, so I'm making a bit of everything. I thought today we'd take a picnic to the beach. It will be cold, but I'll bundle them up. Then we can stop by the shop for a treat if Jessi says it's okay. She's quite intense, isn't she? But I love the shop. It's so well done, Cillian. You really changed that space for the better." She seems genuinely happy to have the Littles here, excited at the prospect of taking them for a fun outing. Gods, don't let her be secretly evil. Please let this mom be a good one.

Cillian leans against the counter and folds his arms. "That's great, Mum. Do let us know if you decide to run away to Tibet or Madagascar or Shangri-la as a change of plans, though. We'll need at least five minutes' notice."

Her reflexive smile is tight and defensive. "Give me a moment and I can make you all eggs. You still like them sunny-side up, right?"

Cillian doesn't answer. He pulls out the necklace instead. She flinches as it winks in the light. "What is this?"

"Toast?" Her glance at me is accusatory. I wasn't supposed to bring Cillian into it.

"It's too late," I say. "I'm sorry. We have nowhere else to turn."

Cillian moves to block her path to the toaster oven. "This is our only lead. You *owe* me this. If we don't find these people, our friend will die."

His mom's hands tremble as she reaches up and smooths the wrap around her braids. "What—what can this have to do with your friend?"

"The people wearing this symbol took him. And it can't be a coincidence that Da's puzzle is the same pattern. Was he involved with this before he died? Were you? *Are* you? Because they're all zealots, and you've spent a lot of time trying to find God or religion or whatever."

The kettle whistles, and Cillian's mom shuffles around him to pull it off the heat. She pours five cups of tea and pauses on the sixth, raising an eyebrow at Doug. He shakes his head, and she sets the kettle back on the stove. We each get a mismatched mug. I take Jade hers, not wanting to let Cillian's mom away from where we have her cornered. Jade's face is bruised, her lip swollen, and I catch Doug staring at the damage with an unreadable expression.

Cillian's mom wraps her hands around her mug and turns to face us, leaning against the counter with the same physical posture I've seen Cillian do a hundred times. "Your father isn't dead."

Cillian chokes on his tea. "What?"

"In my defense, I never said he was dead."

He sets his tea down on the tile counter. We're all frozen, unsure where this is going. "Yes," Cillian says, "you did."

"No. I try not to lie to you. If you remember, all I ever said— all I have ever said—is that we lost your father. I meant that literally. We lost him."

"I think we should sit down." Rhys takes Cillian's elbow and leads him to the worn pink sofa. I can't tell whether Cillian looks like he's more likely to pass out or murder someone. I sit on his other side, both to support him and to keep him in place in case he does decide to strangle his mother.

Esther sits on a chair across from us, balancing her mug on her knee and staring down into it as though the tea leaves might reveal an easier way to tell this story.

"I was a student of fairy tales. Grad school. I wanted to teach. I've always been interested in oral traditions, the stories we pass down generation to generation. Why we tell the stories we do. I traveled the Irish countryside, asking for regional variations of the tales of fair folk. I found the same general information in every single one, but some of the towns and villages had details—very specific details. A hill you should never visit at night. A path that should never be walked alone. A house that was abandoned two hundred years ago and still stands unclaimed to this day. I could sense the power behind their fear. It wasn't terror—it was self-preservation. It had all the same rules and practical steps as my spells. And that got me interested. I went to one of the abandoned houses at night, made a protective circle, and I waited. At midnight, a portal opened." She pauses, then looks up at Doug. "I'm sure none of you will be surprised to learn that our world contains—contained— gateways and portals to other worlds. These weren't fairy paths and fairy doors. They were openings to other dimensions. Hell dimensions. All the stories about keeping your loved ones safe from ageless, unknowable beings who would take them and never return them, or return them so altered you wouldn't recognize them, were true. They were just about demons, not fairies. Same concept, different name."

"I like 'fair folk' better than 'demon.'" Doug shrugs. "Has a nicer ring to it."

"It does, doesn't it? But most of the folk were far from fair. I was lucky that first night. Nothing came out, and I ran as fast as I could. Then I picked my next move very carefully. I wanted to prove my theory was correct. That we were telling ourselves stories about demons, that the Irish had always known about these connections to other worlds and had been protecting themselves for generations. So I found a village with stories about one specific fairy. The Sleeping One, they called him, because he had no name. Once a year, every year, every single person in the village left. They abandoned their homes, their businesses, their lives. When I asked why, they couldn't tell me, other than that it wasn't safe. And sure enough, a cursory search of newspaper archives from that annual date showed missing persons going back decades. So that year, when they all fled, I set a trap."

She sips her tea, frowning. "It was arrogant. But I was young and ambitious, and I wanted a demon. It turned out I was even more ambitious than I meant to be, though, because I didn't catch a demon that day." She sighs, looking out the window at a place and a day far from our own. "I caught a god."

It's Rhys's turn to choke on his tea. "You caught a god?"

"A minor one. But yes."

"Wait," Cillian says. "There are gods—plural?"

"Yeah." I shrug. "It depends on your definition of a god, but there are countless hellgods, some midlevel benevolent ones.

Powers-that-be that sometimes fiddle with our own earth. We're not sure whether they still have access now that magic is dead."

Cillian leans back into the couch, rubbing his forehead. "So all this time, when you said 'oh my gods,' you weren't being cute. You were being accurate."

"I like to cover my bases." I gesture toward Esther. "But when you say you caught a god, what do you mean by that?"

Cillian's mother has refocused on us. She's watching Cillian with careful concern. "I was quite good at magic. I drew from a variety of sources. Irish, English, Nigerian. The traditions melded in surprising ways, and I drew a lot more power than I would have had I specialized in only one like my college coven wanted me to. There's a lot to be said for knowing your heritage. When the god stepped into the village to look for a sacrifice, he stepped into my trap. My nets fell on him, binding him to this world and to me. But once he was there and I had him, I didn't know what to do with him. I panicked." She swirls her remaining tea around in her mug. "I defaulted to my British training, and I invited him to sit down for tea with me. We talked. He had been visiting earth for countless generations, siphoning power. Like we were an outlet and he was recharging himself. It takes a lot of energy to sustain godhood."

"Naturally," Jade mutters. "Can't be all-powerful without a lot of power."

"So you had a bound hellgod and you were drinking tea. Then what?" Cillian isn't looking at her, or any of us. His eyes are fixed on the floor, and his hand is gripping the necklace so tightly it must be cutting into his palm.

"Well, we . . . we hit it off. He was really interesting, and quite charming and handsome."

"Mum." Cillian's hand twitches. "You are not telling me my father is a hellgod."

"A *minor* one. But yes. Technically. Though he resented it when I referred to his home dimension as 'hell.' He felt it was reductive." She takes a prim sip. "He did quite like being called a god, though."

Rhys lets out a long, controlled breath. "Then you brought him back here and played house with him."

She shrugs. "I couldn't let him go, knowing what he was. Eventually his power would drain. If he spent long enough here without sacrifices, he would become human. I debated the morality of it, of course. Of deciding this ageless creature should no longer be able to do what he was designed to do. But that had to be weighed against the countless generations of people who had been sacrificed to him. And, well, I liked him. It was lonely, being the only witch in Shancoom. Honestly, he was happy. He had been doing the same things for so long they had ceased to have meaning. Watching him discover the world, feel things as a human, was really wonderful. He never tried to break the binding, never asked to be free. I loved him, and I really do think he loved me, too. When I fell pregnant, he—well, when I say he glowed with happiness, I mean it literally. He was thrilled. He had been alone for so long too. We had that in common. And we both wanted you, Cillian."

Cillian is silent. I can't imagine what must be going through his head. Aside from the decidedly complicated question of whether a hellgod bound by magic can give consent, the sheer fact that his parentage is half not of this world would be enough to set anyone over the edge. I reach out and take his hand in mine, squeezing.

"So what went wrong?" Jade asks.

"Everything was normal. Happy. I had the magic shop. He volunteered with the local police force, helped out in the shop, took over the bulk of the parenting and housekeeping. But then a few years ago, I came home early with a headache and caught him in the shed with Cillian. They had that triangle receptacle. I didn't know where he got it, or how, but I recognized the symbol from the town where he'd crossed over. A circular courtyard in the center where he'd appeared had an old stone pillar with the symbol carved on it. I had thought it was a Celtic relic, but it wasn't. It was *him*. His symbol. He was teaching Cillian how to manipulate it, and then—then it started glowing. It terrified me."

"Why?" Cillian asks. "You knew what he was."

"I didn't know what *it* was. I didn't know if he was using it to siphon energy from you like one of his sacrifices. Or if . . . or if he was trying to make you into whatever he had been." She grips her mug, her posture rigid. "Either option scared me more than I'd known was possible. I had gotten complacent, so used to him and in love with our life together that I let myself forget who and what he was. And for the first time I wondered if maybe he had *let* me bind him. Maybe I had been the one without power all along. I was so distracted, that night I forgot to redo the binding." She shakes her head. "I don't know. Maybe I forgot on purpose. I was in over my head, and I was scared for my child. On that very first day with him, over tea, he told me he'd kill me when he got free. He said it with a smile, casual

and cheerful." She shivers. "But when I woke up in the morning, he was gone. He just left. I think—I really do think he
loved us. In his own way."

"Why did you lie to me?" Cillian's voice breaks. "Why did
you let me think he was dead?"

"He's not the same as us. He's an ancient creature, infinite. And
when he was no longer tied to us, he had no choice. He had to go
back to what he was. But he loved us. We're still here. If he didn't
love us, if his time with us hadn't changed him, he would have killed
me. So I let you think he was dead. It felt kinder than knowing he
couldn't stay. That he went back to his own dimension."

Rhys frowns. "He went back? Just like that?"

"I never saw him again. I don't know what else he would
have done. He hated how noisy it was here. Going by his old
calendar, he was due to return this spring equinox, but he can't,
obviously."

Cillian stands, pacing. "This is so messed up. This is all so
messed up. I—I don't have time for this. We don't have time.
What's the triangle thing?" He shakes the necklace, our only link
to Leo's captors. "Why do they have it on necklaces?"

"If I had to guess, I'd say they worship him." She makes a dis-
tasteful expression, as though something is sour or rotten. "It's
tacky, really. Maybe they're trying to reach him."

"Like Eve," I say, "trying to make a new hellmouth."

Jade leans back in her chair, her expression thoughtful.
"Could be what they need Leo for."

Rhys nods, his expression intent as he ponders these new
developments. "They heard what Leo's mum did and want him
to do the same thing."

"Would that be so bad?" I'm genuinely curious. "I mean, he's Cillian's dad."

Cillian shakes his head. "Any god who runs an operation that uses other living creatures for parts isn't a benevolent god. Plus, he's missed every single birthday and Christmas even though he knew exactly where I was and could have come back to earth any time before magic died. Even if it was just for a day. He might be a god, but he's still a deadbeat dad."

Cillian's mom looks sad. Then she shakes her head, her expression resetting into firm disapproval. "Cillian's right. It wouldn't be good if he came back. Especially now that there's no competition. He used to talk about how he didn't stay because he could only stand to be here for a day at a time with all the other powers and demons competing. They all sort of held one another at bay. If a god—any god—could get a foothold here now, they'd have no rival. It would be bad." She gestures to the necklace dangling from Cillian's hand. "I don't know that it's much to go on. The triangle is his name. It's a symbol, or a receptacle. I'm not sure. He would never talk to me about it. All this time I've been studying, trying to learn more about various gods, about their power."

"Why, though?" Cillian stops his pacing. "You want another boyfriend?"

She recoils as though he struck her. "I did it for *you*. Because I worry. About the parts of you that are him. He can't be here for you, so I wanted to learn as much as I could. That way, if you are like him, if you do . . . change, then I can be here to help you navigate whatever comes up."

"But that's just it, Mum. You haven't been here. I've been

alone. I don't care about the parts of me that are him. I care about the parts of me that have been so scared and so alone." He doesn't turn away when Rhys stands and takes his hand. He shifts so their shoulders touch.

"I'm so sorry," she whispers, tears brimming in her eyes. "I wanted to take care of you. But I made the wrong choices. I'm so glad—I'm so glad you've had a family here, while I was gone. And I'll try my best to make it up to you."

Cillian clears his throat, trying not to cry. "I don't care if my father was some big bad bloke from another dimension. I take after you, anyway."

She laughs, then stands and wraps Cillian and Rhys up in a hug. "At least you have better taste in men than I do."

I don't want to be the reason this family reunion is disrupted, but Leo can't have much time. And I have to find Artemis. I have to stop her. "How do we find them, though?"

Cillian's mother releases him, straightening and pulling reading glasses from around her neck. She puts them emphatically into place. "Oh, I've done the research."

Rhys's face is nearly beatific as he looks at her. "Can I see it?"

"Next time, dear." She pats his shoulder. "I have so much to show you. But for now . . ." She reaches into a cupboard and pulls out a recipe book. When she opens it, it's revealed to contain hundreds of pages of notes in a cramped but efficient hand. "If they're trying to reach him, they'll go to his traditional seat of power, of course. It's a little village about two hours from here. We can start searching there."

"It's more than we had before." Rhys sounds excited.

I wish I could be excited too. But part of me hopes we don't find them. That we never find them. Because if we never find them, I never have to face Artemis. But if we never find them, Leo will die.

I think of Sineya stabbing me over and over in my dreams. Maybe she was just preparing me for what real life as a Slayer is like.

27

IMOGEN WON'T STOP HOVERING AS WE weapon up. Doug wrinkles his nose every time she's nearby.

"I'm coming," she says.

"You don't have to. I know you didn't get the fight training."

Her grin is as sharp as the series of throwing knives she sheathes onto her belt. "I've got your back, Nina. To whatever end." She hands me a wickedly curved sword. I take it, staring at my warped reflection in the blade.

Doug frowns at the selection of weapons. "I don't know how to use any of these."

I lower the sword. "You aren't coming." Whatever happens today, nothing will ever be the same. I can barely think. If I do, I start worrying about what I'll do when I see Artemis, and I can't afford to worry about that. The darkness inside me, once roaring and seeping and insistent, is comforting now. At least when I let it wash over me, I don't have to feel anything.

Doug toys absentmindedly with the gold hoops in his ears. "Sean hurt me for years. And until now, I was okay to let it go, because I was free. But he hurt you, and you're my friend. Nobody gets to hurt my friends. Besides," he says, shrugging, "I want him to know I get to go to a Coldplay concert before I defeat him."

I snort. "How can I argue with that?" I would rather Doug stay here, where he's safe, but none of us are safe here. We know that now. He's choosing to fight rather than hide, and I can't blame him for that.

My mother is sitting in a chair we dragged into the gym for her. Whatever sedatives they meant to hit me with were designed for a Slayer. She can't walk in a straight line yet. "And you're sure the Littles are safe?"

I sheathe the sword. It makes a satisfying sound as it slides into place. I try not to imagine what sound it would make going into a body. "Yeah. You know Jessi won't let anyone hurt them." She's keeping them at Cillian's house. If we don't come back, she'll take care of them forever. I'm certain of that.

Rhys is poring over Esther's collection of legends in the corner, letting Cillian do the weaponing while he does the research. Doubtless we would have had a lot more information to go on if I hadn't let Artemis walk out with that book. I've made so many mistakes. I can't afford any others.

"Has Ruth woken up yet?" Jade asks.

Rhys doesn't flinch, exactly, but the way he turns the pages has a desperate sort of precision.

"No." My mother delivers the news matter-of-factly. That single syllable holds all my fears. Ruth might never wake up. And it's my fault. And everyone knows it now.

I strap the sword onto my back. My belt is a special Watcher design; the finest Italian leather, complete with stake-and-knife-size loops. I load up. "I'm leaving the tiny purple demons here. They did a good job before." Or at least an okay job. Artemis managed pretty free range. I can't figure out how she got past them, and I can't understand their mandible-driven speech to ask. But they're better than nothing. I'm leaving Pelly here too. It's not designed for fighting. It's been in the medical center, a gentle guard over unconscious Ruth. And my mother is going to stay with her too. We debated for a long time who should go, and normally I would have voted for my mother. She has more real-world combat experience than the rest of us combined. But we don't know when she'll be back to full fighting force, and we won't leave Ruth unattended.

"Where are you going?" Chao-Ahn asks. She's in the door-way with Maricruz and Taylor. I didn't factor the three Slayers in at all. They didn't ask for any of this. They only wanted a safe space, and I couldn't give it to them.

Rhys looks up from his book. "Gotta fight a cult so we don't end up having to fight a god."

"My da," Cillian offers, a bemused frown on his face. "The god, I mean. Not the cult."

"More gods?" Maricruz throws her hands in the air. "We already fought three with Buffy. Why can't monotheism be a thing? I'm so tired of gods." Taylor flinches violently at the B-word. Maricruz pats her distractedly, her eyes on the weapons pile. "You didn't make us fight to defend the castle. Even though we could have helped."

"You would have protected the Littles, if it came to that. That was more than enough." I heft a duffel bag. It's filled with holy water and crosses. They used vampires on the assault here, though we'll reach the village during daylight, so who knows. Best to be overprepared, though. A prepared Watcher is—well, frequently still a dead Watcher. But at least a well-armed, thoroughly knowledgeable corpse.

What is a prepared Slayer? Taylor might hate the very mention of Buffy, but I need her. I wish I had been able to reach her on that dark shore. Would she understand? Would she be able to help me? Or would she see the same failure and corruption in me that Sineya does and put a sword through my belly instead of sitting down for a chat?

Tsip leans over my shoulder. "Can I have any eyes I find? It's my birthday."

I take a deep breath, steeling myself against the instinct to elbow her, to grab her and throw her into the wall. It's not fair that I have to fight feeling this way about demons and people I care about. "You said yesterday was your birthday."

She smiles slyly. "Every time I shift into the void beyond reality, I'm unmade. And when I come back, I'm remade, all brand-new. So . . . every day is my birthday."

"I'm glad I didn't make you a cake, then. Fine. You can have any nonhuman eyes you find. Except for Leo's or Doug's or anyone who is fighting on our side." I'm not sure if that was necessary to add, but her slightly disappointed nod makes me think it was.

"I am coming," Chao-Ahn says.

"Me too." Maricruz folds her arms, angling herself away from Taylor's shocked and hurt expression.

"What?" I turn from Tsip, taking in the three Slayers. They've already been through so much. And I can't guarantee anyone's safety. "You don't have to."

"Exactly." Maricruz smiles at me. "Ever since I became a Slayer, no one's given me a choice. It was go here, fight that, don't die. You didn't ask us to do anything, much less command us to do anything, other than stay safe. And you know what I realized hiding in that closet?"

I shake my head. I have no idea.

"Hiding *sucks*. Gimme that stake." She holds out her hand, and I toss it. She flips it over her hand, catching it in a neat trick. Her sweet face is transformed, and I can see how much power she has simmering under the surface. "Let's get our slay on."

"You can't leave me!" Taylor's voice is high and tight with panic.

Maricruz turns to her, her face softening. She reaches up and tucks Taylor's hair behind her ears. "I'm not leaving you. I'm going to work. And I'll be back. You have to trust that I'll come back, okay?"

Taylor nods, numb and silent. "What am I supposed to do?"

"Watch over Ruth." My mother stands, shaky but determined. "Call us if there's any change."

"Mom—"

"I'll patrol."

I sigh. I know she'd be safer inside, but I can't exactly forbid my mother to do what she does best. "You remember where the medical center is?" I ask Taylor, and she nods.

"She likes being read to," Rhys says, his voice soft. He doesn't look up. "Anything with romance in it."

"I won't leave her side." Taylor walks out. What would it feel like to walk in the opposite direction from this fight?

From every fight?

There's nothing in me that could let that happen. Not my Watcher training, not my Slayer abilities, and certainly not the humming dark *extra* that is already gathering somewhere deep inside in anticipation of what's to come.

"Should we talk about the elephant-size prophecy in the room?" Imogen asks. Everyone freezes. They're all so deliberately not looking at me they might as well be. Imogen quotes it from memory. "*'Girls of fire / Protector and Hunter / One to mend the world / And one to tear it asunder.'* So we all get the stakes, right?"

I wish it weren't true. I wanted that prophecy to be checked off, averted, officially off the books. But maybe Artemis and I are doomed to clash again and again until one of us finally succeeds. Will it be the world breaker, or the healer? And which one am I? Artemis betrayed us, yeah. But I'm the one with actual demon inside me.

Rhys clears his throat and pushes his glasses into place. I flinch, waiting for whatever he has to say. However harsh, I deserve it. But he surprises me. "No world is ending today. We've been averting apocalypses for generations; ours won't be the one to fail. Our top priority is to rescue Leo. Without Leo, all their plans fall apart."

"Why rescue him?" Jade holds up her hands in anticipation of my anger. "Hear me out. He's already dying. And he as good as told us all he's fine with it. So if it's a choice between letting them use him, or stopping them from bringing Cillian's hellgod father to earth, which do you think Leo would want us to do? Which would you want us to do? I know what I'd pick."

He told me it wasn't my choice when I talked to him. That he'd rather die than hurt anyone again.

I imagine myself a hollow shell, filled with nothing but the dregs of demonic power I never asked for and can't control. It's easier than feeling what I'm about to say. "If we can't get him away, we kill him."

With the addition of the two Slayers, plus Cillian, Tsip, Jade, Rhys, Doug, and me, we end up having to take both cars. I don't like leaving the castle without a vehicle, but it can't be helped. It's part of why my mother has no choice but to stay. There's really not room with all the people and weapons we have to take.

She stops me as we head out. "Forgive her." She doesn't have to specify who she's talking about.

"How can I?" I whisper. It's not an accusation. It's a genuine question. How can I forgive Artemis for what she's done? How can any of us?

"She's been through so much."

"We went through all the same things. And I . . ." And I could easily have killed her, or killed Von Alston, or killed any of the cloakers. Maybe the extra darkness isn't demonic. Maybe it's me. Maybe Artemis has the same thing, and she's stopped fighting it. Maybe she's still my mirror image, just a few steps farther into a blood-soaked future.

"She's your sister. Nothing changes that."

"She changed it." I shake my head. "I'll be careful. But I'll also do what I need to in order to protect the world. Artemis herself told me to make that choice."

There are tears in my mother's eyes. "I've failed you both."

I don't have time to comfort her, and I don't know how. She already lost her husband to the evil in the world. How much more will she lose? How much more will we all? "This is what we were born to, Mom. We can't live with one foot in the darkness forever without it catching up to us."

"No." Her voice is fierce, stronger. "We don't live with one foot in the darkness. We live with our shoulders against the door, holding it shut so it doesn't flood the world. Don't forget that. Remind your sister, if you can. And be careful." She hugs me, and I rest my head on her shoulder for a heartbeat. We've all lost so much. Too much. And it's not over yet.

Before I can start doubting my resolve, I turn and leave. She's wrong, though. Maybe Watchers are the ones holding the door shut. But Slayers have to walk through it in order to work.

I'm in the back of the smaller car with Doug. Cillian drives while Rhys reads certain passages of Cillian's mother's research to us. "According to this, he has three forms." He pauses and looks up at Cillian. "What is your father's name?"

Cillian shrugs. "Da."

"What did your mother call him?"

"My love."

"What did his friends call him?"

"Mate. Buddy. Pal. Chum. I don't know. I actually can't think of a single time I ever heard someone call him by a name. I was a kid, though, so maybe I didn't notice."

"Or maybe he doesn't have one. Or he doesn't have one that

human voices can say. Interesting. Well, as I was saying, three forms. And when he reaches the third form, he'll be unstoppable. But your mother doesn't seem to know what that means, or what form he's currently on. It's not much help." He hums to himself, an atonal thing he does without realizing it while he's focusing. "I can't find any specific weaknesses. I wonder why they call him the Sleeping One. Maybe because he only visited once a year?"

"If Jade were a god, that would be her name too," Doug says. His voice is laced with fondness. Maybe her extreme efforts to keep him safe—even though he's no longer supplying her with artificial happy—mended something between them.

Doug gives me a meaningful look. "And speaking of sleeping, when was the last time you did?"

I lean my head against his shoulder and close my eyes, certain I won't fall asleep.

As in every other part of my life right now, I'm wrong.

"Come *on*!" I dodge the obsidian knife as it tries to find my stomach. "I want to talk with Buffy!"

Sineya glowers at me, the effect amplified by the white face paint she wears.

"It's not my fault I have extra demon!" I twist, then run. I find myself in my childhood bedroom, the purple flames that haunted me for so long frozen. The floor is neatly lined with bodies. The bodies I created out of living people. I stand, shocked, and take them all in. There are the expected ones, but so many new additions. Rhys. Cillian. Jade. Doug. Chao-Ahn and Maricruz. My mother. Leo.

And Artemis.

She's laid out in the center, the others forming a triangle around her.

I came here to—I wanted to—I needed to—

I can't look away from the bodies. They're here because of me. This is my fault. They're all dead because of me. Because I couldn't keep them safe.

I look down in my hand to see a knife, coated in sticky black blood. I didn't just fail to protect them. I killed them. There's movement behind me, and I turn, slamming my knife into Sineya's stomach before she can get me. But it's not Sineya I've stabbed.

It's Buffy. Her eyes widen in shock, and then go blank. She slumps, limp in my arms.

"No," I whisper. "No no no no." I lay her next to Artemis and I don't know what to do.

"Hey, kid," a woman says. I turn to see the same brunette with pouty lips and big brown eyes who took me to the Slayer rave what feels like a lifetime ago. "Come with me." She takes my hand and tugs me away from my carnage.

"It's not—I didn't—"

"Hey, no need to explain. If I had a dollar for every time I've stabbed B in my dreams—or just my daydreams—well, I'd have a lot of dollars. And if she had a dollar for every time she stabbed me in real life, she'd have . . . one dollar. So I'm coming out way ahead."

I half expect her to drop me off at the rave, which is the last place I want to be. I can't think straight, the dream storm getting closer and the atmosphere crackling with the promise of destruction. It's almost here. But instead of the rave, she takes me to an office. There are a couple of flags, a neat and tidy desk, a closet, and a big set of cabinets.

She sits in the office chair behind the desk, putting her booted feet up on it. "He hated it when I did this." She smiles, but it's sad.

"Where are we?"

"Somewhere that made me feel safe back in the day, when I needed it most. I was pretty broken." She purses those full lips, stained dark red. "Not sure I'm any less broken now, but I'm better at handling it, you know? Tell me why Sineya's been gunning for you, why you bring that storm with you here, and why you thought B deserved a knife in the belly."

"I didn't—I didn't realize it was her. There were all the bodies, and I just reacted."

She nods. "Been there. Only my insta-stab reaction wasn't a dream. I ran straight here after. I almost destroyed everything, myself included, because I couldn't handle the darkness."

"I have more than you, though. So much more. Leo gave me extra when he—"

She holds up a hand, cutting me off. "So?"

"What?"

"So what? What does that change?"

"Ever since he gave it to me, I've felt different. Wrong. So mad and so scared and so guilty."

"And what does feeling that way get you?"

I can barely breathe. "I don't know. But I can't handle having extra darkness. It was so hard to accept being a Slayer, and now I have to face even more?"

"Change we don't choose is hard. Trauma puts things inside

your soul you never asked for. Sure, sometimes it's demonic. But sometimes it's just growing up."

"I've done terrible things, though."

"Did you think you'd get through life as a Slayer living in sunshine? That you'd never have to spill blood? That you'd never have to grapple with the death that's your calling?"

"You don't understand."

"Oh, honey, I do. I promise. We live in the darkness. Fight it or embrace it. But accept that even in a world of powers and gods and Slayers, nothing is going to magically heal you and make you the person you used to be. And would you want it to, if it meant sacrificing everything you've learned and become?"

My voice breaks. "Maybe." I wasn't happy, but at least I still had Artemis.

She considers it. "Fair enough. I might too. But we don't have that choice. We're Slayers. We're imbued with darkness. We live in it, and with it, and sometimes it's more than we can handle and we become it." A figure flashes next to her, a pleasant-looking middle-aged man in a suit. She doesn't look at him. A knife appears on the desk, an ornate, double-bladed, wicked-looking piece meant to kill and cause as much pain as possible in the process. "You can't go back. You can't undo whatever triggered this extra bad you're struggling through. So discover the new you. Learn to live with her. To love her, when you're ready. And find people who will go on this journey, too. Because not everyone will, but the ones who do—you fight for them and they fight for you."

"I still wish we could hit reset, though. Start over."

"Nah, not me. Then I'd be back in jail. Or worse, in Boston."

"Oh my gods." My Watcher research finally clicks into place. I've been so distracted I didn't put it together. "You're Faith."

"In the flesh. Well, sort of. I guess not really, because, dream. But yeah. You know that I know what I'm talking about." Faith leans forward, her dark eyes boring into mine. "You can't handle the pain and anger inside you? Welcome to the club. You're so much more than that, though. Maybe you messed up. You'll mess up again. But you're doing the best you can, and that's not nothing, you know?"

"But what do I *do*? I don't know how to fix everything."

"You can't. Not ever. Part of this job is recognizing that. There's evil in the world, and suffering, and loss, and there's *nothing* you can do to fix it all. So you do the best you can, and then you figure out how to live with it. Because you have to keep going, even on the days when it feels impossible, and it would be so much easier to just . . ." She trails off, looking to the side where the man is smiling warmly at her. She shakes her head and he flickers out of existence. "The darkness isn't going anywhere. But there's a difference between walking through it and *becoming* it. It doesn't control you. You got more of it than you should? Good. Use it. Use it all."

She picks up the knife and tosses it to me. I catch it. In my hand, it's shifted from a wicked tool of pain into a simple wooden stake. "Do the job," I say.

"Do the job. Save the world. Don't lose what makes you *you* in the process. And, above all, look good doing it." She winks at me. Then the desk disappears, along with the office. We're in a cemetery, but it doesn't feel menacing. It feels right.

"Thank you." I wrap my arms around her.

"Oh, sweetheart, I am not a hugger. Okay. Fine. But do not tell the other Slayers. A girl's got a reputation, you know." She pats my back. "You got this. Five by five. And next time you're in London, look me up, okay? We'll go get drunk. Wait, how old are you?"

"Oh my god, Faith," a familiar voice says. "Are you *hugging* her?"

"Dammit, B, *now* you show up?"

I straighten as Faith shoves me away. Buffy is standing with her arms folded, amused. She nods at me. "World still ending?"

"Yeah. Or ending *again*, I guess."

"It does that. You good?"

I look at Faith. If she can do this, so can I. "Not yet. But I will be."

"Look at you, Faith, being all mentor-y."

"Shut up." Faith rolls her eyes. Sineya appears behind her, glowering.

"Go on," Buffy says. "We got this. You've got places to be." She turns and intercepts the First Slayer, and I open my eyes.

When I wake up, unstabbed but still unsettled, we're nearly to the village. I wish I could have dragged Faith and Buffy out of the dream and into this car. They'd be able to fix this. They'd know exactly what to do.

I want to laugh at this newfound confidence in the most notorious Slayers in history. A year ago I would have lectured myself about their unreliability, violence, poor decision making, and general bad apple–ness.

I look out the window, wondering how they've survived this

long. Not only facing the evils outside, but the ones inside, too. If they can do it, surely I can. Can't I?

The village appears like a growth of mushrooms in a lawn. This area of the countryside has loads of these small remnants of bygone eras. Most of them are barely clinging to life via farming and tourism. But the younger generations are abandoning them for the greater job opportunities of Dublin and other cities. This one's not on the way to anywhere else, all by itself at the end of a long, wandering road.

And, unlike the waning villages elsewhere, this one seems especially, *aggressively* abandoned. Overgrown dead weeds, chipped and faded paint, sidewalks and walkways eaten by plants. Cillian slows way down as we work our way deeper in. Nothing is boarded up. There are cars neatly parked, the wheels covered in cobwebs. There's even a stroller on the sidewalk. It was like everyone up and walked away at the same time, leaving everything exactly as it was.

"Pull over." There are two children's bicycles lying on the pavement. No kid would leave a bicycle like that. Back before my dad died, Artemis and I spent every summer day on our bikes. I can almost feel the sunshine, the wind, my tennis-shoed feet furiously pedaling to leave her behind and her shouting at me to wait up.

I get out of the car and walk to the bikes. There's nothing there. Except . . . I crouch, looking at the concrete. There are two scorch marks. And ashes.

My stomach clenching, I look up at the store. It's an ice cream shop. A bell chimes with rusty weariness to mark my entrance. The power is off, dust hanging in the air. There's nothing and no one in here. The scent of spoiled milk is more a memory than anything else. I peer over the counter where someone would stand to serve the ice cream, and sure enough, there's a scorch mark and some ashes.

I back out.

I don't want to see anymore. The stroller haunts me as I climb back in the car. The second car of our convoy is idling behind us, waiting.

"Something bad happened here," I say. "Maybe ten or fifteen years ago." I wonder if the news reported on it, or if everyone in this part of the country just sort of . . . knew. That sometimes people disappear. And sometimes towns do. Esther figured it out with her fairy-tale research; she's probably not alone.

"Is that why everyone left?" Cillian's hands grip the steering wheel so tightly his knuckles are bloodless and pale.

"They didn't leave."

Rhys's eyes widen. He shudders once. "Maybe . . . maybe when he was free, he wasn't so happy on his way out of our realm."

"We don't want him coming back," Doug says. "We really, really don't. Right? I'm not alone in this."

I shake my head. "Not alone."

No one gets out to explore. Cillian continues steering us through town. It's built like a wheel, all the lanes like spokes leading out from the central point. His mother had drawn a diagram of it. An ancient stone in the center of a grassy meadow. No one ever tried to take it down, or build there. They knew what it was, and they respected it. They were careful.

And now they're all gone.

"Well, this is a problem." Cillian brakes as several cloaked people detach from the shadows of abandoned buildings to step into the road and block our way. They all have shock sticks. Their hooded expressions are hidden from us. "What do I do?"

A car comes screaming around a corner ahead of us. The cloakers aren't so fanatical they're willing to be bowling pins. The car squeals to a stop, and my mother and Cillian's mother climb out. "We got this!" my mother shouts.

Cillian's mother is holding a canister of pepper spray in one hand and a club in the other. "Don't let him come back, okay? Whatever his third form is, we don't want to find out. The portal was the stone at the very center of town. Destroy it. And if that doesn't work, well, break everything else until something does."

Cillian nods. "Thanks, Mom."

She beams at him, then shouts a battle cry as she chases after a few of the confused cloakers, followed by my mother.

We make it all the way to the center of the town without any more foes. But once we're there, a single figure is blocking our way, his back to us as he stares at the rock in the middle of the meadow.

He doesn't move. Cillian slams on the brakes and stops just shy of him. He's white, wearing a pin-striped suit, his hair straight and dark, neatly trimmed. He turns around slowly, tilting his head as he takes us in.

"Da?" Cillian says.

"Oh god," Rhys says, not inaccurately.

28

CILLIAN'S DAD LOOKS LIKE THE PHOTO
of him from Cillian's shed. He's an Orlando Bloom look-alike.
Not long-flowing-blond-locks Orlando Bloom, but normal dark-
haired handsome Orlando Bloom.

And when I say he looks like the photo, I mean he looks *just*
like the decade-plus-old photo. Cillian's dad has not aged a day.
Perks of hellgodhood, I suppose. Cillian's dad is looking at him
with a puzzled, vague expression, like he can't quite place where
he knows him from.

He sees me and gestures for us to follow, then turns and
walks into the meadow. The earth swallows him. He disappears
into it from one step to the next. We climb out of the car and
hurry forward as one. It hadn't been visible from our vantage
point, but the whole meadow has been excavated. A subterranean series of tunnels greets us, with Cillian's father already disappearing down a metal walkway.

"What do we do?" Rhys asks.

"It's a trap, right? It has to be a trap." Jade puts her fingers through the brass knuckle portion of a knife hilt. The members of the second car join us.

I peer over the edge. The metal walkways I can see are all empty. "But why? He doesn't need us for anything. He's already here. We failed, I guess?" I can't figure it out. He wanted us to follow him, and he certainly didn't seem worried or alarmed that we were here. This whole plan is a moot point. The hellgod is already here, just . . . wandering around in a really nice suit. Does that mean Leo is dead? Or does that mean he isn't?

I shrug. "I have no idea what's going on. But I want to find Leo, so I say we follow the god. Maricruz, Chao-Ahn, and Imogen, will you stay here? Guard our backs? Tsip, stay with them. You can pop in and out and warn us if anything goes down."

Chao-Ahn and Maricruz nod, gripping their weapons. But Imogen shakes her head. "No way. I'm coming with you."

"Me too," Doug says.

Jade pulls out a bag of what I assume are explosives. "GQ Hellgod might already be here, but someone should destroy the stone thing just in case. Keep Doug safe. If anyone hurts him, you'll answer to me."

"Don't you mean *they'll* answer to you?" Rhys asks.

"No, *you* will, because I'll kill you if you let anyone hurt him."

Doug grins, black lips in the fullest smile I've seen since I told him about the concert tickets. He leans in to kiss her, but she pulls back. "Not right now! This is beatdown time, not happy time."

He laughs and jumps into the tunnels. Jade and I share a nod. "You have the training," I say to her and the Slayers. "You all do. You got this. But if it comes to it, run. I won't lose anyone else."

Maricruz grins, twirling her knife. "I forgot how much fun the waiting is. It's like being at the top of a roller coaster. I want to puke and laugh at the same time."

Chao-Ahn rolls her eyes. "Americans," she mutters. She gives me a worried look, but then shakes her head as though resolving something. "Watch out for the storm. It wants to swallow you. And the rest of us."

The storm. The one that's been chasing me in my Slayer dreams. Thinking about Arcturius's prophecy, I have to wonder: Is the storm coming for me, or am I the one bringing the storm to everyone else? I jump into the tunnel. Imogen, Cillian, Rhys, and Doug are all already there, waiting for me.

"I feel like you should give us a pep talk," Doug whispers as we stare down the dark tunnel waiting to swallow us.

"All I can think of are really terrible puns about gods."

"All I can think is *Oh god oh god oh god*, so, about the same," Doug says.

Cillian grips a baseball bat with firmly violent intentions. "He's just a predator from another dimension. Nothing special, right?"

Rhys puts a hand on Cillian's shoulder. "You're okay with this? With whatever we might have to do?"

"I cried myself to sleep for years because I thought he was dead. He left us. Left me. I'm fine with it." He pauses. "I'm not fine. I don't know when I'll be fine again. But whatever he is, he's hurt—he's killed—a lot of people. Being my dad can't outweigh that. We have to stop him."

"We have to stop anyone in there." Rhys gives me a heavy look.

I swallow and nod, then draw my sword. I can't think about Artemis. I have to think about anything else. I'd rather face a hellgod than what I might have to do when I find Artemis. "Well, then. You know what Nietzsche said: God is dead. Let's put his philosophy into action."

"I can't decide which surprises me more," Rhys says, loading his crossbow. "That we're about to go fight a god, or that you actually paid enough attention in our one philosophy course to remember that Nietzsche quote."

"Come *on*." Imogen rushes ahead of us, practically skipping. "It's finally the end, and I can't wait anymore!"

Doug leans toward me. "She smells really, really off."

"We'll look out for her." But I'm sure none of us smell appetizing to him. Dread fills me as I contemplate the featureless tunnel leading into the dark. Will Artemis be there? Will Leo? And what will I do when I find them?

Before I can be left behind, I jog to the front. I won't let Imogen bear the brunt of an attack. Rhys brings up the rear, with Cillian and Doug protected in the middle. If it were up to me, we'd leave Cillian and Doug behind. But this is their fight too. It's personal for all of us.

The tunnel curves sharply. There are temporary lights strung too far apart, so all they do is create deeper, more disorienting shadows. Nothing jumps at us. No fangs or blades greet us. We walk unchallenged. At last the tunnel reaches what I assume is the center of the meadow above us. It opens into a huge, brightly-lit cavern.

The first thing my eyes settle on is the triangle puzzle thing like Cillian's. It's suspended from the roof of the cavern. Only instead of being small enough for a child's hands, it's big enough for an adult to climb into. And instead of being empty, it's filled with glowing, pulsing, quivering light. Next to it, on a catwalk connected to the doom triangle but not leading to our own catwalk, is Leo. He's chained in place with his hand duct-taped to the point of one of the triangles. He's *also* glowing.

I glance down. At the bottom of the cavern, discarded like empty husks, are dozens of demon bodies.

Leo looks across the cavern and sees us. "I'm sorry." His face is anguished. "They said they'd kill you if I didn't come with them. And then . . . they would have taken you next, just like my mother did. I had to choose."

"I thought you couldn't drain energy on your own?" I shout across the echoing space, angry with him for trying to protect me yet again by leaving. And so devastated for him for what he's been forced to do.

"'*Can't*' is very different from not wanting to." Sean appears on the other side of the cavern from some other tunnel. He's wearing a slick suit, his hair pulled back into a ponytail. He smiles. "Leo was perfectly happy to let his mother do the dirty work and survive off her. But my girls figured out the right motivation."

"They were bad demons," Honora says from behind us. We turn as one, weapons raised, but she holds up her free hand. One arm is splinted. "The ones he drained. We only picked the ones you'd be obligated to kill as a Slayer. Or at least, if you were a real Slayer. And if Leo were a real Watcher. Some of us haven't forgotten our jobs."

"Does your job include serving a hellgod?" I ask.

Honora tries to give me a haughty, dismissive look, but there's something shifty and—dare I say—uncomfortable behind her perfectly lined eyes. "I don't have to defend myself."

"That's where you're wrong." I swing my sword so she ducks. While she's distracted, I kick her in the shoulder. She careens off the catwalk, unable to stop her momentum. She bounces against the side of the cavern, rolling a few times before managing to catch herself one-handed against a rocky outcrop.

"What the hell?" she shouts. "I was trying to have a conversation."

"Are we ready?" a new voice asks. It's Cillian's dad. He's on a catwalk across from us. Our catwalks aren't connected. The one we're on curves around and goes back into another tunnel. Leo's isn't connected to ours either, but it isn't connected to Cillian's dad's catwalk. Sean is on the same catwalk as Cillian's dad, and Leo is joined by—

Artemis walks out to stand next to him. She looks down at Honora, and her face shifts in concern. "You okay?"

"Grand." Honora grunts, slowly pulling herself up the side of the cavern.

There's a muffled boom above us. Dirt and debris rain down. The cage swings and sways but doesn't fall. We all hold our breaths, but the cavern ceiling holds. And, unfortunately, so does Cillian's father's body. So blowing up the stone didn't make a difference. Sean gestures to a couple of goons, and they run off to see what happened. I hope Jade is ready.

"Why did you let them in?" Sean asks the hellgod.

He appears confused by the question. "She is yours." He points to me. "But now there are two of her." He thought I was

Artemis, and that's why he let us follow. Score one for being identical. "One of any human is still too many. Why did they make two of this one?"

"When did you get back?" Cillian takes a step forward so he's got a direct sight line to his father.

His father tilts his head. He's scratching idly at his arms, opening up welts that close almost as fast as they appear. "Who are you?"

"Fecking hell, Da, it's me. Cillian."

Still no recognition appears on the hellgod's face.

"I'm your son!" Cillian shouts.

"No." He holds a hand out so it's level with his side. "The child is this tall. And he has longer hair than you."

Cillian's laugh is harsh and angry. "Kids grow. Do you have any idea how long you've been gone?"

His dad raises his hand slowly as though adjusting his measurement of Cillian. He appears deep in thought. "I never left."

"Yeah, you did. You left us. Mum and me."

He shakes his head. "I never left the earth. I had so much time to think. So much aching, crawling, buzzing time. Why leave? Why struggle back and forth? I did for so long because it was too loud here—so loud, so loud, all the voices and claws and hungry mouths sucking at it—but I had gotten used to the noise. *You* were noisy." A brief, dreamy smile flits across his face, but then it goes back to a neutral expression so lifeless it's almost terrifying. "I stayed. And because I stayed, I was here when the doors all shut. When the noise was cut off. Only I am here now, and it's time."

"Time for what?" Rhys's crossbow is pointed right at his boyfriend's dad.

"For my third form. For my final form. For earth to have a god once more."

"Bit of a monopoly." Sean grins. "Used to be more competition, yeah? But we partnered up, and it's been good business for everyone. Once the Sleeping One here is fully awake, we'll use my network to spread his word, and before you know it, my products and his worship will be in——" Sean twitches, then looks down to see the crossbow bolt embedded in his shoulder. "Bloody hell, you *shot* me."

I turn to Rhys, but his weapon is still loaded and trained on the hellgod. Doug looks at me, his crossbow no longer loaded. "I've had to listen to a lot of his speeches over the years."

Sean staggers back toward the tunnel he came from. "Enough!" he shouts. "They're wasting our time. Take them." The pounding of dozens of sets of feet surrounds us with metallic rumbling as black-cloaked minions pour into the cavern. They're behind us and in front of us, totally blocking any paths we might take.

Tsip pops into existence in front of me. "Just so you know, you're surrounded. Okay, bye!"

I don't have time to ask if Jade, Maricruz, and Chao-Ahn are all right before Tsip disappears again. Teleportation is wasted on her.

"Keep my son," the hellgod says. "I am curious about him, and he should see what happens next. The rest can go."

"You're letting them leave?" Sean sounds outraged. His shoulder is bleeding and I'm sure quite painful, but Doug didn't hit him anywhere that would kill him.

"Why should I care about them?"

"Because." I stand on the edge of our walkway and calculate distances. "I'm a Slayer."

Cillian's dad smiles. "A Slayer never killed a god."

"Nope," Rhys agrees. "But a Watcher has." He fires his crossbow. The bolt lands with deadly precision exactly where a human heart would be. The hellgod pulls the bolt out. It trails a shimmering gossamer substance that evanesces into nothing as it hits the air.

"Triangle thing, right?" I turn my head toward Rhys.

He nods. "When in doubt, break the big glowy thing. We'll add it to the Slayer handbook."

"Go," Cillian says. "We got this."

I take one step back, then push off the edge and leap. I soar through the air, covering the distance between catwalks in a way no normal person could. Maybe even no Slayer could. Faith's right. If I have extra, time to stop hating myself for it. I'm going to use *everything*. I land hard between Artemis and Leo. I swing the sword toward her, but she takes a step back, holding up her hands. "By all means."

"We're not done." I can't even stand to look at her, knowing what she did. It makes no sense. None of it. But Leo first. I slice through the duct tape, then set my sword down and break the chain holding him there. He stands, full of life and fury. I know it's awful how it happened, but seeing him restored is still like cold water on a parched throat.

The fight on the catwalk behind me is raging, awkward and treacherous with the drop beneath all of them. "You good?" I ask Leo.

He nods. "They need help."

"I'd toss you, but even I'm not that strong."

He smiles at me, something so hopeful and warm bursting through the sadness and desperation there. We haven't lost each other yet.

"I have a better idea." He jumps, grabbing the bottom of the triangle doom device. It swings, and he uses his own weight to increase the momentum.

"Be careful!" Cillian's dad shouts. For the first time, he has the sense to look nervous.

"Watchers, duck!" Leo releases and flies through the air. He sails over our friends' heads and then lands hard just past them. So hard, in fact, that the catwalk groans and buckles beneath him. He jumps back as that portion of it detaches, taking most of the zealots with it. They tumble down the side of the cavern toward the bottom. Leo turns and joins Rhys, Cillian, Imogen, and Doug fighting the remaining zealots. Which leaves me with my sister.

"Is it ready?" she shouts, ignoring me.

"We'll come to you! I know the way!" Leo pushes through their remaining attackers, tossing them off the catwalk with ease, and my friends run into a cavern.

"No," the hellgod says. "It must be shifted into the divine transference configuration."

Artemis huffs in frustration. "Translation?"

"Translation is," I say, twirling my sword, "I still have time." I swing with all my might at the side of the wretched triangle thing. My sword connects with a ringing blow—and then my hands and arms go numb. The sword clangs to the catwalk, my arms useless.

"Nina." Artemis sighs. "Honestly." Then she punches me in the face.

ARTEMIS

EVERYTHING IS SPINNING OUT OF CONtrol. Nina was never supposed to be here. She was never supposed to see how it happened. She was never supposed to be in danger.

Artemis wanted to protect her from that, at least. But it's too late. She needs to protect Nina, she needs to help Honora, she needs and she needs and she *needs*. The Sleeping One was right to see that in her. She needs so much, and until she gets this power, she'll face this exact situation until Nina dies, or Honora does, or Artemis does. She'll watch Nina get left behind in flames. She'll watch Honora being hurt by people she can't fight.

Once, when presented with an impossible situation, she chose Nina. And because of that, she lost the role that should have been hers. The training. The power to make decisions for herself and others. She's never forgotten what it felt like to hold Nina in her arms while the world burned around them. It wasn't real—it was a magic-induced hallucination to test whether she could make the hardest sacrifice—but Artemis saw and felt everything. Those bastards made her test as close to what had actually happened as possible. The world even burned violet-black, just like their room.

She chose Nina. She chose wrong. And she knows Nina will never make the right choice either.

This time she's choosing power over Nina, so she'll never have to make that choice again because no one—*no one*—will be able to hurt her. And only then will everyone else be safe.

Nina is in her arms again. The world isn't burning. Yet. Artemis won't fail.

29

"NO FAIR," I MUMBLE AROUND THE swirling stars of pain and confusion left behind after Artemis's fist gave my face a handshake. "Cheating." My arms still won't work, and Artemis is obviously taking whatever performance-enhancing demon cocktail Honora favors.

"Will you calm down and *wait*?" She hauls me to standing, then holds me up, my back against her. Her arm around my neck. A blade against my—

Oh. Not holding me up. Holding me hostage.

"How could you?" I'm not crying because of the pain in my face—which is tremendous but temporary. "She helped raise us. She knitted you a scarf last Christmas. She's Rhys's grandma."

"What are you talking about?"

"Ruth! She was an old lady who never hurt . . . well, she probably hurt a lot of things, but she never hurt us."

"You have a concussion." Artemis sounds concerned but distracted. "I didn't mean to hit you that hard."

"Artemis!" Rhys shouts as he, Leo, and Cillian race onto our catwalk. Leo is still mildly glowing—or it could be my spinning vision giving him a halo—and Rhys has his crossbow reloaded and pointed at my sister. Which also means pointed at me. Imogen is behind them, next to Doug.

"I need to know how to make it work." Artemis jerks her head back toward the glowy doom triangle. "I know the basics, but the book didn't have any diagrams."

"You slit my grandmother's throat," Rhys says, his voice cold.

"What the hell, Rhys? Nina, is that what you were talking about? Ruth is dead?"

"Don't play dumb!" Rhys's hands are shaking.

"Point that elsewhere, please." I eye the crossbow. My arms are still numb, but my fingers feel like they're being stabbed by a million hot lava needles, so that's probably a good sign I'm going to get movement back. Or a sign my fingers are about to fall off. I give it fifty-fifty odds. "Artemis, drop the knife. No one here wants to hurt you."

"I do," Rhys says.

"But we will if we have to," I continue, glaring at Rhys.

"You all think—you actually think . . ." She takes a deep breath. "After everything. Figures. I don't have time for this." Artemis jabs the knife, poking me with it. "Cillian. I see the way you're looking at it. You know how it works, don't you?"

Cillian shakes his head, but then nods. He can't quite look away. It's exactly the same as the puzzle his dad let him play with when he was little. So whatever needs to happen to make it functional . . . I suspect Cillian can do it.

"Why are you helping a hellgod, Artemis?" I ask.

"I'm not helping *anyone*. Cillian. Do it."

"No!" I shake my head.

There's a shout and a scream. I can't look to see, but it sounds like my mother and Cillian's mother. Inside the caverns.

"Rhys?" Cillian sounds terrified.

For one second Rhys seems torn. Avenge his grandma's attack, or protect my mother and Cillian's after having lost his own without a chance to save her. I can't nod at him because of the knife placement, but my eyes communicate enough.

He swings his crossbow toward the tunnels. "On it! Leo, with me! Imogen and Cillian, don't let Artemis move." They turn and run back into the tunnels.

"What now?" Cillian's hands are trembling, his crossbow shaking. He keeps glancing to the side, trying to see what else is happening without taking his eyes off Artemis.

"Do what Artemis asks," Imogen says, putting her hand on Cillian's shoulder. Doug looks alarmed and unsure what to do. He can't spit and hit Artemis without also hitting me, and we need me clearheaded.

"What?" Cillian turns to her.

"Jade blew up the stone and nothing changed. Nina tried to break this thing, and it didn't work. We don't have any plays left here. We can't lose Nina. Artemis has already shown how far she's willing to go. Whatever happens, we'll deal with it. Besides, Mister Hellgod over there can't reach it. He's not even trying. He doesn't expect us to be able to do anything. So we improvise." She grins. She's handling all of this really well. Or she's lost touch with reality and is so far into panic mode that she's actually calm.

Whichever it is, Cillian shouldn't listen to her. I shake my head, but Artemis yanks me to the side, then drops me over the edge of the catwalk. I yelp, but my fall is broken as she grabs one of my useless arms and holds me there, dangling. The drop probably won't kill me, but it's far enough that even I'll get hurt. And I don't know how I'll get back up here to help. Honora rolled off the side so she had things to grab on to. I'll fall straight down.

"Save her!" Doug says, panic altering the desert landscape of his face.

"I'm doing it!" Cillian edges past Artemis, his hands up. He pauses in front of the doom triangle, studying it. Then he reaches out and takes hold of one of the corners. I don't think it will move—I hope it won't—but the way he slides it triggers a smooth progression of shifting sides. He manipulates it faster and faster, falling into a rhythm like someone who's done a Rubik's cube hundreds of times. The corners spin and spin until they shimmer, the lines disappearing into pure light. And then, suddenly, it all clicks into place. It looks almost the same, but everything is inverted, and the glow is brilliant, concentrated. Now it's a pyramid, the side nearest the catwalk open like a door.

Artemis looks down at me, tears in her eyes. "You weren't supposed to be here. I'm not sorry for anything I've done, but I want you to know that you were supposed to be far away." She blinks rapidly, trying to clear her vision. "I always thought Mom saved me first because she loved me more. But she saved me first because I was weak. That's why you got left behind. And someday soon, you're going to die. Mom's going to die. Honora's going to die. I'm going to lose everyone I love just like we lost Dad because I'm not strong enough. Because I was never chosen. I'm choosing myself today. I'll save *everyone*."

Cillian shakes his head as though coming out of a daze. He slowly backs away, eyes drawn to the light.

Leo and Rhys reappear. "We couldn't find them," Rhys says, then stops, staring in alarm at the new configuration.

"We need Jade and her explosives!" I shout.

"On it!" Doug runs toward the tunnels.

"Give Nina to me," Leo says, his voice gentle. "Nothing's been done yet that can't be undone." He takes a step toward us. "I understand, maybe more than anyone else. Give me Nina, and then we'll figure it out from there."

"The hell we will," Rhys says. He pulls his trigger. Artemis drops her shoulder, dodging the bolt, then swings me up and throws me right into my friends. They catch me, everyone falling except Leo. He holds me.

Artemis steps backward, knife up as Rhys scrambles to untangle himself and reload his crossbow. "You never trusted me. Any of you. And you, Nina?" Her voice breaks, but then goes hard and cold. "What did I expect? Watchers don't take care of their own. It's up to me." She puts her hand on the side of the hellgod's cage.

"What are you doing?" Cillian's father asks. For the first time, he sounds alarmed. "You cannot use that."

Artemis doesn't look at him. She turns toward me and shakes her head, her expression exhausted but determined. She tightens her ponytail like she always does before a fight. "Ending it."

And then Artemis steps into the light.

A blinding pulse throws us all to the metal grating of the

catwalk. Leo covers me, trying to shield me, but it's like the light is everywhere, in everything. Even with my eyes closed, I can see it. I can *feel* it.

It recedes like a wave from the shore, leaving me with the sensation that I'm still covered with little grains of light. "You okay?" I ask Leo.

He nods, eyes squeezed shut. "I'm sorry. They would have taken you. They made me choose, and—"

"I get it. We can talk later about how impossible it is to have to weigh the value of one life against another. Promise. We can also fight, because I'm not over everything you did. But for now, you're back, and I'm glad." I brush my lips against his cheek and stand. My eyes are dazed, my vision photosensitive and covered with spots like I've been staring at the sun.

No. Like I *am* staring at the sun. And she's standing on the end of the catwalk. I can't focus on Artemis. The light coming off her is so brilliant I have to look to the side of her in order to be able to see. The doom triangle behind her is a melted husk, totally ruined.

I shake out my hands. They're still tingling and mostly numb, but I have movement.

I step toward her. Maybe it's easier this way. She's less like my sister and more like the monster she's apparently become. "I'm not going to let you hurt anyone else. I can't."

She laughs, drops of liquid sunshine raining around me, warm and layered. She sounds like herself, but multiplied, amplified, and . . . happy. So, so happy. I can't remember the last time I heard her sound this happy.

"I did it! Oh, Nina, I did it. I fixed everything. None of us have to be scared, ever again. I never have to be scared again. I can feel it everywhere. Everything. I can feel everything, but it doesn't touch me."

I have to stop her. I promised everyone I would. I promised *her* I would. If she tried to murder Ruth to get this power, what will she do to keep it? *Girls of fire*, I think, watching as my sister burns brighter and brighter.

A phone is ringing insistently in the background. It feels absurd that someone would be calling us at this moment. "Nina!" Imogen shouts. "You have to stop her! Before it takes over! She'll become just like him, and we'll all die!"

I look at my sister, wielding all the power of a hellgod. And I know—I know what she did, what she's done. What she could do now. When she tested to be a Watcher, she was given a choice: save me, or save the world. She chose me. And she made me promise that if I was ever faced with the same decision, I'd choose neither. I'd choose myself. I know that's not the promise Imogen is referring to, but it's the only one I can think of.

How can I save myself if it means hurting Artemis?

"Nina!" Rhys shouts.

I pick up my sword from the catwalk. We have to weigh lives. Can my sister's life really outbalance the whole world? If this is it—what I'm supposed to do—where are my instincts roaring to life? The coiling, seething darkness that demands I fight and rage against everything around me? I reach for it, wanting to cloak myself in it so I can lose the parts of me that would never let me do what I need to do right now.

I'm desperate for anything to shield me from this pain. To keep me from feeling everything. The pain of what I need to do.

The pain of knowing what Artemis chose. The pain of every-thing in this whole bleeding and broken world. Even if it means surrendering myself to absolute darkness. Anything is better than feeling powerless to avoid what has to be done.

The darkness is waiting. It rises to meet me, ready to wash over me and drag me from the shores of myself, just like it pulled me from Buffy again and again in my dream. I lift the sword.

And I pause. Anything is better than feeling powerless. But to be powerless is to be human. To be vulnerable is to be human. Being *more* than human doesn't have to make me less human.

Artemis ran from us; she even ran from herself. She wrapped herself in as much power as she could find. If I do the same, how am I helping anyone?

Artemis raises her arms, and Leo shouts a warning. But she's holding them toward me as though asking for a hug. She never asks for hugs. She never asks for anything. Gods, she must have spent so much of her life being terrified. My mom was right. Because while we went through all the same things—our father's death, our mother's emotional abandonment, the fire, our life of training and then hiding—I did it all with her protection. No one did that for her.

How broken must she have been to decide leaving was her best option? To betray and hurt and try to kill people who had cared about her? To chase down a *god* in order to feel like she had a purpose again?

I drop my sword. I care about all the wrong and evil she did. Of course I care. But it doesn't change the fact that she's my sis-ter, and I'll always love her, and I'll always be there for her. "I'm so sorry. I'm so sorry you felt like you had no other choices."

"You don't have to worry anymore. Not about anything." She takes another step toward me but freezes. She's trembling. No, not trembling. *Vibrating.* A low hum accompanies it, and the light begins to build again. I turn and shield my eyes as another pulse hits us, threatening to throw me off the catwalk. I bear the brunt of it. It's worse than being electrocuted. I feel fuzzy and numb and in pain everywhere.

"Artemis, stop!"

"I can't," she gasps. "It burns. I can feel it all—so much. Too much. I can't hold it."

I stumble toward her. "You had the book! Tell me how to make it stop! Tell me how to help you!"

The catwalk shakes as someone lands on it. Cillian's father stands up from his long jump. "She cannot hold the power of a god. It will burn her alive." He pauses, frowning. "Without a container, it will burst free and burn everyone."

"Everyone in this room?" I have to get them out and then figure out how to help Artemis.

"Everyone, everywhere." He shrugs, unconcerned. "The whole world. I am not a benevolent god, and my power is not kind."

"The whole *world*?" All my jokes about apocalypses come back to haunt me. This is it. This is our prophecy. Arcturius never saw Eve's mini hellmouth. He saw this coming, even if I didn't. *Girls of fire / Protector and Hunter / One to mend the world / And one to tear it asunder.*

This is how the world breaks.

Cillian's father stretches a hand toward Artemis, holding his palm up as though offering something. "I will take it from her."

I look at Artemis. She's still vibrating. "Will taking it away hurt her?"

He looks confused by the question. "No. It will kill her."

"Then I need another option!" I have to get between Artemis and him, but there's no way around her, and I'm afraid to touch her. If hitting the doom triangle with a sword left both my arms numb, I can't afford to be out of commission now because I brushed up against her.

"She took what is mine. I will take it back." He steps toward my sister, calm and measured. A flash of shiny hair and black sweater flies through the air and slams into him, tackling him off the catwalk and carrying him all the way to the other end of the cavern. Honora tumbles with him down the side until they hit a ledge. She looks up at me, face bloody and desperate.

"I didn't know! I didn't know. She was so sure she needed it. She promised she could handle it. I just wanted her to be happy." Honora pauses to punch the hellgod as he tries to rise. "I got him. You save her!"

I nod and turn back to Artemis. She falls to her knees, the light building again to almost unbearable levels. I don't know how many more pulses until it kills us. Until it breaks free from her and kills everyone.

"Leo, can you take it back?" I don't turn around, keeping my squinted and watering eyes in Artemis's general direction.

He sounds as worried as I feel. "Maybe. Probably. But the pyramid thing was an amplifier. The power's so much more than what I put in there. Even if I can hold it, I can't hold it for long. It'll have the same effect on me. We need something to transfer it into."

"We can play hot potato until we figure out where to put it."
I turn and hold my hand out toward him.

"Oh, come on!" Imogen shouts. I look at her, confused.
"After everything she did, you're still trying to help her?"

"Nina!" Rhys is backing away from Imogen, his crossbow
raised and trained . . . on her. He has his phone in his free hand.
"My grandma woke up. It wasn't Artemis."

"What?"

"Artemis didn't try to kill her. Imogen did."

Imogen flicks her wrist, extending her sleek metal baton.
She swings it up, catching Rhys under his chin and sending him
sailing off the catwalk and down into the cavern.

"No!" Cillian screams. He scrambles back along the catwalk,
looking for a way to get to his boyfriend as Rhys tumbles down
the side and lands at the bottom near the pile of demon corpses,
still and unmoving.

"If you want a prophecy done right," Imogen growls, turning
toward us, "you do it yourself."

30

IMOGEN PULLS A KNIFE OFF HER WELL-stocked belt and throws it at Leo. He dodges, but she pulls another, bigger blade. She's between Leo and me, blocking him from getting to Artemis. I want to help him, but that would mean leaving Artemis unprotected.

"I spent my whole bloody life trying to keep their prophecy from coming true. Protecting the world." Imogen ducks a swing from Leo, dodging nimbly around him. I hope she'll try to sweep his legs or push him—I know from experience gravity's claim on him is so intense both are impossible—but she's been paying attention. She moves faster than him, blades whirling, making sure he can't get past her. "But you know what? The world sucks."

Leo rushes her. She twirls away with a dancer's grace, then, to my horror, grabs his arm and uses his momentum to spin him right off the catwalk. He looks at me as he falls over the edge, his horror mirroring my own.

He'll be fine. He has to be fine. But now I'm on my own. Against . . . Imogen?

"I don't understand." I keep myself between Artemis and Imogen. Imogen is barely breathing hard, knife still in hand. "You're my friend. You've always been my friend."

"I've always been there for you, that's true. Because I was assigned to you. To kill you, actually. Well, one of you." She shrugs. "My mother decided to take a shortcut and go for more power since the Watchers wouldn't let her just mercy-kill one of you. The prophecy needed two, after all. And it's not like your mother didn't have a spare."

"The fire at our house!" The realization is horrible, but then I do the math. It doesn't match up. "But your mother was already . . ."

Imogen smiles. "Yes, after my mother died horribly, the mantle was all on my shoulders. The fire should have worked, but no, you two just had to survive. And then your mother ran back to the Watchers. I waited for years. I couldn't risk getting caught and missing my chance. If I wasn't there to do it, no one would. And, god, they were so protective of you two."

I'm braced for attack, but she's just standing there. After the last blast from Artemis, I'm still shaking and off balance. I don't feel anywhere close to myself. "The fire was you. You. You're . . ." My head is spinning. "All this time, you wanted us dead?"

"Only one of you. I would have killed Artemis, if it makes you feel any better. But then last fall happened. And for a few brief moments, I thought that was it. I thought it was your apocalypse, and that we had failed to prevent it. That I had failed. And you know what? I was *relieved*. Happy, even. Because all these years my job has been protecting a world that couldn't give a shit about me or my mother. I'm sick of it. I'm sick of all of it. Your prophecy was the very last one in the book, and I'd hate to deny the earth its grand finale."

"You can't be serious!"

"*Follow your instincts, Nina,*" she says, her voice a syrupy sweet corruption of herself. "*If you feel like it's right, then it's right.* I even made your sister a murderer, and you still forgave her! All you had to do was shove that sword in her stomach and release the power to end it all. God, you are *so* hard to corrupt, you know that?"

I shrug. "Hufflepuff." My mind is reeling, but I finally realize why she's telling me all this. Why she isn't attacking. She doesn't need to. She only needs to delay us all long enough that the power becomes too much for Artemis. I draw a stake and throw it straight at Imogen's head. The blunt end hits her forehead, snapping her head back. She staggers, then rights herself.

"Actually, I know which one of you I can kill, finally. It's pretty obvious who the world breaker is. I won the bet with my mother. She never did pay her debts, though." She moves a wrist in a lightning-fast flick, and a sharp pain hits my shoulder. I look down to see a knife embedded in it. "If it's any consolation, you'll only beat us to the finish line by a few minutes."

"What about the Littles? You took care of them. You can't want them dead." I tug the knife free, hissing at the pain. If I were in charge of treating myself, I would have cautioned myself not to remove the knife until professional help was available. But I'm not in charge of treating myself. I'm in charge of fighting Imogen. I need to get Imogen out of the way so I can figure out how to help Artemis. A quick glance over my shoulder reveals my sister trembling so fast her edges are blurring. Her eyes are

squeezed shut, and she's got her arms wrapped around herself
like she's trying to hold it together through sheer force of will.

Imogen laughs. "Like they're really better off growing up? I'm
doing everyone a kindness. Putting this whole spinning hellhole
out of its misery. Did you ever think about why every *other* dimension is a hell, but somehow ours isn't? Joke's on us. We're the original hell dimension, baby. We're just too stupid to realize it." She
launches herself at me in a flurry of fists and kicks and flashing
blades. My shoulder and the disorientation from Artemis's dis-
charge slow me down. I'm fighting to keep her away from Artemis
but not to kill. Imogen is holding nothing back.

She grins, swiping a knife across my forearm as I try to block
her. I get in a kick to her side, but she twists, absorbing the blow
and elbowing me hard in the face. I stagger back. A searing pain,
and I look down to find yet another knife sticking out of my
lower abdomen. How many knives does she have?

I tug it out, my hands slick with my own blood as my brain
registers yet another stern caution for removing a knife from a
wound without any way to stop the bleeding. I can barely see
Imogen because of the light behind her.

Oh no. Behind her. I let her get between Artemis and me. I
can run and tackle her off the catwalk, but then Artemis will
be up here alone. I don't think I could get back to her in time.
I'm going to have to throw Imogen off, even if it kills her. I rush
her, but she's ready. My vision is dazed by Artemis, so I don't see
Imogen's club as she swings it at my leg. I fall to my knees, my
right one unusable with pain. I grab for her, but she dances back
toward Artemis. There's the particular metallic click of a gun
being cocked.

"No hard feelings. I'll see you on the other side, okay?"

I hang my head. I have nothing left. I lost. Artemis protected me for so long, and I couldn't return the favor. "I'm sorry, Artemis."

Imogen screams. I look up to see two blindingly brilliant arms encircling her. Imogen's clothes light on fire, and in the blink of an eye, she's consumed. Where Imogen was is only Artemis.

She meets my eyes and smiles, an agonized expression through gritted teeth. She's all blurry, literally falling apart. "Saved you."

I crawl to her, and she drops to her knees.

"Kill me," she whispers. "That might stop it."

I wrap my arms around her. She tries to push me away, but I hold her tighter. It's searingly hot, but I'm stronger than Imogen. I'm stronger than anyone except Artemis. I hold her against the vibrations, and, to my surprise, they calm down. "I've got you, and you've got me. We're strongest together."

She squeezes me back and holds me up while I hold her in place. All the darkness in me, everything I've been through, all the ways it's changed me. It wells in me, carrying me past what I'm capable of. We're here because Artemis walked in her own darkness for so long, feeling like she was the only person who could face it. But Buffy and Faith showed me the truth: We're not alone in the dark. Not as Slayers, not as sisters, not as friends. Not when we hold the people we love as close as we can. The heat is unbearable, but for Artemis? I can bear anything.

"Nina!" The catwalk rattles as Leo runs across it. He puts a hand on Artemis's shoulder. "I can take it, but I need somewhere to put it."

"Give it to me." Cillian's father's voice rings through the cavern. He drags Honora onto the catwalk and drops her. She groans, twitching. "I am the only option."

"You're not." Cillian emerges from the cavern. His face is streaked with blood and dirt. Rhys limps behind him. "I'm half god. Let's give it a shot."

Cillian's father radiates menace and power. "I will kill your friends one by one while you watch, and then burn away your humanity to see if anything is left in the ashes of my divine—"

Honora kicks him so he once again falls off the catwalk. She rolls onto her back, breathing hard. "Save her."

Leo puts both of his hands on Artemis while I hold her. I don't know if it's going to work, and for a few blistering seconds I'm sure it won't. But she gradually goes still and colder until she collapses into my arms. I check her pulse, desperate, barely able to see with the burned light images on my vision.

Her heart is beating. She's still alive. I cry, cradling her. Cillian rushes to Leo, who is as blindingly brilliant as Artemis had been. Leo puts both hands on his shoulders. "Are you sure?" he gasps.

Cillian swallows hard but nods. "Better me than the hellgod who wants to kill you all."

Leo puts his forehead against Cillian's, and he slowly dims. Cillian gets brighter, but not in the unstable way Artemis and Leo did. He seems to somehow come even more into focus, every feature in perfect clarity, to where I could swear I can see each eyelash from here. He's high-definition in a fuzzy world. His skin isn't brown anymore so much as metallic, gleaming in the harsh cavern lights.

"You good?" Leo falls back and sits.

"Yeah. Yeah." Cillian looks down at his own hands in wonder. "I——I think I got it."

"It will overpower you!" Cillian's father shouts from where he's clinging to the side of the cavern. Each exit has been filled by one of the remaining zealots. Two of them have my mother and Esther at knifepoint. My mother looks at Artemis in my arms, and I try to smile to reassure her, but it's weak. The zealots all have crossbows trained on us, and none of us are in any shape to fight our way out.

"You cannot hold it forever!" the hellgod shouts. "You are a *bastard*, a half-breed, and I will kill everyone you love while you watch. I will bleed them dry while you——"

"The third form," one of the black-cloaked zealots chants, pointing. But they aren't pointing at Cillian's dad. They're pointing at Cillian. They all drop to their knees. Cillian rolls his eyes.

"No," his father screams. "I am your god! I am the only god left in the world! I will kill everyone you——"

"Can you stop him, Nina?" Cillian looks at me, desperate.

I don't even know if I can stand up. "I'm——I'm tapped out. And you saw how little the crossbow did to him. I could . . ." Decapitate him? Would he be capable of recapitating himself? He might not be at full power, but he's still a hellgod. "We can try?"

Cillian's eyes are brimming with tears. "You were a pretty good dad for a while there," he says.

"You do not deserve anything of me. I will tear that one you seem to love limb from limb," the hellgod answers, pointing at Rhys. "But first, I will end the one who made this all possible." He leaps through the air, grabbing the edge of the catwalk where my mother and Esther stand, unarmed. He pulls himself up and reaches toward Esther. She and my mother back up but trip on the kneeling zealots behind them.

"Nina!" Cillian cries, terrified.

I don't know what to do. We can't have come this far to watch this happen now. But I can't get over there in time. No one can.

No. Not no one. "Tsip!" I shout. She pops into existence on a catwalk across the cavern.

"You can take someone beyond reality if they don't mind all their molecules being dissolved?"

"Yes!" She nods enthusiastically.

Cillian points at his father, tears streaming down his face. "Do it."

She shrugs and disappears. Cillian's father has one moment to look truly godlike in his wrath as he looms over our mothers before Tsip pops in next to him and then pops him right out of existence.

We all sit in the ringing silence left in his wake. Tsip reappears empty-handed. I feel a sudden rush of relief that she's actually empty-handed and not holding any eyes. This is already too much trauma for Cillian to process.

"Are you okay?" I ask him. I know his father was an evil hellgod who was going to kill all of us, but he was still Cillian's dad.

Cillian shakes his head. His brow is furrowed, but he still looks more like he belongs as a display of fine art in a museum than a real person. "My da died a long time ago. That wasn't him. Not really. It had to be done."

Across the way, my mother helps Esther stand. Esther is

crying as she turns to hurry back through the catwalks to find us.

I'm struck with the thought that Cillian turned out to be the only one of all of us actually qualified to be a Watcher. He was faced with an impossible choice, and he chose the world. But we'll be here for him, forever. We're his family. And I think he knows it.

Rhys walks hesitantly to his boyfriend. He keeps adjusting his glasses like somehow it will change the way Cillian looks. "So. Erm. You're . . . a god now?"

Cillian looks down at his hands. "Guess so. That or I'm totally off my nut and none of this is actually happening."

"It's happening." Rhys takes Cillian's hand in his own. "What about what he said—that you won't be able to hold it?" Everyone looks at me like I'll have an answer. For a moment I'm horrified that we've traded an immediate apocalyptic problem for the same problem in the near future. Then Leo shifts closer to me, and I realize *I've done it*.

I've saved everyone. Everyone I could, at least. Not poor lost murderous Imogen, or Cillian's father, if any of him was left in the hellgod's mess of a brain. But Faith was right. I used every ounce of power I had, the good and the bad, each part of myself. And we all came out on the other side. Including me.

"Two birds, meet one stone!" I lean back, laughing in relief. "We have a half god who will need siphoning and a half demon who can't stand the idea of harming even demons by draining them." I gesture to Leo and Cillian.

They look back at each other appraisingly. Cillian shrugs. "Could work."

"You sure?" Leo asks.

"You can be my chief minion." Cillian laughs at Leo's horrified expression. "No? Head zealot. High priest."

Rhys shakes his head. "God, you're the worst."

"You can still call me Cillian. We'll save 'God' for formal occasions." He's joking, but his expression is still a bit shocked and raw. Rhys pulls him close and hugs him tightly. Esther bursts out of a tunnel onto our catwalk and wraps them both in her arms. She's murmuring something quiet and broken that I know isn't for me, so I don't try to hear.

My mom sits next to us, and I lean against her, but I don't let go of Artemis. I'm not letting go of her for anything. Plus, I'm bleeding quite a bit from my various stab wounds and frankly not feeling very mobile. Just exhausted and grateful. Leo lies back, his head brushing my leg. I finger-comb his hair away from his eyes, and he closes them, smiling. He looks stunned but happy. It's not lost on me that only a few hours ago he was ready to die, but now he has a way to live without harming anyone. Sometimes we get happy endings.

Speaking of happy endings . . . "Where's Doug?" I ask. "And the other Slayers? And Jade?"

"Here!" Chao-Ahn elbows one of the still-bowing zealots out of the way. "We are fine! A few vampires in the tunnels."

"Done and dusted!" Maricruz twirls her stake again.

Doug and Jade appear on the opposite end of the cavern. They're holding hands, laughing. Jade gazes proudly at Doug. "No worries about anyone stopping us on our way out. Sean and his crew are quite incapacitated. Blissfully out of it."

Doug holds up Jade's hand. "Also the police will find him with an extensive array of bomb-making supplies in his car, not to mention an entirely illegal arsenal of weapons." Jade curtsies.

Honora drags herself across the catwalk. She looks so genuinely worried for my sister. There's a lot I can't—won't—forgive her for. But I can't deny that she loves my sister. She tried to help her. All this time I thought it was Honora forcing my sister into associations with hellgods, but I suspect it was the other way around.

"Is she okay?" Tears are streaming down Honora's face, making tracks through the smears of blood and dirt.

"Do you . . ." I grimace, the words foul on my tongue. But I push on. "Do you want to come back with us? Help me make sure she gets better?" Artemis is going to need more than just physical healing. It will take a long time, and everyone who loves her should be there to help.

Honora closes her somehow still perfectly lined eyes as she bends her head and brushes her lips against Artemis's forehead. "Yeah. Yeah, I'd like that. Thank you." My mother reaches for Honora, and Honora collapses into a hug, crying.

With the other Slayers helping, we manage to limp out of the caverns and into the sunshine. I can't believe it's the same day. I help load still-unconscious Artemis into a car and then close my eyes, feeling the weak winter sun on my skin. Everything feels tender and raw, like the worst sunburn of my life. But it *feels*. We are still here to feel. Whatever it is we have to, whatever it is that comes. We'll feel it all, together.

A hand slips into mine, and I don't need to open my eyes to know whose it is. I lean my head on Leo's shoulder.

The prophecy that loomed over Artemis and me since before

our birth is done for real now. But, more than that, I finally understand Artemis's pain—and my own—enough that I think we can help each other. I hope we can. It's time to heal. After all, together we saved the world.

And it hurt. A lot.

EPILOGUE

SPRING IS SLOWLY BUT SURELY NUDGING
winter out of the way. Artemis and I sit on the stairs to the castle.
I'm braiding her hair back from her face. I've been watching tuto-
rials. Every day the braids get more elaborate. Old Artemis never
would have let me, but this one does. Maybe only because she
isn't up to fighting me off yet, but I'll take it.

It's been two weeks, and we're not sure how much better
she's going to get, or how quickly. Everyone is walking softly
around her. The general consensus is she already paid the price
for what she did, but we all have a lot of healing ahead of us. I
spent years studying how to heal bodies; now we're all going to
work on how to heal the hurt we can't see.

"How can I do it?" she says.

"A fishtail braid? I'll teach you later on Maricruz."

"No." She shakes her head, then rests it against my knee.
"This. Everything. *Life*. How can I do it as me?"

I rest a hand against her forehead. She apologized for what
she did, but it was as distant and lost as her eyes when she said

it. I'm ready to really talk. I hope she is too. "What's wrong with you?"

"I'm not strong enough, or smart enough, or good enough to exist in a world this broken and evil."

"That's not true. You saved me."

"Because I had all the power of a hellgod."

"No, I don't mean from Imogen. I meant all those other times. All those years. You saved me time and again. Not only by protecting me, but by making sure I never felt the weight you did. You worked so hard to keep my life as happy as possible, as filled with love as you could make it. That was you, and only you. You did it for Honora, too." I only wrinkle my nose a little bit at this. There's a lot I'll never forgive Honora for, but she fought a god to protect my sister. I can deal with having her here, knowing what she's willing to do for Artemis.

I asked Honora the other day in a rare moment alone as we prepared dinner—I still don't know how to feel about Imogen's memory, but we definitely miss her meals—how she was doing with everything. She shrugged and said it was her turn to support Artemis through some bad times. And that, if it had worked, my sister would have made the most kick-ass goddess ever, so it was worth a shot.

Artemis clenches her fists. "How can it ever be enough? Dad was . . ." Her voice breaks. "Dad died. I don't want to die, or to watch you die, or Mom die, or Honora die."

I put my hand on her head, stroking her hair. "Everyone dies eventually. Nothing we can do will prevent that. I mean, unless you fancy life as a zompire, in which case, grrrr argh," I growl. It doesn't elicit a laugh. I sigh. "Dad wasn't a failure. He was everything he was supposed to be. I wish he would have lived longer, but he lived *right*. I'm proud of him, and I know he'd be proud of us. The world is messed up, yeah, but it's also pretty great sometimes. We can't spend every moment afraid of what's waiting for us." What's waiting for us out in the world, or inside ourselves, as I've learned. I wish I could take all Artemis's fear away, but it's part of her. She'll have to learn to live with it in her own way too.

I tuck a loose curl behind her ear. "Besides, we don't love you because you can protect us. We love you because you're you. Me, and Mom, and everyone in the castle, and Honora."

"I hurt her, though. I never should have asked any of that."

"Pretty sure she gets it."

"I hurt you, too. And I didn't do it for you, or for Honora, or even for the good of the world. I did it for me. Because I couldn't be me anymore."

"I understand." I do. I was willing to throw myself into the darkness to avoid actually feeling what I needed to. "But we're not alone. We have each other. We have a whole castle filled with people who love us. We were always supposed to stick together. Slayer and Watcher." I squeeze her shoulder as she looks quizzically up at me. "I know you didn't want to be a Watcher anymore, but I could sure use one."

"What about Leo?"

"I mean. Um. Not a lot of actual training going on there."

She snickers a laugh, then her face falls. "How can you trust me? After everything I did?"

I slip down so I'm on the same step as her and we're face-to-face. "You hurt me. Really bad. And understanding *why* you did it doesn't change the fact that it cut deep. But it also doesn't change the fact that I love you, I'll always love you, and I'll always be here for you." I want to ask her if she feels the same, but I won't push her.

She puts her arms around me and pulls me close for a hug. This one doesn't feel like it's burning me alive. It feels fragile. But that doesn't make it weak. It makes it precious. "What if I have to leave again?" she whispers. "What if I can't find myself here?"

"Then I'll let you. I'll even let you take your favorite coat. But no more books from the library. Those are off-limits." I say it like I'm joking, but she incurred a lifetime ban from both Rhys and a fully recovered Ruth. "And as many times as you leave, you can come back."

"Thank you." She relaxes a little more into the hug. I luxuriate in the closeness, in knowing that we can't ever lose each other. Not really. Until she speaks again and ruins the moment. "You really do need a Watcher, though. I can't believe Imogen almost beat you."

"Hey now! She's been secretly evil for years! That's a lot of training!"

"Exactly. Next time—"

"Oh gods, no next time. None of our other friends have been plotting our deaths for the last decade. Unless you steal another book, and then I don't know if I can stop Rhys from destroying you."

"Okay, okay, not next time. Next *threat*, you'll be ready. We know what goes bump in the night. We're going to be ready, together."

"Together." I release her as Honora bounds up the steps.

"They're playing football," Honora says, "and no one is there to critique their terrible form. Come down to heckle and fill out these college applications with me." She helps Artemis up and puts an arm around her as they navigate the stairs. She also flips me off behind Artemis's back.

"I hear America has good colleges!" I shout. "Or Australia! Maybe you could do an exchange program in Antarctica?" This time Artemis flips me off too.

I laugh, then lean back and observe the castle grounds. Ruth is helping Jessi push the Littles on the swings while the tiny purple demons chase each other in circles. Pelly is dozing in a patch of sun next to them. Cillian and Rhys are playing Doug, Tsip, and Jade in the aforementioned game of football, which seems to be more about arguing with one another than actually trying to score. Maricruz and Taylor are working on a patch to grow a garden next to the makeshift football field. Honora guides Artemis to a chair and tucks a blanket around her, cuddling in next to her as they watch the game and shout commentary. My mother opens the door behind me. She pauses, and I can tell she's looking at Artemis too. They're working on their relationship. It's weird to be the one who's closer to Mom now. But I don't mind it. "Can we go over some logistics for this month's schedule? We'll have to shift things now that Chao-Ahn is going home."

"Schedule meeting in ten minutes!" I shout. "Be there or be on bathroom cleaning duty!"

"I call babysitting on Jessi's days off!" Maricruz shouts.

"I don't take days off!" Jessi shouts back, violence in her tone.

Maricruz laughs brightly, and I'm not dreading the schedule, or talking with my mom, or any of it. I don't feel like I have to avoid anyone, or pretend to feel anything I'm not. I'm okay with feeling everything I am. The happy parts, the dark parts, and everything in between.

"I'll be right there." I stand, stretching. "Just let me help Chao-Ahn load the car."

At the bottom of the stairs, a hand shoots out of the shadows and grabs my wrist, spinning me off the path and into Leo's arms.

"Hey," he says.

"Hey," I say.

He looks good. Better than good. He looks amazing. Cillian sometimes gets a little jumpy—buzzing, he calls it—and Leo drains the excess. It might not be a permanent solution, but it's working for now.

"Seems like you need more training." He frowns thoughtfully down at me, his hands around my waist.

"Excuse me?"

"You should have sensed I was there and blocked my attack."

"You're assuming I wanted to." I go on my tiptoes and press my lips to his. We had a lot of talks. *So you're part demon* talks, and *so you thought you could die instead of having a fight about all your lies* talks. Painful talks, but good talks. And now Leo and I both have someone who knows exactly what it feels like to worry you're going to hurt the people around you. Who understands having to work to keep the angry and predatory parts of yourself under control. We don't have to be ashamed. We can be proud. Because it's hard, but we do it. Together.

A few moments—or minutes—luxuriating in the feel of his mouth on mine pass before I pull away, remembering I came down here for a reason. I twist free of Leo's grasp with a laugh, then hurry to where Cillian's mother is helping Chao-Ahn load everything. She'll take the Slayer to an airport and help her get on her way back home. One of these days I'll go to London to meet Faith in person. Maybe even San Francisco to meet Buffy. But for now, dreams are enough. I have plenty of Slayers in my real life too.

"I am ready." Chao-Ahn loads her small pack into the car. Then she turns to me. "I was afraid to face the monsters of my home—my past—for too many years. Thank you for helping me find my strength again."

"And thank you for helping me face my storm."

"See you in dreams?"

"No more ice cream, okay?"

She laughs and hugs me, then climbs into the car. Taylor waves forlornly, but everyone else has already said their good-byes. Sanctuary might be permanent for some of us, but it makes me happy to see someone take what they need and then go back out into the world.

I'm surprised as another car pulls up just after Esther's car disappears. A young woman, maybe a couple of years older than me, her nose pierced and her expression intense but haunted, leans out the window.

"I hear you help Slayers." Her fierce tone is belied by the slight tremble in her hands as she grips the steering wheel. "Take them in."

Prophecies and ancient forces have tried to claim me. Generations of tradition have tried to steer me. Trauma and fear have tried to stop me. But today, right now? I'm exactly who I'm supposed to be. I smile. "Welcome home, Slayer."

ACKNOWLEDGMENTS

Liesa Abrams, Sarah McCabe, Jessi Smith, Michelle Wolfson, Sarah Creech, Kekai Kotaki, Cassie Malmo, Ian Carlos Crawford, Zoraida Cordova, Caleb Roehrig, Slayerfest 98, Stephanie Perkins, Natalie Whipple, Noah, my three children, my parents, my in-laws Kit and Jim, Buffy Summers, Faith Lehane, the cast, crew, writers, directors, producers, and everyone who brought Buffy to us, as well as the authors, graphic novel writers, and artists who continued her stories off the screen:

You know what you did.

(Thanks for what you did.)

ABOUT THE AUTHOR

KIERSTEN WHITE is the *New York Times* bestselling author of many books for teens and young readers, including *And I Darken*, *Now I Rise*, *Bright We Burn*, *The Dark Descent of Elizabeth Frankenstein*, *Slayer*, and *Chosen*. She lives with her family near the ocean in San Diego, where she perpetually lurks in the shadows. Visit Kiersten online at kierstenwhite.com and follow @kierstenwhite on Twitter.

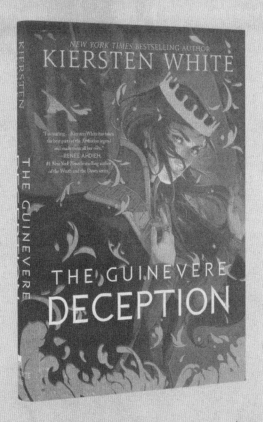